GAVIN & THE BODYSNATCHERS

MICHAEL A. DUFFY

Dufflington Books 2021

Cover Design by Josh Duffy
joshduffy.co.uk

Gavin & The Bodysnatchers
Copyright © 2021 Michael A. Duffy
All rights reserved.

ISBN: 9798475011546

For my cover designer

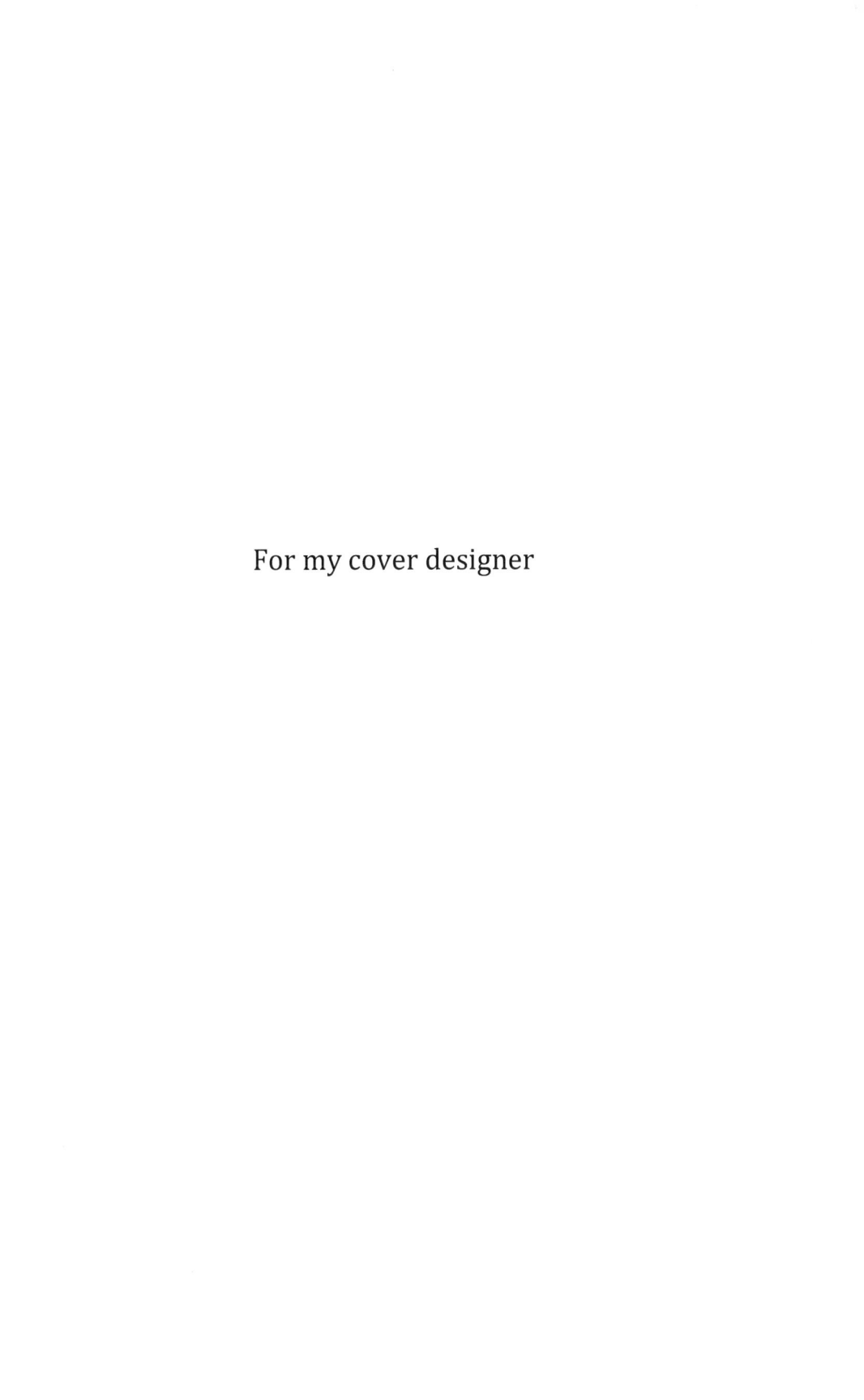

ACKNOWLEDGEMENTS

'**H**ey aspiring novelist! Wanna write a best seller? Then *write about what you know!*' Well, that's what all the Creative Writing self-help books tell you. Sounds easy, right? But not if your life has been as dull as mine, meaning you don't know very much at all. Well, who wants to read an entire novel about hair-loss, anyway? As moving and as tragic as that might be.

Nope, if I wanted to hit the best-seller charts, I needed to get thinking - these days, an effort in itself. OK, I've been to work for most of my life, I eventually brilliantly recalled. I *should* know a bit about that. But then, the commercial world is mostly tedious, is it not? The only thing I could remember about it that was mildly interesting was the extreme behaviours of some of the more 'challenging' bosses I've had to endure over the years. ...Aha! *Light bulb moment,* no less – and the novel 'Gavin & The Bodysnatchers' then poured from my keyboard like a fast-flowing stream.

In a long career, I've worked for many half-decent bosses, don't get me wrong. Some were even quite good – one or two even better than that. But every now and then a proper stinker - either directly or indirectly – would come along. Only funny if it were my colleagues in the department next door who'd inherited the new horror, not me.

Still, I couldn't help noticing that having corporate power seemed to bring out the worst in some people - liberally showering around their untamed and mostly unpleasant character traits. Oh yeah, and leaving trails of human devastation in their wake. I confess, I might have even come to see it as a kind of masochistic pleasure to witness first-hand, the unbridled egomaniac, the bully, the narcissist, the dictator, the micro-manager and even the occasional incompetent nutter. Some of them were so talented, they managed to be all of the above and still not get sacked! Some even got promoted.

But I survived! Though what rich pickings for a novel, I finally concluded - as my own career-inspired character of Bryce Brimstone was born, the archetypal terrible boss. It seems everything happens for a reason, after all.

So, to those select few who I personally consider having been my most horrendous ex-bosses - each with your own morale-sapping, manufacturing plant of misery - I'd like to thank you all. Without your input, showing me the least favourable side of how to behave at work, this hopefully entertaining piece of creative writing could not have been born.

Not only that, but for me, writing this book - *where the bad boss may well go down* - has been a cathartic experience. I am sure that for many people still out there in the corporate world, catharsis will also be achieved by reading it.

All the best, folks,

Michael A. Duffy

DISCLAIMER:

'Gavin & The Bodysnatchers' is a work of fiction. Any resemblance to actual events or persons, living or dead, is entirely coincidental. Except in the case of you, Kevin Midgely-Moore. You're all over this book – and you know it!

1
- NO JOKE SHOP -

Some towns deserve to be rained on. So, it was justifiably raining that morning in Drabbleton, Lancashire. But grey drizzle, a half-arsed kind of purposeless rain, was all that Mother Nature could really muster. This once proud industrial town, formerly at the hub of Northern England's manufacturing glory, had been 'redesigned' by architectural Muppets in the Sixties. Pink cladding on breeze blocks, pretty as a pig in a tutu, was supposed to paper over many sins. Then all the makeshift colour drained away. Greyness ruled and besides, buildings built for twenty pence really can't be expected to last. People feared the rain. The whole shoddily rebuilt town might be washed away at any moment.

The highest chimney in the town, however, still stood. Belonging to Brimstone Mill, a Victorian cotton factory built in 1850, this giant tower stood like a Viagra propelled phallic symbol. An enduring monument to a time when the town could still get it up. But today, local business flopped. Commercial ventures came and went. Failed shops were boarded up and graffitied. Closed factories saw life only in car parks overrun by riotous dandelions. So many windows smashed, all roof lead stolen.

Unemployment would have been higher, but most young folk with anything about them buggered off as soon as they could. The remaining workforce were what they were. The *Drabs of Drabbleton*, as they were known throughout the hills and valleys of Lancashire. But that jibe was slightly harsh. A few of them still had a pulse and wanted to live a bit. Some even ventured beyond their own sofas. One or two, on the extreme of the spectrum, even dreamed of one day *being somebody*.

Gavin Hargreaves, for one, could remember such a dream - as the bailiff walked out of his shop with yet another box of repossessed fancy dress wigs. However, life had generally been a bit shit for him in recent times, what with his divorce in his mid-thirties and his simultaneously bankrupted retail establishment. It wasn't his fault that his Irish missus, Marie, had left him for Drabbleton Town FC's dishy Italian goalkeeper. After all, the guy was on two grand a week, plus had developed two packs towards a rippling six pack - pretty good at thirty-four years of age. But it *was* Gavin's own fault for converting his neighbourhood's much-loved chippy into a retro joke shop. Drabbleton had done stink bombs, itching powder and whoopee cushions back in the Sixties. Nobody wanted to go back there.

Even the ten-foot-wide replica of a clown's spinning bow tie that Gavin had erected on the roof had failed to reel in the punters. It was ex-stock from Blackpool Illuminations, bought from a commercial auction site. But to date, it had never actually lit up, so the planned Grand Lights Switch-on Event had never got round to happening. Still, the local kids were fond of it for stone throwing target practice, especially when it was in spinning mode. Most of its glass was therefore shattered inside a week, meaning the chances of the illumination illuminating were as bleak as the Drabbleton sky itself.

All this was two years back now, when a casual passer-by also observed a black bin bag full of clothes being thrown out of an upstairs window of 21 Mayfair Avenue, a Seventies built Council semi. Just prior to this, through the cardboard walls, the following conversation was heard by next door.

'I bought you a scratch card to cheer you up.' This was Gavin again, a presently grubby, bearded and track-suited bloke, moderate height, slightly overweight, mid-thirties. His mop of curly light brown hair looked like it had been permed in a tragic Seventies style, although - unfortunately for him, so he'd always thought - the curls were quite natural.

'Thanks. But it'll take more than a fifty quid win to make a difference.' This was Marie, petite bottled-blonde, pixie hairdo, tiger-stripe onesie and neon branded trainers.

'Go on, scratch it. I've got a good feeling about it.' Gavin smiled and crossed his fingers for luck.

'We never win anything,' said Marie despondently as she then scratched away the silver concealing panels with an oversized, pink nail file.

Gavin sat on the edge of the sofa, watching on patiently. This was going to be great - he just knew it.

'Six stars! We've got six stars!' Marie suddenly squealed, springing in the air like a hyper-active bunny rabbit. 'What does that mean? Quick!' She fumbled the card, trying to read the prize run-down on its back cover.

'Six stars! *No way*. It only means we've won a million, that's what!' Gavin hollered, punching a fist with apparent joy.

'A million quid? Jeez that's feckin' amazing! Wow! Wow!'

Marie threw her arms round her husband, momentarily forgetting all about their recent marital difficulties. This win might change *everything!*

Gavin was laughing along, hugging his animated wife in return. What a glorious moment!

'Aha!' he then sang gleefully. *'Gotcha!'*

'Whadayamean?' said Marie, still in her ecstatic bubble.

'I mean, gotcha! It's a *fake scratch card!* A new line in my joke shop.' He flinched expecting the mug his wife had suddenly picked up to come flying his way. Marie's face turned from sunshine to thunderstorm in an instant and payback was inevitable.

'You bastard! You absolute swine,' she cried. She didn't throw the mug though. Only its contents. A hot wave of coffee splashed hard against Gavin's face and shoulders.

'Whoa! No need for that. It was just a bit of fun!' The drenched one looked hurt at the blatant overreaction. 'I was just showing you what a good laugh you can have with stuff from the shop.'

'If I'd have had my hairdresser's scissors in my hand, I'd have feckin' stabbed you, never mind the coffee.'

'Bit harsh love, it's a *joke*.' The wet husband dried himself down with a tea towel off the maiden by the radiator.

'You're the feckin' joke.' Then the agitated petite blonde, in pocket rocket mode, did actually throw the mug. Gavin ducked and it smashed against Marie's Robbie Williams photo-frame on the wall. She wailed. 'Now, see what you made me do, Gavin Hargreaves! Well, I'm leaving you. I'm leaving you for good!'

Five minutes later the bin bag went hurtling through an upstairs window. The passer-by, PC Duckworth of Drabbleton Police, tutted in mere resignation. Another day, another *domestic*. Nothing for him to bother getting involved in.

'What the hell, Marie? What you bin-bagging *me* for?' he heard the householder yell as he then ambled off on his way.

'Cos you deserve it, that's why!'

'But you're the one leaving *me*!'

'Oh, don't you go confusing me with all yer clever talk.' Marie stamped an angry foot.

'I'm staying here. So, I need *my* clothes in *my* bedroom.' Gavin snatched his favourite hoodie, currently ketchup stained, away to safety.

'Are you calling me an eejit now?'

'I never called you an eejit.' Gavin raised his arms, surrendering in all innocence.

'Typical you, descending down to cheap insults.' Marie stamped the other foot.

'I didn't...' Gavin realised this was an argument going nowhere - *best to change tack.* 'Stop, now!' He grabbed the second bin bag that his animated, departing wife was loading with his socks and underwear.

'Look at the state of these boxers,' she grumbled, eyeing the shabby items with disdain. 'Even the bin bag's too good for them. Disgusting.'

'Well, money's been tight.' He snatched back the tatty pants. But she'd embarrassed him. When a man is down on his luck, then underwear is the first thing to go. She should have known that, or so Gavin reckoned.

'Take a bit of pride in yourself, now won't you? You've gone to the dogs long ago.' She puffed her cheeks despairingly.

'Harsh.'

'But true,' Marie hissed as she wrenched back ownership of the second bin bag but immediately threw it at Gavin, hitting him in the face - although little harm done. 'Right, I'll be packing a case then.'

'Makes more sense.' He retrieved a second old pair of boxers and, on second thoughts, decided they should stay in the bin bag. Looked like today was a day for goodbyes.

'So you'll be wanting me to go now, is that it?'

'No,' Gavin was in knots. 'No need for any of this, love. What happened to *for better or worse?*'

'Well now, there hasn't been much of the *better*, has there? You're nothing but a non-stop comedy juke box, so you are Gav Hargreaves.' Marie now busied herself packing a battered suitcase she'd retrieved from the top of a wardrobe. She spotted the *I love Dublin* heart sticker on the suitcase lid and resisted the temptation to burst into tears.

Gavin knew by now he would have small luck in getting through to his currently snarky wife of ten years or so. But he felt he had to try, though his words - even to his own ears - sounded like a scratched record. Meanwhile, Freddie, the couple's nine-year-old son had come inside from the backyard and had crept up the stairs. He half hid behind a door, in silence, picking off flaking paint and wishing that adults could at least try to be nicer to one another.

'Come on, you did know all this was coming, did you not?' Marie went on, a little less shrill. 'I did say I'd be giving Alberto up *if*. ...If you could prove you'd make a go of that stupid junk shop of yours.'

'Not a junk shop - a *joke shop*,' Gavin bleated in defence.

'It looks like a junk shop to me. But there's no joke in being skint. Just my pathetic wage from the hairdressers to live on. ...And there was another thing,' - she paused to search her malfunctioning memory. 'Now what the feck was it?'

'The joke shop just needs time to get noticed, that's all. Just a bit of time.'

'Funny how your chippy didn't need any time to get noticed. Steady as clockwork that place was. And it didn't need a feckin' useless, giant, pink bow tie stuck on its roof to pull in the trade.'

'It was a chippy, Marie,' Gavin spoke patiently. 'A bow tie would have been stupid. A giant cod, maybe...'

Marie face-palmed herself. She was ignored. Because Gavin still had hopes for his joke shop business, well kind of. But he also realised that maybe he should have stuck with his old chippy. Well not *maybe*. He definitely should have. He'd disposed of his steady livelihood in pursuit of quirky stink bomb dreams. There was no other joke shop that he knew of within a thirty-mile radius. But now he knew why. He might as well have been the guy trying to set up a video rental store in the age of streaming. The golden era of joke shops had long gone. Though he wouldn't let Marie know he knew that, that much he did know. But she knew alright.

'Besides clever clogs, joke shop stuff might be kind of old fashioned to you, Gavin continued his defence. 'But there's whole new generation of kids who don't know about fake dog poo or prank spiders. It's like a whole new world to them. But they need to get used to it. See, nobody bought Marmite when it first came out,' he persevered. 'But did Mr Marmite give up? No, he stuck at it. And today, some people actually like Marmite.'

'Not better than a chippy tea though. Go on, who likes Marmite better than a chippy tea? Marie feigned spitting the offending assault on her tastebuds from her mouth. 'Feckin' Marmite!'

Gavin waved his hand dismissively - he'd run out of steam, so it seemed. But Marmite versus a chippy tea, yeah, she had a point he supposed. 'Ah, it's all going over your head,' he finally retreated. 'I'll sort it with the bank.'

'You mean the bank that'll be sending in the bailiffs?'

'How do you know about that?' Gavin was genuinely shocked that Marie was in on this particular crisis. She clearly knew more than he knew she knew. That was supposed to be a confidential matter anyway.

'Sharron Butler, one of my customers at the hairdressers told me. Then Mukesh in the corner shop when I was getting me fags. The whole of Drabbleton must have been knowing before me. Well, I'm only your feckin' wife, am I not? But not for long, God willing, if I promise to go to mass on Sunday.'

'I said I will sort it, love.' But even Gavin knew that was unlikely. Though throughout life, he'd always worked on the basis that promises made with all good intentions at least buy you a bit of time to have a good think. Best to take the heat off, at least temporarily, while a master scheme can be hatched. But Marie wasn't having it this time, merely recalling a further misdemeanour, according to her book anyway.

'Oh yeah...and join the gym, that was the other thing I'd be having you doing. You promised to join the gym.'

'What, thirty quid a month?' Gavin was shocked at even the thought of such a profligate expense.

'You've got proper fat since you opened that joke shop.'

She scowled at the spare tyre that a man aged thirty-five should be ashamed of.

'Comfort eating. Jaffa cakes,' he confessed quietly, breathing in. With no customers to serve what else was there to do?

By now, the dubiously blonde yet still cute Marie had Gavin floundering on the ropes. It wasn't always so. He'd first met her when on holiday in Dublin just over a decade ago. Only 20 years of age, she was a local of the city, and a thing of enchantment to Gavin from the very off. Smashed on Tequila and Guinness, he told her she was the most beautiful girl he'd ever seen in his entire twenty-five years on the planet. By that he knew he meant she was the most beautiful girl to ever have shown him the time of day. He was grateful for his luck, batting out of his league as he believed he was.

Gavin's Lancashire charm even finally persuaded Marie to venture over the water to be with him. But Drabbleton had few selling points for a life-loving girl like her - she soon began to think that said charm alone was not enough to keep her in this grim part of England forever.

But then Freddie, possibly unhelpfully, decided to come along. As a devout Catholic, abortion was out of the question for Marie, despite her relative youth. So, a ten-year roller-coaster ride of a marriage began. But now the ride was practically over, and it was time for its dizzied passengers to stand on their unsteady feet and walk away.

Marie's packing was almost complete, well she'd got all she needed for now anyway. She'd be at Alberto's place in the better part of town - minuscule part that it was. So more stuff could be ferried over in coming days if her new boyfriend would lend her his BMW, that is. He normally did.

'No wonder I'm leaving you for a professional, international athlete.'

'He plays for Drabbleton Town FC, Marie. It's not like you've copped off with Cristiano Ronaldo!'

'Jealous. Jealous. Jealous. Goodbye Gav...'

'Is that it?' mused pensioner Bob next door, addressing his grey, old mongrel and soulmate as the voices beyond the party wall grew silent. 'I think she's off for good this time. That's our fun over for a while.' The nosey septuagenarian seemed genuinely disappointed that the free soap opera he'd always tuned into from next door was likely to be over. He sighed and reached for the TV remote.

'What's on the box, Rocky?' Rocky wasn't that bothered, to be honest.

*

Out in the front garden, late next morning, pensioner neighbour Bob Horsefield encountered Gavin getting into his decade old rust bucket estate car, while Rocky was taking his usual morning piss on Marie's rose bed.

'She's gone then?' said the diminutive Bob, hardly a question.

'Aye, I suppose you heard.'

'Aye...what you gonna do now? Fancy a brew?'

'No mate thanks. Stuff to do.'

'I've got Jaffa Cakes.'

Gavin leant against the bonnet of the motor he wished, after all these years of thankless toil, would be an Aston Martin - his sense of purpose momentarily lost.

'Ha, Jaffa Cakes,' he weakened, defences destroyed. 'Go on then, five minutes won't hurt.'

Though they'd been neighbours for seven years or so, Bob and Gavin had only spent time together on and off. With an almost forty-year age gap between them, they really only had a couple of things in common - and pitying one another was one of them. Gavin had felt sorry for Bob as he'd never found love again once his wife had left him. Bob had felt sorry for Gavin because his wife still hadn't left. Bob didn't like Marie at all.

'Am I invisible now?' Bob had grizzled to Rocky many a time when Marie had blanked him in the Co-op when he'd been buying his *Daily Mirror* and she'd been off in a world of her own, buying *Hello!* magazine. How she envied the glittering lives of all those celebs in that glossy. Perfect lives. With money. Although now she was seeing Alberto, she reckoned she was one step closer to living the dream. All she needed next was for her two-pack beau to get signed up by AC Milan and they'd be minted. Then she could spend all day taking her spandex clad bod shopping in the retail temples of Italy's most prestigious fashion houses. But for now, along with *Hello!* magazine, she'd just shop for a pizza for Freddie's tea. That way, if the move to Milan came off, her son would be already accustomed to Italian food.

But now, here in his neighbour's cosy front room, Gavin supped on a welcome cuppa and decimated an entire cartridge of Jaffa Cakes. Bob, meanwhile, had something on his mind.

'Maybe you shouldn't have turned that chippy of yours into a joke shop, after all.'

'You were all for it at the time,' Gavin protested, remembering that a love of old joke shop wares was the other thing the two men had in common. 'In fact, we've sat in this very room looking at *Joke Shop Planet* magazine together and choosing the best fake dog poo and *Blue Mouth* sweets.'

'I know, but I shouldn't have encouraged you,' said Bob, scrunching his nose. 'How many times are folk round here likely to buy chips? How many times will they buy *Blue Mouth* sweets? Bloody 'ell, lad, it's just maths.'

'They're a laugh though, *Blue Mouth* sweets,' Gavin smiled, consoling himself. 'I gave one to Marie once. She had to use a whole tube of Colgate to get her teeth clean. But her tongue stayed blue for a week.' He then chuckled like a schoolboy, finally infecting his neighbour too with the giggles. 'But yeah, I know,' he straightened up, 'I wasn't to know that parents just don't let their kids have proper fun these days. Kill joys, most of 'em.'

'Don't go crying after the good old days,' Bob sighed. 'The good old days were not all that they're cracked up to be. I was there!'

He certainly was. In fact, Bob still had something of the look of the old rock 'n roll *Teddy Boy* about him, still even occasionally wearing his velvet trimmed, drape jacket and drainpipe pants. But nowadays his once gravity defying quiff was much depleted, his mourned for washboard stomach had been replaced by a bubble pot belly - and he'd long since swapped his suede, creeper shoes for comfortable sheepskin slippers. Whatever though, he still had a bit of sting left in him. Enough at least to now release the bee in his bonnet.

'You know what, lad? And I'm only saying this for your own good. You remind me of one of those kids on that Alan Sugar programme. What's it called?'

'...*The Apprentice?*'

'Aye that's the one. *The Apprentice.* You're like the nice but not very bright kid on there whose project is something simple - like to organise a piss-up in a brewery, or something. But he even manages to balls that up. Against all the odds. Like having a gold mine chippy in Drabbleton and shutting it. Not clever.'

'It was hardly a gold mine,' Gavin sulked.

A pointed finger was then held up in a menacing fashion towards the beleaguered apprentice.

'Gavin, I'm sorry. But *you're fired.*' Bob held the stern pose for a few seconds, then laughed, a release.

'I was a ringer for Sir Alan then, the old sod. What do you reckon? Just like him, wasn't I, Rocky?' The sedentary, shabby dog seemed marginally interested, but then got up from the rug he'd been half-dozing on. He slowly limped over towards the house guest, who noticed its deformed left hind leg - remembering the story of how this had been caused, years earlier. A losing skirmish with an aggressive German Shepherd had done the lasting damage.

Gavin looked suddenly close to tears and Rocky nuzzled his snout into the morose visitor's leg in a show of instinctive doggy sympathy. Bob felt he'd maybe been a bit harsh there, despite sensitivity not being his strong point.

'Eat your Jaffa Cakes lad. Chocolate. Endorphins and all that. *Daily Mirror* said so. You'll feel better then.'

'Aye, I will.'

'Anyway, you're far too old to be on *The Apprentice,* so ignore me. I'll be in my retirement flat soon and you won't have to put up with my bollocks anymore.'

Gavin sat there looking at his shoes, feeling sorry for himself. He didn't clock Bob's last proclamation. Too busy reflecting on thirty-five years of living the best life he could, but now everything gone - business, wife, child, even his own self-respect had one foot out of the door.

Bob somehow accepted being ignored and suddenly felt further reparative action was needed.

'I'll get us some ale from the kitchen.' Rocky raised his figurative ine eyebrows, maybe fearing the worst. Gavin didn't protest, 1ough both men knew that lunch time drinking rarely ended well .. ind here.

Then over the next couple of beery hours, as Bob studied racehorse form in the sporting pages of the *Daily Mirror*, Gavin poured out his broken heart. He still loved Marie and couldn't bear the thought of only getting to see Freddie a couple of days a week. Yeah, it had been a stupid mistake to convert his modestly profitable chippy into a loss-making self-indulgence. And he shouldn't have put on weight. Not when he was being compared to he of international, athletic prowess, *Amazing Alberto*, by the lovely Marie.

'Are you listening, Bob?' Gavin paused on the threshold of the second hour of his marital woes monologue.

'Eh?' Bob jolted himself back into a pose of fascinated concentration.

'If I'm boring you, well just say.'

'No, it's great. You get it all off your chest lad. Fancy another beer?'

Through the window of Bob's council semi, Gavin then noticed the erect chimney of the Victorian Mill, built by James Brimstone in 1850. That self-made cotton entrepreneur was still Drabbleton's all-time wealthiest and most successful son after well over a century since his death. Gavin had 'done him' in school and somehow remembered the locally much told story of Brimstone's success and philanthropic nature to boot. A model wealthy citizen who employed most of the townsfolk on fair terms. He'd also paid for most of the town's construction too, including neat, terraced houses for his workers and the ornate Victoria Park where they could relax, admiring the beauty of nature - and even the odd duck. A statue of the great man stood to this day, outside the Athenian influenced grand Town Hall, once again constructed and paid for by Brimstone himself.

'Y'know that James Brimstone fellah? He must have been like Drabbleton's Alan Sugar. Back in the day, like.'

'Aye, I suppose he was.' Bob wasn't exactly following his neighbour's train of thought. 'Why are you saying that?'

'I was just looking at the chimney of his old mill. Drabbleton were nowt until James Brimstone came along. Everyone learns that at school.'

Bob squinted through the window to also view the looming chimney, but he couldn't see it properly without his specs. 'James

Brimstone *made* Drabbleton alright. But he'll be turning in his grave if he can see the shit-hole that it's turned into today.'

Gavin suddenly seemed to steel himself, as if something important was trying to hatch in his slightly befuddled brain. He was on his fourth *Carlsberg*. Bob had been generous.

'I hope this isn't the beer talking, but the answer is here, right in front us every day. That giant, bloody chimney.'

'Aye it's an eyesore alright. It nearly got demolished once - by me, as it happened, in my steeplejack days. But then the heritage people put a stop to that at the last minute.'

'If one man can build a whole bloody town...'

'A shit-hole.'

'It wasn't in its heyday. Drabbleton were proper grand. Well, if one man can do all of that, then surely I can do a little something. Maybe like one of Alan Sugar's apprentices. One of the good 'uns anyway. You know, *make something* of myself again.'

'I think you should just calm down, lad. I wouldn't have given you my ale if I thought it'd turn on the dreamer in you again. Remember the joke shop.' Bob found himself once again shaking his head wearily.

'What? For fighting back from adversity. That makes me a dreamer?'

'I had a little dream once,' Bob sunk into a sadness of his own. 'I wanted a window cleaning round and me own ladders and a little red Ford van. Mavis would have loved that. Maybe she'd have stayed and me not being able to give her kids wouldn't have mattered.'

'Oh sorry, I never knew why she left you. You never said,' Gavin muttered, feeling awkward.

'No matter,' said Bob, brushing away his romantic history with a dismissive hand. 'But imagine that. *Me*, a business entrepreneur.' He puffed out his chest with pride, caught in the wistful daydream.

'Sounds impressive,' Gavin assented, sharing the momentary fantasy as if it were reality. 'But what happened?' he continued, moment over.

'Went on a training day, didn't I? With my brother who has a round in Trapton. I went up the ladder and was fine with the heights. No problem for a steeplejack - of course.'

'Sounds like it suited you.'

'You'd think. But then I got spongephobic.' Gavin looked blank, surprising Bob by his ignorance, so that further elucidation was necessary. 'You know, *spongephobic* - fear of sponges. I look at a sponge and it looks like an alien creature. It's like cleaning windows with a soggy ET. Aarrgghhh! Just couldn't stomach it.'

'Ah, bad luck mate.' Gavin slowly moved his head from side to side in sympathy.

'Gutted, I was. So, I just carried on with me day-job as a steeplejack. Until all the mills closed down and there were no chimneys needed sorting - or blowing up.'

Gavin looked puzzled. *Blowing up?*

'Y'know, demolition by explosion. As I said, I would have collapsed Brimstone Mill chimney if it wasn't for the heritage folk,' Bob continued, seeing his neighbour had finally caught on. 'So then, Mavis never did get to see me as Mr Big,' he then lamented, looking more than a little crushed.

'You are only five-foot three mate.' Gavin was just being honest.

'Not big in height, dimwit. Big in *business stature,* y'know.'

'Right...,' said the neighbour, belatedly on the ball.

'Then maybe my childhood sweetheart wouldn't have left me for Ken the plumber. See, he did have his own business. Jammy git. Once he'd got Mavis, he had everything. And they had a daughter too - then a grandson to cap it all.'

Bob blew a very snotty nose into a hankie, picturing a family life and business empire that hadn't meant to be. 'So that's what I'm saying. Dreams can kill you mate. Round here any road - as you well know.'

But this sad tale had only served to make Gavin more determined. Mavis went, all those years ago, but what had Bob done about it? Here he was, forty years later, a lonely pensioner living with a limping old dog. Gavin had heard enough. Bob's predicament, then the beer talking - and maybe even the spirit of James Brimstone - combined to inspire him. But he was starting to feel newly focussed, invigorated too.

'I'm going to build a proper business. Just like James Brimstone. I'm going to be *big in Drabbleton!'*

Bob took pity on the misguided ambitions of relative youth.

'Too many Jaffa Cakes with that beer, lad. I should have said. Them endorphins...'

'I've got a dream, Bob. A dream.'

'Martin Luther King had a dream. Didn't end well for him.'

'Bollocks!'

Then Gavin got up and swiftly left Bob's somewhat overly cautious and restricting environs, dream intact in his pocket. In just two years' time Gavin Hargreaves would be in an entirely different place. Entirely different. But meanwhile, Bob shouted after him through the PVC window he would have opened further if only the Council had been round to fix its rusted hinges.

'Yeah, and that one from *Les Miserables*, she had a dream too. Didn't end well for her either.'

But Gavin was deaf to all reasoning. His destiny was waiting.

2
- TROUBLE AT T' MILL -

The philanthropic business empire of James Brimstone had continued in good hands, down through the generations of industrious and smart sons and daughters, until the 1960s. By then the cotton mills of Lancashire were entering their final years of terminal decline. Thousands of immigrants from India and Pakistan were encouraged to find work in the cotton industry, mainly to allow the factories to operate overnight - their last chance of becoming economic once more.

In the late Sixties, under the custodianship of James's great grandson Cornelius, the once mighty Brimstone Mill began to operate 24/7 in order to survive. But the workforce was not at all keen on the new working patterns and complained bitterly to Cornelius, who, with too soft a nature gave way to them. Which meant him subsidising the loss-making mill from the much-dwindled family fortune. Until, in July 1970 - with all family money spent - the factory closed its gates for the final time. The global cotton industry was leaving Lancashire forever and hundreds of other mills in the region soon closed too. But in Drabbleton, in particular, it was Brimstone's Mill that had been the economic mainstay of the town for 120 years. Without it the place was devastated. Fifty wilderness years had followed.

The remaining family assets of the Brimstone empire passed on, a couple of years later, to Henry. They said Cornelius died of a broken heart, feeling himself responsible for the failure of the historic business. But now it was left to Henry, his son, to make something of what was left.

Unfortunately, Henry possessed the poorest business acumen of all of James's descendants. Now this particular great, great grandson thought he had pulled off a great, great deal by buying a TV manufacturing plant. But the company's specialty, black and white televisions, weren't exactly flying off the shelves by the mid Seventies. Without the capital to convert the business into the *World of Colour*, his business collapsed in 1978. Two years later, penniless Henry had committed suicide, aged forty - but not before he had provided the world with a son, Bryce, by then ten years of age. His newly born daughter, Alice, sadly never got to know her father at all.

Bryce Brimstone, however, was an entirely different animal to his father. He had hated his teenage years spent in relative poverty. With all family money gone, his mother, Elizabeth, had to seek support from her own parents to help get by. But support, although freely given, was modest.

The first thing to be sacrificed was Bryce's place at Graveston Hall private school, Lancashire's world-renowned cathedral of learning for young gentlemen. Just approaching secondary school age, Bryce was forced to swap the gay Pink and Navy striped blazer of Graveston Hall for the utilitarian, polyester sweatshirt of Drabbleton High. How *embarrassing* - he felt utterly humiliated.

Inevitably, although quite tall for his age, he was bullied by older boys of the school. Graveston Hall kids were always ripe for a good kicking by Drabbleton High's meanest foot soldiers, and now they had one of them in their very lair - every day could be torture day! In fact, the broken nose, they'd inflicted on their victim early on was still with Bryce today - an unsightly twisting of bone and flattening of flesh that was the only blemish on an otherwise quite handsome face.

Another favourite prank of Bryce's tormentors was to hold his head down a lavatory bowl and then flush the chain.

'Feeling flushed, Brimstone?' some anonymous bully would scorn. This sadistic ritual happened over and over again. Until one day, five years later a poor boy's head was brutally shoved into the bowl. But this time the bowl was full of a substance it is quite unwise to wash your hair in. This was a new twist to the ordeal dreamt up by the new champion bully of the school. That bully went by the name Bryce Brimstone.

To say that Bryce was the antithesis of his ancestor James would be an understatement. While James would try to take care of the weak, Bryce had much fun trying to crush them. James fell in love with Anne, his childhood sweetheart and they eventually enjoyed a lifelong and monogamous marriage. Bryce somehow managed to ensnare a string of girlfriends, on account of his flashing brown eyes, jet black, lustrous locks, and tall, athletic, though burly frame. But he treated them all badly. *Sex dolls* he called them, usually to their face when he became bored with them - usually within a few weeks. Or even days.

James, of course, had a shrewd nose for business, a trait that had sadly evaded Bryce's father, Henry. But this was the one thing that the founder of the Brimstone empire and his great, great, great grandson had in common. Bryce indeed had an instinct for commerce and an unbridled appetite for success. As he disinterestedly traversed through his studies, leaving school with below par qualifications, he hatched a vague plan to seek his fortune. To his mother's part distress and part relief, he vacated the family home at just eighteen, hitch-hiked down to London and blagged a job as a junior in an estate agency. It would be over thirty years before he would return to Drabbleton - to attend his mother's funeral and to comfort his sister, Alice.

Somehow his sister seemed to be the *soft spot* in his life. Ten years her senior, he had tried to be a decent big brother to her, always battering to a pulp any friends who dared to upset her as a child. Then, as an adult, battering to a pulp a useless husband, Malcolm Compton, who had begun to drunkenly abuse his oddly treasured sister. But today she was no longer Alice Compton, on divorce reverting to her original family name - Alice Brimstone.

For her part, however, Alice was the only person who seemed to be able to get through to her brother. The only one who could occasionally prick his mostly insensitive conscience. And for that he was sometimes even grateful.

'How could you have possibly lived in this dump of a town for all these years?' Bryce impatiently asked of Alice at their mother's funeral wake. He was staring, it seemed with almost contempt, out of the window of a modest hillside bungalow with a clear view ahead of Brimstone Mill. 'Turning fifty makes you think things over. What about this decision, or that decision? Did I do the right thing?'

'You always think you've done the right thing, Bryce. I can't imagine you ever admitting you made a mistake.' Alice smiled sweetly as she attempted to dilute the bile.

'Yeah? Well, the best decision I ever made was to escape this sewer hole. When I was young, I think I'd rather have prostituted myself on the streets than spend even one more day here.'

'I think you've had better business ideas. Women aren't that desperate, even in Drabbleton.'

Bryce was starting to enjoy his sister's spirited showing. He'd missed that. He wildly smiled.

'What about the men, darling? Now they *are* desperate, ha ha! Mind, isn't this the town where men are men and sheep are nervous?'

Alice, for her part, was tolerating him.

'Wow, Bryce Brimstone made a joke. Obviously stolen from a Christmas cracker.' Which it probably was.

Bryce raised a middle finger to his sister and knocked back what was left of his large whisky.

'Actually, the menfolk of Drabbleton were devastated to see the young you go,' Alice continued, feeling a tad encouraged, maybe like a gutsy lightweight boxer trying to score the odd point against a heavyweight. 'People have been mourning for years.'

'Very funny... Yes, I am sure some were glad to see the back of me. Losers mostly. The *Drabs of Drabbleton*.'

But Alice's mood darkened.

'What you mean like Pete Harrison who had a nervous breakdown at school because you kept trying to drown him in the biology pond?'

A suppressed guffaw from her brother.

'Ah, Pete! I did rather like him, actually. Or he would still be in that pond.'

'Or Martin Rishton whose mother you had sex with in the school car park.'

'Hilarious! ...A malicious rumour. Can't be proven.'

Alice found herself quickly losing patience.

'Who else?' she pressed.

'Mmm, so many to choose from.' Bryce ran his fingers through his ample locks, deep in thought. 'Well actually there was that Dinesh kid, little Muslim insect,' he finally laughed. 'Stuck his head through the school railings. They had to get the fire brigade to get him out. Classic. Oh, and wasn't he the one I imprisoned inside a wheelie bin, then sent him reeling down The Hundred Steps? Vintage stuff!'

For the benefit of non-residents of Drabbleton, The Hundred Steps was a steep incline of Victorian stone paving that rose from Town Hall Square up to the outer edges of the commercial area itself, climbing at a ridiculously challenging angle of forty-five degrees. A narrow, pedestrians only thoroughfare, although only the bravest and fittest of the town ever bothered to traverse it.

Looking very pleased with himself and his selective childhood reminiscing, Bryce topped up his whisky glass. Turning around he noticed his sister had left her space beside him and was making small talk with a couple of the other funeral guests.

She found him out in the garden later, after everybody else had gone home. Still with a drink in his hand.

'You should be ashamed of yourself.'

Bryce looked at his glass.

'I'm not driving. What's the problem?'

Alice was happy to correct him. He seemed to have made a bad day worse for her and had barely spoken of their lost mother at all.

'I meant because of all that ...all that, well bullying quite frankly.'

But her brother wasn't too pleasant a drunk.

'Don't lecture me, Sis. What do you know? You've never known *wealth* - and what it's like to lose it. Our family had lost everything by the time you were born. What a lucky charm you turned out to be.'

'I'm going in.'

'No wait, you started it. I'd had to leave Graveston Hall. Treated like shit at that awful state school. Trodden into the ground. Until I learned to fight back. The strongest win, Alice. It's just the law of Nature. Not my law.'

'Survival of the fittest?' There was a sarcastic yet weary tone to Alice's voice.

'Exactly.' he huffed. 'Don't pull your face, that's how it is. So here I am back in town after over three decades, *filthy rich*. Ha! Unashamedly so. I taught myself to win, Alice.'

'Father would have been so proud of you.' Turning on her heels, Alice strode back to the house. She'd heard enough of this.

'Whatever... Good old bankrupt father. Thanks for *everything!*'

Alice tried her best not to listen as she escaped. She did hope he'd be away first thing on the train back to London. Bryce was a master at outstaying his welcome. Usually within twenty-four hours, in her view.

*

He'd phoned to apologise around lunch time the next day, once the hangover had started to subside. He was indeed heading off on the London Express, well via the local branch line's connecting train. Drabbleton was far from being a mainline town.

Feeling some kind of inexplicable sibling pull, Alice had found herself agreeing to meet him at the station for a farewell coffee.

She'd ordered her standard latte by the time he came bustling into the small rail-side coffee shop, checking his watch and silently admonishing Time itself for letting the morning slip by so quickly.

'You here already? Had to take phone calls,' he said by way of apology for his tardiness. Not much of an apology really, but Alice wasn't expecting one.

A couple of minutes later he joined her at the Formica topped table, suddenly offended by the cafe decor that probably hadn't altered since he'd left town as a teenager all those years ago.

'Look at the state of this place,' he grumbled. 'A station can tell you a lot about a town. Proud gateway into its heart, isn't that's what it's supposed to be?'

He sighed as he spotted two dead house flies on the windowsill next to them.

'Disgusting hole - there certainly needs to be some changes round here. Nothing a Biblical flood wouldn't fix.'

He slurped on his super-sized Cappuccino, leaving a moustache of frothy milk on his lips. Then he savaged on a gargantuan Danish Pastry like he'd not eaten for days.

'Good morning, dear brother. How's the head?'

When he could manage to speak again, mouth finally empty, Bryce got straight down to business.

'Actually Sis, I was wondering when the Will was being read?'

Alice took a deep breath. Her brother didn't mess about, did he?

'It's not being *read*. Mother's estate is not Buckingham Palace you know. It's just her tiny bungalow and a paltry few Premium Bonds.'

'Of which we're no doubt getting half each.'

Alice sipped on her coffee, calming herself. A side of her might have even been enjoying knowing she was about to score one against her brother.

'Well, no actually. You are not in mother's Will. It's here if you must know everything right at this very minute.'

Alice had thought to bring the Will with her, anticipating that Bryce would ask about it. Fishing it from her bag she handed it across the table. Her brother rapidly scanned its contents.

'Bloody cheek. I am disinherited. *Bloody cheek indeed!*' Alice wasn't sure if he was exaggerating his apparent incredulity.

'You don't need the money. Mum knew that.'

'Hardly the point. It's the *principle*. I'm hurt.' Bryce pushed away the small remains of his pastry. Surely, he wasn't sulking? Whatever, Alice felt she had the upper hand now.

'But I do need the money, Bryce. Now I'm single again at the tragic age of forty-two - and Malcolm is finally out of my life.'

'And I'll kill him if he dares to return.' Bryce couldn't help crushing his now empty polystyrene cup.

'Thank you.' Alice really meant that. It was the only good thing Bryce had done for her in her adult years, *persuading* Malcolm to leave. 'But I'm going to settle down here now in Mum's old home.'

For some reason Bryce was then gleefully smiling. His mind was ticking over so quickly Alice could almost hear its cogs and levers.

'Then you owe me!' *Reel her in, Bryce!*

'What?' Was he playing, or was he serious, she couldn't tell.

'You owe me, Sis. Blatantly stealing my inheritance. Well, I might let one that go...'

'Really?' Alice didn't believe he really would.

'Yeah, well, the least you can do is start by coming to work for me!'

'Never!' She meant it. She couldn't bear to even think of being under her brother's control on a daily basis. She liked him away in London, with the odd drunken text late at night being his only communication.

'Sis, I mean it.' Bryce did look like he meant it too. Alice had rarely seen him looking more serious. 'Question. The best time to buy assets are when, my dear?'

Alice looked blank - she'd never even thought about such a dull subject.

'Answer. When the price is rock bottom. When you can take those assets and transform them. Having a brilliant business brain - that's erm me of course. And some great products. Millions are there to be made.'

'I don't know what you're talking about, at all.' By now Alice certainly wasn't liking the way all this was heading. She threw her last drop of latte down her throat.

'I've bought it back. Brimstone Mill. It's back in the family, it's mine.'

'What? How? Oh, you've just totally lost me.'

'I'm starting up a sales operation there. Call centre and warehouse. Drabbleton's prodigal son is finally coming home!'

A sense of dread permeated through Alice's entire body.

'I need someone who knows the town. Someone I can trust. That's you, Sis. Isn't it just brilliant?'

Bryce leaned over the table and gave his sister a voracious kiss on the cheeks, triumphantly punching the air. Alice sank in her seat.

3
- VINDALOO -

It was hard for Gavin Hargreaves to look at the fascia board of his old shop. Two years had passed since Marie had left him and since the bailiffs had finally repossessed not just the odd box of stock, but the entire beleaguered joke shop as well. Yet when he looked across the street, in his mind's eye he didn't remember *Gav's House of Fun,* but instead still he read the words on a fondly remembered earlier sign: *Gav's Chippy - Drabbleton's Finest Fish Bar.*

But today, anyone without Gav's mind's eye, just using normal eyesight, would read a completely different sign: *Star of India - Fish, Chips, Curry.* One day, yes one fine day, *Gav's Chippy* might be back, fantasised its previous owner, as he opened his former shop door. Stepping inside now, he was immediately warmly greeted by different owners - the owners *for now* at least - behind the steel serving counter, Dinesh Patel and his petite wife, Mishka.

'Ah Gavin, how are you, my friend?' asked Dinesh, broadly smiling as he organised freshly fried fish in a hot display cabinet.

'Not so bad, not so bad,' the nostalgic customer replied, concealing the inner melancholy he felt would never fade. Mishka smiled at him as she efficiently took a telephone order.

'The usual Gavin?'

'Yeah, please Dinesh,' he nodded. 'Actually, our Freddie's coming round any time, so a small sausage dinner too.'

Dinesh winked and got to work while Gavin marvelled at the culinary breadth of the menu stretched across the back wall. It was hard enough keeping up with the English chippy menu, ninety per cent fish, chips and pies. But Tandoori, Tikka Masala, Vindaloo, Korma, Rogan Josh, Kofta and more and more - it all sounded high maintenance stuff to Gavin.

'And how is work, my friend?' Dinesh breezed on, always attempting to make initial polite conversation. But Gavin didn't really think there would be genuine interest in the tedious goings on inside a Call Centre. He brushed off the question.

'Fine, fine...'

Then Dinesh, twinkle in eye, leaned across the serving counter to ask a better question he really was more interested to learn the answer of. He whispered, hoping his wife wouldn't hear.

'And how is sex life?'

'Same.'

'*Same*? How long is it now, two bloody years?' Dinesh tutted woefully as he stirred chips in hot oil.

'Twenty-seven months, but I'm not counting.' Gavin shrugged a shoulder. Couldn't be helped. He'd last had sex with Marie about three months before she'd ditched him for Alberto Assini. Then after she'd gone, he wasn't really interested in any other woman for quite a while - he was just kind of mourning her loss. In the past year, however, that had started to change. At thirty-seven years of age and in slightly better shape after a bit of weight loss effort - just fewer Jaffa Cakes really - he'd started thinking he'd like to test the water again. Whilst his past business difficulties, Marie leaving and now his low wage had all combined to dampen both his libido and his sexual motivation - he was finally up for a change. He certainly didn't want to grow old alone, like his old neighbour Bob.

'I will give you extra chips. For get up and go.'

'Thanks. That'll work.' Gavin smiled, appreciating this concept of *life coaching plus chips* that his Indian friend was cornering. Dinesh seemed to have an easy way about him and waiting customers were often heard telling him all about their marriage problems, money woes, bad backs, bad neighbours, whatever. His takeaway was now a hub of the community, a proper little talking shop - and its owner was proud to be at the centre of it.

'But how's business for you, Dinesh?' Gavin asked, happy to change the subject away from his non-existent love life. But he was maybe hoping for a less than beaming smile to cross the late middle aged, yet relatively handsome face across the serving counter. And why did Dinesh always wear a crisp white shirt and smart tie underneath his protective overall - *in a chippy?*

'Booming, yes very good indeed. Your Call Centre co-workers have wages again. There is life in Drabbleton once more. So, I think I will only sell it back to you now for half a mill. Ha ha!'

'Half a mill, give over. Two fifty.'

'Never!'

Gavin didn't have two hundred and fifty thousand pounds. Neither could he borrow it as his credit record had been shot to pieces by his first business failure. Then, following on from his James Brimstone inspired proclamation, two years ago round at Bob's - that he would become *Big in Drabbleton* - Gavin had actually dabbled with a subsequent business idea. He'd become a children's entertainer. Start-up costs were low - just a helium canister really, as he had plenty of balloons left over from his joke shop, hidden from the bailiffs. So even he, in his cash-strapped state, could afford that outlay. His bookings were slow but steady, until at one kid's party he started letting the little 'uns breathe in helium so they could talk in a funny, high-pitched squeak. They loved it! But then one of them got into breathing difficulties and ended up in A&E. Two more fainted. So, he let off a stink bomb, an attempt at an hilarious distraction - surely a winner. But nobody found that funny at all and two more kids then threw up all over the *Bob the Builder* birthday cake. Word swiftly got round the gossiping mums and dads of Drabbleton and consequently bookings completely dried up. So that was the end of *Balloon Man Gavin.* Another heroic failure.

With hope of self-employment triumph seemingly knocked out of him for now, he'd settled for a job in a Call Centre. But the wage was meagre - and he was still paying off some debt from his closed shop too. So, Gavin lived a frugal life for now, a chippy tea being one of his only few treats.

Dinesh knew all of this. But Gavin's financial lot was never spoken of, too awkward a subject to broach. All the same, the pair had regularly exchanged banter over the past couple of years - well ever since the Patels took a new lease on the premises really. Gavin kept telling Dinesh he would one day make him an offer he couldn't refuse and buy back *his* chippy.

'It is not your chippy,' Dinesh would reply, smugly grinning away. 'It is a far better thing now. It is the *Star of India* chippy. And never again shall it turn into a rubbish joke shop that nobody wants.'

'Dinesh, I have advised you to be polite to our customers,' Mishka would usually mock scold. 'We apologise Gavin, but you see, I am married to a monster!'

All three usually laughed, well it was all good-natured stuff. Dinesh would give his slender wife a reluctant kiss and Gavin would say his goodbyes and leave, usually with a complimentary extra sausage for Freddie on the nights the now eleven-year-old was staying over. But tonight, before that customary ritual could be completed, the growling engine of a silver *Chelsea Tractor* pulled up outside the shop. A sharply dressed, burly gent in his early fifties disembarked. His crisp long wool overcoat and expensive Oxford shoes were obviously well outside of the pricing range of all Drabbleton outfitters. Both Dinesh and Gavin seemed to shrink literally by inches as the tall, foreboding presence burst into the shop.

'Telephone order for Bryce Brimstone.'

'Of course, Sir,' Mishka politely replied and got to work packing up a generous stack of pre-prepared, Indian meals. Dinesh, meanwhile, quietly slid away, disappearing into the storage room out back.

'Evening Mr Brimstone,' said Gavin, nervously addressing his employer of the past couple of years.

'Ah Hargreaves...I thought you were on overtime this week.'

'No, not tonight, sir. It's Friday. I've got me son coming over.'

'How delightful.' Brimstone replied, hardly sincerely, as he threw three ten-pound notes onto the counter. Mishka promptly collected them. 'Well make sure you hit target this month. We don't want to be having another *chat*, now do we? You know, if I were in your shoes, Friday night or not I'd be in work making sure I hit target.' He stared hard into Gavin's eyes. They seemed to glaze over, so he thought. *Not much going on in that brain!*

Mishka passed a large bag of delights over to Brimstone which he took without ceremony.

'Thank you.' He abruptly barked. 'Have a lovely evening, Hargreaves.'

A flourish to the door. Then he was gone.

'Sorry, I'll finish your order, 'Mishka seemed flustered. 'Shouldn't have let him push you out.'

'No, no... obviously. It's fine.' Gavin waved a casual hand trying to emphasise his understanding of the situation. When Bryce Brimstone wanted anything in this town he always went straight to the front of the queue.

Neither he nor Mishka spoke further. Dinesh failed to reappear.

★

As he meandered home that evening - preferring to walk to and from work to help keep his weight in check - Gavin couldn't help noticing the looming Brimstone chimney in the distance. He felt a little enslaved at the Call Centre now housed in that mill, the days were long and his duties sometimes grim. This wasn't the path on which his *Epiphany* moment - round at Bob's two years back - was supposed to take him. So, he was in an entirely different place alright. But not the one he had hoped for.

He knew Sir Alan Sugar would have still been waiting to be impressed. But the new, flourishing business that Gavin still hoped to grow was not even on the drawing board. So, it seemed only practical, in such circumstances, to get a quiet little job for now. Some kind of transitional gig, until he finally worked out how to start up the next Amazon or Apple. That said, even securing humble forms of employment was easier said than done in job scarce Drabbleton.

So, he was actually initially grateful to Bryce Brimstone for setting up business in the town and for himself being lucky enough - along with a couple of hundred or so others - to be taken on. After two years of working there now, he was maybe less grateful. Although for another year at least, while he saved up a bit, this would have to be his lot. Despite his grumbles, he had learned to accept it.

Somewhere in his heart, however, just the flicker of a fading dream somehow managed to live on.

As he waited at a pelican crossing, swinging his takeaway bag and starting to anticipate eating its delicious contents, a small, light blue hatchback car pulled up to allow him right of way. He waved to acknowledge the driver, then noticed it was Alice Brimstone, the HR woman from work - sister to Bryce. She was smiling at him as she then gave a little wave back.

'She's nice,' Gavin said to himself. 'Though well out of my division.' But as he then crossed the road, he was pleased with himself that he was at least weighing up the opportunities. Alice's car sped away and he thought nothing more of her.

Around the corner and now home. He immediately noticed a gleaming BMW monster parked outside his abode. Marie was getting out of the car, along with Freddie, who was retrieving a small overnight bag from the boot. The driver's window wound down and the deep voice of an Italian accent was heard.

'Ciao Gavin. How's it going?' Marie's partner of over two years held up a hand outside of the car window and a polite high-five was exchanged.'

'Nice one Alberto,' Gavin replied, in nothing other than friendly tones. 'Good luck in the Cup for Saturday.'

'Ah, cool, man. *Grazie.*'

After initially hating Alberto, in recent times Gavin had come to quite like the guy, if a little begrudgingly. He'd looked after Marie, obviously financially - well he earned enough as a footballer, even for lowly Drabbleton Town FC. But he seemed decent enough too.

Freddie had obviously benefitted from having a little more money in his life than his dad could provide - a steady supply of Xbox games, a cool bedroom and brand-new football kit every season. What more could an eleven-year-old want? And Marie seemed happy too. That was important to Gavin.

'Hiya Dad,' smiled Freddie. 'Fancy playing *Grand Theft Auto?* I've brought Xbox!'

'A takeaway and a games console. Looks like it'll be the perfect boy's night in,' Marie smiled at Gavin as he pecked her cheek. He briefly clasped the hand she dangled by her right side, just out of Alberto's line of sight. She swiftly pulled it away - a brief awkward moment, but nothing more, Gavin thought. The ice had thawed between them, certainly after the first more difficult year of separation. But Marie knew that her ex-husband hadn't entirely moved on. Still, she was glad they were now just both trying their best to accept the practicalities of bringing Freddie up - albeit via shared custody. Although Gavin would have currently preferred a bigger share.

'Have you heard?' asked Marie, seemingly unflustered. 'That lovely boss of yours has only gone and bought the football club.'

'Bloody hell, he thinks Drabbleton's a *Monopoly* board. He's going to buy everything round here.' Gavin scratched his curly beard in dismay.

'I hear he is a bit of a bastard, no?' asked Alberto. 'Oh well, I think I am bigger than him, ha ha!'

'Yeah, but he fights dirty, so watch out mate.' Gavin scratched the beard a little more. 'But all the best with that one. You'll need it.'

'Lookin' on the bright side - with all of *himself's* money maybe Alberto will be in for a big fat pay rise,' Marie added, sunny optimism in her voice.

'Ha ha, good luck with that one an' all.'

Gavin was genuinely amused. A *pay rise,* ha ha! Bless 'em, poor innocent souls. He left them to their dreaming and got on with his takeaway tea and Xbox fun, together with his young son.

4
- JOBSBODY -

Each morning, on his way to work, Gavin walked past the Atheneum columns of Drabbleton Town Hall, a grand building these days aesthetically out of sync with the cheaply constructed Sixties shopping precinct it sat glumly beside. Beyond the Town Hall's steps stood the imposing bronze statue commemorating the town's original philanthropic benefactor, James Brimstone.

'Morning James,' Gavin would always say as he passed by. It was a simple daily ritual that kept him in touch with his dream - to one day escape from his dead-end life and make something of himself. In recent months, however, the *good mornings* had sung out a little less chirpily - work life making a damn good attempt at breaking his spirit.

Just around the corner, the imposing gates of Brimstone Mill would draw him in. He'd find himself looking up at three hundred feet of red brick, historic chimney stack and the proud ensign flying from its apex flagpole. Installed up there since the first day of his acquisition of the factory, the flag was embroidered with one upper case word bearing the new owner's family name: BRIMSTONE.

Today, like most other days, Gavin felt his footsteps slow as he approached the gates, and his shoes appear to fill with lead. But on entering the giant ground floor of the six-storey mill, long gone were the industrial weaving machines of its cotton heritage. Today, rows of flat-pack desks were huddled together, each workstation partitioned away from its neighbours by felt-padded, bright red screens. Banks of beige PCs, seemingly from a computer world of yesteryear, awaited their morose users - themselves soon to be hooked up, via headphones, to the dreaded *Dialler*.

Within one minute of an operative 'clocking in', by placing a hand on a glass topped fingerprint reader, that staff member had to be settled at their desk, ready for duty. So today, sixty seconds after Gavin registering his presence to the system, an alert sounded on his PC and said Dialler piped through his first call of the day. A cold call as usual, or *outbound customer opportunity* as they were known in-house. He took in a glimpse of an old family photo pinned beneath his monitor - it captured Marie and himself in happier times, along with a much younger Freddie. *Action*:

'Good morning, is that Mr Kevin Brinkley?' Gavin began, sunshine coating his vocal cords.

'Who wants to know?'

'Uh oh, bad start,' Gavin said to himself. 'Mr Grumpy on Line 16.' He upped the sunshine. 'It's Miracle Sleep Consultants here, your GP has referred you to us.'

'No, he hasn't'.

'Yes, he has indeed. Dr erm...let me see in the notes...' Gavin searched that imaginary document.

'Dr Entwistle?' Mr Brinkley finally suggested. *How helpful.*

'Ah yes. Brilliant. Dr Entwistle.'

'Then stuff off. He died ten years ago.'

Line dead, Gavin recorded his first result of the day into *Sales Winner*, the revenue recording software: 'No sale'. In his headphones Sales Winner's AI voice spoke to him. 'Gavin, please record the reason for the missed opportunity.'

Gavin sighed as he typed his reply. 'Dr Entwistle inconveniently died before referring customer.'

'Failure recorded and logged. Here is another opportunity,' said AI, coldly. The Dialler then promptly delivered call number two.

'Good morning is that Mrs Doris Beecham?' continued Gavin, still in sunny mode.

'If this is a nuisance call go away.' But Gavin's experience ensured he immediately recognised weakness in the old female voice. He proceeded with vigour on the doctor referral nonsense, quickly to discover that Mrs Beecham did indeed have the nocturnal issues that her GP had allegedly enrolled Miracle Sleep Consultants to help her with. Well, as the *Sales Winner* software only contacted customers aged sixty-five or over, there was always a good chance that sleep would be an issue for some reason or other.

'Well yes, with our *Mattress Miraculous IV* I am absolutely certain that your husband will stop snoring. And research at Oxford University's Faculty of Slumber recently proved that this mattress reduced spinal deflexification by over ninety per cent!'

'That sounds good.'

'It's more than good. It's excellent. Deflexification is a well-known cause of back pain and insomnia.' The cold caller was practically humming now.

'I might have that...*deflexi-something,* or whatever you said.'

Gavin could sense a deal was closing. 'And you can buy-now-pay-next-year at only thirty-nine per cent APR. Here at Miracle Sleep Consultants, we do like to make it easy for our customers in every possible way.'

'Lovely,' said Mrs Beecham. 'I'll take one.'

'Marvellous, a wise choice,' Gavin gushed, slightly ashamed of himself. But he had to live somehow. 'And can I interest you in the Queen Elizabeth mattress topper at only £99.99? That's half price, today only. The *royalty* of mattress toppers. You don't want to be spoiling a £2000 mattress investment with one night's little accident. We all do it, of course.'

'Do you...erm do it.' The voice was enjoying the prospect of this lovely young man's possibly secret disclosure to come.

'Yes, of course. But no problem, as I've got the Queen Elizabeth topper which goes straight in the wash next morning. Comes out spotless and smelling fresh as a daisy.'

A few moments later Gavin was enjoying typing into *Sales Winner*: 'Sales opportunity completed. Amount: £2099.98.'

'Congratulations Gavin,' said the AI. 'Next call coming.' The Dialler was already queuing up the next opportunity. Relentless.

Gavin hated that Dialler with its mechanical serving up of potential customers all piped into his ears, all day, without respite. To escape, he was allowed one ten-minute break in the morning, one in the afternoon plus a thirty-minute lunch break. Any additional toilet requirements had to be logged onto his screen so that wages could be appropriately docked. If the Dialler put through a call that he didn't answer, for example because he was speaking to Krystyna, the Call Centre manager, he had to log his explanation. If he touched his own mobile phone, and was spotted, he knew that meant instant dismissal. Only when the Dialler went offline for IT tinkering, which happened a couple of times a week, would he have a chance to share a few trivial words with his pod neighbours.

Sometime on this particular morning, the Dialler had one such brain fart and the spanner men of IT ambled onto the scene, scratching heads, looking clueless. If they needed encouragement, then a jarring voice was soon booming at them via the PA system.

'Offline for seven minutes!' Bryce Brimstone yelled. 'Third time this week. Mr Connors, my office!' One of the three IT guys turned a little green and looked up at the giant windows of a mezzanine floor office. Up there, taking advantage of the panoramic view of his minions, Bryce stood there nursing a simmering temper. IT Manager, Pete Connors, was soon climbing the exposed steel staircase up to Brimstone's lair, much in the manner of a condemned man approaching the scaffold. The entire Call Centre nervously watched his ascent, only relieved it was not them being summonsed. Five minutes later, accompanied by Security, Connors left the building, never to return. Brimstone had given Connors every chance to sort out the Dialler's glitches, he believed. His latest IT Manager complained, like all his predecessors, that the second-hand kit he was forced to work with was a decade beyond its useful life. But he was wasting his breath.

'What's the point in me paying you handsomely to sort out shit if it keeps happening!' Brimstone had remonstrated to him. 'If I had a brand-new system then I wouldn't need you, would I? Because shit wouldn't happen. So, congratulations, you've just talked yourself out of a job.'

For the workforce downstairs, the fact that Pete was just whisked away as a *persona non grata,* without any 'goodbyes' or 'good lucks' just felt menacing and sinister. It made them feel disposable too. Which of course, in the world of Bryce Brimstone, they were.

But while the Dialler was having a rest, Gavin had a rare chance to talk to three of his direct reports, those sitting closest to him. He was a Team Leader now, since being promoted a few months back when the former job holder on his 'Blue Bank' went off with stress. This meant he earned £1.02 per hour more than the country's minimum wage. It also meant he was under Brimstone's radar now, as Team Leader was the minimum level of management that his employer would bother addressing. Was that £1.02 per hour really worth it, Gavin had often wondered? Life had certainly been more stressful since his little promotion.

'How are we all doing today?' Gavin addressed his foot soldiers, with a genuine smile.

'On target, boss,' chirped back young Kirstie, a recent graduate and still enthusiastic.

'Nearly on target, boss,' said Deepak', another fresh-faced newbie. 'Two sales down, but I'll definitely make it up this afternoon. Definitely!'

'Good lad, let's keep on track.' Gavin imagined a day when Deepak would have his job. It probably wouldn't be long now.

'I'm miles off Gav, sorry. My head's all over the place.' This was Sandra, a forty-three-year-old wife to Tim and mother to two teenage girls. Tim had been diagnosed with cancer a couple of months back and had recently started a course of chemotherapy, one that wasn't going too well.

'OK, you just do your best our Sandra. Maybe we can catch up later for a chat. I'll book us a one-to-one on the system.'

Sandra looked relieved. 'That'd be nice, Gavin. Thanks.'

'Anyway seeing as *Doris the Dialler* is down, anyone got any good jokes?'

Gavin's somewhat optimistic question was met with puzzlement on the faces of his colleagues. When was the last time that a *joke* had been told at Brimstone Mill Call Centre? None of them could remember.

'Well, I've got one,' Gavin beamed. 'A guy goes to the doctor's and says you've got to help me doc. Since I got my new job, I keep getting this ringing in my ears. Doc says, oh dear, where do you work? Guy says *in a Call Centre...* Ha ha!'

But none of his mini audience seemed to share his amusement. Gavin was expecting at least the odd smile, but no. In fact, their faces grew stonier by the second, until Gavin realised that somebody was behind him. Turning around, the displeased face of Krystyna Kowalski, the customarily brusque Call Centre Manager, was there to greet him.

'What is going on?' she asked, in her clipped Polish accent, hands on hips and unimpressed.

'Krystyna, good morning, how are you? Gavin attempted an overly cheery response, but his voice could not disguise the little rush of anxiety that ran through his body. 'I was just telling a little joke. You know, to boost morale.'

'Why would joke help?'

'Well happy workers are productive workers. Don't you have that saying in Poland?'

'No. We have *hungry* workers are productive workers. We work, so we eat. Jokes not necessary.' Krystyna flashed over an intolerant half-smile before quickly straightening her face.

'Well, I can see that's one way of looking at it,' Gavin placated.

'It is the best way. Nobody starves. Anyway, come with me. Mr Brimstone wants to see you.'

She turned on her heels and set off towards the *Staircase of Doom*. Kirstie, Deepak and Sandra looked at each other with trepidation. Was their Team Leader, not too bad a bloke after all, going the same way as Connors?

'He has task for you,' Krystyna called back over her shoulder. Gavin sighed with relief, a task to be done meant work would inevitably continue - he had a future, even for the short term. Though seconds later he felt his body tense as he approached the steeply pitched, steel stairway. Brimstone menacingly peered down at him from the giant window above as Gavin slowly ascended.

Dead man walking, he thought to himself, flimsy confidence about his prospects weakening further. *I'm dead man walking.*

★

Bryce Brimstone sat on an oak framed, executive swivel chair, positioned behind a huge Gothic style desk, himself now facing the back wall. He always enjoyed allowing a few seconds of silence to pass, helping build almost touchable tension in the room, before spinning round to face whichever minion had been summonsed and staring them hard in the eye - the famous *Brimstone Glare.* What a giggle to see the pond-life squirm!

'Right, Hargreaves, Krystyna, take a seat,' he finally boomed.

The two visitors obediently squatted on their lowly set chairs, these deliberately designed to ensure all guests sat in a much subordinate position to the alpha gorilla up there on his rock.

'OK. *Operation Weed Out the Weeds.* Are you with me, Hargreaves?'

'I have not yet had time to explain,' said Krystyna, in matter-of-fact monotones.

'Well waste my time, why don't you. But do you want to explain *now*, Ms Kowalski?'

Gavin's line manager looked more than a little crestfallen at Brimstone's displeasure, but she did her best to continue without letting this appear maybe too obvious.

'Mr Brimstone says all gardens have weeds. We are a garden. We have weeds. We must use weed killer and they must be gone.'

Gavin couldn't recall seeing any gardens inside the walls of Brimstone Mill. Just Victorian cobbles and modern tarmac. Brimstone clicked a mouse and on a large projection screen a Power Point diagram was displayed.

'This chart shows the ten members in your team,' Brimstone went on. 'I have a similar chart for all twenty odd Team Leaders. Ranked by performance, we have a league table of operatives. At the bottom of the table are your poorest performers. Two of them have failed to meet target for three months in a row. Explain.'

Gavin saw two names there, Sandra O'Malley and Sean Thompson. Meanwhile, at the top of the charts young Deepak had a gold star next to his name. He hesitated, fearing any words he offered would be cruelly misinterpreted.

'Mr Brimstone is waiting,' prompted Krystyna. 'These two names, we have spoken about them together, no?'

She was right, of course. The efficient Krystyna had pointed out the shortcomings of Sandra and Sean in his last Monthly Review with her.

'Today, Hargreaves, it is your job to take some responsibility for once. Which one of these will be leaving us today? O'Malley or Thompson? We must weed out the weeds! Choose.'

Brimstone glowered as he watched Gavin's squirming discomfort, the visibly perspiring lackey sinking further in his seat, if this were possible, given its already close proximity to the ground.

'Look Mr Brimstone, I can turn these two around. Sandra has problems at home. Her husband has cancer, God bless them both. As for Sean, well he lost his mother.'

'Two months ago,' added Krystyna coldly - also unhelpfully, thought Gavin. He was disappointed in her.

'I can't choose from either of them,' he fretted. 'They are both very good people.'

Krystyna sighed impatiently. Brimstone closed the Power Point slide, looking almost bored.

'Very well then. If you are too spineless to choose, then I will do it for you. Both are fired.' Brimstone looked pleased with himself as he shooed Hargreaves away. 'You can go home tonight Hargreaves knowing you could have saved one of your beloved cohorts. If only you'd have shown *leadership*. Team Leaders are the Call Centre Managers of tomorrow. That's the plan, eh Krystyna?'

'Yes, Sir.'

Gavin thought Krystyna was on the verge of saluting Brimstone when she'd just said that. But Gavin knew he'd regret this forever if he didn't say more. He just had to say more!

'With all respect Mr Brimstone, you are going too far this time,' he finally managed to blurt out, expecting his employment to be instantly over. Brimstone raised an eyebrow, said nothing, but then quickly swung his swivel chair around to face the wall. Elongated seconds of silence ensued. Gavin and Krystyna exchanged puzzled looks. But when the swivel chair suddenly faced them again, Brimstone was grinning wildly.

'That's it, ha ha! A bit of spine. That's what I'm looking for, Hargreaves.'

But Gavin had indulged the swivel chair game quite enough today, instead now propelled on by some kind of determination stirring from within. He would continue now.

'People of the town hoped they'd see a bit of the old James Brimstone in you when you turned up here. The Brimstone name means something in Drabbleton, even today. Firm management, we were expecting that alright. But we were expecting *firm but fair*. Not this.'

'Ha ha, you *Drabs of Drabbleton* are so entertaining.' Brimstone seemed genuinely amused. 'Actually, I think it's demonstrably *fair* that my money is helping to drag this half-dead town back to its feet. People haven't exactly been queuing up to do that in recent years, have they Hargreaves?'

'Well no...'

'Don't confuse being *fair* with being *nice*. Business doesn't need nice. Because niceness is just *weakness* in my book. My father was nice, and the family lost everything.'

'But still...' Gavin tried, but his rattled employer wasn't to be interrupted at this point.

'Enough now. Enough!' Brimstone clenched a fist and smashed it down onto the desk. The left side of his face twitched until he then composed himself and then smiled weakly.

'But then you've come in here Hargreaves, and you know I actually like this fighting talk. Although...have you quite finished now?'

Gavin shrugged his shoulders. He couldn't win this battle, not today. Not here, like this. Brimstone saw his resistance crumble and his own smile grew stronger.

'So, you just go downstairs and fire those weeds of yours ...and maybe, just maybe, I will plan better things for you here. Are you understanding me, Hargreaves? Opportunity knocks!'

'Yes Sir,' Gavin mumbled as Krystyna looked on with suspected jealousy. She wasn't liking this sudden shine Brimstone had taken to her subordinate. She was supposed to be the *Golden One* around here.

Team Leader Hargreaves solemnly descended the steel staircase, down from the Executive Suite. The eyes of fellow workers below scrutinised him, looking for clues as to whether he'd been sacked or not. Krystyna left his side as he approached his section. Gavin stood before his workstation and glugged on a plastic water bottle. Again, he was aware of anxious eyes - all wondering *what was going on?* Finally, he took a deep breath, hating himself just a little.

'Sandra, have you got a minute, please?'

★

Gavin was so glad to feel the fresh air on his face as soon as he'd signed out from Brimstone Mill for the day. He briskly walked beyond the factory gates trying his best not to dwell on the grim events of the day.

Just across the street, he saw Tim's car and then Sandra embraced in the arms of her husband, she in tears. Tim's face turned to fury as soon as he spotted Gavin.

'Judas!' he yelled out, shaking a fist. 'You should be ashamed of yourself, letting this shit happen!'

Gavin chose not to engage. He quickly crossed the cobbled thoroughfare, avoiding all eye contact with the O'Malley's. Not for the first time today, he felt quite sick.

Unknown to the conflicted Team Leader, someone in an upstairs office saw this little scene play out from the vantage point of a large factory window. Bryce Brimstone chuckled to himself. This had been a fairly good day at the office for him. Sometimes, he had to admit, he just loved his work.

5
- LOOKING UP -

Promptly on the dot of 7.30 am the following morning, Alice Brimstone joined her brother in his office for a scheduled meeting. She'd finally agreed to come and work for Bryce these past two years for a couple of reasons. Firstly, she hoped to temper the excesses of his somewhat unusual management style. Secondly, he offered to up her current salary by fifty per cent. Even so, it was with some reluctance that she had resigned her position as Human Resources Manager at a local mail order company and taken up the new role Bryce was offering to her- Head of HR, here at Miracle Sleep Consultants Ltd.

This morning, like on many mornings, Alice was less than happy with her elder sibling.

'What's all this I am hearing about from Krystyna? This *Weed Out the Weeds* stupid project of yours?'

Bryce smugly observed his sister's consternation. He expected he'd have to handle this.

'I knew you wouldn't like it.'

'But I am Head of HR. Well supposedly so.'

'Your point being?' Brimstone knew exactly what the point was. He was just enjoying goading his sister. Just another bit of sport at the office.

'This idea totally undermines me, that's what. I'm supposed to be consulted on disciplinary matters. I have set in place due processes - so that staff would receive a series of verbal and written warnings before they are dismissed. Dismissal being the measure of last resort. But now, you're ignoring those lawful policies and just firing people on the spot.'

Bryce reached for a somewhat thick pamphlet sitting on a bookshelf beside him. Alice knew what it was as she was its author.

Miracle Dream Consultants - Staff Handbook. He flicked through its pages from start to finish in a couple of seconds.

'Blah, blah. Blah. Yes, read it all. But I did find your disciplinary road map a little on the long side, dear sister.' He blew dust from the pamphlet's cover. 'May I suggest a re-write. Just a headline, really. *Fail and be fired*. Nice and simple. Everyone can understand that.'

'Welcome to the Wild-Wild West!' Alice sneered. But then she remembered that she'd promised herself beforehand that she wouldn't lose her temper. Bryce would *want* her to start getting emotional at this point. But then she would only lose momentum and the meeting would degenerate into one big sisterly sulk. She needed to keep making salient points and not get wound up by this deliberate provocation.

'We will end up in an industrial tribunal, very sordid. You mark my words.'

'My risk, Alice. My risk.' Brimstone allowed the HR booklet to *accidentally* fall into a bin beside him. 'Oops!'

'Very funny.' Alice wondered right then if it would be for the best if she simply resigned. But she knew she had bills to pay, like everyone else in the company remembered at times like this. Instead, she simply made a mental note to start looking for another job.

At that point a weak knock of the door signalled the arrival of a third person that Brimstone was expecting at this early meeting. Permission to enter granted, one somewhat bewildered Gavin Hargreaves tentatively entered the office.

'I got your text last night,' Gavin mumbled.

'Of course, Hargreaves. You replied as well! Now sit down, man. Sit down.'

Alice and Gavin exchanged pleasantries, at the same time blankly exchanging glances at one another, wondering why they'd been asked to attend together this morning. Over the course of the next five minutes, they would soon find out.

'Now nobody interrupt, hear me out,' Brimstone demanded as he stood up and started to pace his office. 'Alice, you are great at recruiting people - and training them. Not so good at getting rid of your mistakes. Hargreaves, I've seen something in you of late. A bit of spunk if you like. But you need to up the mental toughness if you're going to get anywhere in business. So, I've decided...together you will be my *Team H&F*.'

'And what is that, exactly?' asked Alice, almost wearily - while Gavin was just happy to keep his simple bewilderment to himself. 'Team H&F?'

'Alice, you will *hire* people.' Bryce grinned, loving his plan. 'And Hargreaves, you will *fire* them. Team Hire & Fire. Genius!'

'Sounds horrendous,' Alice predictably bemoaned. But on the brother and sister see-saw, Brimstone knew he was up in the air celebrating now, his sister anchored down at ground level.

'I know you'll do it, all the same, dear Sis. While you Hargreaves will be *The Enforcer*. You are going to be feared by everybody working here. Nobody will want to be called to a meeting with you because that will mean only one thing. *Disposal*.'

Brimstone rolled his eyes into his head as he feigned slitting his throat and gasping for a final breath. He then cracked the bones of the broken nose that seemed to be somewhat double-jointed since they were squashed by school bullies, all those years ago. Just for effect. All for the fun!

Gavin couldn't help merely gawping. This was hard to take in all at once. But this did sound something like the *Job from Hell,* at least he had processed that much.

'You'll go onto a proper management pay scale, of course. With a bonus, depending on how quick you get through the deadwood.' Brimstone raised two thumbs up towards Gavin, the lucky jackpot winner. Hargreaves would appreciate the cash alright; his boss had already calculated as much. He had a young kid after all, as Gavin's HR file helpfully revealed. So, money usually talked, well in Brimstone's experience anyway.

'Erm, can I at least think about the offer?' Gavin looked at the giant window of the Victorian Mill built into Brimstone's office. Would it be so terrible to jump?

'Not the dynamic response I was hoping for. But yes alright, meet me here at 5.00 pm sharp with your answer.'

Gavin took his cue to leave. He'd leave the window leap for now.

'Now send Krystyna up when you're back down there,' Brimstone ordered of Alice. 'She can get on with driving sales if she's free from dealing with the deadwood. I'll have *Mr Enforcer* here for that.'

★

After collecting a vending machine coffee, Gavin joined Alice in her cavernous windowless office down in the basement of Brimstone Mill. He immediately noticed that the room smelt damp and cold as fluorescent strip lights flickered into action. In the middle of the expansive concrete floor, a Formica topped desk and three plastic chairs looked decidedly lost. Mildew-stained walls tried to remember the last time they'd seen a lick of paint. Surely Brimstone should find a nicer place than this for his sister, Gavin concluded, as she tried to fire up a portable gas heater.

'Let me have a go,' he offered, as the heater's ignition failed to respond.

'Thanks. The central heating doesn't extend down to the cellar, I'm afraid,' Alice giggled unsteadily, slightly embarrassed by her less than palatial environment. 'Never mind, Bryce has promised me a room with a view when the first floor is finally refurbished.'

'It's stuck,' said Gavin trying to turn an awkward lever on the heater. Alice quickly knelt next to him. 'You need to press that red thing too.'

'Yes...success!' The fire ignited, but when Gavin turned his head, he instantly felt it was in an intrusive proximity to Alice's. Their noses almost brushed against each other. Gavin jumped to his feet. 'Sorry!'

'What for?' asked Alice, smiling maybe a little too awkwardly. She remained kneeling by the heater, looking up at Gavin. He noticed her large brown eyes, not for the first time. Kind eyes, he thought. Beautiful even. They were set off by contrasting jet black and shiny hair - a family trait, it seemed - cut into an angular Cleopatra style bob.

'Oh nothing,' Gavin flummoxed. 'Glad that's sorted, it's like a blinkin' fridge in here,' he mumbled, quickly clinging to a change of subject. Alice looked puzzled and rose to her feet, taking her plastic cup of insipid coffee over to her desk. Her visitor, looking strangely awkward, clumsily pulled out another chair to belatedly join her.

'So, what are your thoughts re that job offer?' Alice enquired, some kind of empathy there in her voice. 'Sounds like the proverbial poison chalice, don't you think?'

'I wish your brother would just head off back to London and let us all get back to our miserable former lives.' Gavin then scrunched his face as the bitterness of the coffee hit him.

'He won't be doing that. He's got Roxanne looking after all his property empire down there.'

Gavin's face made it clear this was all new to him.

'Roxanne, his wife of seven years or so.' Alice helpfully filled in the blanks. 'But they're not close. Far from it. Well, she's young enough to be his daughter for a start.'

'Dirty old bugger.'

'Precisely! Married her when she was just twenty-one, just after she'd done the front cover of *Vogue*. Bit of a supermodel. But he bit off more than he could chew with that one. He can't handle her, and that's saying something. Part of the reason he's scarpered up North. To escape.'

'Blimey!' Gavin really couldn't imagine Brimstone struggling to handle *anybody*.

'He's only stayed married to sweet Roxanne so that he doesn't have to shell out a settlement that would cost millions. He knows she's a shameless gold digger and he's been suckered in. So, he's prepared to play the long game, hoping she'll blink first. If she comes to him, he's hoping the divorce will cost a lot less.' Alice laughed at the thought of Bryce succumbing to the lethal combination of lust and greed that had delivered a complete wreckage of his personal life.

'Couldn't happen to a nicer bloke,' Gavin shared the amusement.

'Quite. Unfortunately for the likes of you and me he's had to find a distraction for now. So he's gone and got all fixated about trying to make the Brimstone name great again round here once more. Big ego thing. He hates the idea that it was our father who finally lost the Mill too. He wants to put it all right. But he's going about it in all the wrong ways.'

'You're not kidding.' Gavin then noticed a flip chart hung skew-width on an easel. In thick felt pen somebody had written the words 'Respect at Work'. One of Alice's training courses, no doubt. She was clearly trying to run a department that didn't really belong in her brother's business, so Gavin surmised. *Pointless*.

Alice leaned across the desk towards him and fixed on him with a gentle stare.

'Can I trust you, Gavin? Well, I'm thinking of looking for another job. You seem like a decent man. Maybe you should do the same.'

He fidgeted with his beard, disappointment etching his face. 'There's no other work in Drabbleton. Not for someone with my CV, any road. Failed joke shop owner, then flop of a children's entertainer - and now this. Maybe it's different for you.'

Alice sighed.

'Maybe. But I don't like to see decent people getting crushed by Bryce. He's setting you up for failure. Don't trust him.'

'That's something, coming from his own sister.' Gavin was genuinely surprised at her candour. Maybe she'd taken a bit of a shine to him - he was willing to take that, for sure.

'Yes, I suppose it is. Take it as a bit of friendly advice from me, that's all.' She turned towards her PC monitor and logged on, looking even a little upset. Gavin realised the meeting was over.

As he walked across the now busy Call Centre floor, he realised his head was in a muddle. But he did think that Alice had been very nice to him with that little confidential chat. And those engaging brown eyes, well wow! She was a few years older than him, he reckoned. Still, very attractive all the same with her neatly cropped, glossy black hair and very trim figure. *But she's out of your league, forget it,* he said to himself. *Brimstone's lovely sister isn't going to go for you!*

★

Gavin felt his stomach in knots as 5 pm approached. But then at 4.55 the tannoy's harsh blaring made him jump in his seat.

'Hargreaves.' A one word summoning of a minion to his office. Brimstone sounded in a foul mood. The beckoned one felt the sympathetic eyes of his colleagues, sending moral support, or simply fearing for him, as he rose to ascend the steel stairway.

Have these steps gone steeper? He felt his sudden breathlessness getting out of control. So he paused outside of Brimstone's office door before knocking, taking in deep breaths attempting to calm himself as best he could.

'Come!' His master's voice boomed before he'd even knocked. Gavin tentatively entered, but then tried to steel himself the best he could. He did want to make a decent showing in here.

'Hargreaves, good. Well, let's get down to it. What's your answer?'

'Erm, I would like to hear a bit more about the role, for a start,' he mumbled almost indecipherably. 'If that is OK with you, Sir.

Sir, why did I call him Sir. I feel like I'm in the headmaster's office, aged eleven.

'I thought I'd made that clear,' Brimstone barked, rolling his eyes. 'Still, for the benefit of those with learning difficulties in the room...' – a desk was punched - 'your job would be to take the twenty or thirty worst performers each month off to a consultation room. Then consult with them that they are fired.' Brimstone laughed at his own spontaneous little joke - *consult with them that they are fired, indeed, ha ha!* 'Then take the next twenty or thirty on the brink of failure and deliver a so-called final warning. We've got to have warnings apparently, according to *Miss Prissy Knickers* downstairs. Then fire them the next month. And so on.'

'Maths isn't my strong point, but don't you think we'll run out of people,' Gavin wondered, calculating that this could indeed be a real possibility.

'Never!' the amused CEO guffawed. 'There's a never-ending supply of *Drabs*, isn't that the case? Nowhere else for them to go. And Alice can keep 'em coming. She's good at that.'

Brimstone suddenly disengaged. 'Excuse me a minute.'

Seemingly distracted by some irritation, Bryce rapidly rolled up a copy of the *Drabbleton Bugle* that had been sitting on his desk. Gavin soon realised that an irked bumble bee was flying stupidly against the window, desperately trying to overcome the physical impossibility of penetrating glass. The constant drone of the attempted escapee had certainly annoyed his boss, who strode purposefully towards the small nuisance.

'Die! Die! Die!' Brimstone yelled rhythmically, each syllable in sync with his battering of the wriggling bee, now brought down onto the windowsill. 'Die! Die! Bloody die!'

The creature croaked, buzzing no more. Brimstone seemed delighted. 'And *don't* interrupt one of my meetings again!' The bee probably wouldn't.

'Now where were we, Hargreaves?'

Gavin hesitated, before he was only interrupted anyway.

'Ah yes. Can we shake on it then? The job?'

Brimstone offered the handshake to the newly promoted confused one who seemed too busy glancing over at the crushed bumble bee.

'Yes, alright then,' he muttered. 'But I was going to ask? Can I have a trial period?'

Brimstone vigorously shook Gavin's hand and patted his shoulder repeatedly - with not much less force than he had used to kill the wretched bee. 'Trial period? Yes, yes. Goes without saying,' he grinned manically. 'If you try it and I don't like it then you're out. I always like a *trial period*.'

Before Gavin had time to think what to say next, Brimstone had shoved a piece of paper into his hand, one entitled *Management Pay Scale*. A number at least twice that of a Team Leader's remuneration had been circled in red ink.

'Amazing!' Gavin couldn't help gulping. 'That's a generous offer.'

A hundred fizzling thoughts went shooting through his head. Being able to treat Freddie without Alberto having to step in, holding his head high with Marie, her maybe seeing him differently again, being able to buy a decent car, maybe get a movie subscription for his telly. Even start saving towards buying back his chippy from Dinesh. All good things. Brilliant, even. All he had to do was go through the motions of this unsavoury job. Yep, on autopilot, not thinking about it too much. Brimstone would undoubtedly be sacking all these unfortunate under-performers anyway, even if he wasn't going to be there to assist. At least he could maybe do it with a little humanity.

'Good, you will earn it though, believe me. I pay my management handsomely. It makes them all never want to leave. In return I reserve the right to make their lives an utter misery.' Brimstone laughed loudly once more. He did enjoy repeating his favourite sayings. All of his managers had heard that last line many a time.

'Hopefully, I will do a good job and that won't be necessary.'

Brimstone laughed again, as if his minion had made a counter joke. He then went on. 'Just one more thing, Hargreaves. You're going to love this.' Striding over to a spacious, walk-in stationary cupboard in the corner, he swung open its double doors. 'Dah, dah!' he sang, in unison with the big reveal. 'For you!'

'No way! I am not wearing that!'

Gavin goggled the highlighted contents of the cupboard, his jaw dropping.

'No,' he blathered. *'No way!'*

It was amazing what people would put up with it just to secure a wage, Brimstone had long since realised. Especially here in the Land of Little Prospects, Drabbleton. Upping the stakes on this, however, was where the real fun might be had. As Hargreaves stood there gawping, he wondered one thing: how low would he go? How very low, indeed?

6
- DIPSTICK MAXIMUS -

The next morning at 7.45 am Gavin, as per usual, checked himself in a hallway mirror before beginning his fifteen-minute walk - through the town centre - to work. But today, his reflection looked back at him with some dismay. It didn't much like the steel helmet of a Roman Centurion at all, despite its ornate bronze decor and striking bright red plumage. Thankfully, for the wall mirror, it couldn't see below head height. So, Gavin's chest armour, skirt and calf strapped leather sandals were out of view. So too was the eagle emblazoned golden shield with its bold engraving that read: '*The Enforcer - Oderint Dum Metuant*'.

Brimstone was testing him; Gavin knew that as he wondered how on earth he'd agreed to all of this. His employer certainly had a persuasive way about him, that was for sure. Persuasion powered by *fear*.

'I want the sight of that uniform to strike dread throughout the Call Centre,' Brimstone had ordered, as the two men had concluded their meeting yesterday. 'And you should walk to the office in it too. Then everybody will know that *The Enforcer* is coming.'

Do this on autopilot, you can do it, Gavin's inner pep-talk advised as he collected his Gladius combat sword and braced himself. Marching out into the crisp morning sun he immediately saw his next-door neighbour out in the garden, off on a walk with grey mutt Rocky. The poor dog's limping seemed to be getting worse.

'Gavin, bloody 'ell. What's this, fancy dress day at work?' Bob laughed, while Rocky cowered behind the recycling bin. 'Nice legs!'

'Yeah, yeah get your laughing over with. It's just a new initiative at work, that's all.'

'Is that skirt from Dorothy Perkins?' This had made Bob's day. *What a show!*

'Piss off or I'll run you through.' Gavin brandished *Gladius* with mock menace and paced onwards. 'In fact, I've been waiting for two years for you to piss off. What's happened to that retirement flat?'

Bob shook his head and spat. 'Bloody paperwork holding things up. But in a couple of months, I'll be gone. Is that that soon enough for you?'

'It'll do, you old misery.' Gavin was tetchy alright. Maybe on his first day as company Centurion he needed to get right into character.

'Send me a postcard from the Coliseum,' Bob laughed as he closed the garden gate behind him. 'The state of him Rocky, the *state* of him.' At least he'd have something to talk about in the newsagents as he went off to fetch his morning paper. *Roman Centurion - what a dick!*

'Morning James,' Gavin sort of mumbled as he soon passed by the venerable bronze tribute to Drabbleton's finest. Recently, he couldn't help noticing the unsettling family resemblance between James and Bryce that was evident in that statue - both men sharing a thick set frame, square jaw and full head of wavy hair. But today, if he could, Gavin was sure that the ancestral Brimstone would be rolling his eyes in despair. *My poor family name! Has it come to this?* Hargreaves scurried along, a wolf-whistle from an amused window cleaner up a ladder following him on his way.

By the factory gates, his path crossed a trio of junior co-workers. They were almost falling over themselves with laughter.

'Hargreaves, you daft pillock!' Darren Eccles scoffed, one of the cocky youngsters from the Customer Retention team that Gavin did his best to avoid. 'You'll get sacked if you walk in wearing that bonkers kit, you thick plank!'

'No, I won't. Mr Brimstone told me to wear it,' Gavin gruffly replied and walked on.

'Are you his bitch now, or something?' Eccles followed up, enjoying the sport, playing up to his two much tickled mates. 'Hey, we've heard the rumour that Brimstone likes to dress up when having sex. Now he's going to ride you up against his chariot, bitch boy!' Eccles gripped on imaginary reins with both of his hands and mimed a breezy gallop.

The raucous laughter and goading continued right up to the main entrance - but as Gavin walked the Call Centre floor towards his desk the ripples of giggling, knowing nudges and barbed comments were at least a little quieter. Then his team colleagues were clearly surprised when he walked straight past their bank and entered a small office underneath the steel staircase. *Where's he going?*

This was Gavin's new workstation, a small grey box with a tiny window too high to see out of. He remembered movies where austere rooms like this would be used as interrogation cells. But when he sat behind his tiny desk he felt a small sense of satisfaction, all the same. This was *his* office, no more open plan cubicles for him. He hadn't exactly *made it* yet, but at least this was a little step up.

Logging on to his PC he was soon inspecting this month's *Poor Performers Report.* Scanning the names of the unfortunates he would have to deal with he paused on one name in particular. He smiled as he highlighted that name in the document. 'Very nice.'

Approaching the Retention Team's bank, above all the mild tittering around him, Gavin once again heard the eager-to-taunt, cocksure voice of Darren Eccles.

'Oh, here he comes - Dipstick Maximus!' Eccles sang out with glee. 'Going for your chariot ride then?'

'Come with me Darren. I am a manager now.' Hargreaves looked deadly serious.

'Yeah right. What costume department manager? You're having a laugh, mate.'

Gavin walked up to Eccles and pushed his own face within an inch of Darren's nose. He glared at him at virtually point-blank range.

'Come with me,' he menacingly whispered.

Darren suddenly looked a lot less comfortable and then hesitantly rose to his feet. But, as he trailed behind Gavin across the floor, he was soon smiling again. The entire Call Centre had begun a slow handclap in time to the Roman Centurion's weird kind of death march. The mirth continued until both Roman and his Anglo-Saxon follower entered the small office, and the door was quietly closed behind them.

Fifteen minutes later eyebrows were raised as two burly guys from Security were seen to enter the same office. What was going on?

Within seconds, Darren Eccles was escorted back to his desk to collect his belongings.

'What's happened, Darren?' asked Urma, a now ruffled co-worker and cubicle bank buddy. *'What have you done?'*

Darren's face was ghostly white. He said nothing to Urma, or indeed to anyone, as he was led out of Brimstone Mill forever.

Gavin emerged from his office a few minutes later. As he walked the floor there was no more tittering, no inane giggles and no muttered jibes. All eyes glued back onto PC monitors with feigned enthusiasm. Silent prayers were sent up that the next tap on the shoulder would not be for them. Hargreaves remembered what the Latin inscription on his shield translated as. Brimstone had told him last night.

Oderint Dum Metuant - 'Let them hate me, as long as they fear me.' For The Enforcer, the work had begun.

★

In the spartan canteen, this not being a normal time for staff breaks, the place was virtually empty. Management could go for breaks at more flexible times and so Gavin thought he'd take advantage of his new little perk. His late lunch had meant he'd had time to sack one more poor performing weed already - and dish out two final warnings to a couple of others. A productive morning.

Only Alice sat there, alone at a table in a gloomy corner. She eyed him with a look of quiet despair as he approached, carrying his lunch tray in one hand and golden Roman shield in the other.

'Do you really have to come to lunch fully armed?'

'Well yes, actually. Your brother insists I must carry my sword and shield at all times.' Gavin smiled sweetly - he was quite ready to swat away any little digs by now. But he was also hoping that Alice wouldn't be too cruel. 'Mind if I join you?'

'What a pantomime,' she sighed as she beckoned him to sit. 'You do realise you look quite ridiculous, don't you?' The Roman soldier nodded in reply, but then laughed hollowly.

'Now then Gavin, I said to myself. At the end of your first month in your new role, what do you hope to achieve? A salary, I answered. Large as possible.'

This seemed to thaw the frost, he reckoned, as Alice smiled back at him, vaguely amused. Even though she was still shaking her head in mild bewilderment.

'I've always admired a man in uniform,' she suddenly twinkled. Gavin looked suddenly hopeful. 'Until I saw you!' She laughed now and her lunch companion willingly took the blow, exaggerating the pain. *But surely, she wasn't serious?* He thought he looked quite good, actually.

'Ah well, the Lord Brimstone giveth and the Lord Brimstone taketh away,' he continued, happy to entertain. He needed a bit of friendly human interaction right now, even if it meant putting up with a bit of gentle stick. Plus, it certainly helped that he found the female opposite so very easy on the eye.

'And talking of the Great One upstairs, you'll never guess what's happened this morning,' Alice teased, suddenly far more animated and seemingly bursting to share a secret. 'This has to be confidential, of course.'

'Of course.'

'He's only gone and received a death threat on Twitter. Fake account, probably. But he's in a right flap about it.' She seemed quite thrilled, despite her brother's apparent consternation.

'No!'

'What do you mean, *no*? You can't believe he's got a death threat, or you can't believe he's in a flap?'

'Both actually.' Gavin quickly concluded. 'Correction, yes I do believe he's got a death threat, but no I can't believe he's in a flap!'

They each laughed, probably not taking the Twitter menace too seriously - but certainly enjoying the thought of Bryce having a bad morning.

'He's making a list of suspects for the police, so he says.' Again, Alice seemed tickled.

'That will be some list!'

They both chuckled. *This is nice,* Gavin thought. A bit of light relief. He was even happier when, fifteen or so minutes later, he got up to put his cafeteria tray away. Because Alice remained at the table, studying him on his way, skirt and all.

'Nice legs though!' she devilishly called over.

'Get lost!' Gavin smiled to himself as he left the canteen. *Thanks Alice!* He felt like he could be *The Enforcer* this afternoon with an extra spring in his step.

★

'Cool Dad. You look cool!' Gavin was pleased to answer the door to his eleven-year-old son and finally hear a lone voice of assent. 'That armour is sick!'

Freddie entered the house, huge grin on his face, leaving his mum on the doorstep with his overnight bag. She duly looked the still-costumed Gavin up and down with some incredulity.

'I've seen it all now,' said Marie finally. 'I thought they were winding me up when I heard about you at the hairdressers.'

'Well, I must have made it now if I'm the subject of gossip under the hair dryers of Curl Up & Dye.' Gavin was feeling his skin thickening by the hour. 'Fancy a cuppa?'

Marie finally managed a smile, weak though it was.

'Oh, mmm, OK then Julius Caesar.' She accepted the quick peck on the cheek.

'Actually, Julius Caesar was an *Emperor*. I am a *Centurion*,' Gavin righteously corrected.

'Same feckin' thing.'

'It is not *the same feckin' thing!*'

Bit like the old days, this, thought Gavin. A bit of harmless banter. Marie joined him in the kitchen while Freddie sat on the lounge sofa, happily scrolling social media. But after five minutes or so of light pleasantries the subject moved onto Alberto.

'I hear your boyfriend's gone and done himself in then?' Gavin spoke, genuinely interested in hearing the inside info on Drabbleton Town FC's star goalkeeper - who'd left the field injured during Saturday's cup match.

'Sensitive subject, so it is, but he's ruptured his *cruciate ligament* - whatever that means. Clattered by his own defender, for the love of God.' Marie rolled her eyes as though the injury was just another irritating thing about *stupid football.* She'd never liked the sport and Gavin had been a bit surprised that she'd left him for a footballer - apart from then seeing that he was gorgeous and recalling that even Drabbleton Town footballers were said to enjoy a tasty pay packet.

'He'll be out for a few months with that, I expect,' Gavin mused. Marie ran a finger through a dust-caked sideboard top, suppressing disapproval.

'Apparently yer lovely Bryce Brimstone says he'll not be getting paid as he's saying the injury was negligence on Alberto's part.'

'Bluffing. I'm sure his agent won't be having that.' Gavin, it seemed, still felt some kind of need to stand by Marie through life's knocks, a leftover habit from the old days. So, he was sounding as convincing as he could be. 'The guy's just trying it on.'

'Yeah, he can't just tear up his contract, like.' Marie seemed grateful for the moral support. 'We said that too. Worrying so it is, all the same.'

'Brimstone just likes to rattle cages. Better get used to it.'

Just then Marie's mobile rang. She quickly scanned her screen to see who was calling.

'Alberto,' she informed Gavin, before walking off into the hallway to take the call in partial privacy.

Freddie then shuffled along the sofa as, next minute, his dad joined him in the lounge. By now, the youngster was busying himself on his iPad - one protected by a skull-and-crossbones cover and the felt-pen inscribed words, *Adults Keep Out!*

'So, what's this you're up to, son?'

Freddie quickly flicked the screen away from Gavin's view.

'Don't tell Mum or she'll do one.'

Oh no, not porn already, Gavin shuddered. 'Is it that bad? Hope it doesn't involve naked females.'

'Dad,' the boy cringed. 'You're just embarrassing.' Freddie purposely threw his head backwards, banging it against the sofa cushion in frustration. He then rotated the iPad, offering up the screen to Gavin. 'See, it's just an app, durr-brain.'

'Oi, less of the lip, sonny. Or iPad goes away for the night.'

'Sorry,' Freddie's petulance was short lived, and his father was most grateful that this was usually the case.

'*Disposals Inc,*' Gavin read aloud, viewing the app's logo. 'So what's this all about?'

'It's just a game really. You put in the name of a friend, or someone, who you really hate. Then they are supposed to get done In by the Mafia, or something. Want a go?'

Gavin laughed. 'No, not really.'

'I put in Connors from school. He's in Year Ten. Keeps bullying us kids in Year Seven. Popped our football today in the yard.'

'Sounds a right meanie. Yeah, nobody likes a bully, Freddie. Do you want me to say anything at school?'

'Well no, *obviously*. Hopefully this app will work, though.'

Gavin sighed. He wished he could protect his offspring, but everyone's kids are going to meet life's tormentors.

'It probably *won't* work son. Just try and toughen up the best you can when the bullies come. Unfortunately, there's a lot of them about. Sometimes it really is worth reporting them. Sometimes.' He put a comforting arm around his son. 'But one day you'll maybe grow up to be bigger than Connors, *then* you can go and stick the nut on him.' Gavin smiled and winked.

Freddie giggled. 'Yeah, I'd love that!' He punched a sofa cushion twice as he went off into a momentary fantasy. 'Dush, dush!'

The father gave his lad a little hug and ruffled his hair.

'Give over,' said Freddie, wriggling free, then continuing to focus on ordering his hitman.

'Close it down, son. Don't let your Mum see.' *Boys together.*

Gavin closed the iPad screen just as Marie entered the lounge, now looking less than happy, but not because of app game antics.

'Yer man there must be having a laugh. Alberto's up the wall! Have you got a minute?' Marie beckoned Gavin back into the kitchen, out of Freddie's earshot.

'What is it?' Gavin knew it wouldn't be good news if *yer man* meant Brimstone.

'He's only gone and ripped up all the players contracts,' said Marie, closing the kitchen door. 'They've got to sign new ones or they're going on the transfer list.'

'A new contract? At least that means Alberto is still wanted.' Gavin clutched for the straws.

'Yeah, but no pay if he's injured. That's what it says. And Alberto's just told me he'll be out for six months. We'll be skint.'

'Surely he's got some savings?' All footballers have savings, course they do.'

Marie laughed a little bitterly. 'Alberto likes to earn the money and live the lifestyle that goes with it. His face cream alone costs more than the rent on this place.'

Gavin winced.

'He bought some trainers the other day. Three hundred quid. A *win bonus,* he said.'

Gavin shook his head but was also quickly calculating that Marie seemed a little too ready to apportion blame here.

'You always look very nice, course you do. But you're never too far away from a designer clothes shop these days, are you, Marie?'

'I like to look my best, what's wrong with that?

Gavin shrugged. 'But what about that boob job? That must have cost more than a few bob.'

'No need to get personal, now!' Marie almost snapped. 'What's it to you, anyway?'

Gavin couldn't help staring at Marie's somewhat over inflated chest. But not the most sensitive subject to bring up, he quickly realised.

'Well, erm - I liked your old boobs probably.' He averted his awkward gaze.

'My boobs are none of your business.' Marie seemed a tad exasperated by the distraction. *What's boobs got to do with it?* 'Anyway, we're usually broke by the end of every month. It's not like he's *Premier League,* now is it?'

'Guess not.' Gavin focussed on making eye contact again but was also aware too that Drabbleton's status in football was quite a few financial tiers down from the riches of the Premier League. But he never expected to be earning more than Alberto this month.

'His agent's onto the lawyers. God, could do without all this!' Marie certainly looked ready to swing for somebody, preferably Brimstone.

'A good lawyer will sort it. It'll all be fine.'

Gavin didn't really know why he'd just said that. Brimstone always knew what he was doing. If his employer did something it rarely backfired. Alberto was likely to be sunk. Then what would Marie do? But for now, she just hit out randomly.

'And tidy this place up, why don't you? It's a right shit tip!'

7
- ALICE IN SLUMBERLAND -

By mid-April in Drabbleton, the Spring leaves were budding on its meagre population of trees, adding at least some natural colour to its grim backdrop of concrete. Gavin was now a month into his job as Enforcer and inside Brimstone's office the CEO of Miracle Sleep Consultants was discussing his progress with Alice.

'So, Sis, you know how much I like to follow your policies and procedures?'

Alice flashed her brother a sarcastic smile to meet his own sarcasm head on.

'Look at this,' he twirled his PC monitor on its pivot so that his visitor could see the Power Point slide on the screen. 'He deserves a warning for this.'

Bryce looked too pleased with himself, Alice thought. She knew this would only be heading one way for Gavin.

'See here,' he pointed a long, stout finger at the screen. 'Week One, ten sackings, but Week Four, only three sackings. What's he playing at?'

'Maybe dear brother, just maybe people are so terrified for their jobs that performance has gone up.' Alice rotated the PC back towards Its owner. She didn't want to see his nonsense charts.

'Yes, performance has gone up,' he replied, frustrated. He hadn't been expecting to hear any logical explanations from his sister. *Logical explanations are usually only excuses, after all.* 'But that's all down to the wonderful Krystyna, surely? Efficiency personified as she is.'

'You mean you'd rather give credit to a woman that you fancy. Everyone in the office knows you've been lusting after her of late.' Alice took evident pleasure in the goading.

'What? That's ridiculous,' Bryce replied, momentarily red faced. 'Krystyna is a model professional around here.'

'Yes of course, a model professional with nice tits and a cute ass.' Alice laughed at Bryce's mock indignation. 'Anyway, congratulations.

You wanted people to be frightened of *The Enforcer*. Well, now they are.'

'There must be at least someone he can dispose of. I'm not happy!'

He could see for himself that his sister was quite pleased that he was unhappy. He needed *Round Two*. Alice cued it up right on time.

'Give it a rest Bryce, you're going to burst a blood vessel.' *Far too smug*, thought her brother, plotting the counter blow. 'Anyway, what's this so-called personal matter you wanted to see me about?'

Bryce rose from his chair and walked to the window, surveying the sombre landscape of Drabbleton, it once again washed grey by a haze of drizzling rain.

'I returned to this wretched cesspit of a town to do something good. Look at the place.' He pointed beyond, seemingly dismayed. 'Nothing the RAF couldn't fix with a few cluster bombs. But I phoned them and they're busy right now, apparently.'

'Very dramatic,' Alice replied unamused. 'What's all this about?'

'We could have done something great together, Sis. But now you've gone and betrayed me,' he snorted and turned on his heels to shoot Alice a lethal look. 'Your resignation. I can't help wondering why.'

Alice had, in fact, felt slight pangs of guilt at her decision. She felt them now too as she clocked the piercing gaze carrying Bryce's disapproval. But she'd secured a new job in the last few days, away from Brimstone Mill. As a result, she was now working her one month's notice.

'I've told you twice already, don't take it personally,' Alice employed her most reasoned tone of voice. Bryce thought she was sounding like the mother from his childhood years. 'I can't work with this bull-in-a-china-shop way you go about things. If you're going to be a blatant bully Bryce, well your sister would at least rather not witness it each and every day.'

'See, that's just you twisting things. Making me out to be such a bad guy when I've turned up here to save Drabbleton.' He sounded bitter alright, but knowing him well, Alice was only waiting for the sting.

'And?' she ventured.

'What do you mean, *and?*

'Bryce, there's usually an and with you.' Alice eyed him with deep suspicion. 'So, what is it?'

Mr Brimstone smiled. He'd set this up nicely. Now for the strike.

'Alice, since you have betrayed me, I decided it only fair that I play dirty in return.' He went for the pregnant pause, enjoying his sister's obvious discomfort. *What has he done?* Eventually, he deigned fit to continue. 'So, you know that Will of Mother's that I am not supposedly in.'

'You're just not.' Alice's tone suggested she had just stamped a foot.

'Invalid.' Bryce smugly grinned.

'What, nonsense! Of course it's valid.'

'Of course it *isn't* my very good lawyer advises - as it has not been *witnessed* darling. Just signed by Mother. People who download free documents off the internet should at least have the sense to do things properly. Schoolgirl error dear Sis, I am surprised at you.'

Alice felt more than a little stupid, for sure. Her stomach was unhelpfully tying itself into painful knots, perspiration clearly dampening her brow.

'Just leave it Bryce. You don't need the money.'

Bryce tutted at her, admonishing the carelessness.

'But my lawyer advises that a robust claim, contesting the Will's legitimacy is bound to succeed. As equal surviving heir to the estate, then Alice, my dearest, half of your house is mine.'

'You're despicable,' Alice virtually spat, now on her feet. 'I won't sell it.'

'No, no,' Bryce smiled in mock kindness. 'I wouldn't drive you from your home. Do you think I'm a *monster*?' He laughed wildly. 'But you shall pay a robust rent against my half share.'

'You just have to control people, don't you?' Alice derided.

'Of course,' her brother replied, looking genuinely baffled that there could be any other way. *'Isn't that the whole point?'*

When Alice left the Executive office, the steep descent of the steel staircase felt in tandem with the plummeting of her mood this morning. Only three and a half more weeks and she would be free to walk away. She could hardly wait. Away to her new job - the details of which she was still keeping secret from Bryce. She couldn't bear the thought of his further derision. OK, so it was hardly her dream career move, but the new opportunity certainly had a bit of potential there to make a difference. And it wasn't *here* with her brother. She'd embrace it with all of her being.

★

Shift over for the day, Gavin braced the wind and steady drizzle on his fifteen-minute walk back home. That afternoon, he'd just had to sack his thirtieth victim, quite a milestone, he'd thought. Ken Norris had offered up a fair excuse, but it's no good turning up at a Call Centre if you've lost your voice.

'I blame that flamin' Italian goalie of ours. We're out of the cup 'cos of him. No wonder I lost me voice, I was screamin' at him the whole match,' Ken had managed to croak. He was getting his voice back now, a few weeks on, but last month's sales target had been badly missed. 'I'm glad he's injured. Prat!'

Gavin felt Ken's dismissal to be particularly unfair - the performance aberration was only temporary, after all. He was an otherwise solid worker. But as far as Brimstone was concerned there was a *zero-tolerance* policy towards missing targets. The only person, so far, who didn't get fired was Jenny Talbot. But only because she had died during her shift, the shock of actually making a sale killing her off with a heart attack.

Brimstone had still wanted to fire her posthumously, all the same. Alice had managed to calm him down, but still had to deduct one hour's pay from Jenny's final pay packet for clocking off early.

Just as Gavin was thinking about the likelihood of the rain perhaps rusting his armour, then so resolving to rub it dry as soon as he got home, a sharp toot of a car horn sounded from behind. Turning around he saw Alice's little blue hatchback approaching, its driver waving to him and smiling. The car pulled up beside him.

'Fancy a lift? Your helmet plume is starting to droop!' She giggled, but he was absolutely fine about the harmless fun. In the circumstances, he'd definitely be grateful to escape the relentless rain. So, moments later he was depositing a very wet sword, shield and helmet inside the boot before then settling down in the front passenger seat.

'Thanks for this,' he said, wiping the excess rain from his face with a tissue.

'No problem. Mayfair Avenue, that's you, isn't it? Top of the *Monopoly* board,' Alice smiled.

'Yeah, they had a cruel sense of humour whoever came up with that, didn't they? *Lavatory Lane* would have been better, sad to say.' 'Gavin laughed a little too bitterly at the irony. 'Never mind, hopefully I won't be there forever.'

'Oh really?' Alice failed to disguise the mild surprise in her voice. 'Where are you off to then?'

'Oh...I've got my dreams.' A passenger train crossed a pollution sullied Victorian railway bridge that they were about to pass under.

Gavin imagined himself on board, suitcases and all, leaving town forever for a much better place. 'See, maybe somebody on that train is off for a new life in some glamorous far-off location.'

'I doubt it. Isn't that the Accrington train?' Alice said, dryly. 'Not much glamour there, I'm afraid.'

'True.' Gavin sighed. He needed to start thinking bigger, he knew that. 'But anyway,' he finally added, after a glum pause for reflection, 'you're leaving. Just read the announcement on email. I'm a bit gutted about that.'

'What, really?'

'Of course. Who else can I moan to now when His Majesty is off on one?' Gavin rhythmically punched the palm of a hand. *'Hargreaves you must fire more people. Fire more people, I'm telling you.'* It maybe wasn't the best ever impersonation of Bryce Brimstone, but it made Alice laugh anyway.

'Very good,' she approved. 'Yes well, short and sweet though it was, I thought you and I made a good team.'

They both stared ahead at the rain drizzling down the front windscreen, smiling through their private thoughts.

'What's your next move then? Or is it a secret?' Gavin felt finally relaxed next to his driver.

'Well, I'll tell you. But promise not to laugh.'

'I promise.' Gavin patted his heart to demonstrate his sincerity.

'I'm taking up a newly created role. *Tourist Development Manager* for Drabbleton.'

Gavin guffawed mercilessly. Alice bit her lip.

'Seriously? Tourist Development Manager?'

'Yes, I'm serious. Go away!'

'Sorry - sorry.' Gavin could see his amusement wasn't going down too well. But surely Alice had to be pragmatic. 'I just can't see how you're going to promote this dump to the world, that's all. *Drabbleton - Britain's biggest shit-hole.*' He used his hand to paint an imaginary billboard in the sky.

'I'll remember that line. Might even use it, thanks,' Alice recovered. She'd been expecting reactions like this and would just have to handle it, so she'd prepped herself. 'But I had to get away from Bryce somehow. He's not impressed though. You wouldn't believe the private manoeuvrings he's been up to at my expense.'

'I probably *would*.' Gavin pretended to growl like an angry dog. 'Grrrr!'

'Very good, nasty - quite.'

Alice did have a lovely smile, her admirer mused. She continued, unaware he was staring slightly. 'But I do need to keep a roof over my head at the end of the day.' A crease of anxiety now appeared on her forehead.

'Tell me about it. Look, sorry to laugh,' Gavin backtracked, suddenly feeling a bit mean. He remembered the miserable work he was doing just to keep the wolves at bay - and him feeling increasingly ashamed of himself with the passing of each week. Here he was, the willing executioner of people's livelihoods and yet that bribe of a nice salary kept him coming back each day to reload the guillotine.

'Good luck with the job,' he finally added, trying his best at empathy. 'If anyone can do it, you can.'

'Cheers Gavin,' Alice, thankfully, sounded more than grateful.

'I mean that, actually.'

'Really?' She seemed very happy to take the approval.

'Of course.' Gavin turned to face the passenger window, before almost mumbling his afterthought. 'I'll miss you around the place. I really will.'

'Oh...' Alice seemed to be pondering, 'maybe we can stay in touch then.' There was certainly some eagerness in that suggestion. Even Gavin could hear as much in the pitch change of her voice.

'Yeah, could do,' he muttered, trying not to sound embarrassingly keen.

'Right then,' said Alice, also now deciding not to sound too keen in return.

'Right then...' A clumsy silence ensued. 'Well, this is me,' Gavin vigorously exhaled, realising he'd just been holding his breath for ten seconds. He pointed towards the somewhat overgrown tiny garden fronting his house, wishing he'd at least had chance to cut the lawn before Alice saw it.

'Right then,' he repeated. 'Top of the *Monopoly* board,' he smirked, but then paused awkwardly again after the car had come to a halt. Alice leant forward over her own steering wheel, then turned her face so that there was eye contact. She raised an eyebrow. *Well?* Gavin failed to respond. His Lancashire charm was in need of a polish, for sure. *Oh, what the Hell*, thought Alice.

She quickly leaned over and pecked his cheek.

'Right then,' said Gavin touching the spot on his face where the kiss had been briefly planted and smiling slightly inanely.

'See you round,' said Alice cheerily.

'Aye, OK.' *I don't know what to do.*

Gavin finally decided to simply go. So, he inelegantly left the vehicle - getting an armour plate momentarily stuck in a seatbelt strap - before retrieving his Roman paraphernalia from the boot. He then stood waving at Alice's car as it tootled away up Mayfair Avenue.

He realised there was this thing called *excitement* suddenly running through his veins. It had been a while. He stood there, until the car was fully out of sight, happily taking in the moment. Bob Horsefield from next door was at his window, obviously both nosey and curious. He shrunk quickly out of view, behind a curtain, when the Centurion spotted him.

Just then Gavin's mobile rang. It was Marie. His heart sunk a little. Maybe he was finally getting over his ex.

'Hi Marie...'

'Ah, so that phone of yours is actually working then? I've texted you three times today.' The caller sounded stressed.

Gavin knew he'd been avoiding replying on purpose. He also knew that Marie wasn't stupid. But what could he say?

'I have been working. Haven't had a minute all day.' He at least tried to sound convincing.

'Oh well, never mind,' Marie backed down. Getting what she needed right now was going to be more important than scoring points. 'Here's the thing, anyways. I don't know how it's happened, but Alberto says we're about a grand down on our rent this month. I thought we'd be OK, but you know me, I'm no good with money.'

'Ah, you're very good at spending it, I seem to remember that much,' Gavin tried to joke - though it was one carrying a serious edge. He knew what was coming. But it was important to him that Marie didn't think him a total walk-over.

'But that's the whole point of money, is it not? To *spend it*. That's what money's for.' Marie hated it when her ex sought out the moral high ground.

'Surely Brimstone's going to pay Alberto some sort of a wage? What's his agent saying?'

'It's all going to take time. In the meantime, we're basically brassic.' Then Marie's tone of voice suddenly steeled. 'I don't like to bring it up like, but you have been a bit light on Freddie's maintenance for the past two years now. Me and Alberto laughed it off while his big fat pay packets were coming in regularly. But it's suddenly not funny anymore. This is going to maybe hurt Freddie too.'

'Below the belt.' Gavin felt that one alright.

'Sorry, but that's the truth.'

Very sensitive subject and Gavin was on the retreat. He thought he and Marie had shared a kind of unspoken understanding that his up to now paltry wages meant he couldn't put in much for Freddie. The subject had always been mercifully avoided.

'This is the first month I've earned a reasonable pay packet myself, as you know,' he batted back.' But I have already said I'll do more now I've had a rise. Can't do a grand, though. That's silly money.'

'How much then?' The voice sounded as though it was sinking.

'Five hundred?'

'Five hundred? A bit rubbish that. Considering how much you owe.' Gavin hated hearing disappointment in his ex-wife's voice, bringing back too many bad memories from the past.

'But maybe you could up your hours at the hairdressers?' he suggested, realising he was clumsily turning defence into attack. 'Three days a week is hardly killing you.'

'None of your business, my career,' Marie clipped back, feeling the wound.

'OK, but maybe then you and Alberto could find ways of cutting your cloth for a bit.' On the spot himself, embarrassed and guilty, Gavin suddenly felt this whole thing about to spiral out of control. 'Why don't you just sell a *Rolex*, or something?' he blurted out, half-laughing, almost instantly regretting the expanse of his big mouth.

'Feck you, Gavin Hargreaves.' The phone went dead.

'Damn it,' he muttered, not wishing the call to have ended that way.

The Centurion put his phone away, just getting a final glance of Bob ducking behind his curtains once again.

'I can see you spying on me, nosey old bugger,' Gavin shouted, although he immediately regretted that too. He knew he shouldn't be taking his frustration out on old Bob. But why was there always *something*, he wondered? Some people had happy lives, well that was the rumour sometimes incredulously whispered around Drabbleton. But nobody in this town could actually come up with the physical evidence to support that fabled truth.

8
- DRESSING UP, DRESSING DOWN -

Three days passed and no sign of Bob Horsefield, which Gavin thought unusual. He normally saw his pensioner neighbour out and about with Rocky, or at least him taking in all the comings and goings of the good folk of Mayfair Avenue through his front window. He wondered if the old man might be ill or something and eventually concluded that he had better check. So on this particular morning he left the house - again fully kitted out Roman soldier style - five minutes early. He cut across the little lawn he shared with his neighbour and first stuck his nose against the window of next door's front room. Nope, no sign of life. But as soon as he rang the doorbell, Rocky was barking as usual. A good sign. Then a shadow of a small figure could be seen slowly approaching through the front door's textured privacy glass.

Bob opened the door, unshaven and hair unkempt, in pyjamas and a dressing gown that had seen better days.

'Oh, it's you,' he grumbled, eyeing Gavin's uniform up and down with a bewilderment that would never fade.

'Aye, it is,' Gavin nodded, trying to muster a smile, but realising it was just too early at 7.40 am. 'I was just checking if you are OK. I've not seen you about the place.'

Bob looked puzzled. *What's it got to do with you?* 'Nowt wrong with me lad.' But a bout of coughing interrupted any further elucidation that may or may nor have been forthcoming. 'Bloody chest,' he grouched, coughing fit finally over.

'You should go to the doctors with that. I know you won't have been.' Gavin knew that his neighbour believed that going to the doctors only made you *more ill.* You go there with just one thing wrong with you. They send you for tests and then there's three things wrong with you. That was his theory, anyway.

'Bloody doctors. All they do is look at their computers. They could get a monkey to do that. And monkeys don't get six figure salaries.' Gavin realised he might have triggered one of Bob's angry rants. Doctors, immigrants, Council Tax, etc, etc...so many subjects to rant about and not enough hours in the day.

'All the same, you should go,' Gavin reasoned, hoping the bee would escape the bonnet.

'I'm just a bit run down that's all,' Bob suddenly murmured.

Gavin scrutinised the old man almost with suspicion. It was certainly odd to hear him admitting that there was anything wrong with him. Maybe it was Gavin's fault?

'Well look, sorry for yelling at you the other night,' he offered with genuine contrition. Bob, however, didn't like people going soft on him.

'Give over, it were nowt. I'm used to your generation being rude bastards.'

'That's alright then, I'll yell at you more often.' All settled then - *sorted*, thought Gavin. But then Bob suddenly looked troubled as he mumbled on, addressing his slippers.

'Aye, but if you must know I'm supposed to be moving out next month.'

'Yeah, you've said.' Gavin tried to remember how long Bob had lived at this very same Council house. Hadn't he told him it was something like forty odd years?

'I'd seen a nice little retirement flat out near Victoria Park. The one I'd told you about.'

Gavin couldn't recall the exact details.

'I've signed the contract and paid me deposit.'

'Sounds nice.' Well Bob was now in his mid-seventies and living alone. All seemed very sensible, Gavin was reckoning. But the old man began coughing again. When that latest bout subsided, a shroud of stress seemed to cover his face.

'Yeah, but I'm worried sick. Don't know what to do.'

'What's up?' Gavin could tell it was bad news. Bob was shaking his head in disbelief.

'After I'd paid the deposit, they sent me another pack with all the rules. And they've only got a *No Pets Policy* in there.'

'That's that then. You can't be going through with that.' Gavin momentarily imagined Rocky abandoned by Bob. *Nah, would never happen!*

'Of course I can't. I'd never leave this old lad obviously,' he said, looking down at the big-eyed creature, gammy leg and all, at his feet. 'So, I tried to cancel, and they said if I did, I'd have to pay six months' rent. I can't afford that.'

'Well obviously.' Gavin's mind was racing. Surely something could be done. You can't rip off old people like this. 'Do you want me to have a look at that contract?' he offered, trying to be at least of some use.

'That'd be good of you. Come in.'

As Bob went off to make a brew, he left his neighbour on the lounge sofa, next to the sideboard which still carried a photograph of Bob marrying Mavis back in the early Seventies. *Some people never move on*, Gavin quietly reflected, hoping he himself would somehow escape a similar fate. He then picked up the glossy brochure from Paradise Gardens Retirement Homes and got down to business. At the back of the cardboard folder was the contract, all duly signed. In the small print, Gavin eventually spotted the *No Pets* clause. A bit ironic, as there was also an idyllic picture of a silver haired woman cuddling a Labrador on page three.

Gavin finally looked at the back cover and saw that the business's legal details were set out at the bottom of the page. Paradise Gardens Retirement Homes Limited - *A Bryce Brimstone company.*

'It's him again!' Gavin's face fell. 'Unbelievable!'

'Oh, I know,' said Bob as he entered the room with his mug of tea. 'He's buying up retirement flats now. I'd heard he's a tough old git. Didn't realise he was a crook though, as well.'

'A greedy, cheating bastard, that's what he is,' Gavin fumed.

'He wants shooting that fellah. If I had a gun, I'd do it.' Bob bent down to playfully ruffle Rocky's ears and continued to speak, but now in a fake childlike, high-pitched voice. 'I would, wouldn't I Rocky? I'd shoot the bugger. Yes I would, who's a good boy, then?'

*

The Roman Centurion was soon on his way to work, by now realising he was likely to be a few minutes late after the diversion at Bob's. He'd have taken his car, but he didn't have a staff car park pass - which Brimstone charged monthly for. Gavin simply refused to pay for something that every other company in town gave out for free. Not that there were that many other companies in town to compare. Never mind, he'd take the ten-minute pay deduction and maybe a flea in the ear from *you know who.*

His stride today was purposeful and hasty, not just because he was late. He'd decided he needed to take the proverbial bull by the horns and tell Brimstone that all this had to stop. All this hard sell in the Call Centre, all these daily firings, all this strangling of Alberto's livelihood and this blackmailing of poor Bob. The people of

Drabbleton had had enough. No longer would they stand by and tolerate this oppressive behaviour. They would rise up. Just see if they wouldn't.

His pace quickened as he rehearsed the barbed lines that would tell his dictatorial boss what's what. He imagined Brimstone in tears, begging Gavin for forgiveness and maybe even reforming forever - say in the manner of Mr Scrooge after he'd been visited by the *Ghost of Christmas Past.*

Then Gavin allowed himself to consider an alternative scenario, however unlikely. Best to consider all options. One where Brimstone, in a hysterical rage, would maybe throw him down those steep steel stairs outside of his office. At the foot of said stairs Security would be waiting to collect his injured body from the floor. He would be stripped of his Centurion's uniform and cast out, wage deprived forever, onto Drabbleton's unforgiving cobbled streets.

His pace slowed. Good plan in principle, but possibly needed tweaking. *OK then. Right.* So, on second thoughts he definitely would be tackling Brimstone. But maybe not today. Best to tweak the old plan and choose the moment wisely.

But Gavin had realised, if he was truly being honest with himself, that the only reason for prevarication was that he was basically shit scared of the imposing CEO of Miracle Sleep Consultants. And that fact didn't sit comfortably with him at all.

As he struggled with his long-winded deliberations, he felt a loud clunking sound as something had obviously made impact with his shield. He quickly turned around and saw Darren Eccles and another young lad he'd recently fired - Stuart Pickering - throwing large stones off a building site in his direction. He raised his shield to deflect the next round of incoming missiles.

'Oi Dipstick Maximus,' Eccles called over. 'You traitorous snake. Have a brick for your troubles!' Gavin ducked and the projectile hit a car window which shattered on impact.

'Turning on your own. You scumbag!' Pickering chimed in. Another stone came arcing over, this time batted away by the trusty Roman sword now drawn from its golden scabbard.

Gavin's temper quickly surfaced. OK, he might be temporarily lacking the guts to take his frustrations out on big shark Brimstone, but these two small fish were definitely getting it!

'Aaagggghhhh!' he bellowed, a blood curdling battle cry. Waving his sword, he manically sprinted off in the direction of the building site across the road. 'Come here you two. I'm gonna chop your bollocks off!'

The two twenty-somethings looked horrified. They hadn't expected the angry revenge of the Great Roman Army to be heading straight for them. They quickly scarpered. But Gavin spurted on. He knew he would catch them, little sods. *I'll run them down.*

'Come back, you little bastards!' Olympian mindset he may well have had, but Gavin's body then inconveniently reminded him that he was a thirty-seven-year-old of relatively sedentary lifestyle. He bent over, supporting his upper body with hands on knees. 'Useless old git!' he chastised himself, completely out of puff. Eccles and Pickering ran off into the distance, their laughter and catcalls fading away as they disappeared from view.

Gavin just needed a few moments to get his breath back. He doubled over on a rotund plastic waste bin. A scrawny middle-aged bloke was passing, clearly intrigued by the Roman Centurion's epic chase that he'd just witnessed by pure chance.

'Is this a film, mate?' he enquired of the costumed soldier.

'No, it's not a film,' Gavin replied in a tone that said *go away.*

'It looks like a film. Where are the cameras?' The scrawny one looked curiously around, trying to spot Steven Spielberg maybe sat on a director's chair up on the roof of the butcher's shop.

'It's not a film,' Gavin grunted.

'Is there anyone famous in it?'

'I said it's not a bleedin' film!' Gavin slammed his shield against the plastic bin. Boom!

'*Some people.* I was only asking.' Mr Scrawny walked off in a huff. Gavin simply cursed. He'd be even more late for work now.

*

Calendar Meeting Request: 11.30 am. Bryce Brimstone. Thirty minutes.

Gavin sighed and clicked on *accept*. 'What does the Grim Reaper want now?' he wondered aloud, having pretty much fired everybody who'd missed target for the last month. Surely, he couldn't be in trouble for that. Maybe he was just going to get a rollocking for being late. *Whatever*, sigh.

Alice popped her head round his office door, big smile on her face.

'Hi, just a quickie but you'll never guess, *His Royal Highness* has had two more death threats. Two different Twitter accounts, apparently.'

'Blimey, I'm seeing him at 11.30. I hope he doesn't think I'm one of them.'

'He's trusting nobody. That's what he's saying.' Alice raised her eyes towards the ceiling.

'Even if he doesn't think it's me, I'm sure it will have put him in a rubbish mood. Damn.' Gavin stared at the meeting request on his screen, its subject line left blank. 'Damn.'

'Not like you to be overly bothered about him. What's up? said Alice, clearly a little concerned.

'Oh...just had a bad start to the morning, that's all. Had rocks thrown at me on the way to work. Darren Eccles and Stuart Pickering. Everybody in town probably hates me.'

'Not entirely *everyone*,' she smirked. 'But are you OK?'

'Yeah, yeah... I ducked.'

'Good idea - well done. Both of them were on your removal list though, so I suppose that's fair game for Drabbleton.'

'I'll remove them from the planet if I can catch the little buggers. Good job for them they can run faster than me. Swines!' he grumped, wallowing in the misery of his physical deficiencies.

Alice merely laughed again as she imagined him wildly legging it down the street, Centurion outfit and all.

'Oh, never mind, a spot of lunch might cheer you up?' A bright and breezy yet spontaneous suggestion.

'Yeah,' he replied, suddenly perking up - and slightly surprised at the offer, as the pair had never done lunch before. 'Yeah, that would be very nice.'

'It'd be good for us both to get out of here for an hour,' Alice smiled before adding a little wave and disappearing.

'Great,' Gavin called after her. *Not all bad news today then!*

But the rest of morning's hours, right up to the 11.30 appointment with *Misery*, did seem to drag by painfully slowly. He was really looking forward to going out for a bite with Alice, but what a wretched hurdle to have to navigate first. He busied himself with mind-numbing administrative tasks to distract from thinking about it too much. Until the PC clock did inevitably trudge its way to 11.28, at which time he took a deep breath before hauling his reluctant body off to see his Master.

On reaching the Executive Office, at the top of a stairway that seemed unusually steeper, Gavin saw a pale yellow post-it note attached to the door. 'Do Not Disturb!' it warned in scrawled black ink. He looked at the time on his phone - 11.30 am sharp. He wondered what to do. The post-it might have been put there ages ago and forgotten about. Plus, if Brimstone clocked him as being late for the meeting, he could only imagine the tongue-lashing tongue to come. The office door was a Mill original, solid oak and reliably soundproof. So Gavin's eager ear to its surface was a waste of time. Nothing could be heard from beyond. But what if he barged in, interrupting an important business meeting? He'd be dead for that too.

One little post-it note. One big dilemma. His quickly concocted solution was to wait here outside until his phone's clock ticked forwards to 11.32 - a kind of token compromise. He expected he'd get only a mild mauling for being just two minutes late. In the meantime, any prior meeting in there might have reached its natural conclusion.

Yet 11.32 arrived right on time, as expected two minutes later, but no developments. Gavin took in a sharp intake of air and knocked on the door. No reply. He counted down from ten... *Three, two, one.* He knocked again, but this time only as he simultaneously opened the great oak door and stepped swiftly inside.

He gawped.

Brimstone had Krystyna pinned face down and doubled over on his desk. They were having sex - rough and unusual. *Rough* because Brimstone was pulling back Krystyna's hair as she screamed and he continued grunting like a giant gorilla, thrusting his manhood into her from behind - mustering all the strength that his colossal frame could summon. *Unusual*, as they had both seemed to have chosen costumes for the occasion. He sporting some kind of dog suit, she dressed as a sweet, young schoolgirl in a red cape and blonde plaited wig.

'Ooh, ooh, ooh,' groaned the big dog, rhythmically, leering and slobbering.

'Aah, aah, aah,' moaned the thirty-something 'schoolgirl' on the counter-beat.'

Gavin was standing in the middle of the floor, but he realised that neither of the otherwise intensely occupied persons in the room had yet sensed his presence. He was instinctively drawn towards a furtive retreat, tiptoeing silently backwards. But not being particularly experienced at reversing, dressed as he was just now in half a suit of armour, his scabbard unhelpfully hooked itself around a floor lamp which was sent crashing to the ground.

Brimstone looked up, horrified and gobsmacked.

'Hargreaves!' he roared. Gavin froze.

Krystyna screamed and slumped behind the desk out of the Centurion's view, simultaneously scooping up discarded underwear as she fell.

Brimstone stood glaring at the intruder. *For fuck's sake, he could have at least put his cock away,* thought Gavin.

'What are you staring at Hargreaves? Have you never seen *Little Red Riding Hood* getting serviced by the *Big Bad Wolf* before?'

'Actually, no...' Gavin warbled. *Fuckin' hell, his cock's massive, put it away for God's sake.*

'Sheltered little imbecile. Get out! Get out! Wait for me outside.' He shooed the clumsy and unwelcome intruder away. *Finally, he's putting it away. Thank God!*

Gavin quickly restored the floor lamp to its upright position and darted out of the office, gently closing the giant door behind him.

'Thank you,' he meekly offered, as he turned the door handle. *Thank you? What did you say that for? Prick!*

Just outside the office were a couple of plastic chairs, a meagre waiting area. He sat down on one of them, dreading being called back to face his boss's wrath.

He didn't have to wait long. The huge door creaked open within five minutes, when it was then apparent that Little Red Riding Hood had miraculously metamorphosed into Krystyna Kowalski, Call Centre Manager. In her crisp, navy business suit and white cotton blouse she purveyed an air of calm business efficiency. Very serious. Yet, still very attractive, Gavin couldn't help but notice. But who would have guessed at her apparent enthusiasm for amateur dramatics on the side?

'Good morning, Gavin,' Krystyna breezed, as though nothing at all had just happened.

'Good morning, Krystyna,' the accidental witness replied, perfectly fine with that pretence.

'Go in now,' she ordered, before then flashing Gavin a mischievous smile. 'He is in foul mood. Your fault.' She seemed to be enjoying the prospect of her colleague's terrible predicament and he, in turn, was quite sure he heard her giggling as she merrily skipped off down the stairs. But he knew it was time to face the dreaded one, however ghastly that might turn out to be, so he rose from the plastic chair and gingerly entered the Chamber of Doom. Five seconds later he was standing before Brimstone's desk, awaiting the worst.

'Right, I've got one thing to say to you and one thing only!' Brimstone boomed, now thankfully also out of role-play costume.

I'm fired. Let's get it over with.

'If there is a post-it note on my door that says do not disturb, then do not bloody well disturb.'

He stood up and leaned over his desk so that he could firmly knock-on Gavin's skull three times. 'Hello. Anybody in there?'

'Yes *OK*,' The underling pulled away from the mild but still painful assault, regretting his removal of his armoured helmet for this meeting. 'But I wasn't sure if it was an old note that might have been forgotten, or something'

'I see. You're still having difficulties, aren't you? So come with me?' Brimstone came from around his desk and literally frogmarched Gavin back into the waiting area. The now infamous post-it note was still on the door.

'What does that say?' the booming voice patronised. 'Well?'

'Do not disturb,' came the weakest of utterances.

'Very good. Progress. Right ...you wait here until that note is no longer on the door. Understood?'

Gavin nodded. Brimstone promptly stepped back into his office, slamming the door behind him, and leaving both the hapless employee and post-it note alone together outside. Hargreaves gave out a huge sigh and sat back down on the plastic seat. *What a palaver.*

He waited. And waited. He kept looking at the post-it, but no developments. Up in the exposed rafters above him he spotted a fly struggling in a giant spider's web. The large inhabitant of the web descended on cue and demonstrated its skills as an accomplished killing machine. Gavin felt sorry for that fly. He knew the feeling.

Precisely twenty minutes since he had retreated to his office, Brimstone reappeared. Without making eye contact with Gavin, he removed the *do not disturb* post-it and scrunched it up in his fist. He then stepped back into his room and promptly closed the door once more. Seconds later, a timid knock was made on oak.

'Come,' the voice inside barked. Gavin entered and gingerly approached the Executive desk.

'Sit.' The order was immediately complied with. 'See, now that wasn't too difficult, was it? We have learned something today.' Brimstone smiled, pleased with himself for administering such a splendidly easy to follow lesson.

But Gavin felt there was more trouble for him to come. So, when sitting outside just now, he'd decided to get onto the front foot as soon as possible.

'I just want you to know, what I saw earlier will remain strictly confidential. My lips are sealed.' Gavin mimed zipping said lips.

Brimstone let out a huge belly laugh. 'Good God man, I don't care who you tell. You can put in on the front page of the *Drabbleton Bugle* for all I care. As long as you say I have a big ding dong.'

Gavin looked shocked.

'And I did see you looking, so don't deny it!' Brimstone laughed again. 'Anyway, sermon over.'

Is that it? thought the lectured one. *Is he not going to fire me over this?'*

'Hargreaves,' Brimstone moved on, 'did you know I am getting death threats?'

'Yes, I have heard.' Gavin could feel his face now being scrutinised for the slightest twitch of guilt. 'Nothing to do with me,' he blurted without any suggestion having yet been made that it was.

'Interesting. Are you nervous Hargreaves?' Brimstone leaned forwards across his desk, increasing the intensity of his stare.

'No,' came the clearly nervous reply.

'Then keep your leg still.' Gavin realised his right leg was trembling rhythmically. He grabbed it and brought it to order.

'I can see a trace of sweat on your brow. You appear to be clammy. Your body seems to be telling me more than I could expect to hear coming from your mouth.' Brimstone smiled, enjoying the interrogation preliminaries. He turned his PC monitor around on its pivot so that his visitor could then see a Twitter page that he'd readied.

Gavin frantically scanned the profile page, wondering why he was being shown it. The death threats were crude and direct.

'I haven't reported it,' said Brimstone calmly. 'I've got more chance of catching the vile perpetrator if it's not removed.'

Hargreaves felt his body suddenly tense as he saw the author's username: *Dipstick Maximus.*

'Any idea who this Dipstick Maximus fellow could be?'

'No sorry. No idea.' Gavin immediately thought about *Darren Eccles.* He was definitely having him now.

'And then there's this one.'

Gavin's eyes widened as he read aloud the second username. '*The Enforcer.* Well, that's me. But it isn't of course.'

'Oh really? It certainly sounds like you.' Brimstone sounded like he felt that he'd got his man. 'Krystyna has already told me that the young chaps round the Call Centre have christened you *Dipstick Maximus.* You need to fire them to prove your mettle, but that would be for another time. And of course, *The Enforcer* is your Roman moniker, a name I have carefully chosen for you. Very bold of you to do this.'

'I'm not even on Twitter,' Gavin bleated.

'Unlikely. The police will be here in the next five minutes. I purposely kept you outside with all that post-it note nonsense as they told me they'd be about twenty minutes getting here. But you're going down for this Gavin Hargreaves. Death threats are taken very seriously by the Crown Courts of our glorious land.'

Gavin felt his breathing growing more rapid, out of control almost. His skin felt sticky and his chest tightened. *Oh God, I'm going to have a heart attack.*

'I'm innocent. I'm being set up,' he managed to simper.

'Save it for the judge,' Brimstone scoffed, banging down a fist on the desk. 'Gavin Hargreaves, I hereby sentence you to *life imprisonment.* Take him down.' The impression of an Old Bailey, despotic beak was rather good thought the speaker.

'Please. Even you must see all this doesn't make sense.' Gavin knew he sounded desperate but was already realising he was wasting his time with protestations of innocence. Maybe the police would be easier to convince than his habitually unreasonable boss. Well, *wouldn't they?*

'Go on then, I suppose life imprisonment might be stretching it a bit. But you could certainly get five years for this,' Brimstone continued to toy.

'Five years? Surely not.' Gavin covered his face with his hands. His accuser silently observed his discomfort for a good half-minute, savouring the moment. Until...

'Ha ha ha ha!' Brimstone was suddenly creasing up. 'I got you there, didn't I? Sucker!'

'What?'

Brimstone was gleeful now.

'Of course I know it's not you on Twitter. Somebody with half a brain is trying to frame you, moron. Well, everybody you've fired obviously has it in for you, I wasn't born yesterday. I just thought I'd invite you up here to have a bit of fun.'

'That's *terrible.*'

'Oh, don't be a softie. Your face, ha ha! What a picture.' Then Brimstone decided he should adopt a high pitched, simpering voice to impersonate the pathetic Hargreaves. 'Five years? Surely not! Let me lick your boots my lord as you beat me some more!'

'You're terrible too,' Gavin gulped, feeling the weight of humiliation dragging him down.

'Well, I'll take that as a compliment,' Brimstone cheerily replied. 'OK now you can go.' He casually flicked his hand to dismiss the crushed insect.

'But what did you want to see me about?' Gavin just hoped there'd be *something* else and all this just hadn't been some ritual humiliation. But no...

'That was it, *stupid*. Aren't I allowed a little *entertainment* around here from time to time?' Brimstone watched Gavin's face fall yet again. 'Oh, don't be all namby-pamby about it. I'm still paying you for this morning, for God's sake - not that you've done much work. Now go.' Another wave of dismissal was sent towards the irritant.

Gavin picked up his shield and helmet from the side of the chair, rose to his feet and marched out of the office. He thought he might burst into tears, but luckily managed to steel himself just enough. He then decided he was going to slam the door behind him in a gesture of final defiance. It only took him three seconds to reach said door. But that was enough time to reconsider. He closed it meekly behind him and went off to maybe bury himself six feet under.

9
– YOUNG WIFE, OLD WIFE –

Brimstone remained in his office vexing himself over a spreadsheet. Unhappy about the financial state of play of his burgeoning Drabbleton Empire he concluded he needed to redirect some capital out of the London side of the business - the side efficiently controlled by his twenty-eight-year-old wife, Roxanne. He didn't expect his suggestion would go down too well but needs must. He scrolled his phone and clicked on an image of a striking blonde woman, pouting lips - possibly recently filled - and heavy mascara setting off huge eyelashes and amazing green eyes.

The phone rang out for far more than enough time to have been noticed at the other end. Bryce sighed. But then Roxanne's clipped voice finally answered.

'Yes?'

'Oh, I thought you weren't going to pick up,' Brimstone half laughed.

'I nearly didn't. But mother always taught me not to be rude, so you can thank my childhood indoctrination for that. 'Roxanne's sultry voice was Home Counties posh, refined by a Swiss Boarding School education and a First-Class degree in Astrophysics from Cambridge University. Well, that's what her Wikipedia page said. Although certain alumni of Grimley Comprehensive School in Brixton were certain she had been in their class, then expelled at fifteen for snorting a line of coke during PE. But regardless of education pedigree, she'd naturally fallen into a modelling career for real, with her drop-dead gorgeous looks that the likes of *Vogue* and *Cosmopolitan* couldn't get enough of. And it had to be said, whether or not her erudition had been polished at Cambridge or a Brixton Comp, this beauty certainly came with brains - this latter talent not always to the liking of her fifty-two-year-old, far less clever husband.

'I was wondering how my beautiful wife was on this fine morning?' he beamed.

'You want something. What is it?'

'And how is...what's his name, Spencer?

'Spencer is history. I have Dimitri now.' Roxanne remained in monotone.

'Well, I hope you have told *Dimitri* that you have a husband who adores you - and who would be devastated to learn of your clandestine misdeeds?' Brimstone was pantomime acting and he knew it. So did she.

'Oh Bryce, please do not be a baby. We agreed two years ago now that we could see other people.'

'Did we?' Brimstone sounded deliberately vague. 'Yes well... I didn't actually think we were serious about it, Cherry Pie, obviously. I haven't so much as even looked at another woman while I have been up here. My ding dong has been sadly silent.'

Roxanne sighed wearily and looked down from the grand window of her Knightsbridge mansion drawing room. A sweeping Georgian Crescent of similar opulent houses bathed her eyes as a silver Bentley motor car purred to a halt below and some mean looking Eastern European VIP was ushered towards the colonnaded entrance of the property opposite. One of the black-suited bodyguards saw Roxanne at her window. He smiled and nodded. She half waved in return - but then imagined Bryce suffering his contrasting, dreary courtyard view and the shabby northern town vista beyond its gates. He had taken her to see Drabbleton on just the one occasion last year, but she promised herself never to return. It was literally another world for her - and one so suffocating she wished she'd never bothered to have set foot in it. She had told Bryce that she'd felt her life force draining insidiously away every hour she'd been there. Only serious *Harrods* retail therapy would compensate her for that lost weekend in her life - and her husband therefore subsequently paid dearly.

But by now she was controlling the London business interests, not merely shopping for designer dresses and jewellery. Although she still indulged in that too, of course, and at regular intervals. She had negotiated with Bryce that she would manage the property portfolio in the city while he could then play his absentee local-hero games up in Drabbleton. However, in exchange for her management duties - and he knew she was good, no problem there - she wanted full budgetary control. She would run London, including holding the purse strings. He would do whatever it was he was doing in Drabbleton's grubby backwaters. Bryce initially agreed, knowing the arrangement was not legally binding, as all the property assets were still in his name. But he soon learned that Roxanne took the term *budgetary control* very seriously. He had found himself having to plead with her for his own money on more than one occasion. The alternative, an expensive divorce and nobody to manage London.

For her part, Roxanne agreed to remain Bryce's trophy wife, if in name only. She hardly had to see him now that he was away on his ridiculous Northern adventure. She had her sexual freedom, an entrepreneurial business life and the trappings of a dazzling existence amongst the rich and super rich of Knightsbridge. If she played the long game - and he remained complicit - she would outlive the old bastard. Then she'd inherit everything. Divorce meant only half, or even less, if she didn't manage to sleep with the judge first. For now, though, her patience waned.

'Seriously Bryce, let's get to the point. I've got to get Antoinette off to the groomers by 12.30.' Antoinette was Roxanne's current toy, a Pomeranian lapdog which she carried with her virtually everywhere. Multi-million-pound property transactions took top priority 24/7 for Mrs Brimstone, of course, except when it came to serving the delicate needs of pampered bitch, Antoinette.

'Heaven forbid Antoinette's coiffured coat missed its appointment with - who is it this time - *Vidal Sassoon?* Brimstone sneered.

'Boring, darling. Please get on with it.' By now Roxanne was almost gritting her teeth.

'OK, OK,' the baritone voice on the phone suddenly sounded a little less composed. 'Well, I need five million from the Chelsea town houses sale. Cash flow up here is letting me down a bit, have to say. Got to settle an acquisition for those retirement flats I told you about. Plus, I've seen a parade of shops.'

Roxanne tutted. She was managing an amateur, that's how she saw it. 'Yes, but why, oh why, are we buying real estate deep up the backside of Northern England when I have spotted a prime warehouse conversion opportunity here on the river?'

'*Buy cheap*, Roxanne,' Brimstone replied, sounding more confident again. 'This place has ...erm bottomed out, if you'll excuse the pun. The only way is up, you mark my words.'

'Even further up that God forbidden backside, you mean? Roxanne sneered. 'I could make a million on that river development, just flipping it within six months, cosmetic makeover and all. You know it.'

'You're the expert at cosmetics, darling, I'll give you that much.' Bryce instantly regretted the dig, but he couldn't help it.

'Again, boring.' There followed a long sigh until Roxanne seemed to resign herself to instigating Plan B. 'But this takes you to the limit.

I made a contingency that you would do this, even though you promised to make no more cash calls after you'd bought that stupid, useless football club. However, I knew you'd be back.'

'Bit harsh darling,' Brimstone protested, though quietly relieved about that contingency thing.

'I can move some money around and still do the river development. But it will be tight. Still, I will manage,' Roxanne continued with business-like resolve. 'But if we do your latest Drabbleton misadventure, then that's it. No more money comes out of London. Or I'm out. And you know what that means. See you in court.'

Brimstone could hardly know that numbers were simultaneously flying around Roxanne's calculator of a brain, and she really wouldn't settle for only a fraction of a fortune. The long game was her game, but her outsmarted husband just couldn't seem to see it. She only wished she'd have married some millionaire who was *even older.*

'Yes alright. No need for nastiness,' the wary husband interjected. You do know I'm still hoping we're going to patch things up one day, you and me.'

Silence.

'Maybe a weekend in Monte Carlo will help smooth things over, for a start?' he cajoled.

'Yes, very kind of you, darling. I like Monte Carlo. I am sure Dimitri will too. But where would *you* go? She smiled at Antoinette, stroking the small dog's lustrous coat.

'Highly amusing... Anyhow, can you arrange the five mill?' Brimstone knew when there was a time to scratch back. This wasn't it.

'Very well,' Roxanne sounded almost disappointed that her morally subdued husband failed to take the bait. 'I will get it transferred this afternoon. But don't think I approve!'

'Love you darling! Goodbye, kiss-kiss!' Brimstone finally mock gushed.

'Goodbye Bryce.'

Roxanne promptly ended the call and returned the gold-plated iPhone into her weekday Gucci handbag. 'This old thing,' she grumbled as she noticed a millimetre long blemish on the leather. She was wiping the scuff mark with a tissue when, five or so minutes later, her impeccably turned-out personal assistant knocked and then entered the drawing room.

'Yes Penelope, what is it?'

'Mr Sidorov for you, Mrs Brimstone,' said the twenty-something doll.

'Ah yes, as expected. Show him in.'

Penelope nodded and left the room. A few seconds later a slickly suited gent appeared in the door frame. It was Dimitri, the bodyguard Roxanne had just acknowledged from her window as he was obviously concluding his duties for the morning. He was tall, mid-thirties, jet black hair greased back.

'Lock the door,' said Roxanne, by way of an order. She slowly approached her visitor who was clearly relishing the much-practiced sensual steps of an international catwalk veteran. *She is beautiful*, he thought as he turned the key without taking his eyes off her.

'I have ten minutes before I must take Antoinette to her appointment,' she pouted as she reached him, stretching her long, toned arms around his neck. 'How might I fill that precious time? I would hate to waste it!'

She kissed him full on and bit on his lip. His jacket seemed so easy to slide away from his wide chest, revealing a shoulder holster complete with handgun.

'I will try to think of something original,' he replied with a knowing smile, removing the holster.

'Good. I like originality.'

Antoinette barked, a little jealous of the lost attention. As Dimitri unzipped her owner's Gaultier dress the little creature yapped again - but then suddenly realised she would have to give way. She'd seen this scene before - and many times too, involving many different gentlemen. She scurried across the room to go hide under an 18th Century Queen Anne chair, trying her best not to hear the ensuing ecstatic grunts and moans of human sexual intercourse. *My God, they're like animals*, thought Antoinette, as her owner let out a lustful scream, though thankfully now out of view.

★

Meanwhile, in what some would argue may well be a less glamorous location than Knightsbridge, London, Bob Horsefield opened the front gate of 23 Mayfair Avenue, Drabbleton, accompanied by Rocky on a lead. He'd got dressed and smartened himself up too since this morning, even back-combing what were left of his old grey *Teddy Boy* locks, adding a bit of Brylcreem retro styling too. Now clean shaven and sporting his best white shirt and tie - underneath a vintage, velvet collared jacket - he'd decided to try to give a rest to moping about his accommodation woes, well at least for a couple of hours. So, he'd hit on a most suitable distraction. It would do him good.

A fifteen-minute wait at the nearby bus stop and, late as usual, along came the spluttering Drabbleton Circular single decker bus - billowing out, as it was, surely illegal levels of diesel exhaust fumes. Coughing through the thick smoke, both he and Rocky fumbled aboard, where a free bus pass was brandished entitling them to lungs full of pollution for no charge at all. Such was the social generosity inherent in Drabbleton's crumbling transport system.

No matter, Bob and dog were mobile, heading off on an annual journey, one which had become a kind of ritual really. How forty years had flown by. A decade is practically nothing, Bob was reasoning. So only four lots of those and there's your forty years gone by right there. Almost in the blink of an eye. So sometimes, if he put his mind to it, he could still feel the raw pain of the day when his dearest Mavis had walked out on their marriage of fifteen years - four decades ago to the month. Seemed like only yesterday.

Since then, around the anniversary of her departure, give or take the odd day - as he wasn't obsessive or anything - he would habitually board this very Circular bus service bound for Buttermilk Avenue. In fact, looking at it now, this could have been the very same vehicle for each of those forty years too.

Buttermilk Avenue, in the Riverstone part of town, was about a fifteen minute's bus ride away. There, rows of neat Sixties bungalows fronted by miniature, manicured lawns held onto a tradition of neighbourhood pride in appearances. A tad twee for some maybe, but certainly a contrast to much of the unkempt and decayed parts of town. In fact, Buttermilk Avenue was once locally known as *Garden Gnome Gardens*, which Bob thought told you everything about the kind of people who lived there - well apart from one person, that is.

Because it was here, in this very cul-de-sac, that dear Mavis had set up home with Ken the plumber in May 1982. As she and Bob had shared a childless marriage, there'd been no particular reason to have kept in touch - and they hadn't done so. They'd never even spoken since the day she'd left when she'd rejected once and for all a loving but quite infertile husband for her new plumber lover – one who had functional pipes on many levels.

But it's not every day that a childhood sweetheart walks out on you, not someone who you'd first had a crush on aged six, who you'd dated from age eleven up to engagement, aged eighteen, and finally had then married, aged twenty - a marriage lasting a further fifteen years. And could have lasted longer too. Until along had come Ken. *Bloody Ken, wife stealing bastard!*

So on that basis, Bob felt he practically had a right to walk past number 21 Buttermilk Avenue just on the single occasion each year. All this being totally cut off from the love of his life was just cruel and inhuman. So he'd kind of kept up, in his own sweet way. Therefore, he'd known about the daughter that had come along within a year of Mavis's departure. He'd even thought this daughter ironically looked a bit like him and imagined her calling him Daddy. He'd seen Ken's white vans getting posher and newer each year - business obviously prospering.

After twenty odd years went by, a new little boy had appeared too. Probably a grandson. Then every three or four years or so Bob had actually spotted Mavis herself - in the garden, or maybe at a window. He'd also clocked her picture in the *Drabbleton Bugle* a couple of times too. She'd become a firefighter, suiting her physical disposition - and on one occasion had caught a falling baby thrown from a burning building. Another time she'd caught a stranded cat that had tumbled out of a tree. She'd always been a large and muscular girl, a good four inches taller than Bob himself. But as the years progressed so had she too progressed upwardly through the dress sizes, so that by her fifties she was twice the girl he'd once known. But only twice as lovely in Bob's view.

These last few years had seen no sign of Ken's white van on the driveway. But Bob reckoned he must have retired from the plumbing game long ago by now. Instead, in recent times, a dinky red saloon had been parked up instead - always spotlessly polished to match the spick-and-span bungalow that was Mavis's little palace.

So today, having left the health hazard of a bus, it was meant to be more of the same. Bob would casually saunter up the cul-de-sac, first one way and then the other. He wouldn't stop to draw attention to himself, wouldn't dare. But each time he passed number 21, he would surreptitiously glance towards the property and gather this year's intelligence. Then he would be gone, keeping a mental record of exactly what he had learned, until the next yearly visit came around. Then, rinse and repeat.

Rocky, being a dog with a doggy lifespan, had only been around for the past fifteen of these annual journeys. But he seemed familiar with the routine by now, pulling ahead on his lead as if helpfully guiding his owner along to his habitual destination.

This year, however, was to be quite different to other years. As they approached number 21, keeping their eyes furtively peeled, both human and dog saw an old poodle up at the top of the drive.

This smart looking, tiny canine looked very pleased to see the somewhat mangy Rocky, in the way that dogs often are when a new backside to sniff comes along. But, sadly for the petite poodle, it was being prevented from joining in on an impromptu rendezvous by an ornate iron gate that spanned the width of a passageway to the side of the bungalow. Still, she stuck her snout through the gaps in the gate and yapped enthusiastically. Rocky then got suddenly excited himself, a rare happening in these his elderly years and barked a happy hello in return.

Bob quickly smothered Rocky's exuberance, crouching down to hold still an animated jaw.

'Shush boy,' he whispered. 'Remember the idea is this is a *secret mission*. Don't you go blowing our cover.'

Of course, he wasn't to know that Mavis had been in her back garden watering the geraniums. She'd casually come over to the gate to see what had attracted her little Petal's attention. When Bob got back to his feet, now there she was in full view looking right at him. He was busted!

'Morning,' Mavis casually smiled to the passing pensioner gent, who if she'd looked carefully might have been more than a little familiar to her. But it is far too difficult to peel away forty years of ageing and decline from a person's aspect inside a few seconds. Not at twenty paces, behind a garden gate anyway. Bob tried not to completely freeze. 'I think they just want to be friends,' Mavis kindly mused.

'Dogs, eh?' Bob managed to shrug. 'Bye then.' He casually waved and tugged at Rocky's lead, the dog on the end of which being clearly reluctant to leave. Petal yapped again at Rocky, who barked sorrowfully in return. *Why do humans spoil everything?*

Mavis watched them depart for no more than a few seconds, vaguely curious about what would make an old dog limp like that. And that old man had a bit of a cough too.

Then, as the Buttermilk Avenue tourists soon both waited for the anti-clockwise Circular bus to take them home, Bob confessed everything to Rocky.

'That was Mavis, boy. My childhood sweetheart who I married. And today is the first time I have spoken to her in forty years.' He punched the air. 'What a day! Next year will have to be bloody good to beat this.'

Although, it didn't seem that Rocky was particularly listening. Instead, his mind was on the mystery, snowy white poodle - and dreaming of what might have been.

10
– THE GREAT ESCAPE –

As Roxanne took her pleasure from the latest rugged male in her life, Brimstone continued juggling his spreadsheet. His was a different form of satisfaction, the naked pursuit of money, but for him equally as fulfilling.

'Ah that's better,' he said out loud when he realised that the insertion of the handy £5 million made everything balance. He picked up his phone, about to call a property agent, and ambled over to the window where he often made his calls. Down below, walking over to her car parked in the mill's courtyard, his sister appeared to be going off for lunch. Bryce thought nothing of it. But then Hargreaves suddenly appeared on the scene and approached Alice as she rummaged in her handbag for a car key.

'Curious,' Brimstone muttered and decided he'd hold off on his call and observe what was occurring down below.

'Are you ready then,' Alice greeted cheerily. But she could see that Gavin looked decidedly upset. 'What's the matter?'

'Your brother,' Gavin spoke bitterly. 'He's just chewed me up for breakfast and spat me out. For kicks, apparently.'

'What happened?' If you want to say, of course.' Alice's first thought was that Gavin had got it in the neck for not firing enough people.

'He accused me of making the death threats. Got me proper worked up. Said I'd go to jail.'

'Ridiculous.'

'Yeah, but then he burst out laughing. Said it was a wind up. He was just having a laugh.'

'Oh, that's awful. Come here...'

She leaned towards him and administered a soothing hug. Gavin felt himself willingly sinking into the warmth of her embrace. The hug tightened so that they were suddenly aware of each other's bodies pressed close. Neither of them had expected it to happen, magical chemicals colliding as they did, but then they were suddenly kissing - a long and tender example of a kiss that made Gavin feel as though all his troubles were being gently spirited away.

As the enchanted moment came to its natural conclusion, its participants giggling in clumsiness, Alice pressed the car remote. The jolt of the doors unlocking then nudged them quickly back to reality.

'What in the Devil's name are you two playing at?' a boorish voice boomed down at them. They looked up in alarm to see Brimstone leaning out of his first-floor opened window. 'None of that kissing nonsense if you please!'

Gavin initially stumbled, shocked by the intrusion. But then he remembered - how could he fail not to - the barking boss having full-on sex with Krystyna. *So that's OK then, but no kissing!* The hypocrisy of the Law according to Brimstone rankled.

Alice, however, seemed to muster a far more combative response.

'Don't you dare yell at me from a window, Bryce Brimstone!'

'I'll bloody well yell at who I like from my own factory window!'

'If you were down here, well I'd smack your face. And if we were in a pub, or something and not work, then Gavin would probably punch you. Wouldn't you Gavin?

'...Erm.'

The Centurion, less attuned to the sudden escalation, seemed to be finding difficulty in switching on his *Enforcer* superpowers. Brimstone sneered.

'Sorry, shouldn't put you on the spot,' Alice muttered to her ally, by way of afterthought.

'Don't make me laugh, Sis,' Bryce continued, 'I don't know what's going on exactly. But you are not to see this excuse of a man. I forbid it!'

'Who are you to forbid anything that is going on in my private life?'

'But it's not in your private life is it. These are working hours!'

'Lunch break!'

'But still on my property!' Brimstone's volcanic ash continued to shower. 'Anyway, I am not having my sister going round with a *Drab*. Now come back into this office this minute. ...Hargreaves, I don't care where you go, as long as it's not with her.'

'Come on Gavin,' Alice quietly beckoned Gavin towards the sanctuary of her light blue hatchback.

'If you get in that car with him Alice, then you are fired!'

'I've already resigned.' She stamped a foot in temper. 'And *this* to the rest of your notice period!' She flicked the finger towards her glowering brother.

Gavin had never seen Alice use profane gestures before. *Wow, she's angry!* The rebellious sister then jumped into her car and slammed the door firmly closed. She auto-wound down the passenger window.

'Are you coming, or what?'

Gavin stared up at Brimstone, despising those blustering red cheeks and furious eyes. He realised he had finally had enough too. He removed his plumed Centurion's helmet and tossed it into the gutter.

'Don't you dare Hargreaves...' Brimstone really could not believe this level of unbridled insubordination. He cracked the bones in his broken nose, an involuntary habit, but sure sign of his anger dial about to trip off the scale.

The Roman shield soon joined the helmet clattering to the ground - then the sword crashed down beside them both.

'That's expensive company property, you moron! Don't go chucking it about!'

Gavin glared back at Brimstone and then gave him one glorious Drabbleton V-sign salute. He had passed out a few similar gestures down the years. But this one was by far the most satisfying V-sign of his life.

'You're fired, Hargreaves!'

'I'm free!' Gavin replied, celebrating the defiance and the joy. He pumped a fist before then throwing in a bold middle-finger salute for good measure. He opened Alice's car door and slid in beside her. As Brimstone watched agog, smoke and fire possibly exuding from his nose and ears, Gavin's chest armour was thrown from the car. It soared gracefully through the gusty Drabbleton air for several seconds before clanging down on top of Brimstone's pristine *Chelsea Tractor*.

'You are double fired!' he exploded. But the ex-Head of HR and the former Centurion were gone, and his words merely faded on the wind.

'Oh my God, what have we done?' said Alice inside the retreating car, catching her breath and trying to still concentrate on her driving.

'That was mad!' Gavin replied, amazed at his own sudden show of guts and resolve. And Alice too, *where did that come from?*

'His face when you chucked away that armour. Priceless!' She laughed, suddenly swerving a little to miss a traffic cone in the road. 'Whoops. I've lost it!'

'Yeah, steady on. We've just escaped to freedom, don't be killing us off already.'

They both laughed, almost hysterically.

'Sorry.'

But moments later Alice's smile straightened. 'Oh my God, I've just realised. I only had a few more days of my notice to work. But you've just lost your permanent job. What was I thinking?'

'My decision.'

'Well, you wouldn't have done it without me egging you on.'

'Yeah well... Hopefully something will turn up.' Gavin's face gradually fell as he was dragged against his will to face the grim practicalities of life - *bills, Marie,* how would he manage? But at least he'd got Alice now. A great start to his hopefully better new life. 'Any road, I'm glad it's all happened.

'All of it? Why's that then?'

'Oh, you know...' Gavin attempted to spit the smothering gag of awkwardness out of his mouth. 'I suppose...well, what I'm saying is I think I might be falling in love with you.'

'And I think I might be falling in love with you too,' Alice replied brightly. She laughed.

'Yeah cool...but we mustn't rush into it, like.' Gavin instinctively turned away and found himself looking at the boarded-up shops of an abandoned precinct as they drove on.

'No, no, not at all. Mustn't rush.' Alice was trying to suppress a wide grin. 'We definitely wouldn't want that at all.'

★

Now that they both had all afternoon to take in a leisurely lunch, Alice decided she'd first like to show off to her newly acquired boyfriend something she'd already been dabbling in up at the Town Hall. So driving into the pastiche Athenian square, she then pulled her car up in a parking bay, just beside the bronze statue of her great ancestor, James Brimstone.

'Afternoon, James,' said Gavin, nodding in respect.

'What you saying that for?' Alice seemed most amused.

'Ah, yeah... I'm always talking to James; didn't I tell you? I like to think he's kind of looking out for me.'

'Odd - but sweet I suppose. Come on.' Alice left the car and indicated that her passenger should follow. As Gavin then walked by the statue of James, towards the Town Hall's grand oak doors, did he sense a slight sparkle in its eye? 'That'd be nice, James approving,' he whispered to himself. 'OK, carry on talking bollocks!' he then quietly laughed.

'Dah, dah!' Alice sang, as she eventually led Gavin into a vast room on the ground floor. It was formerly Council Chambers, but since Council business migrated to a cardboard tower block in the Sixties, this rather grand space had kind of lost its purpose really. But, in more recent times, it had at least regained some part-time usefulness as an *ad hoc* exhibition space.

Gavin entered to see Alice enthusiastically dancing around an entirely disorganised collection of old spinning and weaving machines from the town's industrial past. He noticed a couple of items were labelled up. There was a wooden wheel and frame called 'Spinning Jenny' and a sturdy, wrought iron weaver called 'Lancashire Loom'. On a table was strewn a collection of sepia tinted photographs originally taken in mills and factories through the ages. Gavin looked at the gaunt faces of mill hands who would have worked these machines, dawn until dusk, all those years ago. A tough life to have lived - and he considered that maybe work in a modern Call Centre wasn't so bad, after all.

'See, this is the exhibition I am putting together. First project in my new job,' Alice chirped. *Drabbleton Cotton Town*, it's called. What do you think?'

'Good - I guess it will be very interesting when it's all put together,' said Gavin, much taken by Alice's obvious enthusiasm. Far more verve being shown here than ever up at Brimstone Mill.

'And what do you think of him?' she teased as she hesitated before pulling away a dust sheet from an exhibit set aside in the corner. 'Dah, dah,' she sang again as she revealed an amazingly lifelike waxwork sculpture. To full human scale, and looking resplendent in a fine Victorian gentleman's suit, was a replica of James Brimstone, founder of Drabbleton's once proud cotton industry.

'That's incredible. Bit spooky he looks so real though,' Gavin giggled nervously as he tentatively touched the model's face. 'But very nice to finally meet you, James. I'm Gavin, the one who speaks to your statue outside every day.' He offered a handshake, but it wasn't reciprocated.

'My new boss, Leo, got him commissioned from a sculptor who had worked at Madame Tussauds. Good, isn't he?' Alice brushed off a little dust from James's left shoulder and fastened the single undone button on his waistcoat.

Meanwhile, Gavin scrutinised the model with increased intensity. That thick set jawline, the piercing eyes, the voluminous and wavy hair, there was a family resemblance there that unnerved him.

'Mind, I hope the good folk of the town don't kidnap him and melt him down. Looks a bit like Bryce, sorry to say!' Gavin frowned.

'Well, he is our great, great, great grandfather, not sure how many *greats* exactly,' Alice chuckled. 'Bound to have been some shared genes sent down the line. But no crooked nose,' she added, noting James's version of that particular facial feature was perfectly straight. Unlike that of her brother's, of course, long ago brutally mangled by some anonymous school bully.

'Ah yes,' said Gavin, noticing the same. 'Very handsome. And if I try not to think of Bryce, he's incredible,' he finally enthused. 'Yeah, I laughed at you at first, sorry, but at least all of this is something that people might actually visit Drabbleton to see.'

'I do hope so. Heritage is big business in the tourist industry these days.' Alice's voice sounded full of hope. Gavin felt oddly proud of her. If anyone could make a go of being Drabbleton's very first Tourist Development Manager, then yes, he was doubly certain that she was the girl.

Having re-covered James with the dust sheet, Alice switched off the lights and led Gavin away from her *work-in-progress* exhibition. But she couldn't wait to get stuck in for real when she would finally start her new job a week on Monday. As they then crossed the parquet floored hallway towards the exit, a frail looking chap, around forty years of age, dressed in a bright pink pinstriped three-piece suit came towards them. Alice beamed a smile of instant recognition.

'Leo, hi!'

'Hello Alice, starting the job early then?' came the reply, which left Gavin immediately despising the privileged sounding Oxbridge accent. *We don't talk like that round 'ere.*

'No, no,' Alice laughed politely. 'This is my friend Gavin. I've just been giving him a sneak preview of what we are up to. Hope you don't mind.'

'Not at all. Nice to meet you Gavin,' said Leo, curiously eying the remnants of the Centurion costume that Alice's companion was still wearing. 'But I'm afraid you've chosen the wrong period of history if you were hoping for an acting job in the *Living Museum* section.'

Gavin looked blank. Alice burst out into what was surely forced laughter.

'Ha, ha. Very good, Leo,' she replied, gushing. 'No, I do suspect Gavin here has had enough of dressing up for a while.'

'Shame, said Alice's boss, who was the new museum's chief curator and himself a renowned academic specialising in Britain's Industrial Revolution. 'Nice legs,' he quipped with a cheeky smile.

Interesting. Not usually chatted up by gay blokes, thought Gavin. Not sure exactly how comfortable he felt about that, he did long for later when he could finally take that skirt off forever.

Final pleasantries exchanged, Alice and her retiring Centurion left Leo behind to his opening preparations and were back outside onto the cobbles of Town Hall Square.

'He's gay then?' asked Gavin, a little insecurely. Despite Leo's effeminate personae and annoying accent, with his tousled blonde hair and fine features, anyone could see that here was a very handsome gent. And if he was going to be working alone with Alice? Well...

'I really couldn't say,' came the somewhat surprised reply. 'Does that bother you?'

'No, course not,' Gavin replied, trying to sound relaxed. 'I don't mind gay blokes. Definitely not.'

'Do you actually know any?'

'Yeah, course. I know loads of gay blokes,' Gavin bumbled.

'Loads?'

'Well, ...there's that gay newsreader on *North West News* for a start.'

'So, you don't actually know any gay blokes, do you? TV doesn't really count.'

'No, not really,' Gavin scratched his beard, hoping to dig up at least one gay from his memory's limited Contacts list. A forlorn attempt. 'That said, I will try and meet one or two if it's important to you. I hear the Anchor pub has Gay Night on Thursdays!'

Alice just laughed. *What a fuss!*

'Anyway, fancy dinner, Friday night at mine?' Gavin blurted out, happier to jump back into his heterosexual comfort zone - and change the subject. They were, incidentally, approaching Ted's greasy spoon cafe, home of the best all-day breakfast in Lancashire and yet another Drabbleton top attraction. 'I usually call it me *tea*, but I'll make it posh and call it *dinner* if you're coming.'

'Mmm, would we end up talking about who might be gay and who most certainly isn't?' Alice had a glint in her eye, obviously enjoying ruffling a few feathers.

'No, *definitely* not!'

'OK, then that would be nice,' Ms Brimstone smiled, finally releasing Gavin from the slight squirm of discomfort.

'Great!'

'What will you cook?'

'International cuisine. You'll be impressed.'

Gavin had already plotted that he would be calling on the culinary skills of the *Star of India* chippy to come to his assistance. He hadn't seen Dinesh in a while, so he was dying to break the news to him about his newly acquired girlfriend. If indeed he was allowed to refer to Alice by such a term! Was it even politically correct these days? *Who knew?*

11
- DATE NIGHT -

Gavin had been having a grumble. 'Look at the state of this place,' he'd self-admonished as he'd suddenly become aware of dust and dirt that hadn't previously bothered him for months. 'Bloody hell, lad, you're a disgrace!' It was early Friday morning and he had set out to get his house literally in order before the visit of Alice that evening. He'd fought with a brush against two giant spiders who had taken residence behind the TV, creating web debris reminiscent of a *Haunted House* theme park ride. Then he'd hoovered the carpets, saying hello to remnants of food from previous dinners that he hadn't seen in weeks. He'd cleared the coffee table of a dozen empty lager cans, scooped up empty crisp bags and sweet wrappers - the latter, *Freddie's fault* - and removed three bin bags of rubbish from the kitchen, one of them stinking so badly it could have almost walked itself out to the back yard. He'd even changed his bedding, first time for two months, on the off-chance he might get lucky - and realising that a sophisticated lady like Alice was unlikely to appreciate his stinking pit.

'Not going to happen,' he corrected himself, restraining any false expectations in that department. 'Too soon.' But at least if Alice was having a look around and she saw *clean bedding*, well that might help her relax into things a bit more easily when the time felt right on some future occasion.

By mid-morning he'd already put in three hours of solid graft, and he reckoned the place was maybe now only half the shit tip it was before he'd started. *Not too bad!* Now time to tackle the past week's washing up...

Just then the doorbell rang. Gavin quickly scooped a stack of soiled dishes into the froth filled kitchen sink and went to answer.

'Hi Pat,' Gavin brightly greeted the pointy featured postman, who wasn't really called Pat at all. However, Freddie - when but a toddler - had christened him so. And the name had just stuck ever since.

'Morning Gav, *Recorded Delivery,* sorry pal,' said Pat with a glum voice. He knew that the only Recorded Delivery letters that folk on Mayfair Avenue got were from solicitors, Magistrates Courts and bailiffs. 'From Payne & Cheetham's solicitors. Bastards that they are.'

'Oh, ta...' Gavin sighed as he took the white envelope from the postman and signed on the dotted line, thinking all along that Pat had probably read the letter already. He didn't mind, he was salt-of-the-earth was Pat.

'Bob next door got something similar last week. Trouble with his retirement apartment contract,' the postman tutted wearily.

'Yeah, I know...'

'That's yer Brimstone bugger for you. I'm giving these Payne & Cheetham's letters out all over the place. I'm starting to think he's got something on everybody in town.'

'Ha!' Gavin scoffed bitterly. 'He probably has.'

Pat seemed to be shuffling his feet, growing mildly impatient. 'Well, aren't you going to open it then? It's not good news.'

'Eh? ...oh yeah, alright then.'

Pat's bespectacled stare fixed on the envelope as Gavin tore into it and pulled out a single A4 sheet of luxury laid paper.

'Top quality paper that,' said Pat. 'Those bastards make so much money they can afford that.'

Gavin was busy scanning the letter to extract its essence as fast as he could.

'Bloody hell!'

'How are you going to pay that then? Five grand!' asked Pat, without reading the letter.

Payne & Cheetham's, on behalf of Bryce Brimstone, were *giving formal notice of possible proceedings in respect of compensation for damage to company property.* Gavin read aloud the remaining details of the claim against him.

'Damage to antique Roman Centurion armour, two thousand pounds. Damage to Range Rover motor car hit by armour used as trajectile, two thousand pounds. Compensation for distress and inconvenience to claimant, one thousand pounds.'

'I never hit his bloody car, did I?' Gavin had been blissfully unaware that the last bit of armour he'd thrown from Alice's vehicle had been gracefully carried on the wind before colliding with the roof of said Range Rover. *'Distress and inconvenience,* it's all bollocks.'

'You've got twenty-eight days to pay up. See it says so there.' Pat helpfully pointed out the obvious.

'Yeah thanks, I'd seen that. Oh well, I'll just have to sell me stocks and shares.'

'Oh?' Pat replied, eyebrows raised. 'Have you got stocks and shares?'

'No, course I bloody well haven't,' Gavin shrugged. 'I was joking. So, what am I going to do now then?'

The two men stood there with blank faces, seemingly staring up at across-the-road's gutter where two pigeons sat chatting. But neither the sky, the Universe or the pigeons came forth with an answer. Exactly what to do would have to remain a mystery for now.

★

Gavin had set aside a twenty-five quid allowance for his big date night. A generous budget by his standards and given his new employment status. Yet he knew he'd have to push the boat out a bit to impress Alice. He'd called in at *Bonanza Booze* for a five quid bottle of Prosecco and bought a small bag of tea lights from *Harrison's Hardware* for three quid. This left him with enough for a grand Indian banquet, courtesy of Dinesh.

Half an hour before Alice was due to arrive, Gavin had temporarily forgotten all about his job woes and had walked with a chipper spring in step off to the *Star of India*. He seemed to arrive in no time, busy as he was in his head daydreaming about the potentially exciting night ahead.

'Good evening, Gavin my friend,' Dinesh smiled, as the daydreamer walked in - on auto-pilot - through the frosted glass door.

'Hi Dinesh, Mishka, ...Mrs Rowbottom.' Mishka waved as she wrapped a stack of tin foil trays in paper. Mrs Rowbottom, a rather large woman in her sixties - but dressed as drably as a post-war pensioner, nodded politely. *She looks like a black and white photograph,* thought Gavin. *Devoid of colour.*

'Mrs Rowbottom here is just telling me about Albert's snoring,' Dinesh revealed unabashed.

'Albert, I expect that's your husband, Mrs Rowbottom?' Gavin politely enquired.

'Course not, he's long dead,' came the deadpan reply. 'Albert's my cat.'

Gavin nodded, trying his best to show empathy on his struggling-to-co-operate face.

'Yes, very strange a cat snoring,' counselled Dinesh, wisely. 'I will give you cup of curry powder, Mrs Rowbottom. Give Albert a little sniff of that. Used to work wonders for Mishka's grandfather who was a fellow snorer. That is right, eh Mishka?'

'Oh yes, Grandfather Harjit would snore like a tractor engine,' Mishka happily confirmed. 'But he came to swear by the magic of sniffing Dinesh's special curry powder - so that Grandmother Binita did not kill him!'

They all laughed.

'That's very kind of you, Dinesh. I will certainly try that!' A shadow of colour seemed to flash across the monochrome one's face.

When Mrs Rowbottom subsequently left the chippy, fish, chips and curry powder in hand, she looked like the weight of the world had been lifted from her very round shoulders. Another satisfied customer for Dinesh and Mishka's takeaway and counselling service.

'But Gavin,' Dinesh then said with a twinkle, talking behind a hand. 'How is sex life?'

'Starting to warm up,' Gavin grinned. 'Not exactly all action yet. But maybe soon.'

'You old rascal. I was worried that your man-piece would have seized up, it has been so long.'

'Thanks for the concern, Gavin muttered, grimacing at that thought and hoping Mishka wasn't listening.

'Indian Special Banquet telephone order ready,' said Mishka, all smiles, holding up a carrier bag of hot food towards Gavin. 'Yes, I was worried too. Use it or lose it, Grandmother Binita always used to say. And Grandfather Harjit gave her ten children!'

Dinesh gave a mini round of applause. 'Yes ten, very splendid!'

'Anyhow, good luck with lady friend tonight,' Mishka added with a knowing wink.

'Oh...you know about that?' *Isn't anything secret round here?*

'Of course, it is the talk of neighbourhood. Everybody knows it is Gavin's date night.

Dinesh applauded again.

'Heck...' Gavin marvelled at the efficiency of the Drabbleton grapevine.

'You enjoy it. But sorry to hear about job,' Dinesh's face suddenly took a more sombre turn.

'Yes thanks, but it's all for the best,' said Gavin, not really wanting to talk about that right now.

'That man is bastard. He kills us all.'

'Come now Dinesh,' said Mishka, putting her arm across her husband's shoulder. 'Do not be putting downer on Gavin's happy evening.' She smiled at the wannabe Romeo and lightly waved him to go.

'Why what's up?' Gavin's sudden concern lost him the opportunity for a quick exit.

'No, Dinesh,' said Mishka, now more firmly.

'I am sorry Gavin, but I am beside myself,' the chip shop owner continued, freeing himself from his wife's arm. 'Today I get letter from solicitor. Brimstone bastard has bought our parade of shops. He is doubling rent. We will go out of business.'

'That's rotten news,' Gavin frowned. 'Maybe you can appeal, or something?'

'I don't know. ...But this is same man who used to bully me at school.' Gavin's face made it plain that he had no idea about all of that.

'Don't go on, Dinesh. Please.' Mishka held her hands together, as if in prayer.

'He put my head through railings and threw food at me. He put me in wheelie bin and sent me tumbling down The Hundred Steps in town. Broke my arm, that did. Then he force fed me a donut during Ramadan when I was meant to be doing sacred fasting. But he doesn't even recognise me now. Yet when I see him, all my nightmares return.'

Dinesh turned the chips in the fryer, fighting back tears in his eyes.

'That's all dreadful, I'm so sorry.' Gavin felt helpless. He hated to see people he cared for suffer. 'You know what, this town, maybe all of us, need to do something to stop all of this.'

'I will do something myself - you see if I won't.' There was cold steel in Dinesh's voice. 'Meat cleaver into skull! He mimed out his fantasy with an imaginary weapon in swiftly chopping arm. 'Splat!'

'Stop all this foolish talk. Husband you are scaring me.'

'No, I am telling you in Allah's name, I will kill that man.'

Both Gavin and Mishka looked at Dinesh in stunned silence. The takeaway door opened and in walked a middle-aged man wearing a paint splashed boiler suit.

'Ah, good evening, Jim, how are you Sir? beamed Dinesh, instantly transforming into *Mr Smiley Chippy Man*, before then continuing with his food prep as though nothing at all had just been said.

*

Gavin had managed to navigate home in double quick time, ensuring his Indian Special Banquet for two remained piping hot. As he had passed number 3 Mayfair Avenue, Karen O'Malley - an ex-colleague from the Call Centre - had waved to him from the upstairs window that she was cleaning the inside of. He returned the gesture, but by then Karen had opened her window.

'Good luck tonight, Gavin!' she'd called out before miming a heart shape with her fingers and blowing a kiss.

'Thanks,' Gavin had replied somewhat awkwardly, before quickening his step, hoping to avoid any further public engagement. But just as he'd reached home, a blue Ford Fiesta had headed towards him, horn pipping brightly. In the front seat, Digger and Molly - two old friends from school - were grinning at him and making thumbs-up signs. He'd looked away, part embarrassed, part bemused before finally reaching the sanctuary of his hallway and gladly closing the front door behind him. *Finally, some privacy.* All he needed now was a good luck telegram from the Queen.

But presently, in the kitchen, he was carefully transferring the contents of the tin foil takeaway trays into a mishmash collection of serving dishes that he'd pre-warmed in the oven. Makai Shorba Corn Soup, Lamb Tikka Masala, Chicken Korma, Onion, Bhajis, Basmati Rice, Mango Chutney, and Poppadoms, now all looking delicious in various plates and bowls purchased at ad hoc intervals during his ten years of marriage to Marie. Only the Basmati Rice looked out of place, he thought, sitting there in a *Bob the Builder* dish, a leftover from Freddie's toddler years. *Couldn't be helped* - no more crockery.

Gavin quickly covered each dish in tinfoil, keeping everything warm, and then carefully transported the romantic feast to his small dining room at the back of the house. There, a tea-light illuminated table awaited - a now rickety *IKEA* flat-pack jobby elegantly disguised by a white tablecloth. Hopefully, Alice wouldn't notice the red wine stain he'd covered with a placemat, or the tomato soup stain he'd covered with the salt and pepper holder - or the slight munch-hole a moth had unhelpfully bequeathed, but now cunningly concealed by the Tikka Masala.

'Perfect,' Gavin said aloud, wondering if all twenty lit candles on the table were really necessary. He snatched one away. *Nah*. Then he put it back. 'Perfect'.

Standing in front of the hall wall mirror, he was making one final comb of his light brown beard and curly locks - all freshly washed - when he noticed two unsightly black nose hairs sticking out of his left nostril. He tugged on them with pinched fingers, but they weren't for budging. He tugged again with more force. *Success*, but only at the expense of triggering an involuntary reflex - an almighty sneeze. Then another. The doorbell instantly rang. *Alice*. He quickly opened the door, only an arm's length away, quite unsure if the sneezing fit was over.

Alice was framed there in the doorway looking very sexy, so he thought, dressed in a fairly short black skirt, black, gossamer hosiery and low cut, silky blouse. She beamed out a *hello* smile. Gavin sneezed for the third time - so that a volley of green mucus shot forth from his nose to land unhelpfully on Alice's obviously expensive cashmere jacket. Luckily, he had a tea towel still hanging out of his pocket, the one he'd used to transfer hot food from kitchen to dining room.

'Ah, sorry,' he almost screamed, as he lurched forwards to dab away the snot.

Alice cringed in disgust as she momentarily eyed the abhorrent sight of green gunk sliding down her lapel. The tea towel was forcefully applied over her right breast making her step backwards in mild alarm.

'What are you doing?' She swatted the irritant tea towel away from her bosom.

'Oh, sorry, sorry, sorry...' Gavin blathered. 'I'll take your jacket if you like and sponge it inside.'

Alice looked down at her right lapel with dismay. Green mucus had been joined by a splash of orange Tikka Masala sauce, courtesy of the tea towel.

'I'll take it to the dry cleaners, on second thoughts,' said Gavin aghast, ushering his already dishevelled date through the door. 'First thing in the morning.'

He clumsily kissed Alice on the left cheek. 'Erm...can we begin again?'

'Maybe that's an idea,' came the welcome reply, but not before a moment's hesitation. 'Let's do that...'

Please, nothing else go wrong, Gavin prayed. Then Alice thankfully smiled as she entered the dining room to see the wonderful feast that her thoughtful paramour had promised to cook for her. She finally started to relax.

'Oh, *Bob the Builder*,' she smiled, viewing the plastic cereal bowl in question. 'Unusual, I'll give you that.'

Yet only ten minutes or so later, aided by sweet Prosecco, a far more chilled out mood was really starting to settle in for the evening. Gavin was not unsurprised, though very happy all the same.

'I'm really impressed you've managed to put all this together for me. My ex-husband couldn't cook for toffee,' Alice laughed and took another tasty mouthful of the culinary treats set out before her.

'Ha, ha,' Gavin joined in, scoffing at the lesser man's incompetence.

'This Tikka Masala sauce is divine.'

'Thanks.'

'I always struggle with the sauce. What cream did you use?' Alice almost whispered, as though she was trying to coax trade secrets from some legendary chef.

'It's from the Co-op.'

'No, I mean, did you use double cream or crème fraiche?' She smiled. She wouldn't be put off that easily.

'That second one,' Gavin replied blankly, hoping for the best.

'And the ground almonds, they're really coming through. Sitting perfectly with the tang of paprika. How much did you put in?'

'Quite a lot.'

'Amazing,' Alice gushed, happy to be learning so much. 'You should go on *Master Chef*.'

'No, no. It's just a hobby is cooking. I once owned a fish and chip shop,' said her able host, attempting to move quickly away from the nuances of Indian cuisine. 'Hard work, that was. Cooking for other folk every night. Now I like to cook just for fun.'

'You do it very well.' A toast of the flutes was offered, gratefully accepted.

'Cheers!'

'Cheers!'

Alice smiled and then seemed to be thinking about something. Gavin gazed at her beautiful blue eyes. He could lose himself in those.

'I knew about your chip shop actually,' she said. 'Hey, I was Head of HR. I remembered it was on your CV.'

'Uh, of course.'

'Didn't it used to be where that Indian takeaway is today?'

'That's right.' Gavin knew it. He was about to be rumbled, wasn't he? She was playing with him.

'Maybe you should go and ask for a job there,' she laughed. 'This is far nicer than anything I bet they turn out.'

Gavin blushed with guilt, though a tingle of instinctive relief shot up his spine.

'Oh no, I'm sure their stuff is better.'

'Whatever...This is really delicious. You might get a second date out of this.'

The glasses came together again.

'I'll drink to that,' said Gavin happily. 'Nice one!'

*

As the evening went on and the last drops of Prosecco had drained away, Gavin had rummaged in a kitchen cupboard for the remnants of a bottle of Tequila left over from Christmas. The pair had moved on now from the dining room and were slumped next to each other on the old sofa in the front room - standby Tequila well and truly going down well.

'I'm feeling a bit tipsy, naughty Mr Gavin Hargreaves,' said Alice definitely a bit sloshed. 'If I didn't know better, I'd suspect you of trying to get me drunk.'

She giggled as she stared into the bottom of an empty tumbler, puzzling as to how all the scrumptious Tequila had disappeared already.

'No never. Here have a top up!' Gavin continued to play the gracious host and tipped out the last of his Christmas spirit into her glass.

'Let's have some music,' she slightly slurred. 'Do you have a smart speaker, or something?'

'Not really. I've got a very unsmart stereo player in the loft. Sorry, it's been a while...' Gavin thought about kicking himself. 'Didn't think about music.'

Alice merely looked amused at his clumsiness. She pulled a silver iPhone from a pocket of her short, black skirt, while Gavin admired the shape of the legs on show.

'Here, there's a good signal on my phone. I'll get something on *Spotify*.'

'Oh, very modern,' he was impressed.

'Hardly, how old are you again?'

'Thirty-seven.' Gavin felt embarrassed. He wasn't that old, but he realised he'd completely given up on music. He wondered if Oasis and Blur were still in the charts.

'Oh, bloody hell!' Alice laughed at that age revelation, amused and maybe a little proud of her ability to pull a younger bloke.

The sound of Destiny's Child then came blaring out of Alice's phone speaker. Seconds later both the occupants of the squishy sofa were singing along to the chorus of 'Say My Name', waving arms in the air almost in time. But it sounded like either Destiny's Child or the tipsy sofa duo were singing badly out of tune - whichever, both parties were blasting it out regardless.

'When did this song come out?' asked Alice. 'Must have been just before the Millennium. Takes me back to the end of Uni.'

'Cradle snatcher,' Gavin grinned. I was only studying for my GCSEs back then. Well, I say *studying...*'

'You mean out studying the young ladies... All the same, fifteen- and sixteen-year-old boys.'

'Well, any of them that would let me.' Gavin sighed, reflecting on a track record of mixed performance. 'I wasn't too successful, I guess. Mind, I did get better as I got older,' he added, perking up.

'Did you now?' Alice seemed intrigued, a playful tone coating her words.

'A bit...'

'So, what skills exactly did you get better at?' She turned to face him. The Tequila glass had smudged her lipstick. Her eyes dilated and she playfully ran a hand across his knee - then took it away again. She looked confident and mischievous.

'I wouldn't like to show you just yet,' Gavin knew he had to match the confidence and the mischief. He could do it!

'Why's that?'

'It would be just taking advantage as you'd be just putty in my hands.' He placed a hand on Alice's knee so that his roaming fingers became hidden under the hem of her skirt. He pulled her slightly towards him and hovered his lips over hers. He teased that the kiss might happen...

'Now is that so?' she murmured, breathing more deeply as he slowly undid just the top button of her silk blouse.

'It certainly is....' he cupped her right breast as the longed-for kiss was finally delivered with firmness and not a little passion. He then wrestled her over to him, so she was laid out flat on the sofa - as she tore at his shirt and he at her blouse. He straddled her dominantly, but then paused to view her beautiful legs suddenly exposed by lustful manoeuvres. He ran a hand slowly up her stockinged inner thigh moving so close to Heaven itself - fixated on the rise and fall of her chest and knowing that she really wanted him.

'Ding-dong,' the doorbell cheerfully sounded.

Fuck off!

'Ding-dong, ding-dong, ding-dong,' it persisted.

'Dad!' shouted a young voice through the letter box!

'Oh bollocks, it's Freddie!' Gavin shouted, quickly sitting up and retrieving a tossed away shirt from the rug. Alice raced to fasten a blouse and straighten down her dishevelled skirt.

'What the Hell?' gasped Alice, completely confused and flustered. She'd surprised herself that her body had been so ready for sex and yet now she felt like somebody had just come along and thrown cold water on them both. Which in a kind of way, they had.

Gavin quickly scuttled along the hall towards the front door, finishing off buttoning up his shirt, as the bell rang yet again. The shock of the interruption seemed to be telling his brain he was suddenly less drunk. He swung the door open.

'Hiya Dad,' chirped Freddie, giving His father's waist a quick hug before then breezing past him into the house.

'Evening Gavin,' said the unsmiling Marie. Behind her, Alberto's swanky BMW was parked against the kerb - but no Italian goalkeeper in sight.

'Your flies'll need fastening then,' clipped Marie.

Gavin quickly fumbled to correct the offending gape of his jeans

'What the monkeys are you doing here? I've got Alice round. I thought half of Drabbleton knew that.'

'Not my half. Who's Alice?' Marie seemed vaguely disturbed.

'*You know,* from work.'

'What, that stuck up cow?' Marie chortled unkindly. 'She's a Brimstone girl, is she not? What you knocking around with the likes of her for?'

'None of your business.' Gavin was recalling a sweet moment back then on the sofa when almost twenty-eight months of celibacy would have ended. When he would have got his red-blooded manhood back on track. *He was inwardly screaming!*

'I thought you'd at least have mentioned it - before you started seeing other people,' Marie continued indignantly.

'What, you jealous now?' Gavin sounded incredulous.

'No,' his ex-wife snapped. 'But it would at least have been nice to have prepared Freddie. Instead, he's right in there now and she's probably mostly naked with her bra and knickers thrown across the television set.'

Gavin turned up his eyes.

'She's not like that! But why are you even here?'

'You were supposed to pick Freddie up at 6.30,' Marie quietly scolded. 'We changed nights, remember?'

Oh fuck, Gavin vaguely recalled the proposed change of plan, but it had been a couple of weeks now since that discussion. But then he reconsidered. *Hang on a minute...*

'Marie, no we didn't change nights. You said it was a *maybe* for whatever reason - but then you called it off. So, what the hell are you doing here, interrupting the first date night that I've had since you left?'

Marie looked at Gavin with suddenly helpless eyes and he noticed her bottom lip starting to quiver. Then she just burst into full on tears. He instinctively felt sorry for her.

'What's brought this on?' He stepped down off the doorstep towards her and administered a two second hug, feeling awkward now about touching her - especially with Alice in the house. Marie buried her face in her ex-husband's shirt, instantly picking up on the smell of perfume belonging to another woman.

'Gavin, it's all gone up the wall,' she blubbed.

'What has?'

'Everything. It's all fucked up, so it is!' A second breach in the dam brought the next wave of tears.

Marie stepped forward herself to embrace Gavin. This time, however, he really didn't think hugging was the right thing to do. He firmly gripped the top of her arms, outstretched his own and literally held her at arm's length. She seemed to get the message.

'I'm sorry,' she said, controlling her emotions. 'I know I haven't got the right to do this.'

'You're right there...' Gavin remembered a time when all he wanted was for her to come back to him. That time had passed. Tears wouldn't change that.

He remembered the last time he'd seen Marie cry. It had been on the ferry over to England, in the year 2010. She'd realised she was leaving her old Dublin life behind, all of her friends, all of her family - leaving behind more than a bit of the animated and crazy girl that she'd so far been on this planet. It was a true rite of passage and the tears had come falling.

'I love you, Gavin, me man,' she'd said as they leaned over the rail on deck, watching salty waves crash against the side of the boat. He gripped her tight back then as the waves then washed her tears far out to sea. 'But if this is not going to be forever, then I'll be jumping into this water right now!'

Gavin remembered she was so dramatic back then. So damn *passionate*. But he'd never seen her cry since. Not once - until today. He felt somehow guilty, wondering if the mundane life he'd led her to in Drabbleton had killed off all her passion for good. He'd often longed for the return of that fiery young Dublin girl, with her unbridled zest for life. But he knew that person had long gone, in essence anyway. And this was now...

'Well, I suppose you'd better come in for a cup of tea,' he shrugged. Mundane again. But what else could he say?

Marie was quickly drying her eyes with a tissue.

'Hang on, give me a minute,' she laughed over the last of the tears. 'How do I look?'

Gavin was already on his way back into the house.

'You look fine,' he called behind him. *What's she asking that for?*

Inside the front room, Freddie had already joined the now fully dressed and reasonably undishevelled Alice on the sofa and was busy showing her something on his iPad.

'Right, I see you two have met then,' Gavin said, hoping Alice had managed to sober up a bit.

'Yes,' she smiled. 'Freddie's just showing me an app thingy on his tablet.'

'Great.' Knowing Alice as he did, he knew she wasn't sounding one hundred per cent coherent. But she might get away with it.

Marie entered the room, quickly looking Alice up and down. Gavin tried to read her mind, betting she'd be slightly irritated by his new girlfriend's undeniable mature beauty, but pleased too that she was clearly over forty.

'Hello, I'm Marie, Gavin's wife,' she pleasantly spouted.

'Ex-wife,' came the ex-husband's instant correction.

'Same thing...Lovely to meet you, Alice.'

'Hi,' Alice waved. Now she was giving Marie the shrewd once over in return.

'It is not the same thing,' Gavin mumbled awkwardly.

'Whatever,' Marie smiled through gritted teeth.

Gavin made his excuses and went off to the kitchen to make the tea. It was a risk leaving Marie with Alice, he knew that. Could he rely on his ex-wife being on her best behaviour? Probably not. He ran hot tap water into the kettle so that it would boil all the quicker.

'Alice has just been telling me about the marvellous Indian meal you've been cooking for her,' Marie smiled innocently as Gavin eventually re-entered the front room with three teas and a Coke for

Freddie. He sent his ex a daggered look, and she suppressed a giggle. 'And there was me thinking you didn't cook.'

'I have been on my own these past two years, haven't I? Needs must and all that.'

Marie nodded and continued to smile. Gavin passed round the drinks, hoping her fun was done with.

'Anyway, what's up Marie?' He thought it best to settle right down to business and get whatever it was the unwanted caller wanted over and done with. Alice shuffled herself to the edge of the sofa, as if to rise.

'Oh...sorry, should I go?'

Gavin looked to Marie for help.

'No, no... it's fine. You can stay. I'm sure Gav will tell you everything anyway.'

She calls him Gav, thought Alice. *He's Gavin to me.*

Marie took in a deep breath, seeming to compose herself before starting her story.

'It's Alberto really. Brimstone put him up for transfer. The only offer they got was from some team in Latvia. AC Milan weren't interested, apparently,' Marie mourned the loss of her Italian dream. 'So Brimstone accepted the Latvian offer and now Alberto has no choice but to be after going – just as soon as his injury clears up.'

'Where's Latvia? asked Gavin, blankly.

'Isn't it one of the Baltics?' suggested Alice, knowing exactly that's what it was.

'No idea,' Marie replied. 'But I know the club he's been sold to is called Arsolia FC and it's right by Russia.'

'Arsolia - that sounds nice,' said Gavin, trying to look on the bright side. But then the penny dropped. *What about Freddie?*

'I'm not going to Russia, no way,' His young son then piped up on cue, without taking his eyes off his iPad.

'Latvia,' Marie gently corrected. 'But no love, you're not. You'll be staying here with me. ...Exactly where we'll be living though, who knows for now.'

Gavin looked concerned at that little grenade casually tossed out courtesy of the last comment. *She's not moving back here.*

'You've got a lot of stuff to work through, for sure,' he added, knowing there was nothing he could really do. At least for now.

'I don't know what it means for me and Alberto,' Marie continued, her voice now a little unsteady. 'He wants me to come with him, but I don't want to live in a town called Arsolia in the middle of feckin' nowhere. I'm not leaving Freddie either. It's just that I could actually kill that Brimstone fellah for tearing our little family apart. And for what, I'm asking? Well, just for money, as if he hasn't got enough of the stuff.'

'You'd probably be surprised how many people have said that recently. He's got a whole line of potential assassins gunning for him.' Gavin stopped himself - was this a *big mouth strikes again* moment? 'Oh, sorry Alice. I know he's your brother, but you know what he's like.'

'Don't be sorry on my part,' said Alice in a matter-of-fact tone. 'He'd be getting whatever was coming to him, I'm sure. I'm perfectly aware he's not the most agreeable Brimstone to have ever breathed in Drabbleton's sweet air. Far from it.'

'He's like a monster, you mean?' Freddie helpfully translated.

'Quite,' confirmed Alice.

'Um, if you want a wet job done on him, you should use this app. *Disposals Inc.*' Freddie held up his tablet for all to see.

'I thought I told you to delete that app,' grumbled Marie. 'Besides don't say *wet job*. You're not in the Mafia, for sure.'

'Sorry,' came the half-hearted apology. 'Is *bumped off* OK? Or *take out*?'

'Bit better,' Marie considered.

'But go on Dad,' Freddie raced on. 'If this Brimstone's just a bad guy, why don't you take him out?'

'It's just a game, son. You can't really just dispose of folk on an app.' Gavin bit his lip but wishing you could do exactly that.

'Maybe so, but it would be amusing to see what happens if we put his name into the game.' Alice was laughing. 'I'd even feel better if you get to see his meme or something blown to smithereens!'

'I suppose it would be a gas,' Marie agreed, also now mildly amused.

'Oh go on then, let's have a look,' Gavin relented. They all could do with a bit of light relief, after all. He reached towards his son's iPad.

'Yes!' Freddie enthusiastically squealed with accompanying fist pump. 'Let's do it!'

★

They all gathered in the front room, round a family-life battered armchair that Gavin now sat on as he prepared to enter all the relevant details into *Disposals Inc.*

'Welcome to *Disposals Inc.*,' Gavin read aloud 'Would you like our AI Assistant to help you with your order? If so, say *yes* now.'

'Yes!' they all chimed in unison.

'Hi, my name is Dizzy, your AI Assistant for this ...evening,' a softly spoken female voice greeted them.

'Hi Dizzy,' Gavin replied.

'And who may you be? Say your first name now.'

'Gavin.'

'Hi ...Gavin, I am pleased to meet you.'

Then over the next five minutes or so the new customer answered all the questions patiently posed by Dizzy. Then the whole crew had much fun making a lifelike meme of Brimstone, using template art from the app.

'Looks just like him,' Gavin agreed, looking at work-in-progress now almost complete.

'Nah, make his head bigger,' laughed Alice. 'He definitely has a big head.'

Gavin obliged and told Dizzy all was done.

'Excellent, Gavin,' said Dizzy. 'Here is a summary of your order.

Work required: one assassination.

Customer name and address: Gavin Hargreaves, 25 Mayfair Avenue, Drabbleton, Lancashire, England.

Name and details of hit: Bryce Brimstone, white male, aged 52 years.

Location: Brimstone Mill, Drabbleton, Lancashire, England.

Preferred method of assassination: one bullet to centre of head.

Proof required: one photograph sent to phone.

Framed hard copy of photograph: customer declined

Photo mug with printed photograph: customer accepted.

Social media posts of photograph: customer declined.

Any other family member and/or pets to be included in this order: none. Customer declined our Three for Two Offer.

Gavin, are all these details correct?'

'Yes.'

'Thank you. Now please accept our Terms & Conditions. When you have read them, say OK.'

'OK.'

'I am sorry. You have not opened the Terms & Conditions page.'

Gavin muttered impatiently.

'It's there, Dad,' Freddie interjected. 'Press that!'

'I know, I know,' huffed a father hating to be outsmarted by a child's technology skills. 'There.' He pressed the link which revealed a *War & Peace* version of legalese gobbledegook. '*Blah, blah, blah, yeah, yeah, yeah...*' He closed the pop-up.

'Are you sure you have read the Terms & Conditions?' prompted Dizzy again.

'Yes.'

'Say OK.'

'You said, OK. Thank you for your order and for choosing *Disposals Inc.* Your custom is important to us. There will now follow a short facsimile of the work we will do for you. Goodbye.'

'Boss!' said Freddie. 'This'll be the good bit.' Everybody huddled in even closer to the iPad screen as a virtual animation started to roll. A shadowy character immediately came into view, walking through an industrial building in partial darkness. They then saw he was carrying a large handgun that he was pointing ahead of him. The animation then took on the *point-of-view* of the gun as its unidentifiable owner then crept in beyond an office door, again into a room partially lit. The meme of Brimstone swivelled round to face the gunman, initially unaware that he was about to face his death. But terrified eyes indicated that he had now realised his time was up only in the final second before the gun exploded. A single gunshot to the centre of his forehead was coldly but efficiently delivered. The victim slumped across his desk, now quite lifeless.

Everybody cheered as the app loudly broadcast the repeated refrain of a famous rock song, '*Another One Bites the Dust.*'

'Yes, that was a gas,' said Marie, catching her breath.

'Frightened the fairies out of me,' Alice giggled.

'Cool!' Freddie rejoiced.

'Wow,' said Gavin, closing the app. 'If only, eh? *If only.*'

12
- SERIOUS BUSINESS -

Briskly walking across the Call Centre floor, clipboard tucked neatly under an arm, Krystyna seemed puzzled by the low-level murmuring going on amongst colleagues not currently on the phones.

'Come on people,' she snapped. 'Concentration please, work, work...' She clicked her fingers and the murmuring subsided. Then she noticed three workers clustered together around a particular PC, clearly amused by something they were looking at.

Their faces paled as she approached and young Will, whose desk this was, clicked quickly on his mouse.

'What is this? What is so entertaining this morning? ...Joke?' barked Krystyna. She darted an eye onto Will's screen, but whatever he'd been viewing had been closed down. She torched him a disparaging look, enough to see him flinch.

'Come now, we are not children. Playtime over. Work!'

The Call Centre resumed its atmosphere of productive industry once again, whilst Krystyna headed back off to her office.

Soon she was settled by her own PC when a meek knock at the door sounded and Urma, one of the older colleagues, peeped her head in.

'Come...come in Urma.' Krystyna waved the sheepish looking operative forward. 'What is it?'

'I've just forwarded you a web link that's going round,' said Urma, nervously. 'But I just wanted to warn you first. It's not very nice.'

Krystyna scrolled through her catalogue of recent emails.

'Is this the reason for the furtive giggling out there?'

'Yes. But not everyone is laughing.'

'Aha, got you,' Krystyna added as she retrieved Urma's email from her Inbox. 'Let us see then...'

Urma quietly took a seat in front of her senior manager's desk and waited, somewhat anxiously, for a reaction. She didn't have to wait for long as Krystyna was almost immediately struck by mild panic, breathing rapidly, and gulping on a water bottle.

She read the logo and strapline of the web page she'd just opened.

Fantasy SeXXX - kinky videos, starring YOU.

Urma could see sweat breaking out on Krystyna's brow - a look of dread seizing her face. *Maybe she should just go?*

'Aghhhh...' came the sharp scream as the selected video began to roll. In it Krystyna saw herself - or rather Little Red Riding Hood - pinned to Brimstone's desk enduring a fantasy rape, lustfully administered by the slobbering Big Bad Wolf. She'd known about the secret camera in Brimstone's room, but this was just for their private pleasure, he'd said - or *post-match analysis*, as he'd jokingly called it. But he'd promised to delete the footage that very day - and certainly not post it onto shadier side of the internet.

'Do you want me to get you anything, love?' asked Urma, sympathetically. 'As I say not everybody finds this funny at all. Some of us older ones, especially, think this is horrible - what he's done to you.'

But Krystyna did not answer, she was too engrossed in trying to find clues as to the identity of the poster. It wasn't long before she spotted a grinning picture of Brimstone on his Channel page. Username - *Big Bad Wolf.* But then she cringed as she also saw thumbnail stills of two other girls - previous employees of the Call Centre - who'd each hurriedly resigned. Both were dressed in different fantasy costumes. One a caricature schoolgirl, short, pleated skirt, white blouse and plaits topped by a straw boater - very *St Trinian's.* Brimstone was mounting her from behind donning his own outfit, a full Nazi SS Officer costume, whilst waving a black Luger pistol above his head. He took the same pose in the second picture which Krystyna studied uneasily. But this time he was waving a Colt Revolver, indulging in his wild *yee-haw* ride - sporting Stetson and cowboy bandit gear. His sexual victim on this occasion wore a tan leather mini-dress and feathered headband, *Pocahontas* Indian style.

Krystyna not only felt sick and ashamed, but her racing mind was already wondering if all this meant her professional life in Drabbleton was now over. The thought of fleeing home back home to Poland flashed across her mind. *Escape.* She gulped in a large breath of air, realising she needed to steady her shaking body.

This is a *fight or flight* reaction she then told herself, somehow steeling her inner being against the odds, partly by remembering a distant management training course that she'd once attended. *Breathe*, she demanded, as she recalled the details on how to deal with panic due to a work crisis. She swigged at her water bottle again.

'He thinks I will choose flight. *I choose fight!*'

'Eh love?' came the confused response. 'What you on about?'

Though simmering with inner anger, Krystyna managed to sound reasonably controlled now, although with intentions deadly serious.

'I will have revenge for this. Thank you for coming here, Urma. Now you may go.' She made a brief shooing sign with a hand.

'Some of us women are stopping the young uns from watching it. Doing our best, any road.' Urma hovered for a couple more seconds in silent awkwardness.

'Thank you,' Krystyna finally half-smiled. *Rat poison*, that's all she was thinking as her visitor quietly left. There were rat poison sachets in the basement of the shared Victorian house where she currently lived. On her next shift - the coming Monday - she would collect one and bring it in. Then, in the evening, once the general workforce had clocked off, she'd seize the moment. She knew Brimstone would be working late in his office, as was his habit on early weekdays - the perfect opportunity for the administering of the fatal dose. It was time this despicable monster was disposed of forever.

*

Dimitri Sidorov stood sturdily on the mat in fight mode, his pristine white Karate uniform - tied across the waist with *bone fide* black belt - barely ruffled by this morning's opponent.

'Come on now, give me side kick,' he ordered of the gangly nineteen-year-old opposite, his pupil of the moment. 'Strike with blade of foot, keep toes pointed down.'

The braided haired apprentice pranced around the mountain of his teacher, in classic Karate style, before unleashing a particularly underwhelming right leg kick - aiming high towards the head. Dimitri took an easy side-step and blocked the incoming kick with his left forearm. With his right fist he then punched his off-balance assailant at the base of his neck, twisting his fist at the moment of impact.

'Very bad,' he scolded, straddling his young opponent who had been instantly laid flat out on the mat. 'In real battle, I would punch neck two inches higher - and you would be dead.'

'Ow,' moaned one Lewis Wilson. 'You're too rough, man. I'm only learning.'

'You must learn fast now you are sent to me!' Dimitri walked over to a weights machine onto which he'd rested a water bottle. He sipped on the drink, looking back disdainfully at the still prostrate young man who continued to whinge about a little pain. 'Hah!' he scoffed derisively.

Stepping gracefully into this lavishly kitted out basement gym, Roxanne immediately managed to raise his spirits by virtue of her mere presence - and he raised his water bottle to her, by way of greeting, as she approached.

'Good morning, darling,' she pouted, then kissing him on the lips. She glanced over to Lewis, lying there on the mat and shook a sympathetic head. 'I see the lessons are not going too well.'

'He is pathetic. I don't know how Mr Volkov expects me to work with him.'

'Ah, poor baby,' Roxanne sympathised in a correspondingly babyish voice, stroking her lover's lustrous, waxed hair.

'I am used to ex-KGB partner, or ex-*Spetsnaz* like me - Special Forces killer. But now I get him - supermarket trolley boy!'

'Mr Volkov maybe has his heart in the right place. He wants a good career for his son...'

'*Bastard* son, that is all. From some Soho nightclub dalliance two decades ago. He should have used condom.'

'I think it's good that a powerful man is facing up to his responsibilities. Rare thing these days.' The former supermodel looked pitifully down at the dysfunctional fighting machine on the mat.

'Erm, *excuse me*,' Lewis stirred, pulling himself to his feet. 'I am in the room, you know.'

'Ah Lewis,' Roxanne now smiled in return, 'let's not have two sulking boys in the room at the same time.'

'I'd be quite happy to go back to my job in Sainsbury's,' the young man moped.

'Bodyguard and trainee assassin is better job,' snapped Dimitri.

'A dead-end job, you mean.'

'Not true. There is career progression,' Dimitri replied, suddenly amused. 'To Chief Hit-Man, like me.' He burst out into a belly laugh and Roxanne enthusiastically joined in. Lewis failed to see the joke.

'Now, go get showered,' the Black-Belt commanded, face suddenly once again deadly serious. 'Enough for this morning.'

*

A little later, on her Knightsbridge terrace, Roxanne was sat taking morning tea with Dimitri, the latter now dapper again in black tailored suit. The London sunshine bathed pallid light onto the architecturally splendid roofline set out before them. Fat pigeons watched on patiently, hoping any remnants of espied delicious pastries would soon be making them fatter still.

Dimitri sipped on a delicate Bone China cup; a vessel incongruous with the powerful hand that held it. He eyed his beautiful lover with pleasure and pride. He trusted her by now - unusually so, as he rarely trusted anyone. He'd been open with her about the often-dubious activities of his boss, Mr Volkov - a successful oligarch with many business interests. *Russian mafia?* Roxanne had mused. Dimitri had laughed, failing to reply with the obvious answer, but he had been impressed how nonplussed his lady had been about the revelation.

'In big business there are high stakes,' she'd casually theorised. 'If you want to play at the top table, then you must accept that.'

Dimitri felt drawn to her more than ever when he realised she could embrace danger like this, as did he. Life was for the bold - and the weak would be crushed. In Roxanne, maybe he had found a soulmate.

'You know, apart from his mistake named Lewis, Mr Volkov never makes mistakes. He is a genius. Some of his cohorts are fighting battles from the past - controlling drugs, prostitution, gambling. So *old school.*'

'I look at my neighbourhood at all the Ferrari's whizzing by... all the stunning mansion houses,' said Roxanne, feeding her lap dog, Antoinette, an almond biscuit. 'Old school doesn't seem to have done many of them too much harm.'

'Yes - but live in the past and die like the past, that is what Mr Volkov tells me.' She noticed Dimitri instinctively clenching a fist.

'So, what is the future?' she casually mused.

'The internet. The company already employs an army of hackers - Westerners are so careless with their web defences. Such easy money. Then we have the scammers, all trained as convincing actors who can now seduce full string of rich lady widows at one time. It is unbelievable how keen some old people are to part with their life's savings in the hope of finding love. Pathetic.'

'This has been going on for some time now, internet crime. You could argue that soon it too will be *old school*.' Roxanne sounded wearied. Her lover would have to do better.

'Yes, yes...but Mr Volkov is always one step ahead,' Dimitri continued, upping his enthusiasm level. 'He says that internet has disrupted so many traditional business models. Shopping, gambling, banking, booking holidays, watching films, listening to music - now we can do all online, and save money too.'

'Well give me Harrods over internet shopping, any day,' Roxanne rolled her eyes in disgust.

'I will make an exception for you on that, my darling,' Dimitri laughed. 'But Mr Volkov is now ready to launch his own disruptive internet business. It is currently in *beta*, as they say. But initial trials have been successful.'

'Go on, what is it then? I know you are dying to tell me.'

'It is about ridding yourselves of the problems in your life.'

'We'd all like to do that. What is it, an anti-wrinkles serum?' She laughed. 'I'm in.'

Dimitri scrutinised Roxanne's super-model-esque visage and its sheeny tight skin - she couldn't be serious?

'Assassinations, my dear. Assassinations.' A smug face accompanied that final revelation.

'Oh, very good,' Roxanne perked up. 'You've got my interest finally.'

'Bumping people off. The rich have been doing it for years. But so hard to organise offline. Not everybody has a hitman listed in their address book.'

'A shame, but it's true.' Roxanne shook her head in mock regret.

'Mr Volkov's idea is to bring assassinations to the masses by a way of a handy app he's had developed - *Disposals Inc.*'

'*Disposals Inc*, good name,' Roxanne almost enthused. 'Yeah, I get it.'

'I knew you'd like it. See it's here if you like, be my guest...' He passed over his smart phone, with said app already open and waiting.

Roxanne read from the welcome page:

'*Disposals Inc, your friendly assassination assistant ready to go.* Looks cool.'

'So, I'm wondering,' he playfully enquired, 'just for market research purposes, you understand?'

'Absolutely.'

'If you could choose anybody in the world, whose name would you put into it?' His teeth glistened as the wicked grin was revealed.

'Ha ha, don't tempt me. Well, I can obviously think of one name.'

'Yes, I knew you'd say that,' Dimitri confirmed, clapping his hands. '*Bravo*. I do suspect I know the name of the very man you would wish to dispose of.'

'If I knew I could get away with it, that is.' Roxanne's mind was racing. 'But what if it got traced back to me?'

'My darling, wouldn't it be so much better if somebody else had set themself up for you? Some helpful idiot.' Again, the smug look.

'Of course, but stop daydreaming now,' Roxanne dismissed such nonsense with a throwaway hand. 'You're getting me all excited for nothing.'

But Dimitri was so pleased that he wasn't going to disappoint her. He loved to make this beautiful woman happy.

'Ah...but the reason I've let you in on all this today, my angel, is because I believe your wish is within reach. Let me show you back end of app. Not all boring. Please.' He beckoned to her to pass back the phone.

She duly handed the handset back to its owner who the seemed to be tapping in a long string of encrypted info.

'Hello, Dizzy,' he finally announced.

'Hello, Dimitri, how are you today?' replied the softly spoken AI Assistant.

'I am good, thank you.' The two seemed on friendly terms.

'Please read out the details of last night's orders from Region Six.'

Roxanne looked on, by now captivated.

'Certainly,' replied the helpful sounding AI. 'One order. Assassination. Single bullet to head. Victim name - Bryce Brimstone, male aged 52 years. Drabbleton, Lancashire, England. Customer name: Gavin Hargreaves.'

'No *surely not?* Roxanne giggled. 'Somebody's trying to have him actually killed off? How convenient.'

'It is fun for sure,' said Dimitri, enjoying the moment.

'But *customer name?* Is that the person hoping Bryce gets it?'

'That's exactly it... Gavin Hargreaves. Ever heard of him?'

'Vaguely.' She scanned her memory banks. 'I try not to take much interest in Bryce's backwater affairs. But yes, I do remember him being extra pleased with himself when he told me about forcing some poor guy to wear a Roman Centurion outfit to work. *Hargreaves* - kind of rings a bell.'

'Well, no wonder he wants your lovely husband dealt with.'

Roxanne made a gun shape with two fingers and a curl of a thumb. 'Bang! Gotcha!' Dimitri laughed.

'The app is just in *beta*,' he continued. 'We delete lot of requests at this point - making out it's just game. We're just seeing what level of demand there is for now.'

'And?' Roxanne raised a curious eye.

'Crazy! Seems most people have secret hit list,' Dimitri replied, with some relish there in his voice. 'As I say, Mr Volkov is business genius. But for now, we have just done couple of successful trial hits.'

'Curiouser and curiouser.' Roxanne looked like she was sold.

'So. Do you want me to push the button on this one?'

'Push the button?'

'You know what I mean,' said Dimitri, ignoring the feigned innocence. 'Imagine not having to wait until you are maybe old and grey to inherit all of your husband's money. And with some nobody all lined up to carry the can. Mr Gavin Hargreaves can sit behind prison bars. You can sit on beach in Bahamas. Young, beautiful and filthy rich.'

'Sounds like I could get used to that, I suppose,' she sighed, her mind already imagining powdery sand and the gently lapping waves of a cobalt blue sea.

'Dizzy.' The button would be pressed.

'Yes, Dimitri, how can I help?'

'Order F635, please mark as accepted.'

'And the agent assigned to the project?'

'Dimitri Sidorov.' He smiled knowingly at Roxanne. Hopefully she liked a man who took charge.

'Confirmed. Assigned agent - Dimitri Sidorov. Please wait a moment while I check availability of your Assigned Assistant Agent...'

'Make it Ivan or Borislav,' he muttered. Roxanne was quite unused to seeing traces of sudden anxiety on her boyfriend's chiselled face.

'Lewis Wilson, assigned. Confirmed. Thank you.'

'Damn it.'

'Good luck with your project, order F635. Dimitri, goodbye.'

Dimitri realised that Lewis's induction into the business was being taken seriously by Mr Volkov. He only wished that the shaping up of such an unpromising novice hadn't fallen entirely down to him.

*

Bob was out mowing his tiny front lawn when Gavin came out of next door on his way to the corner shop. Rocky was having his usual pee on the rose bush that Marie once took pride in.

'Do you want me to do your half?' he asked of his younger neighbour, still coughing a little from that nasty bug he'd recently picked up. Both men shared an adjoining lawn, but it was clear that one man was very much a keener gardener than the other.

'Yeah, that would be good,' smiled Gavin, realising he hated this time of year, when rain and sunshine combined to make that nuisance green stuff even more of a pain. 'You need to get that cough sorted out, though.'

'Yeah, yeah,' Bob knocked back the mothering.

'I'll do both lawns next time.'

'Yes, course you will,' Someone had clearly heard that one before. But the older neighbour seemed currently more interested in changing the subject altogether. 'Any road, where's the lady friend?'

'Eh?' Gavin suddenly remembered the consequences of sharing a cardboard-like party wall with his neighbour. *Hope he went to bed early.* 'Oh, Alice? That's her name - no she went home last night.'

'I thought you were going to get lucky there for a minute,' Bob cackled. 'Me and Rocky were rooting for you, weren't we Rocky?' The dog didn't answer. Gavin cringed with unease.

'Couldn't you have put your telly on a bit louder?' he admonished.

'What and ruin your romantic atmosphere? Sound goes both ways, you know. That's called *being considerate.* Besides you were doing quite well until Her Ladyship turns up and ruins our night.'

'*Our* night?' Gavin's eyes widened on reflex.

'It was something different for me an' all. Don't be selfish.'

Gavin realised that Bob was serious.

'So, what else did you hear?' A rattled question.

'Nothing once nag-bag had arrived. I'd had my fill of her grating Irish utterances when she used to live here. So I took Rocky out for a walk.' The disappointment of the previous evening's anti-climax was definitely ringing in Bob's voice.

'Good. You should have done it earlier.'

'Bollocks!'

They could have kept the petty bickering going for much longer, easily - but Gavin was wondering if Bob had any update on his run in with Brimstone's Retirement Flats business. He did hope they'd backed down. He felt he should at least ask, anyway, despite being irked by all last night's noseying.

'Nope, got a summons this morning,' came the reply in answer to Gavin's considerate enquiry. 'They're taking me for six months' rent. Can't pay it. Plus, seeing as I'd given notice on this place the Council want me out. So they're sticking me in a one bed flat in Ashburn Towers.'

'Ah sorry, it's rough round there.' Gavin looked into the distance, beyond the great chimney of Brimstone Mill, to the concrete tower blocks on the hill beyond. It was a part of town to avoid.

'Yeah, I've heard all the jokes. So rough that the Alsatians walk round in pairs, yeah, yeah, all of that. Plus, ten floors up, it is. No use for Rocky.'

'Course Bob, it's all a bit shit, mate.' Gavin looked at the afflicted mongrel limping around the garden and felt sorry for both animal and its crotchety old owner.

'But I'm blaming yer man, Brimstone,' Bob suddenly spat out with venom.' He's got a lot to answer for.'

'Certainly has.'

'Still, I've got something in mind,' Bob continued, tapping his temple with a finger to denote the hatching of a cunning scheme. 'Do you know you can kill a man with a roll of cling-film?'

'Never really thought about it.'

'Yeah, you can. Wrap it round their head and suffocate them. Seen it online.'

'Very good Bob,' Gavin smiled, seeing an obvious flaw in the plan. 'But Brimstone is about six foot three and built like a tank. You are five foot three and skinny as a dipstick.'

'I'll take you on any day.' Bob instantly raised his fists in boxer pose and began a little dance. 'Come on, come on if you think you're hard enough.' But then he began coughing again so that the start of Round One was temporarily curtailed.

'You need to get that cough sorted.'

Bob was pausing to catch his breath,

'Anyway, I know loads of us round here dream about Brimstone getting his comeuppance,' Gavin returned to the subject. 'But you and cling film aren't going to put us out our misery, mate. Sorry.'

He'd tried to bring Bob down to earth as gently as he could.

'We'll see about that.'
There was certainly defiance in that voice, as the old man then coughed out nasty phlegm.
'Yeah?'
'We will!' Yep, defiance and determination too.

13
- GETTING AHEAD -

Dinesh lifted the stainless-steel counter flap of his chippy on his way out of the shop. He had purposely kept the mood light and breezy with Mishka, not wishing her to either worry or to interfere with his intention. Courtesy of regular customers, also employees of the Call Centre, he had learned that Brimstone usually worked on in his office after 6pm, once all the regular staff had left for the evening. Monday night seemed to be the night when he was most likely to stay behind, it being the start of the business week and the day he was apparently most focussed. Nobody had wondered why Dinesh was curious about Brimstone's working practices. It was nothing more than chip shop idle talk, so they imagined. Just passing the time until the chips were ready.

'It is Monday night. Quietest of week,' he smiled to his wife. 'You can navigate the *Star of India* for an hour alone.'

'Of course,' she replied casually, having steered the ship alone on many previous occasions. 'But where are you going that is so mysterious?'

'To see man about dog, as they say. But I hope to be in very happy place when I return.'

'Good,' she cheerily assented. 'I like you in happy place. But don't buy a dog!'

'OK my dear wife, no dog!' he smiled warmly at her again.

'Goodbye Husband. A thousand blessings for your little plan.' She blew him a little kiss.

'Thank you Mishka. I love you with all my heart.' He closed the shop door behind him and then the smile was instantly gone. He walked quickly on, unnecessarily checking a small shoulder bag he was carrying and which hung by his side. He knew very well what was inside. *But just one more look to be certain.* Two items. One newly sharpened butcher's meat cleaver, actually a birthday present from Mishka- *check*. One towel to wipe away blood from weapon - *check*.

In ten minutes time he would reach Brimstone Mill, whose giant chimney seemed to be reeling him in as he walked, ever faster by each minute. Once there he would seek out the Executive Office. Then he would murder Bryce Brimstone in cold blood. A perfect disposal. A perfect pleasure.

★

Krystyna sat at her desk in the tiny office which was her Call Centre private space. The functional clock on the austere stone wall informed her it was 6.20 pm. She'd watched its rotating second hand drag by every minute since the hour mark. In her right hand, resting on her desk, she held a red paper sachet emblazoned with the logo: *Vermokill Rat Poison*. She particularly liked reading the warning on the sachet's rear-side - avoid contact with skin; do not swallow; tasteless to humans; if ingested seek emergency medical assistance; DANGER. HIGHLY TOXIC.

'Perfect,' she said aloud. 'Just what doctor did not order.'

She laughed, enjoying the final ten minutes before her murderous poisoning of Bryce Brimstone would commence. Knowing him to be a creature of precise habit, each evening at 6.30 pm he would leave his office for the Executive Bathroom just along the corridor. She would only have two or three minutes, but enough time to spike his much called-on water bottle. Then she would hide in his stationery cupboard until the poison started to work. In his last moments she intended to reveal herself, inform him of his impending death and then just sit there contentedly, in the chair opposite, and watch him slowly perish. Or rather her revenge seeking 'character' would.

With just slightly less than ten minutes to go now, she decided it was time to change clothing. Hanging up on the door was a costume that she'd thought she would never wear again. But the sweet irony of it all was just too much to resist. So tonight, ladies and gentlemen *et al*, for the final time ever - she would become the legendary, the amazing... *Miss Little Red Riding Hood!*

She imagined a trumpet fanfare in her head as she prepared to take the stage for the performance of a lifetime.

★

After a four-hour-plus journey from Knightsbridge to the North of England, Dimitri Sidorov pulled up his black Mercedes SUV into a Service Station on the outskirts of Drabbleton. At the very same moment, neither he nor Lewis could know that a diminutive seventy-five-year-old local was setting off from his Council semi not far away, along with partner-in-crime mongrel, intent on murdering their own intended hit.

'Come on, old boy,' Bob encouraged as Rocky became distracted by the possible contents of a discarded chippy carton. 'We've got work to do.' A roll of *Co-op* cling-film poked out of a side-pocket of his quilted anorak. The contents of a *how-to* online video played over and over in his head.

'Man, do I need a pee,' bleated a young man's voice from the passenger seat of the Mercedes, now just a few miles south. 'I never knew the North was so far away,' said trainee hitman Lewis Wilson.

'It has seemed longer for me, believe me,' Dimitri sighed. 'You can pee and drink here.'

'And man, what a dump when you finally get here. Who would bother?'

'People with job to do. Like us. Go on then...out.' He shooed his apprentice to exit.

'Don't you need a pee?' Lewis had one foot out of the car but expecting both men would be using the Service Station's facilities.

'No.'

'Why? You got a steel bladder, or something?'

'It is training. In combat field, enemy fire can go on for many hours. Stop for pee and get cock shot off!'

'Ow, man!' Lewis flinched at the thought. 'OK I will hold pee in. It's all in the mind, right? He seemed determined to win favour with his fighting machine mentor, now re-entering the car and closing the door as he settled into the passenger seat.

'Exactly,' Dimitri laughed. 'I will give you one minute, then you give in.'

'No way, one minute!' the young man put aside that last casual dismissal and focussed on suppressing his *need-to-pee* pain. He tried his best to relax. Maybe conversation might help...

'I wish I'd have known all this stuff you've been showing me when I was a kid,' he offered, by way of distraction.

'So, why?' Dimitri seemed at least vaguely interested.

'Always getting picked on by white kids for being black.' Lewis was avoiding any eye contact and Dimitri sensed it.

'But you are not black. You are half white, half black,' he replied, all matter of fact.

'Didn't matter.'

'It does now!' A mild temper was suppressed. 'If you were all black you wouldn't be Mr Volkov's bastard son and wouldn't be getting all this priceless tuition I'm providing. You have opportunity.'

Lewis nodded, mulling over the possible wisdom of that last thought. But he wasn't entirely happy. 'Stop calling me that...*bastard*.'

Dimitri seemed surprised.

'OK, maybe,' he reflected, but was then immediately assertive yet again. 'But start behaving like son of proud Russian businessman who everybody respects and fears. Then I stop.'

'I don't feel like his son,' sounded a disconsolate voice. 'I've only really met him a handful of times.'

'Sometimes being father can be done in different ways. This is his way.'

'I don't know why, but I still want to make him proud,' Lewis mumbled, almost to himself.

'Maybe bit by bit,' said Dimitri, with a tone of what might even be described as *mild encouragement* in his voice. 'You are still poor fighter. But your gun skills, they impressed me. That is why I am even speaking to you.'

They both laughed.

'Yeah, well shootin', it's just like a game really. I imagined I was playing some kind of shoot 'em up thing on PlayStation,' Lewis continued, sounding almost sunny suddenly.

'Killing people in real world - it is not like game.' The reply, by contrast, sounded most grave.

'It will be best for me if I think it's just PlayStation.'

'OK... if it works for you, yes, then go ahead. But this first hit is easy meat. Mr Nobody in Nobody Town. It is like Level One PlayStation game.' Dimitri clicked his fingers, *simple.*

'Sounds alright,' the pupil concurred.

'Good.'

'But now I really do need to pee!' Lewis almost squealed, an urgent situation about to overcome him.

Dimitri guffawed as his passenger exited the car and legged it across the forecourt in search of the gents.

'Weak, but maybe we work on that,' the reluctant tutor said aloud to himself as his current *work-in-progress* darted through the automated glass doors of the building opposite. As he then patiently waited, sipping a water bottle, Dimitri checked out the contents of the glove compartment. Ensuring first that no passers-by were around, he retrieved a *Makarov* semi-automatic pistol and confirmed that it was loaded. It was. Hopefully, Lewis would remember his training when he handed him this deadly weapon in a few short minute's time.

★

At precisely 6.31 pm Krystyna - resplendent in Little Red Riding Hood costume - entered Brimstone's office. She'd given herself the all-clear having watched him just now, down from below, walk across the glass-fronted mezzanine corridor to the Executive bathroom. Once he was out of view, she'd darted up the steel staircase and into his office. With expert precision she now tore open the flap of the Vermokill Rat Poison and carefully administered its entire contents into a plastic reusable water bottle. Closing the lid, she vigorously shook the container - grateful that its black, opaque casing meant any discolouration of the water inside could not be detected. Taking the empty sachet with her, she then tiptoed away to hide in a walk-in stationery cupboard just to the side of Brimstone's desk.

As she settled down, crouching inside the cupboard, she noticed shelves of all the usual office paraphernalia - stacks of A4 wallet files, sheets of copy paper, pens, post-it notepads etc. Then on the back wall she noticed a set of items rarely seen in most Chief Executive's working environments. Not that she would expect to see, anyway. First, she saw the Roman Centurion armour and sword, last seen by Brimstone being defiantly discarded by Gavin Hargreaves. Then, hanging up on coat pegs were a familiar looking series of fantasy outfits. A Nazi SS uniform, cowboy gear, a scanty schoolgirl costume and Pocahontas mini dress - all the props that Krystyna had viewed, only the other day, in Brimstone's uploaded files on the porn video site.

She simmered to control her anger and on hearing Brimstone re-enter his office felt like flying out of the cupboard to punch his face. But no, she realised she needed to be patient, as very soon deadly poison itself would start to work its insidious yet murderous magic.

She watched the stop-watch digits of her phone advance rapidly forwards. Three minutes should do it. But three minutes came and then they went. She leaned forwards and was able to see - through a door-crack - her prospective victim sat at his desk. She couldn't know, of course, if he had yet touched the bottle. But he was merely busy right now, tapping out an email, all seeming apparently normal.

'Maybe I need to bring elephant poison, not rat poison,' Krystyna whispered inside her head.

Four minutes passed. Still nothing. The tension of the apparent delay, coupled with a sudden feeling of claustrophobia, started to make the waiting assassin feel decidedly queasy. *Come on please, just die!*

But five minutes and twenty-three seconds brought with it welcome progress.

'Uggghhhhh...' came the first agonised cries from outside of the cupboard.

Krystyna watched anxiously as Brimstone instinctively swigged on the water bottle hoping to help relieve his sudden and violent abdominal convulsions. He jumped to his feet, gagging, attempting to throw up - but to no avail. Both of his hands gripped his neck as though he were being invisibly throttled by a dark mysterious force. Then he fell back, slumping on his chair, now frothing at the mouth and gargling out indecipherable words.

Little Red Riding Hood entered joyously, stage left.

'What big eyes you have, Grandma,' she chirped authentically in character.

The whole of Brimstone's left cheek was twitching as though he was suffering a stroke. He scrunched his blurring eyes - no longer big at all - to try to make sense of what was happening. But all he could discern was excruciating pain.

'Look Grandma, I've brought you lovely present,' said Krystyna holding up the empty bag of poison.

Her victim struggled for coherence but managed somehow to start whimpering.

'Is that you, Little Red Riding Hood?'

'Yes Grandma. And I've brought you delicious rat poison. Yum yum.' She was holding the empty sachet with one hand, water bottle with the other. 'You have drunk. All gone.' She turned the bottle on its head, demonstrating the container was completely empty.

She was just about to sit down for her much anticipated grandstand view of Brimstone's final moments on earth when she heard footsteps on the steel stairway leading up to the office. As her dying victim seemed to be drifting away into semi-consciousness, groaning and grunting as he went, she quickly made herself scarce. Then, just as some unknown person was entering the office, she crouched down behind the door of the stationery cupboard and spied out through the small crevice as before.

She then saw a small male pensioner advancing towards the chair on which its owner was slumped backwards. Brimstone, with eyes closed and moaning on, perhaps appeared to be having a bad dream.

'No time for sleeping on the job, this is serious sonny,' Bob suddenly hollered, springing into attack mode, and assuming he had luckily taken his quarry quite unawares. Behind him, Rocky let out a little yelp - he wasn't used to seeing such bursts of energy from his human companion, so thought he'd better join in on the action.

Brimstone momentarily opened his eyes and slurred his speech like the last man standing in some drunken tavern.

'Is that you Daddy? Tell me a story...'

Bob was already behind him, deadly cling film unravelling. With military efficiency he then wrapped the plastic film around Brimstone's frothed and gunked-up face and head. Six times the film needed to be rotated for maximum strength - well that's what the YouTube video had recommended. But, after only three complete wrappings, Bob's roll was now empty.

'Damn you, cling film!' he despaired at the empty cardboard roll. Brimstone groaned again. 'Agh!' Bob cried, beating his victim's skull with the now weaponised cardboard tube. 'Die, you bastard. For I am Bob Horsefield at your disposal - the shat on little guy who is finally fighting back!' Then Rocky barked again, bringing up the rear-guard in support.

Bryce Brimstone seemed to be tottering right onto the edge of existence, suffocating under the cling film, his insides burnt out by rat poison. But now Bob, in turn, heard footsteps on those steel stairs behind him. An instinct told him he couldn't be discovered. He would go to jail for the rest of his days and pet dogs weren't allowed in jails. Noticing the stationery cupboard door, he scooped up Rocky and quickly scurried over towards it.

He then froze as he saw Little Red Riding Hood crouched in the cupboard, pointing a gun - the toy Nazi revolver - towards him.

'Shush and get in,' she ordered. 'Or I will shoot.'

'Bloody weird,' said Bob as he put Rocky down and put his own hands up. He certainly wasn't expecting to see a character from a *Brothers Grimm* fairy tale hiding in Brimstone's stationery cupboard. But she had a gun, *surely out of character* - and looked like she meant business. So he obediently followed her command and joined her - along with Rocky - behind the door she now closed quietly behind them.

'Do not worry. I am on your side,' Krystyna whispered to the elderly gent she'd just spied attempting to finish off her own work with a roll of cling film. 'I also want Brimstone dead.'

Bob relaxed a little and stroked Rocky, gently settling him down. Then both himself and Krystyna leant forward to peep through the helpful cracks in the door to see who exactly was about to enter the office - and what they would do about the horrific sight that awaited.

'Yaaaaaaahhhhhh!' screamed out a male voice in full battle cry. Brimstone was now slumped over on his desk, his head twitching in its final death throes. Possessed by manic fury, a late middle-aged man was charging forwards, a butcher's meat cleaver being swung wildly above his head. 'Die Brimstone bastard!'

The meat cleaver came smashing down with a force that ensured half of it instantly disappeared, now lodged inside the unfortunate target's skull.

'Dinesh!' whispered Krystyna, incredulously. She immediately recognised the owner of her - and Drabbleton's - favourite chippy.

'Dinesh!' whispered Bob in amazement. He of course also knew the guy who had thankfully reopened a chippy in the vacated premises that Gavin's failed joke shop had once occupied.

'Come,' Krystyna mouthed to Bob as she quickly kicked open the door with a force that sent it smacking hard against the outside wall as it swung outwards on its hinges. The sudden jolting crack of wood against stone instantly stunned the meat cleaver murderer. Rocky barked menacingly. 'Hands up, or I shoot.'

Dinesh quickly raised his hands.

'Ah, it is Allah's will, I am bad man! I am caught red-handed!' he began to blubber.

'Do not talk nonsense, Dinesh,' snapped Krystyna. 'Meat cleaver entirely unnecessary. I killed Brimstone.'

She triumphantly held aloft the empty rat poison sachet before then throwing it disdainfully at the corpse before them.

'That gun's not real for a start, so put it down love,' said Bob wearily.

'It is real. Do not provoke me. I am killer.'

'Bollocks,' said Bob, quickly smothering the gun and surprisingly wrestling it from Krystyna's usually more assured grip. 'It's a stage prop. Like all of them weird costumes in that cupboard. Is this a bloody office or a pantomime set?' He ran a dubious eye over the Little Red Riding Hood costume.

'OK, you may have point. Gun is probably fake,' conceded Krystyna, trying to smother her obvious disappointment, and quickly massaging the wrist that Bob had just twisted.

Dinesh took down his raised arms. 'Please do not hand me in to police. My wife needs me,' he begged - somewhat pathetically, thought Krystyna.

'Dinesh, relax,' said Bob. 'I killed Brimstone. See ...cling film suffocation,' he confirmed, helpfully pointing out the evidence.

'He was dying already, victim thief!' Krystyna protested. 'I am murderer!'

'But see...evidence that *I* am murderer is still stuck in bastard's head,' cried Dinesh, remaining distressed. At this time, he also wished that Mishka hadn't had the name of their chippy - *Star of India* - lovingly engraved on said chopper, her thoughtful gift for his 50th birthday. He retrieved the towel from his shoulder bag and daintily dabbed the blood-stained handle of the incriminating meat cleaver.

'Just pull the damn thing out, won't you? Don't just stand there!' Bob half-exploded with impatience, pointing at the cleaver and miming an action of yanking it out of Brimstone's skull.

Dinesh took a firm grip of the meat cleaver's handle and pulled hard. But it certainly did not budge. 'Again!' he cried, attempting the extraction for a second time, leaning back at a 45-degree angle, using the whole weight of his body to assist.

'Here, let me help,' chipped in Bob, clasping his own hands around Dinesh's on the handle. 'One, two, three...pull!'

Again the meat cleaver remained stubbornly wedged in the obviously very thick skull.

'I try...' Krystyna joined in, adding a third pair of hands to the job.'
Then they chanted in unison: 'One. Two. Three... Pull!'

One almighty tug and the great Gothic style desk dragged towards them across the old wooden factory floor, dragging Brimstone's body with it. Yet again the stubbornly lodged weapon would not be released from its new housing. Again in unison, they all just happened to release the chopper's handle and, with the counterforce, Brimstone's corpse zinged back into the chair, now left sitting upright.

'I'd say it's stuck that mate,' Bob huffed.

'I am certainly going to jail,' wailed Dinesh.

'We will chop off his head,' suggested Krystyna, enamoured by her sudden, yet inspired idea. 'Easier to hide head than whole body.'

'What, you got an axe, or something love?' Bob had concluded by now that she was a bit nuts.

'No, but I have Roman Centurion sword!'

Three faces all lit up with gleeful smiles.

'Yes please, I will do it,' said Dinesh.

'No, I will,' insisted Bob.

'No, I will,' Krystyna argued. 'I was my idea.'

'Shush, what is that?' Dinesh's eyes grew suddenly wider with alarm. He had now heard something on the stairs outside. 'Somebody is coming.'

'Hide,' said Krystyna frantically, darting back towards the cupboard.

'Yes, yes...' said Bob, quickly following on.

'Room for three?' asked Dinesh politely, pausing on the cusp of the cupboard door. Krystyna grabbed his collar and dragged him unceremoniously inside. Bob closed up, leaving them all out of sight of the mystery discoverer of horrible and bloody murder.

★

Perhaps just less than ten minutes prior to that hasty retreat to the stationery cupboard, Dimitri's Mercedes had parked up just outside Brimstone Mill. The two characters in the car were partially hidden from any passing observer by darkly tinted security windows. So, nobody was likely to have imagined the murderous scheme now being finalised within the confines of two tons of upmarket metal. And in any case, most people would have stayed well away even if they did happen to notice the two shady looking figures inside - hardly the friendliest looking pair. Most people are not *all* people, however. Enter one naively inquisitive Drabbleton local, name of Darren Eccles.

'Nice motor, mate,' mouthed Darren, tapping against the glass of the driver side window.

'What the hell?' grunted Dimitri, sending the unwelcome one the bad eye.

'Wow, *Top of the Range Mercedes Visits Drabbleton.* That'll be the headline in this week's *Bugle*, ha ha! Nice one mate!' Eccles stepped backwards to line up a confirmatory snap on his phone. 'You could buy a house or three round here for the same money as you'd pay for this beauty.'

Dimitri stepped smartly out of the car.

'My friend,' he smiled menacingly. 'Take that picture and you and I, we fall out. Understand?'

'Love the car mate!' Eccles smiled gauchely. 'Just for me Instagram!' He snapped the pic and immediately viewed his phone to see how his spontaneous composition had turned out.

'Give me phone, now!' Dimitri beckoned in agitation.

'Ha Ha, who are you, the phone police?' said Darren, putting the handset teasingly behind his back, quite unaware of the danger he was now in.

'I did warn you,' said Dimitri, deadpan. He approached Eccles with serious menace, snatching the offending phone and throwing it forcefully to the floor. Then, holding the weakling *Drab* by the throat, he stamped on the mobile several times, shattering its screen and then its very structure. Pulling the then head-locked Eccles along with him into the adjacent back alley, he furthermore ignored both any attempts to see reason and all pitiful pleas for mercy. A swift and calculated twist of the clamping right arm rendered the fragile neck broken. Dimitri dropped Darren Eccles' immediately lifeless body onto the cobbles.

'Shit man, that was harsh!' said Lewis, as Dimitri then climbed back into his driver's seat, apparently not even breaking sweat.

'I told you, no witnesses, no exceptions,' replied the seasoned field operative. 'You need to be OK with that. Yes?'

'Fuck man, fuck,' said Lewis banging his head against the passenger window, looking at Darren's corpse, now abandoned in that Drabbleton back alley. But he had already reached a kind of fatalistic conclusion that he really had no say in the matter. This was his new life. He needed to fit in. 'Yeah OK, I get it. No witnesses.'

'Good,' replied Dimitri, seemingly placated. 'OK, go and get him,' he added, pointing to the unfortunate corpse. 'Stick him in boot. My DNA is all over him. We dispose of him in river later.'

'Why me?' asked Lewis, with sulky indignation.

'Because it is no good having dogsbody who does not do dogsbody work.' He smiled sarcastically towards his apprentice.

Lewis huffed, but knew he had to do as he was told. He left the car, efficiently collected the broken necked body, and stashed it in the Mercedes boot, covering it with a blanket. He then silently rejoined his boss in the front of the car.

'Very good,' said Dimitri. 'Well now it is your turn for real action.'

From his coat pocket he produced the *Makarov* semi-automatic pistol, now fully loaded, that he had been keeping aside until now.

'Excellent gun. Treat with respect.'

'PlayStation game, right?' Lewis smiled nervously as carefully took the weapon and placed it inside his hoodie's pocket.

'Level One. ...OK, you know where to go?'

Roxanne had roughly sketched them a kind of map of Brimstone Mill, drawn from the memory of her last visit here. Dimitri had drilled into Lewis's brain exactly where he had to go to find his 'mark'. One single gunshot to the head was all that was required, no need to get gun happy. Oh, and any witnesses would need to be eliminated. Well, of course, that went without saying.

Lewis braced himself, took a deep breath and opened the passenger door.

'If you are not back in five minutes, I come,' said Dimitri. 'So, be back, yes?'

'Got it,' replied Lewis as he closed the car door and turned on his heels. Very soon he knew he would be able to call himself a fully qualified assassin. Mr Volkov might then want to get to know him a bit better. He hoped that would be the case anyway.

★

In the subsequent two minutes - Roxanne's map engrained in his head - Lewis had managed to navigate his way across the Call Centre floor and onto the steel stairway leading up to Brimstone's office. Although he'd stepped carefully, he'd realised that large feet impacting metal inside an echoey mill weren't exactly making for the quietest ever approach to a hit. Still, he wasn't to know that the unavoidable sound of his steady footsteps had already alerted the earnest crew currently at work in the Executive office. These three accidental allies, plus dog, had by now had time to furtively conceal themselves inside the stationery cupboard - each with an eye pressed against various door cracks and crevices, even Rocky.

As he now finally reached the slightly open large, oak door of Brimstone's office, Lewis sensed his heart rapidly thumping inside his chest, sounding louder to him than any of his footsteps. His skin had felt suddenly clammy and as he looked at the gun, held in his right hand, he realised its handle was covered in sweat. Pausing at the door, he dried the gun on his hoodie. He held his breath.

'Come on, Bro',' he whispered to himself, 'Level One PlayStation!'

The cupboard dwellers then saw Lewis purposefully enter the office, gun pointed in front of him - heading straight towards Brimstone, whose lifeless body was still propped up but slumped backwards against his swivel chair. They also noticed that the gunman wasn't exactly looking at his target, but rather holding his head away to the side and scrunching his eyes. It was as if he was simply too squeamish to fully watch the details of a real-life murder - which happened to be the truth, actually. But he did then fire the gun, taking an almost instinctive aim at Brimstone's forehead, thanks entirely to PlayStation practice. The bullet exploded into flesh and bone, leaving a bloodied hole right in the centre of the victim's forehead.

The cupboard people silently gasped. The cupboard dog seemed taken by the feather on Pocahontas's headband.

Lewis slowly turned his head to inspect his work.

'Ah, fuck man!' he blurted out in bewilderment. He looked at the still corpse sitting upright on the chair. His own bullet had been a bullseye, job done. But why was Brimstone's head wrapped in clingfilm and impaled by a meat cleaver. He panicked thinking he'd be in big trouble for messing up the hit. He'd been instructed to take a pic for the benefit of Disposals Inc, so he fumbled for his phone. Lining up the camera shot, he frowned and sighed.

'This is not right, Bro',' he self-admonished. He took the pic anyway, but then thought he could do better. Maybe if he removed the cling film and the meat cleaver from the dead guy's head, he'd be able to make it appear that it was just his bullet that had done the dirty deed. He approached the swivel chair.

Inside the cupboard, Rocky had been playfully knocking around the Pocahontas feather with his nose. Bob had stopped him mucking about the once. But after the shock of the gun fire, he'd totally forgotten about his otherwise preoccupied pooch.

So, his pet mongrel had resumed his carefree fun with the feather, quite enjoying his nose being tickled - until this playful agitation of such a sensitive, wet snout looked likely to be triggering one almighty dog sneeze. Bob caught onto this all too late and could only watch as his pet mongrel silently convulsed the once, then the twice. Then finally...

'*ATISHOO!*' A cacophonous explosion of nasal mucus!

The three instantly alarmed humans looked at each other in mild terror. *We're dead!*

Lewis jolted as he heard the spectacularly loud sneeze. Who or what was in that cupboard? *No witnesses, Lewis* - Dimitri's grave instruction resonated in his head. He stealthily approached the little storeroom, gun pointing ahead of him, turned a handle and swung open the door.

'Whoa!'

His instinct immediately took him one stride backwards when stepping forward themselves out of the cupboard came three mean looking characters, each armed with weapons. A growling, rather snotty dog followed on, by way of back-up. There was Bob, pointing a Nazi Luger pistol, Dinesh, pointing a cowboy style Colt revolver. Then there was Krystyna, menacingly brandishing a very sharp looking Roman Centurion sword.

'Drop your weapons, or I'll shoot,' Lewis flustered.

'We'll shoot you first,' said Bob taking aim at the intruder's heart.

'Yes, there are three of us. Plus dog. Only one of you. Put down the gun,' Dinesh tried to wisely counsel.

'I'm a professional hit man, I can shoot all three of you before you even have time to move,' said Lewis, attempting to gain some composure.

'Yeah?' Bob doubted.

'Yeah!' Lewis confirmed.

'Yeah?' Dinesh doubly doubted.

'Yeah, is right!' Lewis insisted.

'Ha!' sneered Krystyna. 'You are not much of hit-man. You just shot dead body!'

They all glanced over to the multiple times murdered corpse still propped up in the swivel chair.

'I executed Brimstone. He is my kill,' Krystyna gloated as her slightly manic eyes sparkled.

'Rubbish,' protested Bob. 'He wasn't dead until my cling-film got to work.'

'But I saw him move before I cracked his skull with chippy cleaver,' Dinesh pressed. 'I am indeed the killer.'

'You lot is mental,' cried Lewis, totally confused. 'Last chance, then I shoot!'

'Get ready for battle people!' Bob threatened. Dimitri's apprentice carefully studied the black pistol being determinedly pointed at him.

'Hang on, Bro'. That is no real weapon, it's just a toy,' Lewis laughed, hoping he was right. It did very much look like a toy gun to him.

Bob's face fell. He was rumbled. He pulled the Luger's trigger part in resignation, part for the sheer hell of it. But the subsequent sound of gunshot sent them all flinching. Lewis dropped his own gun, holding an apparently wounded right arm.

'You shot me man, what the fuck!' the Disposals Inc hitman wailed, holding his arm.

'Sorry,' said Bob, looking at the supposed theatre prop gun in puzzlement.

'Quick, get his weapon,' Krystyna ordered of Dinesh as she threateningly held the Centurion sword above Lewis's head. The relieved chippy man was happy to obey and quickly collected the gun - which he then pointed towards its wounded owner. Dinesh was now a *two-guns* potential sharpshooter. He looked smug.

'What you gonna do, finish me?' Lewis almost sobbed. 'This was only my first job an' all.'

'We will think about it,' said Krystyna, glad to be back in charge. 'On your knees and we will discuss.'

Lewis did as he was told. Bob and Dinesh looked at one another blankly. *What now?*

'My boss will be up here looking for me any time. You'll be sorry. He is a proper killer.'

'Yeah?' doubted Bob.

'Yeah!' Lewis confirmed, nursing his bloodied limb. 'This arm hurts, man. I'll see you'll be the first to get it. You and that plug-ugly dog!'

'Don't call my dog plug-ugly or I'll bloody well shoot you again!' Bob scowled. So did Rocky.

'Yeah?' said Lewis defiantly.

'Yeah!' said Bob, wildly waving the Luger.

Meantime, Dinesh had detached himself from the Lewis situation and had wandered over to the window, wondering if they could maybe throw Brimstone's corpse down into the courtyard. From there they could possibly get a vehicle and move it away. But a dark suited foreign looking guy seemed to be heading for the mill's loading bay entrance - and not looking very happy at all.

'Excuse me, Sir?' Dinesh politely enquired of Lewis. 'Does your boss have nice black suit and drive big Mercedes?'

'Is right.'

'I think we have a new visitor coming,' Dinesh then fretted.

Krystyna, meanwhile, had worked out a plan.

14
- THE PROFESSIONALS -

Dimitri had heard the first gunshot from inside his Mercedes. *So far, so good.* He then expected to see Lewis appear, mission accomplished, within the next minute or so. Then they could speedily get on their way back down the motorway to London. Home before midnight - and with luck Roxanne might consider staying up to welcome him and more.

The sound of the second gunshot was both surprising and unwelcome. He'd immediately put his Mercedes into gear and nosed it slowly forwards and into the courtyard of the mill. He'd checked that a loaded cartridge was in his own gun before then leaving the vehicle and heading off to support Lewis in whatever pickle he was in.

He'd then found himself delayed by the door of the loading bay happening to be locked. Lewis had entered by a different door, but Dimitri had deliberately chosen an alternative route in to avoid any possible ambush. A window about ten feet off the ground had been left open - and once he'd spotted that he'd nimbly shimmied up a drainpipe and wriggled underneath the opening and into the mill. He'd then brushed his dusty suit down with displeasure. Saville Row tailoring should never be treated so disrespectfully.

Coming in from a strange direction, he'd also been a bit disoriented in this unfamiliar building. He'd tried to invert Roxanne's map in his head trying to work out what were his precise whereabouts in relation to Brimstone's office. Of course, he had finally put all the jigsaw pieces into place, but only at the expense of precious lost time.

But now it was his turn to be ascending the steel stairway up to the Executive Office. He readied his own *Makarov* semi-automatic and approached the oak door he was very much expecting to now be in view. No sound came from the office. He entered carefully, gun first.

'Damn it, what is this?' he cried, before blinking twice, doubting the reality of what he was seeing before him. But it was real alright. Laid out on his front, across the width of the Gothic desk, was the successfully executed body of Bryce Brimstone. Well not the entire body. Just the torso. The unfortunate victim had now been decapitated. Dimitri watched the flow of congealing blood from the neck dripping onto the wooden floor below. Not a gush of blood, however, suggesting the death of Brimstone had occurred quite some minutes ago.

Suddenly a knocking sound. The trained killer readied his gun.

'Boss it's me! I'm in here!' Lewis called out from his temporary prison inside the now locked stationery cupboard. Dimitri quickly strode over to the door behind which Lewis was incarcerated but had now been padlocked on the outside.

'Stand back,' ordered Dimitri as he aimed, then fired his gun at the lock, which shattered immediately. He then swung open the door to reveal his hapless apprentice, his hoodie discarded to reveal the cotton vest he'd been wearing underneath.

'What happened?' asked Dimitri, wondering why Lewis was nursing his right arm, but also sounding less than pleased to see him like this.

'They shot me!'

'Let me see.' Lewis's shielding hand was knocked away from the wound. Dimitri huffed derisively. 'Little scratch. Nothing. So be a man!'

Lewis sulkily left the cupboard, immediately then ordered to sit down on one of the plastic chairs in front of Brimstone's desk. A full debrief was quickly demanded and the younger man did his best to fill in all the details. Three mad people and a dog, two guns and a sword. An argument between them about who had dealt the fatal blow to their common enemy. Lewis being shot and then stuck in the cupboard - while they then...

'She only went and chopped his bloody head off. Ugghhh! Lewis couldn't bring himself to look at the decapitated corpse. 'With a freakin' sword!'

'They are probably professionals,' Dimitri surmised. 'Maybe Brimstone was involved in organised crime.'

'Don't think so,' Lewis replied, shaking his head. 'They just seem so ordinary really.'

'*Exactly* what good agents must appear to be when working undercover. They must blend into background, hardly be noticed.

Until the time comes to strike. Then wham!' Dimitri smashed his fist down onto the desk. 'Yes, only cold-blooded killers can cut off head. We charge much extra for that!'

'I'm never doing that. I will stick to the bullet in the head jobby.'

'But you have failed in even that,' Dimitri scolded, making a caricature of a long face. 'Where is evidence for Mr Volkov? No head?'

'Yeah, well I did take a pic, course I did,' said Lewis, suddenly chirping up, retrieving his phone from his semi-sagging pants, and handing it over for inspection.

'Excellent,' chimed Dimitri, viewing the image. One bullet delivered to centre of head, as ordered. 'Indeed, this is proof. Forward it to me then I will send to Dizzy.' *But what of this cling-film and embedded meat cleaver?* 'Sons of bitches looked like they tortured him before death. Yes, clearly professionals.'

Lewis was handed back his phone and immediately sent the pic on to his boss, deleting it as soon as it was forwarded. This wasn't the kind of thing he wanted to see when casually scrolling through his usually light-hearted camera roll. Then Dimitri was addressing him in the strictest of tones.

'Whatever you do, do not mention any other persons present to Mr Volkov. Very bad for business and so unprofessional that others assisted us on hit. We'd have been expected to take care of that other crew. But now they are roaming witnesses to your involvement. Very bad.'

'You reckon he'd be mad if he knew?' asked Lewis, naively.

'How old are you?'

'Nineteen.'

'Ah, you want to see twenty?'

Lewis nodded as the penny eventually dropped.

'Now we must remove torso. It will be needed. Come on.'

Without asking why it would be needed, Lewis quickly positioned himself so he could lift Brimstone's feet while his boss manoeuvred in place to take the upper body weight.

'OK heave,' ordered Dimitri, but the two men immediately struggled to easily shift the sixteen stone plus lump of dead Brimstone. They made a little headway towards the exit door, but only accompanied by much huffing and groaning.

'Too far to car,' the chief shifter complained. 'Must be easier way.'

Even Lewis himself was surprised by his own quick thinking, though his proposed solution admittedly lacked originality.

'When I was locked in the cupboard, one of them suggested throwing the body out of the window,' he offered. 'But next thing they were cutting off its head. Mental, innit?'

'True professionals. They are outwitting us,' mumbled Dimitri disconsolately, then spotting the literal window of opportunity himself.

'Come. Lift again.'

A couple of minutes later, the interest of Samson, the mill's adopted cat - hunting mice in the courtyard - was vaguely captured. First, he'd heard some sort of kerfuffle going on at a first-floor open window. Then he'd seen the headless body of a human plunging down to earth and thumping against the hard cobbles below. Five minutes later, two other humans were tidying up the mess, putting the now bone-shattered corpse inside a body bag - which itself was quickly zipped up and bundled into the back of a waiting Mercedes. On top of a previously stashed dead body, no less. The humans departed and Samson resumed his hunt, merely bemused at the oddities of the lesser species on the planet.

*

Krystyna's 'plan' had involved firstly, the horrible beheading - completed by herself as winner of an impromptu game of *Rock, Paper, Scissors*. As a first-time decapitator she hadn't realised how securely heads are attached to the rest of the body. So, it had taken her three gruesome, yet mighty strikes to achieve success. When the head had finally dropped into the waiting paper basket, positioned for the purpose by the side of the desk, it had been all too much for Dinesh - who had promptly thrown up. Vomiting directly into the bin, therefore onto the head itself, hadn't been the cleverest of ideas. But seeing as he'd then volunteered to be the one to carry away the sick splattered skull in basket, nobody else had really minded.

The second part of the plan had involved nothing more elaborate than hiding in the Executive Bathroom just up the corridor and hoping for the best.

As they'd sat around waiting for Lewis's back-up to free him and depart - banking on the two gangsters concluding that they themselves had already scarpered - they'd made a necessary pact.

'We must tell nobody about tonight, OK?' Krystyna had solemnly warned. 'Not friends, neighbours ...*Mrs Dinesh*...' she'd stared hard at the chippy man sat on the floor, prize basket on knee. She'd visited the *Star of India* many times over the years and had seen that its married owners seemed very close.

'Yes, of course,' Dinesh had solemnly sworn, miming a zipping of the lips.

'Fine by me,' Bob had also agreed, replicating the mime. 'And he won't say anything, neither.' He'd pointed to Rocky, a trustable dog if ever there was one.

'Life imprisonment. It is a suffering to avoid,' Krystyna had then helpfully pointed out.

'Here, here,' Bob had confirmed. 'My lips are sealed.'

'But I must get my cleaver out of this stupid skull. Then dispose of the head forever.' Dinesh had looked a little overwhelmed by the prospective task, Krystyna then surveying him with concern.

'Look, can we bank on you to do the necessary?'

'Yes, of course,' Dinesh had replied after some considered hesitation. 'I will think of something.'

'Good,' the old pensioner had encouraged. 'That's the spirit.'

Sometime later, from the slightly ajar Executive Bathroom window, Bob - on occasional lookout duty, thankfully having remembered his specs - first heard, but then saw a black Mercedes and its serious occupants leave the courtyard. Krystyna's simple plan had succeeded. They hung on for a few minutes to ensure they weren't being tricked out into the open. But finally, they made their furtive exits, first Krystyna, then Bob. Then last but not least, Dinesh - safeguarding the basket full of sick, meat cleaver and sorry looking human noggin.

15
- TERMS & CONDITIONS -

Around the Tuesday lunchtime, Alice walked with Gavin along the canal side, their hands entwined and their mood a light one. The pair hadn't seen each other since their eventful date last Friday and they'd agreed to meet up again today for a hopefully less interrupted get together.

Brimstone Mill, like many cotton factories, had been built next to the canal - where, back in the 19th Century, horse drawn barges would come to collect its wares. Fine cloth would then head off to Liverpool's docks, then an export gateway to the world. But these days the canal's only usefulness, as far as certain locals were concerned, was as a fly-tipping receptacle. Old baths, prams and sofas regularly went to their watery grave here. And today, as Alice and Gavin wandered along the tow path right by the mill itself, an old fridge came floating towards them - a commonplace sighting they deemed unworthy of even a mention.

Meanwhile, each of them couldn't help picking out familiar landmarks that were built on the hills around them. Gavin saw the State Comprehensive where he had been indoctrinated that he and his classmates were second best. Alice saw the Private Girl's School that she was able to attend in her latter teen years, entirely due to the money her brother had sent home from London. Gavin spotted Victoria Park, where he had lost his virginity to the accommodating Wendy Dutton underneath the bandstand, aged seventeen. Alice caught a glimpse of The Ritz nightclub, where she once regularly danced to Spice Girls and S Club 7 hits - but now prayed that no one would remember. Drabbleton held so many memories for them both, but few people round here liked to talk about the past. Because for many, that's all there was.

Luckily for Alice, however, she was optimistic for the future. She was finally escaping her brother's clutches the best she could, about to set out on a new marketing career, even excited by the prospect of the new love interest in her life. Right on cue, said love interest pulled her towards him and planted a gentle kiss on her lips. *Yep*, she thought, *he's not too bad this one.*

Even Gavin was feeling optimistic, despite his recent job loss. He'd already had an interview at the local chicken processing factory and was pretty sure he'd be offered the role. It was in the carcass incineration unit. Not many people cared to be employed burning the remnants of dead chickens all day. But couldn't be worse than having to dress up as a Roman Centurion to work, surely? Except, the pay was worse. Still, there were promotion prospects, he'd been told by the eager-to-please recruitment manager. Operators of the automated chicken plucker got thirty pence an hour more, for a start.

Besides, he reckoned that being with Alice right now made everything so much more bearable. He had been longing to see her today.

'I couldn't sleep last night,' he confided. 'I was like an excited little schoolboy, dying to be with you again.'

'That's nice,' Alice quietly assented.

'How about you? Could you sleep? Gavin sounded a tad needy.

'Yep. Slept like a baby.'

'Oh...' Gavin hated that. These early dates, when you start to take a risk and put it all out there, only to realise you've just made a complete prat of yourself.

'I always sleep well when I'm happy,' Alice said, sounding very contented indeed.

'And are you?'

'Oh yes, very. Because I finally managed to finish off a *Daily Telegraph* cryptic crossword. First time in ages.' Alice beamed with satisfaction.

'Oh...' Another mild crushing.

'I'm teasing you,' Alice laughed, so clearly amused with herself. 'You big daft lump. Come here, give me a kiss!'

She tugged his jacket so that he was standing in front of her. Then, as the abandoned fridge sailed by and the landmarks of old Drabbleton stared down at them, they indeed shared another tender kiss. It then blossomed, growing more passionate and extending to a length that surprised them both.

'Wow!' said Gavin, as the clinch subsided.

'Quite,' said Alice, smiling.

'Hey, you two! Get a room!' It was Urma from the Call Centre, cackling as she approached along the tow path. The two lovers quickly broke their embrace and shuffled around awkwardly. 'You're like Romeo and Juliet, you two. Walking out of your jobs together. Everybody's talking about it.'

'Word obviously gets round,' said Gavin, maybe a little proud of his apparently now celebrated defiance.

'You're not kidding. Every last one of us in that place would be joining you if we could afford to.'

As it was now the subject of discussion, all three of them found themselves casually looking over towards the factory across on the other side of the canal. Alice then spotted two marked police vehicles in the car park.

'Hello, is there trouble at' mill?' she half joked. Although she seriously wondered what was going on.

'All a mystery,' said Urma. 'The cleaner said she'd found blood in His Majesty's office.'

Alice looked immediately alarmed. Urma checked herself, quickly remembering the sibling status of *His Majesty*.

'Sorry,' she added. 'Me and my big mouth.'

'No problem,' Alice placated, waving a casually dismissive hand.

'So are the police talking to Mr Brimstone, then?' Gavin wondered aloud.

'No, that's the funny bit. Nobody knows where he is,' Urma replied, shrugging a clueless shoulder.

'Sounds odd,' said Alice.

'I'm sure he'll just come waltzing in later with a perfectly logical explanation. Panic over.' Urma laughed nervously, hoping she'd done her best to settle Alice's obvious unease. 'Anyway, must dash. I'm just on lunch.'

Urma then made a hasty retreat and her ex-colleagues sent her off with polite farewells.

'I'm ringing him,' said Alice, urgently retrieving her phone from handbag.

'He's maybe just pulling a stunt on some poor sod. You know what he's like.' Gavin tried to make light of it. But two police cars had turned up at the mill. Probably at least fifty percent of the town's entire police resources.

'Yep ...but still,' Alice muttered as she selected her brother's name from her Contacts list.

Voicemail.

'This is Bryce Brimstone. Leave a message and I may get back to you.'

'Bryce, it's me. Give me a call when you get this, thanks.'

Alice hung up and seemed deep in thought. Gavin hadn't expected to see her so worried about something that could still yet amount to nothing. Maybe she was closer to her brother than he had imagined.

Just then, his own phone dinged. A text. Alice saw him scroll onto some kind of picture.

'What the...?' He was then staring with some disbelief at the photograph that he'd been sent, apparently by the app they'd been messing with the other night. Sat in the chair at his desk, Brimstone was depicted in his quite murdered state - bullet hole between the eyes, cling-film wrapping his face and some sort of chopper embedded in his head.

'Order complete. Thank you for choosing Disposals Inc,' read the caption beneath the photo.

'Oh my God,' Gavin trembled. 'It's happened.'

'What's happened?'

'Bryce...'

'What are you talking about? Alice demanded, her boyfriend's expression of terror immediately contagious. She attempted to view Gavin's phone, but he whipped it away.

'What's the big secret? Let me see.'

'No, no, I can't. I'm sorry, but it's just terrible.' He swiftly put his phone into a pocket inside his jacket. 'Come on, let's go.' He set off briskly walking down the tow path.

'You're frightening me now. Don't just say it's Bryce and walk off,' Alice called out, now a few steps behind him. Her frustration rapidly grew until it exploded. 'Let me see that phone, or I will never trust you again.'

Gavin stopped and turned towards her, his face now ashen white.

'Alice, it was just meant to be a joke...'

'Show me the phone!'

Gavin's flustered mind tried to balance up which were the lesser of two evils. He could keep the image beyond Alice, but then he could already see that they'd fall out about it. Maybe even enough of a fall out, in these early days, to drive a terminal wedge between them. But if he showed it to her, then she would be traumatised.

'Look, I just can't show you this,' said Gavin, gambling on instinct. 'But yes, it is Bryce. The photo shows ...well that he's been shot. He's probably dead.'

'What? Show me the picture,' she demanded. 'Show me the picture, that's my brother!'

'No,' Gavin stayed absolutely firm.

Alice was pounding her fists against his chest in anger, until said anger turned into tears of hysteria and then tears of great pain. Gavin enfolded her with his arms and the two were completely still for a brief moment.

Then Alice surprised him, wriggling into life, wrestling a hand inside of his coat and forcefully retrieving the phone. He tried to grab it back, but she shoved him away from her. She then spun around and doubled over, protecting the handset from any rescue attempt. She opened the image.

Then she screamed - a guttural, unworldly scream. Gavin tried to hold her comfortingly, but she knocked him off with a sharp elbow. She ran away, just a few steps down the path, then turned to face him again. There was fury in her tearful eyes.

'This is your fault. You wanted him dead.'

'It was just a joke,' Gavin tried to reason, his arms held out wide. 'You were in on it too, remember.'

'You knew this was no game!' She nodded her head, as if a burst of sudden realisation had hit her.

'What are you talking about? Gavin tried his best to sound reasonable and calm as he slowly approached the spot where Alice was standing.

Alice threw the phone at him, and he ducked as it whizzed past his head onto the grassy bank to the side.

'Keep away from me! she wailed. 'Just keep away! I never want to see your conniving face again!' She turned again and this time sprinted away. He didn't follow, but simply stood still, bewildered. He watched her speedily climb the steps of a nearby road bridge and leave his sight.

*

Gavin took himself off to Victoria Park, another of the great James Brimstone's bequeathments to Drabbleton made back in the 19th Century. He just wanted to sit somewhere in peace and quiet to try to clear his head. What should he do with this terrible information, inconveniently ensconced in his phone? If he went to the police, would they believe his protestations of innocence? Why would Brimstone be murdered in any case, just because Gavin himself was mucking around with an app? What was in it for whoever had done such a thing.

He found himself sitting on the steps of the Bandstand, momentarily remembering sweet moments with Wendy Dutton all those years ago. Life was simpler back then. She'd told him she loved him; they'd had sex - then she'd casually buggered off with Bike Shop Bill the week after. He hadn't minded. Prospects with Colleen from the launderette had been looking good.

But he realised by now that he'd fallen seriously in love with Alice. These days, relationships no longer seemed to be something that could be casually cast aside like empty chip wrappers. It would be agony for him if he couldn't mend this thing. But how?

Just then his phone dinged again. He dreaded to think what this next incoming text could be. So, his first instinct was to avoid opening it altogether, chancing that *ignorant bliss* would be a good strategy. But then he speculated that it could be Alice. Maybe she wanted to talk?

Then he groaned when he saw the senders name - Disposals Inc. He was being invited to click a link, which scared him a little. Morbid curiosity, however, quickly won the day. Two seconds later, the app that was causing him so many problems today was open on his phone.

'Good afternoon...Gavin. It is Dizzy, your AI Assistant at Disposals Inc.' The softly spoken female robot began her business.

'Hello,' Gavin replied in a voice in marked contrast to Dizzy's cheery tone.

'We do hope you enjoyed our work,' she continued to chirp. 'Now we must ask you to pay the invoice which can be found in your My Account page. Amount due... Thirty... Thousand... Pounds.'

'What? What bollocks are you talking now?' Gavin couldn't decide if this were some kind of elaborate prank - yes, just the kind that Brimstone would try to pull off. Or else, was he really and truly in deep shit?

'I did not understand your last response,' said Dizzy. 'If you intend to pay, say yes now.'

'No!'

'You answered ...no.' Dizzy's AI wheels were whirring away.

'Yes.'

'Yes. You will pay,' she confirmed, sounding more cheerful.

'No.'

'No, you will not pay.' Now she sounded confused.

'Yes ...I mean no. No!' Gavin was getting in a tangle while the heat under his collar was increasing.

'Did you read the Terms & Conditions of our app? Our records show that you did.' Dizzy was now very *matter of fact.*

'Yeah, I said I did. But come on, nobody actually reads the *Terms & Conditions,*' he defied, feeling he was speaking a universal truth.

'Clause thirty-five, sub paragraph four,' Dizzy calmly continued. 'The Customer shall, within 24 hours, pay all sums due for the carrying out of any work done on their behalf by Disposals Inc. Failure to do so will result in further action being taken by the Company.

If you understand, say yes now.'

'Further action?'

'Yes, further action will be taken? If you understand say yes now.'

There was then a pause. Gavin considered his response. Then he had it.

'Fuck off!'

'You said *fuck...off.* Computing.' Dizzy was silent as she searched her memory banks for a translation. 'Ah, intransitive verb: vulgar. If you meant ...*fuck ...off,* say yes now.'

'Yeeesss!' Gavin hollered, grimacing at his phone, promptly closing the app and switching off his handset.

I'm drowning, he thought. *Somebody, anybody - please throw me a lifeline!*

16
- SPECIAL DELIVERY -

Another relentlessly drizzling day had passed in Drabbleton. Still, Bob Horsefield always treated himself to a *Star of India* sausage dinner on a Wednesday night - so he would never let a drop of rain deprive him of that little joy. Besides, he wanted to know how Dinesh was getting on with business relating to the disposal of one decapitated head.

'Good evening, Bob, my friend, how are you?' Dinesh was his usual chippy man, smiling self as the old customer plus dog entered his shop.

'All good, thanks,' replied Bob, everything seeming perfectly normal to Mishka who was busying herself with the cash accounts for the month. 'The usual for me, please Dinesh.'

'Certainly. Mid-week usual for Bob coming up. Sausage on side for Rocky.'

'Perfect.' Bob watched on as Dinesh capably stirred the bubbling oil in the fryer.

'Five minutes for chips, sorry,' the cook apologised, inspecting the still pale, sliced potatoes in his serving net.

'No problem.' Bob stepped back from the counter and, sitting on a wooden bench set against the window, pretended to be glancing at the sports page of the local paper. 'I see Drabbleton FC's manager, Tony Head has got the axe.'

'Ah yes...' Dinesh paused for thought. 'But Mr Head was no good, so it was inevitable the axe would fall.'

Mishka was mildly surprised to hear that her husband had an opinion on football, but then again, this was just chip shop small talk of little consequence.

'I wonder where Head will go next?' Bob wondered aloud.

'I think he is finished. His career is probably in deep freeze for now,' replied the expert football pundit.

'Deep freeze, eh? One way of putting it.' Bob had other ideas. 'Well, I think he'd be better off going far away from Drabbleton altogether.'

'He probably likes it here,' countered Dinesh. 'I think he will stay. He's here a lot. I enjoy seeing him.'

'I don't recall a Mr Head,' Mishka interjected, looking vaguely puzzled.

'Yes, you know - *Tony*. Pay attention please dear wife to regular customers.' Dinesh smiled at his partner in mock admonishment. She pulled out her tongue at him. All in jest. 'By the way, my love, have you seen my 50th birthday cleaver? I need to butcher some beef.'

Mishka sighed.

'It is hanging up where it normally is. You had left it in sink, dearest.' She tutted and rolled her eyes, partly for the entertainment of Bob. 'Your memory is getting worse.

'I'm always losing things,' said Bob in support. 'Senile old bat that I am,' he added, following it up with a brief coughing bout.

'You need to get that on-off cough of yours looked at,' Dinesh advised with typical chip shop therapist's concern. 'It's been a few weeks now.'

'Yeah, yeah,' Bob dismissed. 'It's nothing...'

Five minutes later, the old man was on his way back down Mayfair Avenue - Rocky particularly eager to get home for his regular Wednesday night sausage. But Bob was far more interested in mulling over what Dinesh had just told him about Mr Head than dreaming of his own evening supper. Why would his recent partner in crime be wanting to hang onto Brimstone's head in the *Star of India* freezer? He'd obviously managed to somehow extract the previously stubbornly lodged meat cleaver, so surely it was now a case of *job done*. Bit of chippy oil should have sorted it, no doubt. But for Bob's part, he wanted Brimstone's crown well and truly out of the way. There was no point holding onto incriminating evidence. He concluded that the pair needed to speak again - and soon.

★

It was Thursday morning, approaching noon. Gavin had laid awake in bed for hours, lacking the will power to even go for a pee. But by now, his bladder was bursting, and he just had to go. So, he finally stood over the toilet experiencing blissful relief, one hand on todger ensuring a reasonably steady aim, the other on his phone - which he was checking for about the hundredth time today. But still no communication from Alice. Why hadn't she replied to all the texts he'd been sending since Monday evening? Surely, she'd read at least one out of the thirty-seven of them?

Pee over he despatched off text number thirty-eight.

'Hi Alice, has your phone been dead? Xx.'

Oh well, nothing to do but wait and see. But now that he'd actually achieved the single small victory of getting out of bed, and realising too that he was pretty much starving, he decided that he really needed cook breakfast asap. Well, put in a round of toast anyway, which kind of counted as cooking in Gavin's book. As he trod over discarded clothes and a selection of dirty mugs and glasses lined up by his bed, the doorbell rang. He snatched a grubby dressing gown and was hurriedly putting it on as he bound down the stairs, expending more energy in those mere five seconds than he had done all week.

He swung open the door. It wasn't Alice. Of course.

He huffed.

'Alright Pat,' Gavin managed to mutter.

'Bloody 'ell, Gav, you look rough,' replied the bespectacled postman, squinting at the dressing gowned and generally unkempt looking householder before him. 'Been on the ale, have you?'

'Something like that,' Gavin murmured, all energy seemingly now spent, but puzzling all the same over the five cardboard boxes sitting on Pat's porter trolley - one big chunky one, then four longer oblong cartons.

'Special delivery for you. Weighs a ton, this big 'un,' he said pointing to Chunky.

Gavin wasn't expecting any parcels and so, scratching his beard, checked out the address labels. Yep, weird...it was for him alright.

'Do you want me to wheel it into your hallway? You'll not lift this big 'un on your own.'

'Yeah, great,' said Gavin, stepping out of Pat's way, as the helpful delivery man then pulled the stack of boxes in over the threshold.

'Shouldn't be lifting weighty stuff like this. But they tell me I should be grateful I've even got a trolley.' Pat retrieved said trolley from under the cartons, but then was wincing, holding his back in apparent pain.

'Thanks anyway,' said Gavin, not overly concerned. 'You need to be careful with that back.'

'Aye,' Pat groaned, but then the town's nosiest postman suddenly remembered he was the town's nosiest postman. His back pain magically disappeared. 'Do you want me to open them for you?'

'Nah, it's alright.'

'I don't mind.'

'No, I'll manage, thanks.' Gavin was already thinking about getting his Stanley knife from his toolbox to slice through the generously applied parcel tape. But then he considered that the Stanley knife probably wouldn't be in the toolbox anyway. Putting things away in an organised way was just not his thing. Anyway, where was that toolbox?

'Suit yourself,' sulked Pat. Then he hovered around for a bit just in case Gavin started opening the boxes anyway. 'By the way,' he meandered, 'have you heard about your old boss? The police are treating his disappearance as murder. Just heard about it on local radio.'

'Blimey,' Gavin tried to sound surprised. 'Somebody finally got him then?'

'Looks like it,' Pat replied, enjoying reporting on a rare bit of Drabbleton action. 'Apparently, they found empty gun shells in his office and traces of rat poison in a drinking bottle. Plus, all the blood, of course. I bet they're starting to make a list of suspects.

'That will be a bloody long list.'

'You'll be on it,' Pat looked suddenly serious. Accusative, even. 'Prime suspect.'

Gavin winced and a nervous tic seemed to flash across his face - until the postman just fell about laughing, relishing the harmless wind-up. 'You and most of Drabbleton,' he continued to guffaw.

'Good one. See you then,' said Gavin, not entirely amused, now holding the open door and hoping the caller would be on his way.

'Are you sure you don't want me to help you open them?' said Pat, taking one last look at the boxes. He'd have already had a peek inside alright, but the damn things were so well taped up.

'No, I'm fine thanks,' said the new owner of five cartons, finally seeing the postman on his way.

'You got to be kidding me,' said Gavin, a couple of minutes later as he struggled to peel away the stubborn parcel tape with his fingernails. The Stanley knife had been nowhere obvious, of course, so it had been down to Plan B. Then Plan C had been finally hatched, involving a kitchen knife retrieved from amongst the dirty dishes pile in the sink.   Much better. The chunky box surrendered its sturdy seal and Gavin saw that there was an inner grey, plastic wrapping inside, along with one much smaller package. He thought he'd inspect this little item first, intrigued as he was by its apparently thoughtfully applied gift wrap - sparkly gold paper tied up with ribbon and bow. He was quickly inside...

'What?' he fell back from his feet, slumping down on the sofa. 'Can't be...'

He held up for inspection a bright orange ceramic photo-mug - just like the one Marie had bought for him when he'd turned thirty, back in the early days of their relationship. *Happy Birthday Old Man*, her caption had read, set out under a photo transfer of him drunk and asleep down the pub. But this new personalised mug in his life did not depict himself, or feature anything supposedly funny. Instead, the featured photograph was the same one that Disposals Inc had sent to his phone. Brimstone murdered.

Yes, he suddenly remembered - he'd casually selected the *souvenir mug option* when he'd innocently ordered the supposed hit on Brimstone. But, of course, he'd then thought that was nothing more than a joke.

Very warily now, he then considered poking a tentative nose into the large grey bag still sitting inside the chunky box. By this point he wasn't expecting to see anything good, but it had to be done. Going in nose first wasn't a good idea as the stench of something like rotten food sent his head jerking backwards. So, he quickly turned the bag upside down to rely on gravity to empty its contents without having to actually touch anything.

He gagged as his latest 'gift' thudded down onto his rug - a bloodied human torso wearing a white cotton shirt and tie. He'd seen that tie before, certainly. Bryce Brimstone was the only person he knew who still wore a bright red tie, vestige of Eighties power dressing. Working somehow on autopilot, Gavin then quickly opened a second box, one of the oblong shaped cartons. An amputated human arm was unceremoniously emptied out onto the rug, reuniting itself with the torso to which it once belonged. The arm was also still wearing its owner's white shirt sleeve, together with an engraved ivory cuff link. *BB* read its gold leaf inscription.

Gavin sunk to his knees, covering his face with his hands. He remembered when he was a small kid, he'd often just cover his eyes and hope that bad things would go away. They rarely did - and he was sure they wouldn't now, for sure. So, he finally steeled himself again.

The remaining three boxes were reluctantly tackled, revealing further amputated limbs - one more arm and two legs. Almost the full set of body parts. But where was the head? Gavin started to expect a second delivery, maybe tomorrow. He just hoped that Pat would not be sticking his long nose into its packaging, or there'd be serious explaining to do.

His phone beeped. He was hoping for different, but really knew what It might well be. And so it was - the latest notification from Disposals Inc.

'Good day, Gavin Hargreaves,' began a stern, male voice. 'I am Igor, AI Assistant from Disposals Inc. Credit Control department.'

'Hello,' Gavin attempted to be equally stern.

'You did not pay your invoice for ...thirty ...thousand ...pounds ...within the specified time,' continued the AI in its menacing Russian accent. 'As you have also been recorded saying you will not pay, then Company has had no alternative but to expedite further action. As per Terms & Conditions. If you understand, say yes now.

'Yes. ...But you've sent me a corpse. Well most of it,' Gavin complained.

'Contact our delivery department via My Account to report any missing items.'

'Yeah right.' A bitter laugh.

'We do not dispose of dead bodies on behalf of non-paying customers. *You dispose.* This is further action as set out in Terms & Conditions. But debt is still due. Await further instruction. Goodbye.'

Igor disappeared from Gavin's phone before Disposal Inc's unhappy customer had a chance to either vent his frustration or enquire what the nature of *further instruction* was likely to be.

But before he could reflect on the app's latest intervention further, the doorbell rang. Gavin anxiously eyed the human remains stacked up in a heap on his rug. He hastily grabbed the tweed blanket that lived over the back of the stained and worn-out sofa and threw it over the compromising evidence. Not a bad shot, though one hand still poked out from underneath the edge of the makeshift cover. He kicked it irreverently out of sight.

At any other time than this, the visitor he revealed on opening his front door would have been more than welcome inside. But maybe not quite now.

'Hi,' said Alice, shyly.

'Oh, love...' Gavin gasped with not a little relief, stepping forwards to try to hug her - but she backed off. He retracted his arms awkwardly and then retreated onto his doorstep, not quite knowing what to do or say. He did realise he looked a right state though, there on the step and unwashed for days, still in his tatty old dressing gown at mid-day.

'You can ask me in if you like,' said Alice, breaking the quickly formed ice, but thankfully not mentioning his dishevelled appearance.

'Nah, not right now. It's a proper mess in there,' Gavin laughed nervously and jokily slapped his forehead. Although he immediately sensed his denial of entry hadn't gone down too well.

'Suit yourself,' Alice seemed to mildly sulk. 'Actually, I only came round to talk about the police.' She looked behind her to check on any potential eavesdroppers and a young track-suited woman was walking by the front gate pushing a buggy. 'Look, are you sure you're not going to invite me in?'

'No, can't really. Pigsty and all that.'

Alice sighed impatiently before going on. 'Obviously you've heard that the police have launched a murder investigation following Bryce's disappearance?'

'Yeah, just heard this morning. Sorry.'

'I'm not exactly inclined to protect you. But I haven't decided yet how much I should tell them. So for now, I've said nothing.'

'Thanks,' said Gavin, not exactly sure of how grateful he should appear to be. 'I guess...'

'But I gave them your name.' Gavin's face tensed. 'Once they got digging, they'd have thought it odd if I hadn't mentioned you. How you'd walked out on your job after feeling forced out of it by Bryce, who you clearly must have hated. I had to give them a list of people that I knew might hold a grudge against my brother. Quite an extensive list, in fact.'

'Yeah, guess it would have been,' Gavin smiled weakly.

'So I thought I'd let you know, that's all. Maybe you've got something to get off your chest?' She eyed him quizzically.

'Oh, come on, Alice. You know I'm innocent.' He threw a protesting arm into the air.

'Well, if you're innocent why not tell the police all about the app game?' Alice continued with quiet determination. 'Tell them you thought it was all a harmless giggle. Then let *them* work out what's really happened. It's not as if you've got a dead body hidden in your house, now is it?'

'No, course not. That's funny,' Gavin laughed hollowly. 'Dead body, yeah? As if!'

'OK then,' Alice shuffled, indicating she was off. 'If you're not inviting me in...' She turned towards the gate.

'Alice,' Gavin suddenly gulped. 'What about *us*?'

'We could talk about it inside? she fished for the final time.

'Can't,' said Gavin, feebly.

'You've probably blown it then.' She closed the gate behind her.

'But...' Gavin wracked his brain, although no sensible suggestion as to what he should say seemed to be forthcoming. Instead, he helplessly watched on as Alice's car set off and left Mayfair Avenue. He then covered his eyes with his hands again. But he knew perfectly well that his awful reality would remain.

★

A mezzanine floor, at London's Waterloo Station, allows customers of Romano's Espresso Bar a bird's eye view of the busy concourse below. Here, every day, thousands of railway travellers criss-cross on hurried paths to and from the terminal's multiple platforms. So many people. So easy to blend into anonymity here. Then if a call, say from an unregistered pay-as-you go 'burner' phone, were traced back to Waterloo, who could say exactly who had made that call? At any time, innumerable mobile users crowd the station's cellular airwaves. Could have been any one of them.

This was Dimitri Sidorov's reasoning as he'd invited Roxanne Brimstone to join him for a light lunch at Romano's. Though she'd tied her hair back and pinned it under a hat and employed sunglasses to disguise her beautiful and well-known eyes, Roxanne still attracted too many admiring glances for her hit man boyfriend's liking. The charismatic aura of the former supermodel, dressed sleekly, all in black, was just too hard to dampen down.

'Do you have to look so damn stunning?' Dimitri half-protested, though also quite proud that he was currently the sexual partner of such an alluring creature. He sensed a couple of middle-aged businessmen on nearby tables surreptitiously viewing him with envy. He did enjoy that. 'We are supposed to be blending in.'

'You are lucky I am even here,' said Roxanne in protestation of her own, sipping her espresso. 'A bloody station, I ask you. If you'd have taken me into McDonald's downstairs, then you'd have been history.'

'Drink your coffee. Same price as whole meal downstairs.' Dimitri studied the receipt showing the robust pricing of two micro coffees and paninis, shaking a wearied head in disbelief.

'You certainly know how to treat a lady,' she laughed, verging towards scorn. 'Anyway, let's see it then - the evidence.'

Dimitri smiled knowingly as he pulled a handset from his jacket and opened an image. He passed the phone across the table and a moment later Roxanne came face to face with the photograph of her husband's murdered body. She momentarily recoiled, having to catch her breath, surprising her escort.

'I'm sorry,' she added. 'I've never really seen an actual murdered person before.'

'That is OK,' said Dimitri, covering her resting hand with his. 'I am used to it, so sometimes forget others are not.'

Roxanne made an exaggerated show of taking a deep breath and settling herself.

'Breathe,' she sang in extended monotone. Then she just giggled, seemingly fine again, as if to order.

'OK now?' Dimitri nursed.

'Oh yes, quite hunky-dory, darling.' She smiled sweetly but her companion couldn't tell if there was any irony there or not. 'But I must say, this is a bit of an over enthusiastic job,' she then mildly complained as she viewed the suffocating cling-film, the embedded meat cleaver and the bullet hole. 'I thought this was going to be merely a single bullet to the head?'

'My apologies, my angel,' replied Dimitri earnestly. 'Young Lewis got carried away. First hit.'

'Ah, it's done now,' Roxanne said, dismissively. 'I would have preferred a cleaner job. But there it is.' She then seemed distracted by a raspberry and lemon polenta dessert being taken by a young Italian looking waiter to a nearby table. 'That cake looks divine, darling. Shall we partake?'

'Business first, pleasure later,' said Dimitri, reining her back in, but happy to see she obviously hadn't been too traumatised by the photograph - and the possibly over enthusiastic method of assassination. He passed the 'burner' phone over to her, together with some hand scribble on a scrap of paper. She had been pre-briefed and knew exactly what was expected of her. 'Keep your voice down,' he counselled.

Roxanne then rose to her feet, taking with her the disposable phone. Leaving Romano's - and Dimitri for now - she walked along the mezzanine until she found a relatively quiet spot where she settled herself, leaning against a balcony rail overlooking the busy concourse. She unfolded the paper scrap and read the name written upon it - *DI Tom Slater*. The accompanying phone number was the direct line of the Drabbleton police officer assigned to the Bryce Brimstone murder case. She dialled and waited. Three rings...

'Tom Slater,' the Lancashire accented, mature male voice answered.

'Hello. I understand you are the officer handling the Bryce Brimstone murder?' Roxanne's voice was distorted and warping at a low frequency, being fed as it was through a synthesised filter on the phone.

'That'll be me.'

'I have some information that you may well find to be of interest,' the robotic voice continued.

'And who are you then?'

'I'd rather not say. I have reasons.'

'OK ...OK, that's fine for now. I'm happy to take anonymous tip offs. As long as you're not wasting my time.' Roxanne sensed a frosty edge to the voice. Meanwhile DI Slater - sat in a sparsely populated Ops Room at Drabbleton Police Station - was sending silent signals to his junior partner. Detective Sergeant Judith Haslam was quick on the uptake and picked up a desk telephone. Now she could silently listen in on the incoming call her boss was taking.

'I'm not in the habit of wasting time,' said Roxanne firmly. 'I have a name for you.'

'Oh really? Please go ahead,' said Slater, sounding slightly more receptive again.

'Gavin Hargreaves.' The mechanised informant voice sounded somehow pleased with itself.

'Yes, that gentleman's name is familiar to us.' Slater easily remembered Gavin's name from Alice's list of Brimstone's possible foes. Yet this was the chap who once owned the best English chippy in Drabbleton. Slater had been a regular customer. Nice bloke is Gavin, the DI had thought. Not really *murderer* kind of material. 'Any reason why we should take that information seriously?'

'There is the small matter of the dead body which he is currently hiding.' The robotic caller sounded very sure of itself. Haslam was ready to dart to the car. She looked carefully at the craggy facial features of her boss, waiting for the go.

'Hiding where?' Slater pressed, sounding more interested.

'At his house. Number 21 Mayfair Avenue.' Roxanne killed the call. Keep it brief. Don't get into a discussion. She'd done everything that Dimitri had asked of her. And he, in less than five minutes time, would be walking across Waterloo Bridge and tossing the burner phone into the murky waters of the River Thames below.

'Come on Sir, let's go,' said the animated Haslam as soon as her boss replaced the receiver. 'We can be there in five.'

'Sit down Sergeant, sit down,' replied Slater irritably. He took out a half-eaten cheese and pickle sandwich from a Tupperware container sat on his desk. 'Lunch first.'

'But Sir...' protested the recently promoted, young hot-shot, tall and lean in contrast her short and tubby boss. This could be her first big win, arresting a murderer bang to rights. Not bad for someone used to facilitating errant drivers on the local Speed Awareness Course, her last assignment for the past six months. *So dull!*

'Bloody hell, Judith. If you're going to go running around town every time we get an unsubstantiated tip off from a Dalek, you're going to be busier than a mosquito on a nudist beach!'

'But that caller info sounded genuine, Sir.'

'Yeah, yeah. So did the other two hundred tips we've had since we made this thing public.' He could see that his DS was disappointed in him. *She probably thinks I'm retiring soon, couldn't give a monkeys. And here I am, suppressing the unbridled enthusiasm of youth. Well bollocks!* 'See, the thing is, Sergeant Haslam...I've known Gavin Hargreaves for years. If he's our murderer, then pigs will fly over Drabbleton Town Hall!'

Haslam ignored him. She turned around and calmly called the Telecom liaison people. What was the location of that last caller? Might be a lead.

17
- THE BODYSNATCHERS -

Krystyna had bumped into Bob outside the Co-op earlier that same Thursday morning. She'd been on her morning run, turning heads as her toned physique elegantly jogged by a succession of overweight and generally poorly conditioned Drabs. But then she'd been more than a little alarmed to hear that Dinesh was storing Brimstone's head in his freezer and that he seemed happy to keep it there, for now at least. So, she'd asked Bob to contact the chippy owner and maybe set up a meeting. They'd come up with some pretence if disturbed. But they needed to have that conflab asap.

That's why they'd all congregated at Bob's sometime after Gavin had been watching Alice walk out on his life for the second time in a few days. And it was Bob who'd already come up with their cover story.

'I was walking past The Anchor the other day,' said the host, dishing out a mug of tea to each of his guests in the comfort of his tiny front room.

'That pub on Marlborough Street?' Dinesh suggested. 'Thanks,' he added receiving his hot beverage.

'That's the one,' Bob confirmed. 'They are looking to start a pub quiz night on a Tuesday. If anyone asks, we could say we're together simply for that.'

'But better for us if we don't meet very often at all,' said Krystyna, accepting her drink, but apparently a little tense.

'Yeah course,' Bob agreed.

'But good idea anyway,' Dinesh chipped in. 'Pub quiz team. Krystyna can be captain.'

'Of course,' she agreed, defrosting a tad. 'But Dinesh, let's get to the point. Why keep head when it would be better off in bin bag in canal?'

Their Indian co-murderer hung his head, avoiding eye contact.

'Ah, I am slightly ashamed to say it brings me enjoyment every day. After all those school years of torture and then him returning and quite happy to ruin my business, well who is laughing now?' He then looked directly into Krystyna's green eyes. 'Yes indeed, I look at his head in my freezer several times a day and I say it to his face - *who is laughing now, Mister? Who is laughing now?*'

Bob smiled, appreciating the *schadenfreude* of the situation. 'I like your style, Dinesh,' he said, coming round to the head curator's view.

'I understand the pleasure this would bring,' Krystyna interjected, less amused. 'But you are putting us all in danger by your indulgence. Not acceptable.'

'She's got a point,' Bob reflected although seemingly sorry to say so. 'But maybe you'll get bored one day of saying *who is laughing now*?'

'Never!' Dinesh defied. 'I will never get bored!'

'But you are one of three. Majority rules,' Krystyna asserted. 'I vote you keep head for no more than one week. Less police buzzing around by then. After one week max, you dispose. Agreed?'

Dinesh looked hopefully towards Bob for support. Surely all those Mid-Week Specials counted for something?

'I'm sorry mate, I'm with her.' He scratched his balding forehead ruefully. Dinesh felt the sudden pain of defeat.

Rocky, who had been lying there all the time on the rug suddenly barked. Did that mean three votes to one? Well, no, he was merely barking at the inquisitive face of the next-door neighbour now peering in through the net curtains, eyes squinting to see what was what.

'It's Gavin,' said Bob, sudden agitation in his voice. 'What the blazes does he want now?'

'Wait,' Krystyna started. 'We keep this secret, yes?'

'Yes, nobody must know our part. Keep out of jail. That is what I say. I have not even told wife.' Dinesh sounded quite proud of his zipped mouth.

'Very good,' assented Krystyna.

'I'm with you both, no worries,' said Bob as the doorbell then rang and he went off to see what his pesky neighbour was after.

Gavin had taken the usual shortcut over to Bob's front door, hopping across their shared lawn and spying in through the sitting room window for signs of residency. It was usually just Bob that he'd espy, sitting in his rocking chair with a sleepy Rocky at his feet. But today it was very different. Did this explain why he was so obviously perturbed as he entered the little lounge where Dinesh and Krystyna were sitting together on a sofa? Or was there more to it?

'I didn't know you were all friends,' puzzled Gavin, pinching his beard, still dressed in the oldest dressing gown on Earth. He did know, however, that Bob usually led a most solitary existence.

'Hello Gavin,' said Krystyna calmly. 'We are new Pub Quiz team.' She beamed a smile, revealing perfect teeth, that her former work colleague had rarely seen. But then looked pityingly at his dressing gown and bedraggled hair.

'Yes, starting Tuesday at The Anchor,' Dinesh added, equally chirpily, oblivious to any sartorial malfunction here. 'Bob here put message on my chippy notice board recruiting members. So here we are. You should join us my friend.'

'Erm, maybe,' Gavin hesitated. 'I'll think about it.' Clearly convinced by their pretext, he had more pressing matters on his mind - the real reason for his less than composed disposition. Meanwhile, Bob winked at Krystyna and Dinesh, out of the new caller's view, quietly celebrating the success of his cover up ruse.

'Alice says the police might be coming,' Gavin suddenly blurted out. 'About Brimstone's murder.'

'Why would this be?' asked Krystyna scrunching her nose.

It immediately struck Gavin that he had made a schoolboy error by spouting out such a stupid thing in front of Brimstone's favoured manager and kinky sex partner. She could turn against him at any moment.

'Just to eliminate me from their enquiries, I suppose,' he backtracked. 'It's thought I'll be maybe holding a grudge against the poor murdered guy.'

'*Poor* murdered guy?' Krystyna virtually spat. 'Why feel sorry for him? He deserved to die!'

She's changed her tune, thought Gavin, scratching his beard this time.

'I loathed big monster creep,' she concluded. 'I hope he is in hottest place in Hell.'

'Yes, most suitable place for him,' Dinesh concurred. 'Hottest place in Hell gets my vote too.'

'Mine too,' added Bob. 'Burn the horrible bastard!'

'What? asked Gavin, somewhat needlessly. 'Everybody here hated Brimstone? And we're all glad he's dead?'

'Yeeesssss!' the room cried in unison. Rocky barked.

'Well look,' Gavin continued, relieved to be in the company of kindred spirits. 'I might have accidentally had something to do with Brimstone's murder. And now I'm in a bit of a mess.'

'You?' asked Krystyna, spluttering with disbelief. 'Not possible.'

'Hey lad,' Bob continued, 'don't go trying to take credit for somebody else's efforts.'

'Indeed. Do not take shine off for real killers.' Dinesh was tutting at Gavin.

'But it's true,' protested Gavin. 'I ordered his assassination on my phone. See, look!'

He grabbed his phone and showed them all the photograph of the murdered Brimstone inside the Disposals inc app. Unknown to Gavin, they recognised that scene all too well.

'I only asked for a single bullet to the head. But looks like the killers got carried away,' he frowned.

'Looks like they did very good job to me,' said Dinesh, as his co-murderers nodded both in agreement and approval.

'*You* hired professional killers?' asked Krystyna, now piecing together in her mind the reason for the fourth co-murderer's appearance on the scene.

'Yes, I think. But only accidentally. I thought I was just playing around on an app my son Freddie had shown me.'

'Then what is problem?' Krystyna enquired, not sure that Gavin was really up to mixing it with proper murderers.

'These professional killers, as you call them, demanded that I pay thirty grand for the hit.' Gavin was flustered again.

'Disgusting,' said Bob. 'I know some people who would have done it cheaper.' He sighed ruefully, imagining what a healthier bank balance would look like.

'Whatever.' Gavin waved aside the interruption. 'So obviously I couldn't pay that. That's when they sent me bits of Brimstone's body in five boxes. Everything except his head.'

'No head?' Most strange.' Dinesh silently gasped, the picture of innocence.

'I know,' said Gavin. 'But these boxes are sitting on my front room rug. So basically, Bob...' He gulped. 'Can I maybe leave them with you for a bit until after the coppers have been round?'

'Bloody hell, Gav. That's a big ask.' Bob imagined himself in the dock at Manchester Crown Court.

'Come on, Bob, you must help out,' Krystyna almost ordered. 'Police must not find body or who knows what might happen.'

Mmm, Bob had watched *Silent Witness*, that forensic pathologist drama on the BBC. Anyone who watches *Silent Witness* would know a murderer's DNA would be all over the victim's body unless precautions had been taken. So that means ...*Whoops*.

'Oh, alright then,' Bob conceded, now almost too willingly. 'We can nip round the back and pass those boxes over the garden fence. Stick 'em in my shed for now.'

'Brilliant, mate, thanks very much.'

Dinesh and Krystyna smiled encouragingly. They had a plan.

Without further ado, *Operation Shift-a-Stiff* systematically commenced.

★

DI Slater had long since finished his cheese and pickle sandwich. Nothing much to report from his lunch time read of the *Bugle*. Alberto Assini was being transferred off to Arsolia in Latvia. *Good - rubbish goalie he is too!* On the front page was an old stock picture of himself, looking at least ten years younger - no grey hair then. *Nice one. No Leads in Brimstone Murder Case* bemoaned the headline. DI Slater knew exactly what was wrong with this world. Everything had to be done like yesterday. Whatever happened to patience and doing things properly?

Irritated, he turned to a 'Difficult Level' Sudoku - but after ten minutes had three sevens in the same row. He moved on to the 'Easy Level' grid.

'Judith, you've been to University,' he eventually called over to his junior sergeant, herself working through lunch. 'What bloody number goes in this box?'

She had a quick glance of his newspaper. 'Six,' she casually replied, then got back to cross checking witness statements. Slater looked at the returned grid.

'Ah, course,' he sighed. 'Beginner's luck.' *Nobody likes a smart arse.*

A good half an hour later they were finally in their unmarked police car winding their way over to Mayfair Avenue - for what DI Slater thought would be a complete waste of his time. He wasn't to know, at that very moment, Gavin was busy spraying copious amounts of air freshener into his front room. This after his box shifting buddies had wisely advised that the smell of rotting flesh would not ideally make for a good start to any police interview. And a bit of disinfectant wouldn't go amiss too.

But the body-part filled boxes were all neatly stacked away in Bob's shed by the time Slater and Haslam turned up at the *person of interest's* home. Although Gavin himself was less neat, still in his dressing gown, looking like something the least fussy cat in of all Drabbleton had brought in. He answered the door, disinfectant soaked rag in hand.

'Ah, Tom Slater. Fish and chips twice, mushy peas and gravy,' Gavin grinned as casually as he could manage. 'I've been half expecting you.'

'Alright Gavin, ha ha! Well remembered,' Slater replied, momentarily reminiscing about old chippy suppers of yesteryear. 'But bloody hell lad, did you find that dressing gown in a skip? This is DS Haslam, by the way.'

Gavin and Haslam exchanged nods.

'We could do with a word,' said Slater quietly, almost as if he didn't want the neighbours to know.

'Yeah course, come in,' Gavin replied, smiling weakly. 'Sorry for the mess. Bad night on the ale. Girlfriend trouble, y'know.' Slater replied with a sympathetic wink.

The callers were led along the little corridor towards the kitchen, passing the front lounge door on the way. With luck, they wouldn't notice the pungent cocktail of *Lavender Zest* air freshener and disinfectant permeating from that particular room.

'What's that dreadful smell?' Haslam instantly groaned. She glimpsed into the lounge quizzically.

'Fell asleep last night watching telly. Embarrassed to say, but I woke up being sick on myself.' Gavin quickly closed the door, sealing off the offensive stink.

'No wonder you look rough,' said Slater.

'Yeah, so just been doing a spot of cleaning, sorry.'

'No worries,' replied the DI.

By this time, Gavin had led them into the kitchen where he discarded the disinfectant drenched cleaning cloth into an already overflowing bin. Haslam eyed the dirty pots and pans stacked up in the sink. Then on every worktop, every plate, dish, knife and fork that Hargreaves probably owned sat in untidy heaps awaiting a *Fairy Liquid* bath. It all made her skin crawl. Although Slater seemed relatively at home.

'Fancy a brew?' asked the polite host.

Haslam winced as Gavin checked out his copious collection of unclean mugs, ascertaining which of these might be the least filthy. He was having difficulty.

'No, not for me,' the young sergeant replied, happy to dodge the health risk.

'There's a clean one here,' said Slater, helpfully, passing over the unsullied Disposals Inc mug he'd spotted hiding behind a fungus lined pan. Gavin's eyes widened momentarily as the obvious super-sleuth spotted the vessel's customised picture transfer of one dead Brimstone.

'Bit gruesome that, innit?' the DI casually remarked.

Gavin tried to remain calm. He played the part of pondering over the mug, seemingly reminding himself of its history.

'*Pulp Fiction*...,' finally spouted from his mouth, the best he could do. 'You know, the movie.'

'Never seen it,' said Slater, underwhelmed.

'Or was it *Goodfellas*? ...It's one of them US gangster movie memorabilia mugs anyway. One of Marie's before she left. She was into all of that.'

'Marie?' Haslam gauchely enquired.

'His ex-wife, Sergeant Big Feet.' Slater passed his junior colleague an admonishing look. 'Sorry, she's new,' he winked again towards Gavin.

The kettle was filled and put on to boil. Small talk ensued while Gavin made two coffees - one with three sugars for the thirstier guest, who then unwittingly took the Disposals Inc mug on its maiden voyage.

'Anyway Gavin,' DI Slater finally continued, a little more briskly. 'Seeing as you said you were half expecting me, I guess you know we're talking to people who knew Bryce Brimstone. Just preliminary enquiries, you understand?'

'No comment.'

'Eh?'

'No comment.' Gavin then giggled, if only unnaturally. 'Ha ha, got you there, didn't I? *No comment*. Isn't that what all the bad guys say when they're being interviewed on them cop shows?'

Slater smiled, humouring him. 'Ah yes, *no comment*. Good one.'

'This isn't a formal interview under caution, Mr Hargreaves,' corrected Haslam, gravely.

'He knows that Sergeant,' Slater sighed. 'He'd have probably spotted it if we had cautioned him.

'Just saying...,' Haslam sulked.

'Anyway,' Slater continued, putting the tedious interruption aside, 'we know you walked out on your job. We know you weren't very happy about having to wear a Roman Centurion costume to work. And we know you didn't like being told you couldn't see Mr Brimstone's sister, Alice, by Brimstone himself.'

Gavin looked clearly surprised that this last bit was public knowledge.

'Yeah, Alice told me,' Slater filled in the gap. 'But getting right to the point, we had an anonymous tip off today mentioning your name.'

'We were told you were hiding Bryce Brimstone's body in this house,' Haslam blurted out.

Gavin's face fell. Slater smacked a lower palm against his head.

'Sergeant Haslam, *please!*' Her DI clearly wasn't happy. There was no reason to disclose that information at this point. Didn't they teach them *anything* at Police College these days?

'We don't take all these kinds of calls seriously, of course. So many cranks these days,' the senior officer then patiently continued for Gavin's benefit. 'But now it's out there, I don't suppose you have a dead body hidden in the house somewhere?' He smiled in a way that told the interviewee that this was merely a million to one shot.

'Not that I know of,' said Gavin, lightly stroking his beard and having had time to recover his composure whilst Haslam took the heat. 'You're welcome to look around though,' he held out a welcoming hand - *be my guest.* 'You might find the odd skeleton in the cupboard, mind,' he then laughed.

'Oh yes ...*skeleton in the cupboard,* good one,' Slater tittered. Haslam looked on, bemused.

'But actually, I don't get it,' said Gavin, now suddenly more serious. 'The rumour around town is that you guys think Brimstone was done for in his office.'

'Probably,' Slater seemed happy to confirm.

'If I *had* done it though, then I don't suppose I'd bother to cart his body right across town to my own house.'

'No, exactly!' said Slater, sending a disparaging look to Haslam that said *I told you so!*

'So that traces of blood or hair or his clothing, whatever, would be all over my very own place,' Gavin went confidently on, feeling he was on a roll.

'Exactly! Stupid idea!' Slater scoffed.

'Not when I could have left him dead in his office chair, with a single bullet stuck in his head.' *I close my case!*

'Eh?' Slater suddenly pulled back his head as if dodging a punch. 'What bullet is this?'

'Nobody has said to you that Mr Brimstone has been shot,' added Haslam, sharply, eager to muscle in on the possible breakthrough.

Gavin panicked, spotting again the Disposals Inc mug that Slater was still holding. The evidence was right there in the hands of the police, if only they knew. His brain needed to assume urgent action stations.

'Yeah, course,' a ruffled reply kind of finally blurted out. 'I was just looking at that poor guy on your mug with the bullet in his head. That's why I said it'

Slater turned the mug around to scrutinise the gruesome photo transfer once again. Haslam's nose moved forwards to join the inspection.

'Oh, I see,' the DI finally said, seeming to go with Gavin's reasoning. 'Bit of a sick movie this though, isn't it? Suffocate a bloke, stick an axe in his head, plus a bullet.'

'Horrendous,' Haslam agreed, disapproving of this household's choice of crockery.

'Looks sick to me, yeah,' said Gavin, shamelessly disowning Marie's apparent poor taste - but happy too that the cling-film wrapper ensured that the victim's head was quite unrecognisable.

'Oh well, luckily, real life murders are not always so gruesome.' Slater shook his head somewhat wearily. *'Bloody Hollywood.'*

'Sick bastards,' Gavin agreed.

Then the interview was promptly terminated. *Nothing to see here,* Slater had concluded. As expected, a complete waste of time. But in the car, travelling back to Drabbleton Police Station, it seemed that one particularly keen, young sergeant was thinking otherwise.

'Sir, that was classic cover-up stuff, don't you reckon? We get there and he's actually cleaning his house with disinfectant!' Haslam was animated.

'If you say so, Sergeant Haslam,' Slater jadedly indulged.

'I know why you didn't ask him about it,' she grinned. 'Because we're going to go back with the sniffer dogs, right?' She looked very smug with her case busting conclusion.'

'No, we're not going to go back with sniffer dogs, Sergeant,' came the firm response.

'Oh.' *Why on earth not?*

'I'm more interested in finding out about that black Mercedes that several witnesses say they saw round Brimstone Mill on Monday night. Bit of a posh car for round here. Gangsters maybe? Drug dealers? Probably a better lead than hapless Gavin Hargreaves and his sick-stained carpet.'

Slater seemed to sigh with despair.

'I mean, the fellah can't even dress himself by the afternoon or do the washing up for days, weeks even. Do you really think that someone as hopeless as that would be capable of literally getting away with murder?'

'There's an off chance, maybe,' Haslam retreated. Why hadn't she thought more about that mysterious Mercedes? Damn it! She gave herself a silent telling off.

'Next thing you'll be telling me that his *Pulp Fiction* picture mug was really his souvenir of Brimstone's murder.'

'OK Sir don't rub it in,' said Haslam sheepishly. 'I'll follow up on that Mercedes.'

Her boss was probably right. Although she obviously thought him to be a bit of a dinosaur, she had to concede that he did seem to have the instincts of a good copper. And she knew that, at this stage in her career, there was still much to learn. That said, DS Haslam still thought it might be a good idea to keep a quiet eye on Hargreaves on the side. *You never know!*

*

The newly formed pub quiz team had come up with a name for themselves - *The Bodysnatchers.* Bob's idea really. He'd reckoned that for a start, all pub quiz teams always had a name. But nobody would expect a team of body part removal experts to come up with a moniker so brazen, it was almost if they'd be asking to be put under suspicion. *What a smart double bluff.* Bob was very pleased with himself.

He was less pleased though that it was harder to hear through into next door when Gavin or whoever was in the kitchen. Just the way the houses were configured at the back and the properties sharing no party wall at that point. So, although all three Bodysnatchers had pressed their ears hard against the wall of Bob's hallway, the conversation Gavin was holding with Drabbleton Police was merely heard as indecipherable mumblings. In disappointment they'd retreated to Bob's Centre of Operations - his front lounge - to consider their next steps.

'See, the thing is,' said Bob, growing into the role he'd like to take as the inventive one of the crew, 'we never really thought about our DNA and stuff getting all over Brimstone's body when we chopped off the bugger's head. Or his stupid DNA getting on us. The professional killers who shipped off his body probably did us a favour. We could have all been locked up by now.'

The other two shook their heads in dismay at their own amateurism. Still, couldn't be helped. What now?

'We should destroy clothes we were wearing that night,' suggested Krystyna.

'Oh no, I'm quite fond of this navy cardigan,' said Bob, now wearing the very same piece of knitwear he wore on the night in question - and in fact on many a day. He stroked its well-worn wool lovingly. 'I'll give it a warm rinse.'

'Yes, I am also in favour of the washing,' said Dinesh, always keen to watch the pennies.

Krystyna groaned inwardly. She preferred being Call Centre Manager, where people just did as they were told.

'But we will make sure Gavin gets rid of those body parts,' she insisted. 'If found, there is chance we could be in trouble.'

'That's what I was going to say,' complained Bob, unhappy to be losing the initiative. 'It's them forensic pathologists we have to watch out for.'

'Forensic what?' asked Dinesh, flummoxed. Obviously doesn't watch *Silent Witness*, thought Bob.

'Oh yes, *forensic pathologists*, they collect DNA and stuff from dead bodies,' Bob showed off

'What is this DNA you keep going on about, ...as you are so clever?' Dinesh pressed.

'Come on, *everyone* knows what DNA is. It's obvious, isn't it? Sheesh!'

'I don't know,' Dinesh shamelessly shrugged, looking to Bob for elucidation.

'Oh...it's that stuff. You can only collect it if you're wearing one of them hazmat suit jobbies, for a start.' He searched the air for something else to snatch. He grunted. 'You tell him, girl.' The baton had been awkwardly passed.

'It is an abbreviation for deoxyribonucleic acid,' said Krystyna snippily. 'It resolves embodiment and function of every cell and is unique fingerprint of our very beings.'

'Yeah, what she said, obviously,' said Bob, happy to have helped with Dinesh's depleted education.

'Hey, you sound as clever as that wheelchair brain-box man,' Dinesh complimented Krystyna, ignoring Bob. 'You know - that Stephen Hawkins fellow.'

'Thank you, Dinesh,' Krystyna finally smiled. 'But Stephen *Hawking* was astrophysicist, not forensic scientist.'

'I think this one will be good in pub quiz team,' Dinesh grinned, holding out a hand as if introducing her on stage.

'Yes, but the pub quiz team is not *real*, Dinesh,' corrected Bob, diverting attention away from Krystyna's small moment of glory. 'It is just *cover*.'

'I knew that,' Dinesh mumbled down to his shoes.

'Anyhow, we all agree we will help Gavin. Make sure job gets done,' said Krystyna, getting the crew back on track. The two men in the room nodded assent. 'But no need to tell him about our involvement from Monday night. If police are onto him, he might crack.'

'Yes, help him, but keep mouth zipped. Very good,' Dinesh agreed.

'Sounds like everybody wins,' said Bob. *Good teamwork.*

Just then both a knock on the back door and Rocky's bark signalled Gavin's furtive arrival via the rear garden. Bob scurried off to let him in, the police interview obviously over. So now they would all be together again, sat in a circle in the front room to confirm their next move.

'Did police suspect anything?' Krystyna was eager to know.

'No,' Gavin replied, relief visible across his face. 'Some nutter had rung in anonymously and given them my name. So, they had to talk to me, I guess.'

'Why would someone give your name?' asked Dinesh, wishing to berate the injustice of that very thing.

'Well, I suppose I upset a few people at the Call Centre before I left. People I had to fire, and stuff.'

'A grudge call,' Krystyna nodded. She knew all about unhappy Call Centre people. No doubt her name would be rung in next. She would have to be ready.

'But you are off hook?' asked Bob.

'Think so. For now, at least.' Gavin smiled, if tepidly.

'Excellent, my friend,' Dinesh approved, only seeing upside.

'Then we must move these body parts,' said Krystyna in business mode. 'We have already helped you, Gavin. We too are incriminated. But now we move on.' Her eyes scanned her co-conspirators for assistance. 'Any ideas, people? No idea is bad idea.'

'Bonfire,' Dinesh suggested.

'Bad idea,' Krystyna dismissed. 'Fire might attract attention.' Dinesh felt stupid.

'I was thinking the canal,' Gavin proposed.

'No - police might dredge canal.' Krystyna was realising they were all still amateurs.

'I've got an idea,' said Bob, looking a little self-satisfied.

'Go ahead,' invited Krystyna, hoping for a miracle.

'Thing is,' said Bob, relishing the sudden attention, 'every evening I take Rocky out for his late evening walkies. Don't I Rocky, 10.15 pm every night, after the news headlines?'

Rocky perked up an ear, but soon lost interest. Bob went on. 'We go down Mayfair Avenue and up Baker Street, which is derelict now. There's an old railway bridge there where Rocky likes to stop for a pee and whatever. Every night at 10.27 the same thing happens. Like clockwork. The very same thing...'

'What is that?' Krystyna hurried him along.

'A freight diesel train goes by, carrying coal from the last of the mines in the Trapton area. I've not much to do while Rocky does his business, so one night I counted the coal wagons as they passed under the bridge. Thirty-nine wagons. Next night I counted them again. Guess what?' Bob was now enjoying playing the audience.

'Forty wagons,' Dinesh offered, gamefully.

'No Dinesh, course not forty wagons,' Bob huffed, disappointedly. *Wasn't it obvious?* 'Thirty-nine wagons! Every night it is thirty-nine wagons. The same train, bound for the East Coast docks.'

'And so?' Krystyna pressed, increasingly curious.

'We get those boxes and line them up on the bridge wall,' Bob spoke faster as the excitement of the big reveal took over. 'Then, when the middle wagons go by, say wagon number twenty-one - my lucky number - we knock the boxes off the wall. They say that the coal gets exported off to Eastern Europe. So goodbye Bryce Brimstone. Hello Poland.'

'It is bit unfair to Poland to send him there,' sighed Krystyna patriotically. 'Oh well.' *Needs must.*

'Nice idea, Bob,' said Gavin, all thumbs up. 'Nobody will know who the Devil he is if he ends up there.'

'But what if he is found as they put coal onto boat?' That was the obvious question as far as Krystyna was concerned.

'Not likely,' said Bob. 'I once did a steeplejack job at the docks, up the cranes. They don't have little men running around with spades unloading coal, you know. Course not. The train wagons get rotated upside down by this giant mechanical beast, a few at a time. Tons and tons of coal gets dumped out, straight into the cargo hold of the ship. Nobody's checking the wagons. It's all machines.'

'I like idea,' said Krystyna. Her face sparkled.

'Yes, very good,' said Dinesh, equally sunny.

Gavin's thumbs were still up.

'OK, I propose we meet here, say tomorrow, promptly at ten o'clock,' Krystyna finalised.

'I will get help for Mishka in chippy. Cousin Brinda,' Dinesh added on a more practical note.

'We can maybe use my estate car for the boxes,' Gavin offered. 'They'll go in the back compartment and you lot on the passenger seats.'

He then made a mental note to take his car out for a warm-up spin earlier in the day, tomorrow. He hadn't driven the old girl in a couple of weeks, and she needed to be on top form

*

DS Haslam walked into the Ops Room at Drabbleton Police Station carrying a hot tea for herself. How lovely, she thought, to be drinking from a mug that wouldn't be passing on salmonella poisoning. But no sooner had she sat down at her desk, her afternoon's thirst about to be quenched, a voice called over to her from the door.

'Get your coat Judith, we're off to see a body.'

Haslam managed just the one gulp of tea, but then she was off, trying to close in on her boss who'd already briskly marched off without her along the corridor.

'Have they found Brimstone?' she enquired, trying to catch her breath. *Breakthrough news, hopefully.*

'Nope,' Slater called back over his shoulder. 'It's that missing kid, Darren Eccles. Uniform lads just fished him out of the river, up by Abraham's Bridge.'

The lush banks of the River Walmsley were festooned with the vestiges of late Spring wildflowers. Arriving at the potential crime scene, within fifteen minutes, Haslam had been struck by the prettiness of the crops of bluebells and snowdrops that surrounded her as she edged, with Slater, down a steeply descending path towards the water's edge. Nature had painted such a beautiful landscape here, yet so very near to the man-made eyesore that was Drabbleton. Tranquil and lovely as it was, she felt sad that a beauty spot such as this had been sullied by the death of a nineteen-year-old young man.

Cordoned off by tape, a white tarpaulin had already been erected down by the river side, a temporary shroud hiding Darren Eccles' body from public view. A couple of uniformed officers guarded the scene and exchanged pleasantries with Slater as he passed by. Inside the tent-like structure, Dr Dermot Brindle, an overweight, middle-aged member of Forensics, was examining the pale corpse.

'Morning Dermo,' Haslam began, ignoring the customary whiff of alcohol and fags on the good doctor's breath, then turning to scrutinise the lifeless form laid out on the ground. 'Bit early in the year for a swim?'

'Hey up, Tom,' replied Dr Brindle, while trying to take a photograph of the body despite his flash was unhelpfully malfunctioning. 'Useless prick of a thing!' he grumbled, petulantly chucking the camera onto the grass, and lighting up a fag instead. 'Yeah, probably not a leisure swim, poor sod.' He exchanged polite nods with Sergeant Haslam, clearly eyeing up the new tall, dark female on the scene. *Bit masculine looking though, not really my type.*

Meanwhile, Haslam had her own private thoughts. *Surely you shouldn't be smoking at a crime scene.* He knew what she was thinking, bright young thing. *Tough shit!*

'How long had the unfortunate lad been in the water?' Slater enquired.

'Three or four days, at a guess,' Brindle replied, distraction over.

'His mum reported him missing on Tuesday night,' the DI filled in the gaps, 'after there'd been no sign of him for 24 hours. We weren't taking it all that seriously yet, to be honest. *Young lads,* y'know.' Slater shuffled awkwardly, possibly regretting his complacency.

'Yeah, may well have been in the water since then. I'll let you know after I've sliced him open and gone digging.' He glanced at Haslam with a wry smile, hoping for effect.

'Lovely,' replied Slater, dryly. Haslam turned away, squeamish. *Good job!*

Brindle then had a good old yawn as he seemed to be taking a vague interest in Eccles neck and even made the then considerable effort to kneel now beside the corpse, steadying himself on the turf as he landed. 'Bloody knees,' he grizzled, feeling the creaks.

'So, he drowned?' asked Haslam, more unsettled at the sight of her first dead body than her more world-wearied colleagues but doing her best now to look at it again.

'You OK?' Slater checked in on her, having noticed that the pallor in her face almost matched that of Eccles. But she just nodded briefly and managed to even muster a faint smile.

Dr Brindle barely noticed that little exchange as he roughly continued his preliminary examination, pulling Darren's neck from side to side and pushing and prodding his cold skin.

'Drowning? Too early to say without getting him into the lab. No obvious signs of frothing round the mouth - always a giveaway. But I think his neck here is broken. If he fell off - or jumped off the bridge upstream there - that may explain that.'

'Or if he was pushed off?' added Slater.

'Well, quite.' He was drawn to the signs of bruising on the neck. 'Didn't expect that,' he sighed. 'I'm going to have to get me finger out now on this one.' *What a bummer! I was hoping for an early dart.*

Slater, meanwhile, made a mental note of that particular injury.

'Did you recover his phone?' asked Haslam, her sudden initiative winning an approving nod from her boss for a change.

'No sign of it, sorry.'

Dr Brindle then tried to rise to his feet, but this was clearly a struggle for a man in his shape. 'Here, pull us up Tom,' he moaned, extending a hand towards the DI. The hoist eventually succeeded. 'Ta... We'll get him off to the lab now.' He was rubbing his back, obviously not used to such athletic challenges as standing back up, aided or not.

'Yeah, well I know you're after my first instincts,' Brindle continued. Slater didn't contradict. 'Could be misadventure, maybe suicide. Or somebody has thrown him in the river already dead.'

'Interesting,' said Slater, running over those options in his head. He stepped out of the tarpaulin and eyed the giant arches of the golden brick B-road bridge that spanned the water some fifty yards up-river - just a half mile or so away from the motorway.

'Sergeant Haslam, we're just on the edge of nowhere out here, but find out what CCTV coverage there might be nearby. We need to be looking at Monday and Tuesday maybe. Something suspicious might just turn up.'

'Yes boss,' Haslam was just relieved to be leaving Eccles behind - and the odorous doctor too as she then left the tarpaulin.

'Good - and get the media guys involved too. Anyone with any dash-cam footage who might have been going over that bridge?'

'I'm on it.'

Slater rubbed his forehead. *Mmm, typical Drabbleton. No murders for five years, then two may well have come along in the same week. Bugger!* He had been hoping for a quieter run up to his retirement.

18
- CATCHING THE TRAIN -

Just as Big Ben's bongs had chimed on Bob's TV, heralding the start of *News at Ten*, Krystyna had turned up on the front doorstep precisely on time. She'd then fixated on her watch, tutting impatiently. Two minutes late, along had come Dinesh, then just over three minutes late, Gavin had then managed to make an appearance in his own garden.

'We have train to catch,' Krystyna had grumbled to the late arrivals, tapping her watch. The mild admonishment had apparently been enough to jolt the team into focus. Because then, with military precision, Gavin & The Bodysnatchers had then paced through the back to Bob's garden shed. Then, as pre-agreed, Gavin and Dinesh together had gripped onto the push-through handles of the larger box, the one containing Brimstone's torso. Krystyna and Bob had taken an arm and a leg apiece, one limb under each of their own arms. All five boxes were then on the move. Rocky had supposed to be on guard but had become distracted by a minor rustling sound in the bushes - probably a field mouse. Bob had called him to order.

The male members of this makeshift disposal team were now loading up their carriage into Gavin's old Skoda Fabia estate car, while Krystyna kept a lookout down Mayfair Avenue. All quiet. The larger box fitted neatly in under the hatchback, but two of the oblong shaped cartons containing limbs then only just about squeezed in.

'These are going to have to go on people's knees in the back,' said Gavin, finally giving up on manoeuvring the final arm and leg into the boot compartment.

'No problem said Bob,' who was already jumping into a rear passenger seat. 'Here pass me that,' he said towards Gavin, then accepting a Brimstone limb onto his lap. Rocky the dog quickly jumped in beside him, whilst Dinesh took the cue to run around to the other side of the car. He too then made himself comfy, the other limb filled box across his knee.

Moments later Gavin was in his driver's seat, quickly followed to his left by Krystyna - herself having checked that the coast was clear.

'It stinks in here,' moaned Bob, realising that decomposing bodies in enclosed spaces aren't the most delicate of fragrances.

'Drive, drive!' Krystyna ordered, holding her nose. Gavin obediently turned the ignition key. Of course, he had previously promised himself to take his old car for a warm-up spin. That should have been around 9pm, according to his plan. But then he'd accidentally fallen asleep on the sofa. Well, he hadn't slept well again last night, what with all the upset about Alice and dead bodies turning up on his doorstep. So, he'd just nodded off, knackered. No worries though, his old motor wouldn't let him down. Surely?

'Why does car not start?' Krystyna snapped.

'Give her a minute, *don't stress her out*,' Gavin replied defensively as the engine turned slowly over, but failed to fire up.

'You cannot stress car by talking,' Krystyna barked. 'It is machine!'

'Don't listen to her, Lizzie,' said Gavin softly. He turned the unresponsive key again.

'Lizzie? You have name for car?' Krystyna was clawing her fingers in front of her.

'You've done it now,' countered the protective vehicle owner, turning the engine until the battery finally failed. 'She's upset.'

'She is not upset. *She is car!*'

'Not helping people,' interjected Bob, breaking up the front seat spat. 'How about we try a jump start?' He remembered back to the good old days when it was quite usual for cars not to start.

So, all three human passengers - not Rocky, who'd opted out - were soon on duty, pushing Gavin's lifeless car out of his driveway. At least they were away from the stink. They just needed to get some momentum going down Mayfair Avenue and hopefully Gavin would then engage into gear and the reluctant engine would finally explode into life.

Attempt number one - a failure.

'You need to get more speed up!' Gavin shouted over his shoulder, out through his wound down window.

'We push as fast as we can,' Krystyna fired back. 'You drive better!'

Attempt number two. Almost, yes almost. The car hopped like a limping kangaroo and almost stuttered into life. But then - only another failure.

The three spent pushers then crouched over at the rear of the car, catching their breath. *It was hopeless. Now what?*

Dinesh was nursing a nasty twinge felt in his back, but as he raised his head, he saw headlights approaching - in fact now right on top of them. The lights belonged to a car carrying two men and it slowly pulled up, coming in to rest just behind them. The three struggling jump starters squinted as the silhouettes of two approaching figures were then framed in the headlights, momentarily indistinguishable. But then it became obvious who they were.

'Good evening, officers,' said Dinesh, smiling. 'We are having car trouble.'

PC Duckworth and PC Chabra, two of Drabbleton's finest boys in blue, stood there simply shaking their heads at this pathetic attempt to start a motor vehicle.

'Hello Dinesh,' said the relatively tiny PC Chabra, 'Taking the night off from t'chippy?'

'Ah yes,' Dinesh replied. 'I have been in training with my pub quiz friends.'

'What pub quiz is this then?' the affable constable continued.

'Tuesday nights, at the Anchor,' Bob jumped in. 'We're a new team. The Bodysnatchers.'

Krystyna couldn't believe that Bob was spouting out their private joke to the actual police. She sent him the daggers. He shrugged, seeming to enjoy playing with danger.

'Weird name,' said Chabra. 'Some of us lot down the station fancy joining, actually. The Anchor's our local. We've even come up with a name an' all - *Very PC.*'

'Well may the best team win,' said Bob, convincingly keeping the cover story going - whilst starting to warm to the idea of being in a pub quiz team. Could be the highlight of his Drabbleton dreary week!

Meanwhile, PC Duckworth, the older and much larger of the two constables, was sauntering around the car, apparently mildly curious about the five boxes inside. Reaching the front of the vehicle, he was now standing right by Gavin's open window.

'Evening Sir. What's with all the boxes if you don't mind me asking?' Just as he enquired, the whiff of rotting flesh hit his nostrils. 'Ugh!' he groaned. 'What on earth is that?' He vigorously wafted a hand in front of his nose, a sudden animated state that triggered an excited volley of doggy woofs from Rocky.

'Hey, you've upset my dog,' Bob sprung into complaint mode, coming around from the rear of the vehicle. 'OK, he's got halitosis. But he can't help stinking a bit, poor lad. No need to make a big deal about it.'

'Very rude!' Krystyna joined in with finger wagging action.

PC Duckworth withdrew his large nose beyond the range of the foul smell permeating from Gavin's car and seemed to forget about his interest in the boxes altogether.

'Oh sorry,' he backtracked sheepishly. 'No offence intended.' He offered Bob a conciliatory handshake which was begrudgingly accepted. 'Mind, that smell is pretty bad. You need to get him sorted.'

'I intend to,' said Bob forbearingly.

'Do you want us give you a shove?' asked PC Chabra, eager to offer an olive branch to his prospective pub quiz rivals. 'Let's get this thing started.'

'We would very much appreciate,' said Dinesh smiling at his *Star of India* young regular. *Chicken Vindaloo, Naan Bread and Mango Chutney.*

Within moments, three members of The Bodysnatchers and two members of Very PC were giving it their all, propelling the temperamental estate car at record speed - for a human powered vehicle - down Mayfair Avenue. At that optimum point of acceleration, just when an aircraft pilot would raise a nose to commence take-off, Gavin released his clutch. Second gear was engaged. A stutter. A splutter. An almighty backfire. But then success! The car roared into life and the now triumphant driver assuredly tootled along for a further twenty or so yards - with The Bodysnatchers desperately chasing after him. Lizzie then halted for an *all-aboard* moment.

Seconds later, the two members of Very PC - satisfied at a good job done - were left behind. Yet there they both stood in ignorant bliss, enthusiastically waving off the severed limbs and torso of the murdered Brimstone. And now their chances of being included in Drabbleton Police Force's all-time *Roll-of-Honour* diminished with every wave.

'That was close thing,' Krystyna clipped. 'Now, please no more hiccups.'

Everyone inside the car agreed, even Rocky.

It only took Gavin less than two minutes to pull off Mayfair Avenue and into Baker Street, a half derelict row of unoccupied terraced houses awaiting demolition. These neat little abodes were once built by James Brimstone, back in the day, to house his mill workers. Maybe the ghostly echoes from Drabbleton's more philanthropic times called out to Gavin's car as it went by, wishing him well.

By 10.25 pm, all the boxes containing Bryce Brimstone's body parts had been positioned on top of the wall of the pollution blackened railway bridge. Krystyna checked her watch, confirming that in just two minutes time the nightly coal-carrying freight train would pass underneath - and then they would all literally push all of their troubles away.

'OK, when the train comes, we'll all count the wagons going by, yes?' said Bob, confirming the plan. 'As soon as we've counted to twenty, we all shove these buggers off so that they'll land in lucky wagon number twenty-one.'

'One moment,' contested Krystyna, 'considering likely speed of train and time for boxes to drop down to target, I believe boxes will end up in wagon twenty-two.'

'But they've got to go in wagon twenty-one,' Bob bemoaned.

'Does it matter?' asked Gavin, blowing his cheeks. 'Just send them on their way.'

'Yes, it matters!' Insisted Bob, thumping on a cardboard box to help make his point. 'Because wagon twenty-one is the *lucky* wagon.'

'OK, so we push off boxes just as wagon number nineteen goes by,' Krystyna insisted, settling the debate. 'Then number twenty-one will catch everything.'

'Perfect,' agreed Dinesh, impressed by this Polish genius's mathematical assessment - her assured calculation of speed v distance v gravitational pull. 'Yes, very good,' he celebrated. 'I am so glad we have you in pub quiz team.'

'Alright, do it your way,' Bob conceded. 'I was already considering wagon number nineteen myself, actually.'

Then, bang on time, just as the old man had promised, the rumbling of the coal train came into earshot - and by 10.27pm, precisely, the nose of the mighty diesel locomotive was passing underneath the railway bridge. The crew began to count the passing wagons aloud and in unison...

'One ...two ...three,' their voices barely heard above the clattering of the coal laden wagons on the track below. They were shouting now.

Gavin and Dinesh prepared to launch the larger torso filled box. Krystyna and Bob could manage the arms and legs between them. Their voices tensed as the count neared its conclusion and they edged the boxes ready for the big drop.

'Seventeen, eighteen, nineteen...*Go!*

The boxes were launched with efficient synchronicity, sent dropping towards their intended repository below. Wagon number twenty sped by underneath, with the boxes - as Krystyna had accurately calculated - still mid-air.

Bingo! Wagon twenty-one would surely catch the lot!

Except there was no wagon number twenty-one.

They all watched open mouthed as the rear of wagon number twenty trundled away along the distant track, the last carriage of tonight's train. Brimstone's body parts lay strewn across the railway sleepers below, the cartons having given way with the shock of impact with earth. The crew looked down at their mishap in horror.

'Nooooo!'

'What happened to thirty-nine wagons, Bob?' Gavin quickly censured. *'There's always thirty-nine wagons,'* he crowed, mimicking his neighbour as a parrot. 'Bollocks!'

'Don't go blaming me,' yelped Bob, defiantly. 'I was going to say *lucky wagon seven.* It's you that lives at number twenty-one.'

'What's that got to do with it?' Gavin retorted, fighting off a temptation to pull out his hair.'

'I was just trying to be nice to you, what with all your recent troubles,' Bob now sulked. 'I won't bother next time. No more Mr Nice Guy!'

'Wh-a-a-a-t?' Gavin yanked at his hair after all.

'Children, children, please,' Krystyna interjected in stern schoolteacher style. 'Squabbling does not help. Cool head better.' She pointed to a torso and four limbs scattered across the tracks. 'We need to recover bits of Brimstone.'

'Yes, good idea,' Dinesh agreed. 'But not easy.' He was already eyeing the seven-foot-high steel fence, topped by barbed wire, that sealed off access to the tracks on each side of the bridge.

'I vote we scarper,' said Bob, avoiding eye contact with Gavin.

'Not acceptable,' Krystyna countered, chopping a hand, karate style. 'Our fingerprints are all over boxes.' Bob turned away, sulking further.

'We need to get down there somehow,' Dinesh concluded, without cracking the puzzle.

Bob turned around again, suddenly brighter. 'It's like one of those prison escape movies when you think about it. Where they go over the wall. We just need to tie some sheets together and one of us shimmy on down.'

'That would be great if we were escaping from Marks & Spencer bedding department,' Gavin dissed. 'But here in the real world, where are we going to get half a dozen sheets?'

'We can go home for them,' said Bob, trying to ignore Gavin's sarcasm.

'Good idea,' said Krystyna, mindful that she had better placate the old man, clearly a sensitive soul. She paused to reflect. 'Well, I say *good*. But really that is shit idea Bob. What if other train goes by and driver sees body parts? We need to get down there now!' Another karate chop, this time more forceful.

'I've got a tow rope in the spare wheel compartment,' Gavin offered. 'No spare wheel, but yeah pretty strong rope.' He patted the roof of the trusty rust bucket parked up beside him. *I knew she wouldn't let me down.*

'Tow rope probably good idea with car like that,' scoffed Krystyna.

'Now you don't go upsetting her again. You know what happened last time.' Gavin patted Lizzie again. *Ignore her.*

'Abseiling down rope is surely not easy,' Dinesh fretted. 'I have bad back.' He massaged the offending twinge.

'I can do it,' Bob stepped forward gamely, while Gavin was already fishing out the rope from his car. 'I used to be a steeplejack, remember? Plus, I was in a mountaineering club when I was young.'

'What mountains have you climbed,' Krystyna enquired with genuine interest. That would be her kind of hobby, she thought. 'Scafell Pike? Ben Nevis?'

'Well, we mainly stayed in planning stage, at the time, in the pub. There were three of us. But we gave up on the idea when we found out how much all the equipment would cost.' Bob sighed with regret at another lost dream.

'So, you never actually climbed mountain?' Krystyna probed, now much less impressed.

'As good as, kind of. It's all up here. I know *exactly* what to do and what not to do.' Bob tapped his temple three times and winked knowingly. 'Remember that survival movie on climbing Everest? Well, they got it all wrong. Shouldn't have set out on a cold day for a start.'

'It's always a cold day round Everest, it's a bloody mountain thousands of metres above sea level, dimwit.' Gavin called over despairingly, his head stuck in his boot.

'Who are you Mr Clever Edmund Hilary?' Bob retorted, defending his pride.

'He went to the North Pole, not Everest,' Gavin countered, head back out of the car.

'Prove it!' said Bob, with *check-mate* smugness.

'What do you mean, *prove it?* It's on the internet. I could search it on my phone.'

'Fake news!' Bob proclaimed, swimming in the glow of obvious victory.

Gavin now blew his own head off with an imaginary gun. He had to end it somehow.

'Children, children, once again. Not helping.' Krystyna scolded, but by this time only as she was starting to cheer up at the sight of the long and sturdy looking rope that Gavin was holding in a loose coil around his shoulder. 'OK Bob, steeple-jack skills better than mountain climbing skills in this instance. Congratulations, you can be our volunteer.'

'Thank you,' said Bob stepping forward again, smiling self-righteously and patting his pot belly. 'At last, someone around here is seeing sense.' He restrained the minor cough that may have cast doubt on his fitness for work, then braced himself for action.

Over the next five minutes, the project team got to work fixing one end of the rope securely to the roof rack of Gavin's car. The other end of the rope was then tied in a noose around Bob's torso, underneath both of his arms. But then the eager volunteer didn't like the idea of the noose, feeling it might become too tight once it had taken his weight. So, he decided to simply hold onto the rope instead and his buddies in base camp could hold the other end - adding stability to the roof rack fixing - and then he would simply inch himself down. Rocky looked up at his owner, daring not to imagine how this might end. Bob was by then doing stretches, warming up, attempting to somehow emulate the fitness of the man he was some fifty years ago - when he last performed a mountaineering feat. Or rather, would certainly have performed one if he and his mates could have afforded the equipment.

Gavin then knelt by the wall of the bridge and cupped his hands together to make a step-up for Bob. An admittedly inelegant ascent to the ledge begun, with Bob mainly groaning, huffing and puffing and the other three shoving and pushing his arse and leveraging his legs to get him atop the intended pedestal. Despite lacking obvious athletic prowess, however, Bob was game enough. He eventually wriggled around, manoeuvring himself into a position ready to commence the drop.

'This is it guys,' he grinned bravely. 'Let's go!'

Bob gripped onto the rope as though his very life depended on it, which of course it did.

'We have you,' said Krystyna, as she joined Gavin and Dinesh holding onto the rope. 'Good luck.'

Within a couple of seconds, the rope itself was taut, pulling against the roof rack, but being adequately reined in by the three pairs of hands in assistance. Bob gingerly shimmied, little by little, down the vertical drop, his hands starting to burn a little as they chafed against the cord.

'This isn't fun,' Bob grouched, wishing he'd maybe paid closer attention to that movie about climbing Everest. *Didn't they wear gloves for a start?*

'You're doing very well,' said Dinesh, chief cheerleader.

'Go on, keep going you old sod,' Gavin chipped in, a less enthusiastic supporter.

Bob's head had now cleared the bottom of the arch of the bridge and so he could now see the railway track stretching off into the distance. Any oncoming train would now clearly be in his view. No problem. Just like the train, in fact, that actually was now clearly in his view - a mean looking diesel freight train that had every chance of splatting him like a dead fly on a speeding car's windscreen. He hung there, dangling helplessly in space.

'Train! Pull me up,' he yelled in sudden panic.

The others already knew about the train themselves by now, as the approaching roar of its thundering engine had already assaulted their ears.

'One, two, three, pull,' Krystyna commanded, as she and her cohorts managed to pull Bob a foot further towards safety, with Gavin then winding the loose rope around the roof rack to take the slack. But more needed to be done. 'Again, one, two, three, pull,' she ordered.

Bob couldn't see the train by now, his head up against the stone of the archway. But the proximity of the blaring diesel horn made him fear that his legs were going to be imminently removed from his body.

'Pull again!' He screamed, whipping his legs up into foetal position just at the moment the train appeared, breaking its snout beyond the arch below, then rushing on through with its assorted freight filled wagons. Bob instinctively controlled his flailing legs and pushed himself away from the wall as he then attempted to walk up the stonework, abseil style, hauling himself up with the rope. But the rope itself didn't appreciate this sudden extra force, or the car accessory to which it was attached rather certainly didn't. The roof rack was instantly yanked free of its fixings and catapulted itself towards the wall, striking Gavin's back and head and shocking the other two momentarily - just enough so that they lost the rope. In less than a second, they had caught it again. But that was too slow for Bob's requirement, and he screamed out as he lost his grip and then fell backwards towards certain death.

'Aaaggghhhh!'

Well, certain death would most likely have ensued had the freight train not been carrying its particular load that night, consisting partly of sand. Bob consequently experienced an uncomfortable but comparatively soft landing. Gavin, Dinesh, and Krystyna gawped on as they watched him being taken away by the retreating train. They could see him, laid out flat - but seemingly relatively undamaged - on a large heap of sand being carried by one wagon mid-train. Inside this wagon Bob moved his head to the side and saw that somebody had numbered the vehicle with a scrawl of white paint. *Number twenty-one.* Comforting. But that was the last thing he did see before his body gave way to the sudden trauma of the moment and decided to whisk Bob away into a restorative and gentle loss of consciousness.

'Where will he end up?' wondered Krystyna, looking down the track as Bob and the train disappeared into the distance. She then had a thought to stroke Rocky to allay any doggy concern.

'God knows,' said Gavin, nursing a bruised head and sore back. 'Just hope the old git is OK.'

'Do you need hospital?' asked Dinesh, concerned about the injury he had witnessed Gavin suffering just now.

'Nah... I'm fine,' came the shaky reply. 'Just a bump. Any road, we're not sorted yet.' The three peered over the bridge to check on the remnants of Bryce Brimstone which were still down there, of course, but somehow not having suffered further damage at the wheels of that last passing train.

'I will go down,' said Krystyna decisively. 'I go to gym three times a week. I should have done this in first place. But tie rope better please.'

Gavin nodded, Dinesh too. So, over the coming minutes the rope was this time lashed underneath the two open front windows of the car and then up over the entirety of the width of the roof. With Krystyna finally happy with the stability of the fixing, she nimbly hopped up onto the ledge of the wall and in no time was elegantly abseiling and then shimmying in descent to the tracks below.

'Are you OK?' Gavin shouted down to her, simultaneously admiring her athletic poise as she executed a most graceful landing.

'Yes, OK, but drop further than I thought,' came the reply, as Krystyna brushed down her snugly fitting Lycra tracksuit bottoms.

Until, suitably composed once more, she approached Brimstone's severed right arm, now separated from its broken box. 'Get ready, I will throw,' she shouted, before a shirt-sleeved arm was hurled, Olympian discus style, and sent flying through the air arcing towards the now outstretched arms of her less athletic team members up on the bridge. An owl watched on in awe.

'Good shot,' Dinesh called out approvingly, catching the arm. He quickly deposited it in the back of the car. By the time he was back, a second arm had come accurately whizzing up towards them, but this time Gavin was doing the honours.

'Nice catch,' Krystyna approved. 'Finally, you do something right.' Gavin smiled, though half considered throwing the left arm back at her.

Once the two legs had successfully followed on the flight path of their cousins, Krystyna was puzzling about how exactly to deliver the torso - far too heavy to throw. But first she thought she'd simply hide the collapsed boxes behind bushes in the undergrowth. Out of sight, they'd eventually disintegrate in the rain. She just made sure she removed the address labels first, unhelpfully incriminating Gavin as they were. By the time she'd done that she'd hatched a plan for the torso. This was consequently tied in a tow rope noose so that even the two male assistants, with their pitiful lesser strength, could hoist it up and away, no problem.

'OK ready,' Krystyna finally shouted, having secured the battered and bloodied looking torso to the noose. But there was no reply from her associates on the bridge. 'Hello, remember me!' she called out again caustically. But again, no reply.

Easily explained, as up on road level Gavin and Dinesh were frantically legging it down Baker Street in pursuit of Rocky and the right arm that Bob's pet had taken a fancy to. Obviously sensing that his owner wasn't around just at the moment, the suddenly animated dog had jumped onto the boot ledge, grabbed a potentially tasty arm between its teeth and was now making off with it at top speed - despite his limp. He was doing a good job of it too, as the two unfit humans were fast running out of breath, and he was easily escaping past the row of derelict houses towards the bright lights of Mayfair Avenue. He scampered off into the distance.

'If he is seen like this we may well be done for,' bemoaned Dinesh, before now giving up the chase and holding onto a sudden stitch cramp in his left side.

'Rocky, you little sod, come back here!' Gavin called out, as he doubled over, also quite breathless after a fifty-yard pointless dash. 'Let's get Krystyna and then try and catch him with the car.'

Of course, their more athletic crew member wasn't happy to have been left on a railway line with only a substantial lump of corpse for company. But Gavin and Dinesh ignored her reprimands as, first the torso, and then the carping lady herself were eventually hoisted to safety. Then, all packed up in Lizzie and all aboard too, Gavin did a three point turn and headed for home.

'OK, we have lost one team member, one arm and a dog. Body parts not heading on coal train to Poland. Body parts coming home with us. Pathetic mission!' Krystyna couldn't believe she'd allowed herself to become embroiled in such a hopeless plan with such a sorry bunch.

Meanwhile, last orders had long gone at the Anchor pub and now, along Mayfair Avenue, two young lovers propped each other up as they meandered home after a solid night on the ale. Across the road, the sight of a limping dog trotting along with something in its mouth seemed to be worthy of a mention.

'Eh love,' said the burly young man, as Rocky came nearer. 'There's a dog there with a human arm in its gob.'

'Shurrup,' replied his scantily clad companion, lipstick smeared across her face. 'Can't be a frickin' arm.' She squinted towards Rocky, then squinted again. 'Well blow me. It is a frickin' arm. Cheeky sausage, someone'll be missing that.'

'Don't mess with the dogs round 'ere. They're rough bastards,' said the boyfriend with grudging respect.

'They are! *Bloody* rough bastards.'

The two lovers then stopped for a salacious snog. Overcome by lust and groping manoeuvres, the dog with the human arm between its teeth soon disappeared from their inebriated minds. Just another night out in Drabbleton. Nothing remarkable at all.

★

By the time Gavin was driving his car along the length of Mayfair Avenue there was no sign of Rocky or indeed, of a human right arm. There'd been hope that the absconding mongrel would have been found waiting patiently on Bob's doorstep, but not to be. Eventually pulling into his driveway, Gavin parked up Lizzie and switched off her finally co-operative engine.

'You said dog would be here,' Krystyna complained. 'But I see no dog.' She thinned her lips and folded her arms.

'I didn't say he *would* be here, just that I thought he *could* be.'

'No, you said *do not worry Krystyna, dog will be waiting at door of house*. But all bollocks. Always, all bollocks.'

'There's no point bickering about it,' said Dinesh, from the back seat, a severed arm and leg across his lap. 'This isn't solving our problem. We need a new plan.'

'Yeah Krystyna, stop with the bickering,' said Gavin, self-righteously. 'I should have left you on that railway track,' he bickered.

'And I should have pushed you off bridge.' Krystyna pulled a face at Gavin that didn't say I love you.

'Finished now?' asked Dinesh in parental tone.

'I have,' said Gavin, with pronounced certainty.

'Yes, finished,' mumbled Krystyna, unable to look at Gavin just for now.

'While you two have been at each other, I have been thinking,' said Dinesh, suddenly sounding pleased with himself. 'Solution is simple.'

'Great Dinesh, what is it then?' Gavin just knew they'd come up with something good.

'I cook Brimstone. Make him very delicious Special Curry!' Dinesh was the picture of smugness.

'You ...what?' Lizzie's driver maybe wasn't expecting that. 'Surely that's like *cannibalism?*'

'Yes, very good. Cannibalism is one word,' Dinesh continued, completely undeterred by that irritating detail. 'But Special Curry is another. Well yes, that's two words actually - so who is counting? But when Brimstone becomes Special Curry on my chippy menu, then the fine citizens of Drabbleton can eat the evidence. No more problem.' The chef extraordinaire swished his hands together twice, in rapid succession. *Job done.*

'Brilliant.' Gavin was in. Forget that stupid *cannibal* reservation.

'But body stinks. Too late to cook,' Krystyna fretted.

'No, I am sure cooking will kill all bacteria,' Dinesh sagely advised. 'Look at beef as an example. That is often hung for two or three weeks for flavour improvement.'

'That's right Dinesh, good thinking,' Gavin approved with a big grin. 'But it will take some recipe to make that tough old bastard taste good.'

'It will be a challenge, yes, but I will indeed make him most tasty. I have just the herbs and spices in mind.'

'You sound like cooking expert,' said Krystyna, warming to the idea.

'Dinesh is a master chippy man alright – much better than I ever was. If anybody can make a yummy curry out of lumps of human remains, then he's yer man.' Gavin was already imagining being first in line when Dinesh launched Special Curry Night at his chippy

Ten minutes later the three were carrying four bin bags, quickly retrieved from Gavin's kitchen, into the backyard of the *Star of India*. Dinesh unlocked the back door and, being as quiet as they could possibly be - for fear of waking the sleeping Mishka upstairs - they all tiptoed into the premises. A spare chest freezer was positioned in a dark corner of the little storeroom. It had been covered over with a blanket, as if out of use. Well, Mishka certainly thought it wasn't being used at the moment - although she was quite mistaken.

'In here,' said Dinesh, removing the blanket and lifting the chest lid, indicating his chosen temporary home for Brimstone's torso, legs and left arm. The four bin bags were irreverently emptied out accordingly - not a pretty sight.

'Who is laughing now, Mister?' Dinesh whispered, with an almost wicked glint in his eye, seemingly addressing the one body part that had already taken up residence in the base of the freezer - Brimstone's decapitated head.

'Make sure you put *that* in the curry too,' Krystyna directed, spotting the now frost engulfed head for the first time since *Murder Monday*. 'You promised it would go.'

Dinesh nodded in assent, although without much enthusiasm. While Gavin preferred not to look at the head at all - what with the hack marks of the sword's initial decapitation attempts clearly scarring what remained of the dry-bloodied neck, and its bullet-holed forehead and wide-open, terror-struck eyes.

'Who is laughing now, Mister?' Krystyna decided to join in on the release, not put off at all by the horror view. She relished that.

'I will enjoy butchering him, that is for certain,' the creative chef smiled, now closing the lid, and replacing the decoy blanket.

'Well, it's good to be happy at your work,' said Gavin, patting his friend on the back - although quite relieved that the staring head had been shut away - and then gladly stepping out the way he came in.

'Goodnight, Dinesh,' added Krystyna. 'I look forward to tasting your work. Cook well.'

★

Gavin then agreed to drive Krystyna home, but first they had a quick tour of Mayfair Avenue on the off chance of spotting an old limping dog with a human arm in its mouth. No luck with that - meaning Lizzie was finally pointed in the direction of Brimstone Mill, near to where he knew the Call Centre Manager lived, handy for walking into work.

'So, Krystyna,' said Gavin, hoping he could maybe entice his passenger into journeying pleasantries, 'do you live alone in your place?'

'No, it is house share,' she replied. 'Ten of us in big Victorian house. Mostly Polish, all with room each.'

'So is one of them a boyfriend, or something?' Gavin half-smiled, almost to himself, imagining he was straying off limits.

'You are being nosey, Mr Hargreaves,' Krystyna replied deadpan.

'Sorry.' Gavin focused instead on a changing traffic light.

'No,' his passenger seemed to marginally lighten up. 'No boyfriend. I am off men.'

'That's a shame. You are a very attractive woman, if you don't mind me saying.' Gavin immediately inwardly cringed at that last creepy sounding comment. *Why did I say that?*

'Ha!' Krystyna hooted. 'Are you coming onto me now?'

'No, definitely not,' Gavin fumbled. 'Not that I wouldn't...' He squirmed awkwardly. 'I mean it's not that I can't see that you are attractive.'

'You are getting in mess.' An honest assessment. She also thought that would be the end of it, but no...

'Yeah, I know, sorry...' If he wasn't driving, Gavin would be no doubt talking to his boots. He paused for thought. 'It's just that I'm probably in love with somebody else,' he finally uttered, 'if you must know.' He sighed wistfully. But the truth was out there. 'So that's it really. You could be the sexiest woman in the world, and it wouldn't make a difference.'

'If I were sexiest woman in world, you would be begging for it,' Krystyna cackled wickedly. Gavin hadn't realised that she had a sense of humour. 'Love would go out of window in that case.'

'Unfair.' *Hold your ground, lad!*

'But true. Instead, I am merely sexiest woman in Call Centre.' Krystyna stretched out a long leg into the foot well and stroked her thigh in a deliberately exaggerated show of flirtatiousness.

'I hadn't really noticed,' said Gavin, wishing he hadn't have watched that thigh stroking thing. He was driving, after all - by the Town Hall, as it happened. He nodded as usual to the statue of James Brimstone, trying to distract himself. Alice was due to be starting work in that building on the Monday. He resolved to go and visit her there. It was a public exhibition after all. All good distracting stuff.

'Hadn't noticed? Liar!' Krystyna snorted, having enjoyed making that little impact. Her driver seemed stunned into dumbness. Dead air ensued. But soon, bored of then watching them go by the dreary shops and houses of Drabbleton at midnight, she finally broke silence again... 'Anyway, do I get a say in it then? If you were coming onto me, that is.'

'Well, course. But I am not,' Gavin seemed determined to stay out of trouble. 'Besides, I reckon you're a bit out of my league, love. I'm sure you could pull more attractive blokes than me.'

'I live in Drabbleton. Options are limited. I must be realistic!' Krystyna laughed again, clearly having a bit of fun. 'Anyway, answer would probably be OK, I might have casual sex with you. But no boyfriend stuff.'

Gavin raised an eyebrow and then some. *She's playing you, lad.* 'You just said you were off men,' he noted, struck by the contradiction. Krystyna's playfulness seemed to suddenly disappear.

'It creeps me out that Brimstone was last sex for me. As you unfortunately saw. But it was worse than what you saw as he made recording and uploaded to porn site.' She withered at the memory.

'That's terrible. I'm sorry.' Gavin immediately felt the inadequacy of his words. But what *could* be said?

'Not the first time. He did it with others too.' Krystyna was clenching both of her fists.

'Bastard.'

'And tonight, we have been driving around with his dick in bin bag.' Krystyna forced a laugh. 'I should have cut it off.'

Then they both laughed naturally - a tension release.

'I'm sure Dinesh will be doing that for you.' Gavin paused on that sweet thought. 'Mind, you could always ask for your portion of Special Curry to be *extra special,* if you get me.'

'Ha! I like idea.'

They both laughed again. Justice after all. Gavin drove on up by Victoria Park, itself surrounded by a crescent of once grand Victorian villas, these days all divided up internally into small flats and bedsits.

Krystyna would soon be home. Meanwhile, each of them was silently replaying the little movie in their minds where Brimstone's shrivelled manhood meets Dinesh's sharp knife

'But anyway, you are in love,' Krystyna finally continued, playfulness restored by the comfort of revenge. 'So, I will have to get some other man to help me cleanse Brimstone from my sexy, toned body.' She purred as she now mock-erotically stroked an inner thigh with long fingers, before again bursting into laughter.

'I'm sure someone will come along pretty soon,' said the slightly ruffled driver, admittedly wrestling with the potentially missed opportunity.

'Is sex good between you and loved one?' Krystyna then unashamedly pried.

Gavin, instantly embarrassed, didn't quite know what to say. 'Um... we haven't actually got around to it yet,' he eventually mumbled, pretending to be concentrating even harder on his driving. *Difficult turn ahead.*

'Then this would be recent love?'

'I suppose,' said Gavin, realising how much Krystyna's stern, managerial work persona was keeping her out of the gossip loop at Brimstone Mill. He'd thought everybody knew about him and Alice. 'But I think we've already broken up,' he continued, brushing aside his passenger's knowledge gaps. 'Well, she's broken up with me.'

'So how long since you last had sex?' Krystyna asked, piling on the questions like a court room lawyer.

'That's a very personal question,' the suddenly blushing driver pushed back. But the interrogation was to be persistent.

'You ask me personal questions. Now I ask you.'

'Twenty-eight months,' Gavin gave way, realising resistance was useless. He didn't really know why he was keeping such an accurate count of his downtime though. Did it mean that much to him? *Well probably.*

'Very precise,' Krystyna replied. She liked precision.

'Since my ex-wife scarpered.'

'I bet you really desire sex after all this time,' she curiously probed. 'Assuming you have normal urges.' An inquisitive smile.

'Well yes,' Gavin replied, but sounding almost confused. 'Although I'm struggling to remember what it is like. Sex, I mean.'

'Of course, I understand,' Krystyna smiled again, this time almost sympathetically - although she'd certainly never experienced such a problem herself. 'For me, I think we people have animal desire for sex. It is big drive. So you, my friend, cannot go on like this. If no-sex lover has dumped you, best to move on. You aren't getting any younger.'

'Thank you. I'm only thirty-seven.' Gavin felt ancient.

'Two years older than me. But clock ticks. What if sex organs turn to rust?'

'Well hopefully not for a few years yet.' An unsettled laugh.

'Maybe,' Krystyna then switched into business mode. 'All the same, I need man to wash Brimstone from my skin. Sooner than later. We should do each other favour. One night only.'

'Are you propositioning me now?' Gavin was somehow no longer surprised.

'I remember you did once catch my eye in that Roman Centurion costume,' Krystyna looked to the stars, picturing that passing fancy in her head. 'Very nice legs, ha! So, answer to your question is *yes*. But mine is very practical proposition. I win. You win. One night only and no boyfriend stuff after that.'

'You said you wanted to push me off a railway bridge less than an hour ago.'

'Foreplay.' She cackled again.

'Well, give me a minute to think it over...'

'No,' Krystyna pushed back, emphatically. 'This must be spontaneous for it to work. Give me answer now.'

'I'm thinking...' But what was he thinking? Something like a messy cocktail of *twenty-eight months - gorgeous Krystyna - no strings sex - I love Alice - but she broke us up - sexy Krystyna - no strings sex. WHAT? NO STRINGS SEX?!*

'Now please!' Fingers were drumming on the passenger console.

Gavin's brain had formulated an answer.

'Well, yes then,' he triumphed. Probably.

'Yes?'

'Yes!'

'Good, we have deal!' Krystyna smiled broadly and held out a handshake confirmation to Gavin. He promptly accepted and the arrangement was settled.

★

Krystyna's small two room suite was on the top floor of a Victorian villa on tree lined Park Crescent - the pick of the space in her house share. But then, as Call Centre Manager, she was probably earning more than anyone else in the building and so could afford the most rent. Her rooms were built into the eves of the house and exposed wooden beams created a triangulated structure supporting the roof. Very stylised and Mock Gothic.

A small lounge welcomed you on entry, neatly furnished though minimalist to the point of sparsity. But that night both Gavin and Krystyna had been more interested in the bedroom - and skipping the pleasantries of pre-sex coffee or wine - had soon wrestled each other onto the wrought iron framed bed within. Gavin had already been slightly breathless after climbing three flights of stairs, but soon he'd been breathing heavy as a marathon runner at the finishing line as Krystyna had then torn off his clothes and he hers.

Inside a passionate minute he'd been naked, flat on his back on the mattress and with the similarly totally unclothed Krystyna straddling his thighs with her own. She was, *as billed*, beautifully toned - and her skin gossamer fine and sensuous to touch. She'd clamped onto him with her legs as she'd pushed him inside her, determined to dominate him. No more the submissive Little Red Riding Hood for Krystyna. This sex would be hard and hot, but she'd be in control. She'd thrust herself powerfully against Gavin three times in rapid succession, squeezing his recently retired perky pecker with her well-practiced pelvic floor muscles. Then she'd pulled away, pausing tormentingly, before then going in again. She'd wanted to play him all night, teasing him between the extremities of ecstasy and desperation, as he'd beg her not to withdraw.

But just her second set of triple thrusts had been enough for Gavin. He'd groaned like a dying animal as he'd gripped Krystyna's taut ass.

So here they now were, lying side by side under a white cotton sheet, quickly employed by Gavin to cover over rapidly shrinking appendage. *Game over.*

'Do you always come so quickly?' Krystyna asked, with a mixture of curiosity and frustration evident in her voice.

'Well, there was twenty-eight months of pent-up desire exploding right there, love,' Gavin replied in self-defence. 'But sorry if it was too quick.' He leant over to her, immediately struck by the beauty of her glistening green eyes. 'I could kiss you if you like...'

'Please!' Krystyna scrunched her face and pushed at his chest with a hand.

'Sorry,' said Gavin again, thinking his marks on ten were diminishing further. If that were even possible.

'It was nice, though short,' concluded Krystyna, finally noticing his crestfallen disposition.

'My God, when you did that thing with your legs, I thought I was either going to come or pass out.' Gavin laughed, briefly recalling the wonderment of that very moment. Almost worth the twenty-eight months wait in itself.

'Ha! You are pretty weak. You need gym.' Krystyna made a comedy strong man gesture with her right arm and giggled. *Yes, admirably toned.*

'Fair enough, but you're a very physical girl, that's for sure,' Gavin muttered in ascent.

'I am just happy I won,' she then plainly stated, though with just a hint of smugness.

'What do you mean *won*? It's not a competition.' Gavin tried to sound incredulous but not pathetic.

'Yes, it is. I am too sexy for you, admit it,' Krystyna grinned in self-amusement. 'You can't handle me and would always come first.'

'You don't know that,' Gavin protested, outraged at this unjustifiably justified attack on his very manhood.

'OK, prove it,' Krystyna clipped, reeling him in.

'Prove it?' Gavin stealthily checked on his now floppy equipment.

'Yes, prove it. How long before you go again?'

This was a deep question, one akin to the very meaning of life itself, but one that Gavin hadn't really considered for many a year. Even during most of his marriage to Marie, they'd only mostly done it the once. Except on holidays and birthdays and stuff.

'It used to be almost immediately when I was twenty-one,' he finally managed to proffer.

'Twenty-one-year-old Gavin no good to me,' came the no-nonsense reply. 'How long before thirty-seven-year-old Gavin can go again?' She smiled with ironic sweetness.

'I've really no idea,' Gavin scratched his head. 'Twenty minutes …maybe more, maybe less.' Well, that was his best offer.

'No use. I have work tomorrow. I have weekend shift.' Krystyna flipped around underneath the sheet, pulling it over her shoulder and turning her back on him. 'So, you can leave now.'

Gavin hesitated - flummoxed even.

'Shouldn't we just maybe hold each other for a bit.'

'No,' Krystyna balked. 'Holding is the boyfriend stuff I said is off limits.'

'I mean, I could stay over,' Gavin posed, knowing this to be totally unrealistic before the words had even finished leaving his mouth.

'Certainly not! Just sex was the deal. Now deal is done, so goodnight, Gavin.'

Another dumb hesitation.

'Will we have another deal night?' *Surely it was worth the ask.*

But Krystyna had already closed her eyes, preparing for sleep.

'Probably not. I am off men,' she uttered, sleepily.

'You said that earlier. But we still did it.'

'Life is full of surprises, so nothing is certain, I suppose.' She yawned.

'Well, I think I'd probably like another deal night sometime.'

She just ignored him and pretended to start snoring, eyes still closed. Gavin gazed for the final time at the amazing beauty on the pillow. He quickly dressed in silence and headed for the exit. Krystyna heard her bedroom door creak as he left.

'Goodnight, Gavin. That helped. Thank you.'

*

Gavin swung his car around on Park Crescent and finally found himself heading for home at the end of this unusually eventful and very long evening. His head was spinning. It wouldn't be many a night that seeing a neighbour fall into a freight train wagon while trying to get rid of dead body parts would not be the most memorable episode. But that sex just now with Krystyna. *Wow, she was something.* He couldn't stop replaying the whole erotic, though sadly brief scene in his mind. He also couldn't remember the last time he'd had a casual encounter like this. Oh yeah, there was that girl in the nightclub in his early twenties, fifteen, maybe sixteen years ago. It made him speculate that a lucky night like this would probably never happen again. That made him momentarily sad.

Whatever, he could savour the memory right now though, because he was still living the night itself - and would be until he got home and finally got himself off to sleep. After that the memory would be yesterday's, then the following day's, in no time next year's memory. Therefore, he was determined now to hold on to this final half hour of *tonight* because it had all been so special.

Just then, most unusually for this late hour, his mobile rang. He immediately thought *bad news* and - not having hands free - quickly pulled his car over to the side of the road and switched off the engine. He retrieved the still ringing handset from his pocket.

It was Alice. He tensed.

'Gavin, it's me,' said the gentle voice. 'Sorry for calling at this hour. Are you sleeping?'

'I'm trying to,' Gavin replied, mimicking a drowsy voice that had just woken up.'

'Uh, sorry,' Alice murmured sheepishly. 'I've hardly slept for days.'

'Yeah?' Gavin's head still hadn't stopped spinning.

'I've been missing you.' Alice sounded like she'd been crying, which hit Gavin's guilt button right there. *Ouch!*

'I thought we were done,' he said in monotone, wishing he could just squirm away.

'I think we should talk about it. At least try to.' Alice tried to suddenly lighten her voice. 'I was wondering if you'd like to come round?'

'What *now?*'

'Yes.'

'It's almost one in the morning, Alice.' Gavin heard his voice sound like a vexed parent admonishing a stop-out teenager as he or she drunkenly stumbled upstairs, waking the household.

'Sorry,' she seemed suitably suppressed. Although somehow, she just then sprung right back into life. 'But if it's too late to talk,' she coaxed, 'I thought I'd at least be able to tempt you round here with the offer of meaningless sex.' She kind of giggled, almost nervously.

Two offers in one night. After twenty-eight months of abstention. No way!

'I don't think sex between us could possibly be meaningless,' Gavin tried to say meaningfully - but only trying to put Alice off. He'd thought he loved her. But then, why did he allow himself to have sex with Krystyna? Maybe his defences were just at a low point. Maybe he was just a typical flake. Whatever the reason, he couldn't help but beat himself up right now. *Why am I like this? Why?*

'Oh well, looks like your twenty-eight months wait must continue?' Alice finally sighed, obviously having hoped for more enthusiasm. It had taken a lot for her to have made this call.

'Looks like it,' said Gavin, trying Krystyna's yawning trick.

'You must be cursed,' mused Alice.

'Must be.'

'Right then.' An awkward silence.

'I'll call you,' Gavin eventually mumbled, 'when I'm actually awake.'

'OK, night then.' The phone died as the echoes of Alice's disappointed voice lingered on.

'Night. Bye,' Gavin replied to Alice via telepathy. She'd already gone.

19
- BEN & JIMMY'S -

Bob Horsefield's journey in a sand-filled freight wagon had only lasted less than five minutes when his train had been halted by a routine red signal. Of this, he'd been quite unaware, remaining as he was in his temporary dead-to-the-world condition. But as the train had edged forwards once again, moving slowly past the signal box at Drabbleton South Junction, one Jack Pilkington spluttered on his mug of tea. In over forty years' service on the railways, ensuring the passing safety of many thousands of trains, life had been mostly dull. In the old days he used to chase trainspotters off the tracks, but kids today prefer games consoles to locomotive numbers. No fun there, then. Ten years ago, there'd been a power failure on a signal - bulb out - so if he hadn't had been quick witted enough to have used his red flag, the 10.21 dairy train would have collided with the 10.23 northbound passenger combo and then it would have been a case of crying over spilt milk, literally. Last year, he'd seen a pigeon fail to realise that a couple of hundred tons of oncoming diesel locomotive is worth getting out of the way of. Something to tell the wife. But today, a potential dead body in a passing wagon, that was indeed going to be career headline news.

From his signal box window, Jack had just peered down over all his complicated arrangement of levers and buttons, first seeing Bob's sand wagon trundling on by, and then Bob himself - apparently lifeless. *Action stations,* bloody hell! So then, using his lightning signalman instincts, last used to save the milk, he'd intelligently engaged the next red light down-track and got straight on the phone.

All southbound railway traffic for the remainder of the evening was then suspended as the dancing blue lights of both Transport Police and Ambulance Service vehicles attended Jack's little break from monotony. He was expecting a Signalman Commendation Medal for this, if such a thing had ever existed. Or maybe a mention in the *Drabbleton Bugle* at least - *Quick Witted Signalman Who Once Saved Milk Train Strikes Again!*

But all that Bob had vaguely experienced through all of this was a hazy blur of blue light and the sensation of being lifted onto some kind of bed or stretcher. Voices had been incomprehensibly mumbling in his head, then echoing as they faded off into nothingness. Then back to the darkness.

Two hours later, Bob started to move his head slightly and register light again behind closed eyelids. The silhouette of a shady figure muddied his bleary eyes. He wasn't to know, but this was Nurse Jayne Talbot of Ward Three, Drabbleton General Hospital.

'Hello there,' said a kind voice. 'Are you back with us?'

'Mavis?' Bob managed to mutter, closing his eyes once more. Too much effort.

'No, I'm not Mavis. I'm Jayne, your nurse. Who is Mavis?'

'Where's Mavis?' asked Bob, mumbling into incoherence. Then he fell back to sleep. Nurse Talbot scribbled something on Bob's medical notes and then replaced the clipboard at the foot of the bed. Her patient was well and truly out for the night.

*

The following afternoon, a bikini clad Roxanne Brimstone lay on her stomach on an opulently cushioned, reclined sun bed. Dimitri sat by her side, applying a sensual lotion massage to her bare shoulders, while enjoying looking at the contours of her exquisite body. A gently trickling fountain - sculpted in the form of Goddess Aphrodite - was the only noise that broke the silence. Meanwhile, a sliver ice bucket resting on a pearl laden occasional table housed a half-consumed bottle of vintage Bollinger. Heaven, for these two, could be right here inside this marble clad Athenian temple - itself the swimming pool complex and sanctuary nestled in the basement of the Brimstone Knightsbridge mansion.

But Heaven, for mere mortals, is an ephemeral state and despite all best efforts to sustain moments of bliss, practical matters always seem to interfere. One minute euphoria, the next, dropping back down to earth with a most unheavenly bump. So it was to be for Dimitri, in particular, on this otherwise tranquil afternoon.

'You have very firm hands,' Roxanne purred, as his massage eased away the knots in her shoulders. Well, her business matters could certainly be stressful and not without physical consequence. 'Just to the right please.'

'Here?'

'Yes, just perfect.'

Roxanne then reached over to quaff on the Bollinger as Dimitri continued his skilled duty. But suddenly a frown appeared on a forehead so unblemished that it looked like a crease of skin could never before have appeared.

'I feel bad, you know, that we have killed poor Bryce,' a husky voice expounded. 'I never expected to feel guilty about it.'

'Are you Catholic or something?' puzzled Dimitri. Roxanne just laughed at the thought. 'Then guilt is best left with the Catholics and the weak. Sometimes the strong will take what the weaker have. It is way of world.'

'Yes darling,' Roxanne replied emptying her glass emphatically, 'but it's not exactly nice, is it? My whole week might well be ruined now as I dwell on all of that bullet in the head and hatchet nonsense.'

'Best remedy is to remember you are now filthy rich. With emphasis on *filth*.' He lustfully feasted on her neck, and she giggled with pleasure. Instantly turned on, Dimitri ran his fingers along the inside of her thigh before then grabbing a piece of upmarket ass - only to result in straying hand being slapped as if belonging to a naughty adolescent.

'Later, tiger,' Roxanne gently scolded. 'I like filthy rich. But this can only happen when we get the death certificate and then Bryce's damned solicitor will read me the Will.'

'No problem,' Dimitri casually replied. 'Doctor will write death certificate as police say your husband is dead, presumed murdered.'

Roxanne suddenly sat up, alarmed that her much trusted partner, competent in so many ways, was simply missing a trick here.

'Dimitri, no. Being *thought* to be dead and *presumed* to have been murdered is not the same as *definitely* dead and *definitely* murdered.'

'Seems same to me.'

'No, it is far from being the same,' Roxanne smacked her champagne glass down on the table. 'I've played the clandestine informant for you, phoning the police myself so that they would not detect your Russian accent, despite the voice-box disguise. And I've told them, as you requested, that one Gavin Hargreaves is hiding Bryce's body. But nobody's been arrested.'

'Are you sure, my love?'

'Yes, well they're keeping me informed obviously - as his wife. They've even been round. But I've just played the grieving widow.' She crossed her forehead with her hand in melodramatic style. 'Oh, woe is me!'

Dimitri laughed. 'Very convincing, my darling.' He gave a small ovation, but the lauded actress quickly regained her focus.

'Do we even know that Hargreaves still has the body, come to think of it?' She sounded suddenly anxious.

'The plan was police would find body in his house.' Dimitri was at a loss to understand why Drabbleton's so-called law enforcers couldn't even follow a very simple lead given to them on a plate.

'Yes, well they obviously haven't found him,' snapped back the reply. Roxanne was now rising to her feet and reaching for a white silk dressing gown. 'What if he's rather clever and he's got rid of it somehow?'

'Getting rid of body is not that easy for amateurs. Body will be hidden, that's all.' Now on his feet, he helped Roxanne into her gown. She suited it. Like she suited everything.

'Look Dimitri, we need to know he has what's left of Bryce,' said Roxanne, increased edge in her voice. 'Or no death certificate for me and then no inheritance for me either. Not without years of legal wrangling anyway. I'm not waiting years.' She patted her lover's cheek twice, but more business-like than playfully.

'OK, OK, I will make sure he has body,' Dimitri replied, on the defensive and catching her hand firmly. 'Yes, I will make sure you get that damned death certificate. Leave it to me. It is sorted.'

'Sorted? Promise?'

'Absolutely. Promise.'

'Excellent. I shall leave myself in your capable hands.' She smiled, suddenly chilled again. She liked a man who could take care of problems and so she then threw her slender arms around Dimitri's neck. 'Speaking of which, what were you about to do with my ass?'

Dimitri smiled wickedly, realising his luck was in again. But a second later he inwardly shuddered. This wasn't exactly the plan. The police were supposed to have already recovered the body. *Incompetent morons!* Now he'd have to intervene again to make sure the job was properly done. Hargreaves would be sorry for this!

*

Dimitri decided to use a different London location for the second call to Drabbleton Police Station - one he'd decided to place himself. Despite the accent disguising advantage of using Roxanne last time, he reckoned he'd used up all his credits there. She expected him to sort this alone, therefore that is what he proposed to do, despite any downside. So, taking the Tube from Knightsbridge, he knew that the Piccadilly Line made a direct connection to St Pancras Station. It was there that he was standing now, half an hour or so after leaving Roxanne's delectable company, a new unregistered phone in hand. On the concourse, beneath the vast arched roof - a single span of wrought iron and glass - anyone would justifiably feel dwarfed. So many people swallowed up by that huge structure. And just like at Waterloo, hundreds of little ant-like commuters and tourists busied across each other's paths with every passing minute. To Dimitri's benefit, so many mobile calls both made and taken. He found a quiet corner, out of view of any obvious CCTV, and made his.

'Drabbleton Police, Tom Slater,' the Force's senior Detective Inspector immediately replied, slinging his jacket over the back of his chair. He'd just returned from a meeting at the morgue.

'Listen carefully to me,' said Dimitri, like Roxanne, voice disguised by the robotic vocal synthesiser app. 'I have important information.'

DS Haslam had already got the nod to pick up a slave phone and was also listening in.

'Go on,' said Slater, deadpan.

'This is not hoax. Gavin Hargreaves. Number 21 Mayfair Avenue. Why not arrested?' The robot voice sounded vexed.

'Why should he be?' said Slater vaguely.

'We already told you once. He is hiding corpse of Mr Bryce Brimstone. At house.'

'Who are *we*?'

'Not important. Hargreaves is killer.'

'No, he isn't.' By now, DI Slater had concluded that Gavin's informant was probably a bitter ex-employee of the Call Centre, someone with a score to settle after maybe being sacked by the Centurion Enforcer. He wasn't in the mood to indulge hoax callers.

'This is truth,' Dimitri insisted, almost growling.

'Prove it,' the DI sang dismissively.

The line went quiet. Slater and Haslam could almost hear the processor in the caller's brain whirring away.

'You searched river near motorway. Second body there.'

Haslam glanced at her boss, puzzled by the caller's sudden change of tack.

'Darren Eccles? That's been on the news, hardly a revelation, mate,' said Slater, leaning back on his chair, already losing enthusiasm.

'Also killed by Hargreaves,' the voice stated with utter certainty.

'You're making that up from something you've seen on the telly.' But the DI was now suddenly leaning forward over his desk.

'You can say that. But not on news that Hargreaves broke his neck.'

Slater's interest was finally baited. He'd just returned from a post-mortem update. Dr Brindle at the morgue, between fags, had indeed concurred that Eccles had entered the water already dead - cause of death, first compression to the neck and then severe fracture to the cervical vertebra.

The voice waited patiently for Slater to respond. This was the ticket to credibility surely.

'OK, I'm listening,' the old detective confirmed. 'But how would you know about something like that? Were you a witness or something?'

'Yes. Witness, that is me. But I dare not come forward as he is killer.' Dimitri managed to convincingly add a note of fear to his voice - a half-decent acting debut.

'Look...we can protect people in these circumstances,' said Slater, apparently taking this one seriously now. 'But tell me this.' He paused again. 'If you know Gavin Hargreaves so well, can you describe him to me?'

Haslam smiled at the experienced copper's instinctive guile.

'What do you mean, *describe*?' Dimitri sounded rattled.

'You know, is he blonde or bald? Thin or fat? How old is he?' Slater seemed to enjoy knocking the caller off balance.

'He is Gavin Hargreaves, man from Drabbleton. 21 Mayfair Avenue.'

'That's not much of a description, friend,' he scoffed, winking at his DS. Checkmate.

'Platform Three for the 16.33 train to Sheffield. Calling at Leicester, Derby, Chesterfield and Sheffield.'

Dimitri hadn't realised the train departure announcements would be so damn loud! Well, where he had unfortunately chosen to stand was right by a tannoy speaker and that had hardly helped. He immediately knew the policeman on the other end would have heard that broadcast loud and clear. A Russian curse word silently passed his lips.

'Hello caller, are you still there?' Slater coaxed but only as the robot voice suddenly disappeared for good. The line had been killed.

Dimitri buried his head into his coat and made his hasty retreat across the station concourse, quickly escaping out onto the open spaces of busy Euston Road. Near a pelican crossing he noticed a gridded drain cover, by which he knelt to feign tying a shoelace. The 'burner' phone was dispatched to a watery grave below. He then took a subway back down to the Underground, furious with himself for making such an unprofessional error. If Mr Volkov only knew of such bumbling, then the consequences for himself would be most grave.

Back at Drabbleton Police Station, two detectives looked at one another slightly mystified. What a confusing call. But it was Slater who finally took the initiative.

'What's the exact time, Judith?' he enquired, forgetting about the clock display right there in the corner of his computer screen.

'16.30, Sir.' His junior colleague read from hers.

'Right, well that means we've got CCTV of this caller somewhere. That tannoy thing was definitely at a mainline station.'

'Yes, I know. It's St Pancras,' replied Haslam, clearly delighted with her knowledge of the UK railway network. 'I used to live in Sheffield with my parents. Went to Police College in London. That was my train home.'

'Excellent,' Slater endorsed. 'Bit of a needle in a haystack, but let's get St Pancras's CCTV footage for five minutes either side of that last call. Him coming up with that broken neck stuff out of the blue like that - it makes me more suspicious of him than of Gavin Hargreaves himself!'

'Really?' said Haslam, not quite ready to go that far. 'But I'm assuming Eccles died of a broken neck, then?' She hadn't been with her boss at the morgue, so this was fresh news for her.

'Yep, according to Dr Brindle. Already dead when his body was dumped in the river.'

'Then it is possible that the caller is in on something. Unless it was a lucky guess.'

'Well, I'd definitely like to question him or her face to face to find out.' Slater pursed his lips, imagining that opportunity.

Haslam then seemed agitated, something obviously not sitting well for her.

'That voice, it wasn't the same as the first caller.'

'How can you say that? They both sounded like robots, what's the difference?'

'Syntax.' Haslam checked but could see her boss wasn't with her. 'You know, the way he or she was putting sentences together. Sounded foreign to me. Eastern European, maybe even Russian. But the first caller, that one was English I'd say.'

'Interesting. Good work, Judith.' Slater smiled, thinking they did at least teach the kids something at Police College, despite his earlier doubts. 'We'll send it off to our tech guys to confirm.'

'But why would somebody in London know anything about one Gavin Hargreaves, native of Drabbleton?' Haslam continued, confident and on a roll. She drummed her fingers in thought. Slater merely scoffed - his charge wasn't the finished article, after all.

'Hold the front page. *Shock! Horror! Man from London knows man from Drabbleton.*'

The sergeant secretly pulled out her tongue at her boss for that sarcastic response, he now momentarily distracted by unwrapping a Mars Bar.

'He doesn't actually *know* him, does he? Slater then continued, oblivious to the minor petulance. 'He couldn't describe him at all. Could be a friend or relative of someone in Drabbleton who holds a grudge against Hargreaves. Gavin wasn't exactly popular at the Call Centre for a while, that much we do know. But mentioning the broken neck. This caller is suddenly of interest. Big time.'

Slater munched on his Mars Bar as Haslam was rummaging for a piece of paper on her desk. 'Don't know if this helps. But I got that Telecoms report while you were out. The last synthesised voice call we had pointing a finger at Hargreaves also came from London - Waterloo Station, to be precise.'

'A burner phone?'

'Yeah, course.'

Haslam waited for renewed praise, but none was forthcoming. Just routine coppering after all.

'OK Judith,' Slater seemed to be pondering, as if leading up to some great revelation. 'Looks like our callers could be trainspotters. Arrest everyone in London stood on the end of a railway platform with a notepad and duffle bag.'

'Don't forget the anorak, Sir.'

Slater laughed. Haslam smiled to indulge him whilst turning down a chunk of Mars Bar she was being silently offered.

'Course, Brimstone's wife lives in London too,' Slater continued more seriously, not wishing to milk the corny joke. 'But I'm getting nothing from her on the phone. London colleagues have been round to see her, but say she's just distraught, understandably. I should really go down to see her in person.'

'It turns out the Brimstone's have a bit of a property empire down there.' Haslam was now looking at a different sheet of paper listing the London real estate currently managed by Roxanne - a portfolio of eye watering value.

'Sickening,' said her DI, as he was handed the list. 'There's me thinking I'd done very nicely with my three-bed semi by the canal.' He sat back in his chair pondering the world of high finance - in part admiration, part envy.

'But where do we even start with all this?' Haslam was suddenly starting to feel overwhelmed by the task before them. Slater had already been thinking that more foot soldiers were going to have to be drafted in.

'Chin up Judith,' Slater chivvied, noting her frown. 'We've got to start somewhere. CCTV from St Pancras - *and* Waterloo, come to think of it. Plus get these phone recordings analysed by the tech guys, as I say. Might throw something up.'

'Any chance we might go back to the Hargreaves place with sniffer dogs? Settle this dead body accusation once and for all?' That was the *real* kind of action the fledgling DS was hoping for.

'Judith, dear oh dear, give me strength.' Slater sighed at the impetuosity of youth.

'Sir, surely...' A pointless protest tailed off to silence.

'DS Haslam, it's a serious thing searching somebody's house. The householder might well feel that their privacy has been invaded and it can be very traumatic for them. Especially if they are completely innocent anyway. These searches, which you haven't seen one of yet - well they turn the place absolutely upside down, it's not like a quick look in a sock draw.'

Haslam was a tall girl, but she seemed to noticeably shrink as her superior officer continued her painful inauguration into the *real* world of criminal investigations.

'So, we won't get a search warrant on the back of a dodgy sounding, anonymous tip off. Unless I could stand up before a judge and say I believe there's every chance that Hargreaves is involved. But we've hardly built a case, have we? So that ain't going to happen in a month of Sundays.'

'What could change that?' said Haslam, disheartened for sure, but prepared to stick to her distrust of Hargreaves. 'We've no other leads really.'

'This isn't a lead. Not even a half decent one,' Slater slapped a palm hard onto his desk. 'Not in relation to Mr Hargreaves anyway.'

He then softened his voice, not entirely wishing to discourage the young sergeant he was supposed to be mentoring. He did realise his patience was waning after all these years on the job. 'But if we can substantiate who's making those calls, Judith, and for what valid reason, then that might start to get us somewhere. How *did* the caller know about Darren Eccles' broken neck? Let's see if we can turn up one or both of our trainspotter friends.'

Haslam perked up a little. At least there was *something* to follow up on.

The conversation was then interrupted by the ringing phone on Slater's desk. It was an internal call.

'Sergeant Choudhury, what can I do you for?'

Haslam curiously observed as her DI grew increasingly interested by what he was obviously hearing.

'Yes, come on up. Let's have a look.' Slater turned in his chair, sending a thumbs up sign to Haslam.

It turned out that door-to-door enquiries had uncovered an active doorbell cam on Bow Street, by Brimstone Mill. Digital footage was showing a scuffle between two barely distinguishable men. Frustratingly, for the Police anyway, their ruckus had been partly obscured - by a parked up black Mercedes.

★

Later on that Saturday afternoon, Gavin finally removed his *I Love New York* apron, itself once a thoughtful birthday gift from Marie on account of them both sharing a dream of holidaying there one day with Freddie. Well, they'd actually dreamt of holidaying in Walt Disney World, which when he last looked was in Orlando, Florida. But he knew that Marie would merely insist that the two locations were the *same thing*, so he'd accepted the apron at the time with unqualified thanks.

Whilst they never did get to Walt Disney World, they did have an afternoon out once at Blackpool Pleasure Beach - the best they could really afford, what with Gavin's joke shop then on the rocks. They'd argued in the car all the way back home because Marie wouldn't accept that Blackpool was the *same thing* as a holiday in the USA.

But whenever Gavin remembered to don that *I Love New York, Florida* apron it meant business as far as domestic chores were concerned. Hence it hadn't been worn much at all in the past three years - since it was new, in fact. But today he'd woken up inspired to somehow sort out his life. His twenty-eight-month sex life sabbatical was over. Right now, it was still less than twenty-four hours since he'd last had sex, practically still the same day. *Thank you, Krystyna!* But he knew that was a one-off – and was fine about it too. That said, Alice seemed up for seeing him again – a welcome development, if he didn't let himself get crushed by the guilt thing.

As his thoughts slowly crystallised, detached from the afterglow of last night, he realised that he did still love Ms Brimstone. Very much so – and a good thing too, he reflected. It made him happy, yes despite the G word! And all this positivity was only enhanced by the fact that getting rid of Brimstone's body was virtually in the bag now, thanks to Dinesh's culinary magic. A major problem solved. On a run of good luck, maybe even the Disposals Inc people would just go away when they realised that he was a penniless nobody. Oh, and even that five grand bill from Payne & Cheetham's that he couldn't pay – maybe they'd write that off now, seeing as their client was no more.

All positive stuff, indeed. Well mostly. That's why he'd sprung out of bed this morning, admonishing his old self for living like a pig in a sty that even pigs would be ashamed of. His new self - today's dynamic version of himself - had then dusted, hoovered, laundered, dish-washed, scrubbed, bleached, polished and mopped. Number 21 Mayfair Avenue was now in rare immaculate condition, with even Gavin himself wearing a freshly ironed t-shirt and having sponged off the month-old gravy stain from his grey trackie bottoms.

Not only had personal and domestic hygiene and organisation been on his agenda today, but career matters too had also been tackled. He'd decided to turn down the job offer he'd got from the chicken carcass incineration unit. Where was the Sir Alan Sugar style entrepreneur he'd once hoped to become? That's what he'd asked himself bluntly. If he was ever going to be truly prosperous, he needed to start working for himself, not for other people. That had always been the plan, so *what had happened?* Well, he just needed to raise some seed capital for a start.

Sitting at his dining room table, he'd taken a blank sheet of paper and decided to write down his assets.

1. *2012 Skoda Fabia Estate Car. 132,000 miles. Excellent Condition. Very reliable. Seven careful owners. Value: £1700.*
2. TBC
3. TBC

Right, that didn't take long. But *seventeen hundred smackeroos* - he'd be literally quids in with the Skoda liquidated.

Now, his dear Lizzie had been a very faithful servant these past five years. With plenty of room in the boot for cash and carry supplies needed for his former retail operations, she'd been the queen of her day. But now, a newly inspired entrepreneur like Gavin, was in need of an entirely different kind of motor vehicle. That's why he'd just been pouring over the web pages of *Flog My Motor* on an old laptop. Narrowing his search to accommodate what he considered a not immodest budget, he'd ended up studying the details over and over of a bright yellow vehicle of distinction.

He was ready to literally put the wheels in motion when Marie had turned up at the door. She'd called to collect Freddie's football kit that he'd accidentally left at his dad's, but now needed for a Junior League game on Sunday morning.

'Come in, come in, have a look at this,' said Gavin, enthusiastically leading his ex-wife through the house towards his laptop.

A curious Marie eventually sat down at the table beside him and started to read the web description aloud.

'1995 Ford Transit Mk 5 *Ice Cream Van.* Will start, but ideal for spares and repairs. Price £1300, no offers... incredible!'

'Yes, incredible! That's what I was thinking.'

'No Gavin, I was more thinking *incredible, you must be nuts!* That thing's over a quarter of a century old, for a start.'

'What's the matter with you?' Maybe Gavin had forgotten about Marie's tendency to pee on his chips, especially as far as any of his amazing business imaginings went. Maybe she had a point, based on his dismal track record. But a little encouragement wouldn't go amiss, that's what he thought. 'You're really not seeing it are you? This is a top-quality vehicle, maybe in the need of a little TLC - but it's just the business opportunity I need. Plus, Summer is on its way and what's everybody's favourite sunny days thing? Go on say it!'

She didn't. She just sat down at the dining table, all energy sapped. *Not again,* she inwardly groaned remembering the failed joke shop business that had gone a long way towards killing off their marriage. All she really hoped for out of this was that - whatever Gavin chose to do - he'd manage to keep up with his child maintenance payments.

'Ice cream!' Gavin helped her out with the answer to his last question, a mile wide smile on his face.

'Well, I'll just be keeping out of it then, if it's all the same with you,' said Marie flatly, closing the laptop. 'I'd rather not know about your latest retail master plan after everything we went through last time.'

'Just timing, Marie. Timing!' Today Gavin was irrepressible! 'Ben & Jimmy's started small you know. And now look at them.'

'It's Ben & Jerry's actually.'

'No, you're thinking Tom & Jerry now,' replied Gavin, irrepressibly. 'Easy mistake.

'Have it your way,' said Marie, too disinterested to argue.

'Thank you!' Gavin beamed, feeling good about being right. 'Once I've sold Lizzie and bought this little baby, I'll still have about four hundred quid for stock. All I then need is for the glorious Drabbleton sunshine to do its stuff.'

'Yeah well, lucky for you we enjoy a Mediterranean microclimate here in Lancashire.' Marie smiled at the deadpan cruelty of her own retort, until she noticed she wasn't dampening her ex's ebullience one bit. *Very odd.*

'You're not putting me off, *Little Miss Negative Knickers.* My mind is made up.' He ogled the web picture of the ice cream van. What a money-making machine it was!

'Well, what's made you so cheerful suddenly?' Something was different. Marie needed to know. 'And look at this place. Have you got proper royalty coming round? Or will it be just Queen Alice again?'

'You sound jealous.' Now it was Gavin's turn for a private smile.

'On the happy pills now, are we?' Marie crossed her eyes and grinned inanely. But now Gavin didn't rise to the banter.

'Maybe. But to be honest Alice has been a little unpredictable since her brother got bumped off.' A worry line crossed his brow, and the bouncy bunny in him suddenly quelled. Marie caught onto the mood change.

'I'm not surprised really. We might have all thought him to be the biggest bastard to have walked God's earth, but at the end of the day Bryce Brimstone was her brother.'

'Yeah, I get it,' Gavin mumbled, trying to see it Alice's way.

'But it was a weird coincidence, wasn't it?' Marie's voice was quickening. 'There we all were playing on Freddie's game, pretending to get him knocked off. Then, Sweet Jesus, it only went and really happened.'

She made an explosion sound from the back of her throat and sent her arms and hands stretching to suggest some bomb's massive impact.

'Freaked me out too, for sure,' said Gavin, without vigour. 'But yeah, just a weird coincidence like you say.' He'd thought about it, but had already concluded that there was no point bringing Marie into his tribulations with the Disposals Inc app. No point worrying her - besides, if this were to get nasty then he wouldn't want Freddie anywhere near any danger.

'Oh well,' said Marie, remaining then in sweet oblivion 'It's put everything up in the air for Alberto. Maybe he can get out of the Latvian transfer, not sure. Depends on who takes over the football club, I suppose. Early days...'

'Great Marie, at least that's a glimmer of hope. Better than nothing. It's been a *grand* week in some ways - as you'd say,' added the ex-husband, taken off-track by momentarily remembering his own grand bit of luck only last night.

'I wouldn't go that far,' said Marie, looking puzzled. 'What's that smug look on your face all of a sudden?' She noticed he'd started to grin, hardly on her account, possibly even to blush. 'Come on, I know you too well Gavin Hargreaves.'

'Maybe the curse you left me with has finally been broken.' It was out there!

'What curse? Jeez you do like talkin' out yer arse.'

Gavin was mystified as to why his ex-wife wasn't instinctively on the same page. This was *momentous*.

'The *no sex for twenty-eight months* curse,' he emphasised by deliberately separating each word. 'That swine of a thing. When you left me, you must have cast a wicked spell that I'd never sleep with another woman again.' He wagged a playfully admonishing finger.

'Yeah, evil witch that I am,' Marie disparaged. 'Anyway, don't blame me!'

'Why not?'

'Don't make me say it,' she stalled, but then saw that Mr Smug here might benefit from a bit of Dublin-style straight talking. 'The reason you've not had sex for twenty-eight months is cos you turned into a scruffy, fat bastard with food stains all over yer pants. ...Just a woman's perspective.' She smiled angelically.

'Nah, see,' crowed Gavin, taking her by surprise as he pointed to his trackie bottoms. 'No food stains, freshly sponged today.'

'Congratulations, I'll ring the *Drabbleton Bugle*,' she drily retorted, although secretly a tad impressed. 'But no wonder you're saying Alice is unpredictable if she's gone and slept with you now.

But taking advantage of a vulnerable female is hardly worth getting smug about.'

'Actually Marie, I wouldn't have done that,' came a self-righteous sounding reply. 'Although It was on offer.'

'It?'

'*You know?*' Gavin looked oddly embarrassed. But she knew alright.

'You finally hired a prostitute?' Marie was enjoying the tease.

'Very funny,' Gavin huffed. 'You can sneer, but I'm sort of made up about what happened. Thirty-five is no age for a perfectly able bloke like me to be retiring his tackle. So, two- and a-bit years later, I'm pleased to report that it's finally back in action.'

'Amazing what WD40 can do,' Marie laughed.

'Exactly!' said Gavin, this time happy to share the joke. But then his own smile dimmed. 'But I do feel a bit of a shit about it too…'

Marie widened her eyes, waiting for more. She wasn't used to having marginally interesting conversations with her ex. Gavin cleared his throat and took a deep breath.

'See I slept with Krystyna Kowalski.' Not a familiar name to Marie, as her blank face betrayed. 'Call Centre Manager at Brimstone Mill,' Gavin joined the dots.

'Now then, I suppose if you looked hard enough, the most desperate woman in Drabbleton was there to be found.'

'Desperate? Far from it!' Gavin sniggered in derision. 'She's gorgeous.'

'If you say so,' Marie obviously doubted very much. 'Anyway, I'm very happy for you and the rediscovery of your manhood.'

'Thank you!' *About time*, thought Gavin.

'But go on,' his ex now coaxed coquettishly, wanting all the *goss*. 'I'm interested. What's this so-called gorgeous girl doing getting off with a scruffy old sod like yourself?'

'God obviously loved me for once,' Gavin replied, deflecting Marie's jibe - but counting a few lucky stars that had obviously come his way. 'See, it was Krystyna who actually suggested a one-night stand. She'd been having *man trouble*, long story. I wasn't going to object. But now I'm all Guilty Gavin, because - you probably won't believe me now - I think I've fallen in love with Alice.'

Marie sighed, disappointed with her narrator.

'What are you telling me the Guilty Gavin bit for? I was only after hearing about the sex!' Yep, it had been a long time since the pair had been confidantes, but Marie's interest was likely to quickly wane.

'Well, you and me used to talk,' said Gavin, playing the nostalgia card. 'Truth is though, I'm just looking for a bit of female advice. And seeing as you're here, being female and all, I thought I'd mention it.'

'Mmm,' came the note of scepticism. 'Sounds like you just wanted to let me know you'd broken your duck. Male pride restored!'

'Maybe that too,' Gavin shrugged. He knew that wasn't beneath him in all truth. 'But ignoring my *pathetic male ego...*' - he drew imaginary speech marks around those last words – 'I really don't know what to do.'

'So, you're asking me?' Deadpan again.

'I suppose I am.' He clasped his hands in mock prayer. 'Pretty please.'

'Jeez...' Marie took a mental step back. It had been a long time since anybody had sought her council on matters of the heart. In a way, she even felt flattered. That all said, she reckoned it was time to gather her thoughts. 'Well, if you do love Alice, you just have to ask yourself whether this Krystyna thing was a one off. Or could it happen again - with Krystyna or anyone else, for that matter? If it's just a one off that happened because of one-off circumstances, then grab the love that's on offer from Alice with both hands.'

She sounded definite. Gavin liked that and nodded gratefully.

'You know, it's kinda what I did myself,' Marie then spoke more quietly, as if drifting off on a memory of her own.

'What's that then?' Gavin was gauchely curious.

'Ah, I suppose it won't matter after all these years.' A dismissive hand was waved.

'What? Tell me!' said Gavin giggling, not really expecting anything other than a bit of gossip himself. Marie smiled, staring blankly at the wall, now in a different place altogether.

'The night before my boat sailed over from Dublin - after I'd agreed to make a go of it with you here in England - you'd gone off to bed early, drunk as a skunk. I was staying up with all me mates, making the most of the fond farewells an' all. Anyhow, I was coming out of the bog upstairs and Big Dick Rick O'Connell, an old boyfriend from way back, blocks me way out and asks for a kiss. He tells me I'd always been the love of his life and he was sorry for fucking things up with me. 'Cos, he did, like, he was a proper arse. So, I says, too late Mister. So, he starts blubbering his eyes out, pissed like, telling me he was really sorry about everything. Stupid me, I hugs him in sympathy, but one thing led to another...'

'What thing led to what other?' There was a sudden edge in Gavin's voice. '*Big Dick? Oh Marie!*'

'Well, he did have a lovely cock, I must say. I wasn't going to see that again.'

'You were unfaithful!' the blighted one gasped. *The Sneaky bitch!*

'Jesus Gavin, it was nine, maybe ten years ago.' Marie threw her arms in the air. 'Anyway, we're divorced now, so does it even matter?'

'Course it matters. Our entire marriage was a lie!' Gavin's bottom lip was definitely out.

'Bollocks, will you be listening to the shite that's pouring out of your gob?' She smacked her forehead. 'One, we weren't even married then. And two,' she paused, as if she'd lost track of the second point. But then, no, here it was... 'Two. Our marriage was a loving marriage, Gavin. For a good few years anyway, and that's better than some can say. Plus, we both got a great kid out of it.'

'I'll give you that,' said Gavin, partially reining in the sulk. Marie then looked at him in earnest.

'Good,' she said, emphatically, as animated hands reinforced her subsequent words. 'But what I'm saying is people make little fuck ups that aren't that important in the grander scheme of things. Not when real love is on the line. And as long as they don't make a habit of those little fuck ups - so that lots of little fuck ups turn into *one big fuck up* - then everything should be cool.'

She finally folded her arms, giving them a much-needed rest, sermon over.

'Nice one, Marie,' said Gavin, appreciatively. 'I'll definitely have a think about that.' He was nodding, brain in processing mode.

It was Marie's turn to look a little smug. *How wise am I?*

'But I can't believe you were unfaithful to me in Dublin,' Gavin just had to bleat, spoiling it all.

'Get over it.' No further indulgence was necessary. Marie got to her feet to retrieve Freddie's football kit, most likely from his part-time bedroom. Previous topic now closed.

As she left the room, Gavin's thoughts quickly strayed from romantic complications and back to something far more straightforward - *motor vehicles.* So once again he was staring at the vibrant yellow ice cream van on *Flog My Motor* and imagining glorious sunny days when the whole of Drabbleton would no doubt be turning out for his delicious Mr Whippy.

An annoying notification on his phone then rudely trespassed into his daydream. He grabbed his headset to shut it up. *Damn it!* It was Disposals Inc. Marie being still upstairs he decided to check the message. The AI voice of Igor, the app's Credit Control enforcer, began its broadcast.

'Gavin Hargreaves, you still did not pay your invoice for ...thirty ...thousand ...pounds. According to our Terms & Conditions we can deliver snuffed out corpse to non-paying customers. Say yes now if you understand.'

'Yes,' Gavin whispered into the handset, hoping Marie wouldn't hear. 'You already did that, but yes.'

'You said ...yes. Good. Also, according to Terms & Conditions, Clause thirty-five, sub paragraph eight, I quote: Should the Company wish for the return of any corpse (the goods) previously delivered to the Customer in respect of non-payment, then the goods may be collected by the Company within seventy-two hours of official notification.

Gavin Hargreaves... please consider this message official notification that the goods are to be returned to the Company. Collection due ...*Monday*. You have been allocated an ...*evening* slot.

If you understand, say yes now.'

Gavin shuddered. Nobody had told him the assorted body parts might need to returned. Once again, he kicked himself for not reading those cursed Terms & Conditions, *but who does read them, ever?* His mind had already raced off to the *Star of India* where Dinesh was by now probably adding his final herbs and spices to his Special Curry of the Day.

'That's the day after tomorrow,' he bumbled, realising he was catching his breath. 'Wait. I'm thinking about that. I might not be in then. I've got a dentist's appointment. Yes, that's it, a dentist, yes.'

A brilliant plan. Delay.

'You said yes,' Igor continued routinely. 'Thank you. Collection confirmed.'

The AI hung up and Gavin read the exit screen on the app thanking him, once again, for using Disposals Inc.

'Damn it!' he gulped just as Marie re-entered the room carrying the football kit she'd collected for Freddie.

'OK, that's me,' she said, holding up the successfully retrieved *number nine* jersey, shorts and socks. 'I'm off.'

'Right, see you then,' Gavin muttered without looking up from his handset. He was anxiously trying to track back on the app to see if there was a way to cancel collection of the so-called goods. No luck there, it seemed.

Marie closed the front door behind her, imagining Gavin was miles away on his phone, already sorting out the purchase of that clearly clapped-out ice cream van. *What a dreamer,* she thought. *Won't he ever learn?*

20
- DINNER, BED & BREAKFAST -

By now it was approaching six o'clock and Gavin had decided he'd take a brisk walk up to Dinesh's takeaway to discuss the latest inconvenient intervention from Disposals Inc. He'd already tried ringing, but the *Star of India's* phone was constantly engaged - probably typical for a busy Saturday night, so only to be expected. But he walked on in hope that his friend had maybe delayed the butchering of Brimstone's corpse. Or maybe if there was just a leg or even an arm left, well that would at least be something to surrender. Every little helps.

As Gavin turned the corner at the end of Mayfair Avenue and into Bond Street, a queue of people immediately caught his attention - their thirty or so number trailing beyond the front door of Dinesh's chippy and down past the bookies at the end of the block. Wow, someone was enjoying rich pickings tonight. Not for the first time, Gavin regretted converting his own takeaway into a retro joke shop and missing out on golden nights like this at the till.

As he reached the queue's tail enders, he said hello to Karen O'Malley, a nearby neighbour and ex colleague from the Call Centre - a middle aged lady who, by her near emaciated appearance, looked in need of a slap-up take out.

'Hey, get in line Mr Hargreaves,' she jocularly complained, as Gavin shuffled past her trying read the poster in Dinesh's window, some three shops up the row. 'There's a queue here, you know.'

'I'm not after ordering, Karen - just need to see Dinesh,' he replied with a wave.

'I'll let you off then. As long as you don't bags my order of tonight's special. Only a quid!' Karen's almost gasped with excitement. 'Can't believe he's selling curry dinners for a pound apiece. He'll go bust, surely!'

'Hopefully not! Gavin moved along the line, with Karen's voice trailing behind him.

'Yeah, hopefully not, cos he's a true gent is Dinesh. What a gent!'

It seemed that word had been quickly spreading round Drabbleton of the chippy tea deal of the year, an offer headlined on the handwritten, dayglo green window poster that Gavin could now finally read: *Silly Saturday. Special Curry & Bryce. Only £1.00!!!* He edged further through the queue, finally squeezing into the shop, assuring all the grumblers that he wasn't ordering, just visiting the now very popular owner. Behind the serving counter, Dinesh himself, Mishka and guest server, Cousin Bindra, were all hard at work dishing out serving after serving of tonight's very special offer.

'Gavin, my friend,' Dinesh beamed, very happy at his work, 'how are you?

'Have you got a minute, mate?' Gavin pointed towards the chippy's back room, clearly perplexed.

'You look like you've just seen a ghost,' Dinesh observed. 'But I am very busy now, as you can see.'

He was indeed. Meanwhile, Mishka was handing over another four cartons of tonight's mega-deal to a very happy customer. Then Cousin Bindra, a rotund and jolly looking soul in her mid-fifties, was going big on the sales patter.

'Yes Madam, of course it is Bryce Brimstone in the curry. My dear cousin, Dinesh here, murdered the evil monster and now he is on sale as a Vindaloo.'

'Ha, ha! Very funny,' chuckled Mrs Rowbottom, the regular customer with the snoring cat at home. 'If that were really true, you'd have a queue from here to the Town Hall.'

'But it *is* completely true, Mrs Rowbottom,' insisted a very chipper Cousin Bindra, passing over Mrs R's order. 'Spread the word. Everybody in town who hated Brimstone Bastard, tonight is chance for revenge.'

'I'll be sure to pass it on then, Pet,' the bemused cat lover smiled.

'Ah, Mrs R,' Dinesh then called over. 'How is snoring cat Albert?'

'Brilliant, thank you Dinesh.' She raised an upturned thumb to the takeaway owner/vet. 'That curry powder of yours is worth its weight in gold. Not a peep out of him. In fact, he's so quiet now that on the first night I thought he'd popped his clogs.'

'Excellent, Mrs R. If you need more powder, simply ask.'

'I will, I will,' said Albert's happy owner, waving goodbye.

But Gavin's mood was far out of alignment with all this frivolity. Increasingly flustered, he covered the side of his mouth with a hand and whispered to Dinesh.

'What's she doing, that Cousin Bindra of yours? Is she nuts? She can't be telling everyone you've gone and curried Brimstone!'

'Why not, my friend?' Dinesh replied, completely relaxed.

'Because you'll get arrested for murder, that's why not. Or at least nicked on public health grounds. It is probably illegal to mince and curry up human remains for Saturday supper.'

'Chill, dearest Gavin, chill,' Dinesh tutted, not seeing what all the fuss was about. 'I thought about this same problem very deeply. So, I came up with *double bluff* idea.'

'What?' Gavin was shaking his head.

'Yes, double bluff. If I brazenly tell all customers that this is Bryce Brimstone in lovely Vindaloo recipe, then everybody will suspect I am joking. Nobody will seriously think that I am trying to get away with murder.' He laughed, obviously pleased with his masterplan.

As Gavin tried to process the logic behind his friend's cunning ruse, he was further perplexed by the sight of a marked police car pull into a parking bay just across the street.

'Now you've gone and done it,' he scolded, as Dinesh also spotted the car and immediately felt his confidence evaporate.

'I will carry on with double bluff,' a suddenly nervous voice muttered. 'Everything will be just bobbins.'

Gavin raised an eyebrow. However, neither man could obviously hear the discussion the two officers sat in the front of the now stationary vehicle were having.

'Blimey, what's this queue all about?' wondered the driver, PC Duckworth, as he applied the handbrake.

'He's always busy on a Saturday, is Dinesh,' said regular *Star of India* customer, PC Chabra. 'But I've never seen him this busy.' The queue seemed to be growing by the second.

Just then, a track-suited kid about twelve exited the chippy, loaded carrier bag swinging by his side. He then just happened to run by PC Duckworth's open window.

'Hey son, what's going on in there?' the officer enquired with vague curiosity.

'It's fantastic,' said the young 'un. 'Mr Patel reckons he's gone and chopped up Bryce Brimstone's body and put it in a curry. And it's only a quid a portion.'

The officer recoiled in his seat - could he really believe what he was hearing? PC Chabra beside him seemed to freeze. This was serious stuff.

'A quid?!' Duckworth wheezed, incredulously. 'Only a quid? You're kidding!'

'It's right,' said the kid, running on.

'Bloody hell, mate,' Duckworth said to his shocked passenger. 'We need to be having some of that. *A quid!*'

'I would very much like to gobble up a chunk or two of Brimstone myself,' Chabra nodded. 'He was scumbag swine to my mother at Call Centre. Made her sick with stress.' He then radiated a delighted smile. 'But only a quid as well. Go for it!'

The two officers were now out of their car and Gavin and Dinesh anxiously watched them approach. But both coppers merely waved affably to the two of them as they crossed the road before joining the back of the queue - just two more customers eager to taste the chippy Deal of the Day.

'Better not tell DI Slater about this, or he'll have us!' Duckworth advised his more junior colleague in a whisper.

'Yeah, we'd be done for,' agreed Chabra. 'But all the evidence will very soon be eaten, so try proving that!' He laughed.

'A quid though! Duckworth blurted, disbelief in his eyes. 'Can't get over it.'

Back inside the chippy, realising that the two policemen had simply joined the regular queue, two guilty looking men breathed a little easier once again. It was time for Gavin to ask the question that, by now, he did think would be pointless. He asked anyway.

'Dinesh, is there any part of you know who that you haven't minced up?'

'No, sorry.'

'Just a leg would do?'

'Sorry.'

'A big toe? A little finger even?'

'No, all gone. He minced up like a dream, far more tender than beef. Two hundred servings made. At this rate all sold out by nine o'clock. But why do you ask, my friend?'

Gavin thought about confessing this news to the Disposals Inc app, but this wasn't the time. Besides, thanks to the popularity of Dinesh's own disposal idea, all trace of Brimstone would soon be being processed through the productive digestive systems of two hundred good citizens of Drabbleton.

'Doesn't matter,' he shrugged. 'Anyway, you're busy, I'll leave you to it.'

'Wait, here you are,' Dinesh answered, a sparkle in his eye once more. 'Have this on the house. I couldn't have done it without you!'

Seconds later, Gavin was leaving the *Star of India*, complimentary carton of Curry & Bryce in his hand. So maybe his journey had not been entirely wasted. When he got home, he'd certainly enjoy tucking into this meaningful little feast. Even better, Rocky the dog might have miraculously turned up at Bob's house with Brimstone's filched arm. At least that would be something to surrender. And it was about time he'd heard something about Bob himself too, who was also still missing following his railway misadventure.

'Evening officers,' Gavin then chirped in the manner of a guy without a care in the world, casually passing the still queuing policemen.

'Everything OK with the car today, Sir?' Chabra asked, recognising the chap from last night's jump start episode.

'Yes thanks,' Gavin winked. 'Nice to know we've got Drabbleton coppers when we need 'em.'

'We do our best,' replied Duckworth, lapping up any praise going. 'We certainly do our best.'

⋆

As the hungry folk of the town were sating their appetites on delicious Curry & Bryce, Bob Horsefield had finally regained consciousness over at Drabbleton General Hospital. Nurse Jayne Talbot was back on shift on Ward Three and had called for the duty junior doctor to have a look at her newly awakened patient.

'This is Mr Horsefield,' said the nurse, introducing Bob to Dr Taraji Jamac, a slender figure, looking slightly drowned in her light blue, NHS standard issue, medical scrubs.

'Hello Mr Horsefield, Nurse Talbot here tells me you have just woken up,' she smiled.

Bob was certainly looking a bit groggy, propped up in his bed, sipping on a glass of water.

'I've been out for a bit, haven't I?' He seemed to be trying to focus his eyes.

'Your body has just been recovering, so it seems,' said the young doctor. 'Are you in any pain?'

The patient appeared to be running a mental check through his bits and bobs, checking all departments were in order.

'No, not really,' he finally mumbled. 'My back's a bit achy, that's all. But nothing new there.'

Dr Jamac shone a pen torch into Bob's eyes and then listened to his chest with her stethoscope.

'He has been coughing quite a bit,' offered Nurse Talbot, just as the junior doctor seemed a little concerned by the stethoscope's findings.

'Mmm,' Jamac mused. Well, Nurse here will see if we can get you out of bed and then maybe best to take you off to X-Ray to check for anything broken,' she calmly continued. 'But let's have a look at that chest too. A CT scan - can you arrange for that, please Nurse.'

'It's just a routine cough,' said Bob, not really wanting any fuss. 'It's me back that's hurting if anything.'

'Well, you were found unconscious in a railway wagon. If you *fell* into it, I'm not surprised you've got a few aches.'

Bob shrugged. It was a possibility.

'Can you actually remember how you got into that railway wagon, Mr Horsefield?'

Dr Jamac looked at Bob suspiciously, wondering if the old man had a bit of the mischief about him. Just like her own Grandad, she was thinking, taking on late life adventures that could quickly take him way out of his depth.

But Bob was away with his own thoughts now, though definitely struggling to form any kind of concrete recollection.

'I remember being on the bridge...'

'A railway bridge?'

'Yeah, at Baker Street,' he scratched his head. 'Can't remember why. Long way from home, that is.' He looked at his attendants hoping that they might fill in the gaps, but no help there. 'Mavis would have been wondering where I was.'

'You were mentioning Mavis in your sleep,' said Jayne softly. 'Is she your wife?'

Bob had another good think.

'That's right. She must be.' Then he looked suddenly fretful. 'I think she's leaving me though. For Ken the plumber.' His expression dropped. 'I was so down.'

Dr Jamac's own face creased with concern.

'Sir, you didn't jump off the railway bridge, did you?'

'Don't know,' Bob replied as honestly as he could, only snippets of last night's accident flickering incoherently in his mind. 'If you say I ended up in a wagon, maybe I did jump. I'm stupid enough to do that, I suppose.'

'Oh dear,' said Dr Jamac, writing a note and looking perplexed. 'I'm sorry I have to ask you this, Mr Horsefield. But do you have suicidal thoughts now?'

'Don't be daft,' Bob laughed. 'Don't you go worrying Mavis with that nonsense.'

'You did just say you might have jumped off a railway bridge on purpose.'

Dr Jamac scrutinised Bob's face carefully. *What was going on in the old head of this patient?*

'I don't really remember,' came the crotchety reply. 'I've no idea what happened really. You tell me.'

'What else *can* you remember?' asked the doctor, a little less patiently in return.

'How do you mean?'

'You know, just general stuff,' Nurse Talbot helped out. 'Like where do you live, for example?' She smiled at him kindly. Bob seemed to like her better than this other one.

'Oh, that's easy enough,' he smiled back to the nice nurse. 'Number 21 Buttermilk Avenue, Riverstone, Drabbleton.'

★

Back at Mayfair Avenue, Gavin had found no sign of Bob, Rocky or a severed right arm. Dogs and lost limbs aside, he was growing particularly concerned for his neighbour's safety, yet felt there was nothing he could really do but wait. The old pensioner had never felt the need to buy a mobile, so the obvious easy option was out. And in the circumstances, Gavin felt he could hardly go to the police having to explain Bob's unfortunate plunge into a freight wagon. So, he resolved to give it another day or so, by which time he'd convinced himself the old bugger would probably have turned up. A small stroke of luck would now come in handy too, for sure.

In the meantime, by way of distraction, he'd long since polished off his Curry & Bryce, savouring every little chunk of meat while wondering all along exactly which bit of Brimstone's body he had been guiltlessly devouring. A nose, maybe a finger? Or hopefully a delicious slice of old todger, in honour of Krystyna, of course!

Even better, the satisfying meal had propelled him on to a productive evening too, putting aside his immediate worries just for now. He'd been on the *Flog My Motor* website again and made a next day appointment to view the ice cream van of his dreams. He'd then - not without regret - listed his dear Lizzie in the For Sale section. What a top buy for some lucky motorist! He'd therefore been quite unsurprised when two punters had been immediately bidding against each other for ownership of his quality marque. Another step on the way to seeing the dawning of his Ben & Jimmy's ice cream empire.

It was now time to call Alice. He'd been missing her this evening - dearly so. Even though more blokey, interfering recollections of a beautiful, naked female body - owned by one Krystyna Kowalski - were unhelpfully sullying his attempts at purer thoughts. But Gavin knew he just had to forget about that blue moon, one night stand. He could imagine achieving long term happiness with Alice, who ordinarily was the only woman to occupy his thoughts in a romantic sense. But together, they did need to get over the complicated circumstances of her brother's death. The only way they'd do that is by talking. He picked up his phone and flicked through to Contacts.

'Hi, it's Alice. I can't take your call right now but leave a message and I'll be right back to you. Thanks!'

For the third time tonight, he'd been channelled straight through to voicemail. Was she ignoring him? His insides turned over as he suspected that maybe she was. He then spoke tentatively into his own handset.

'Hi Alice, it's me again. *Again, again.*' He hesitated, laughing nervously. 'I seem to keep calling at the wrong time. ...Anyway, it would be great to hear from you. That's it really.'

He killed the call and sighed. A *mixed-up fuck-up* that's what he told himself he was. But a chance of finding love, here in Drabbleton, wasn't to be sniffed at. So, whatever it was going to take, he was determined to get things back on track with Alice.

★

Bob had been kept in Drabbleton General overnight for further observation. The benefits of landing in a freight wagon full of soft sand had been clearly demonstrable as he'd passed the X-Ray and a physiotherapist's inspection without a hitch. Well in terms of broken bones and injuries, that is. Dr Jamac, on the other hand, was very concerned about the shadow that the CT scan had revealed to be showing up on the patient's right lung.

Concern over Bob's mental vulnerability also remained. A chat with his next of kin, or close family member, was in order. But the hospital had been unable to contact his wife, who Bob had seemed so keen to get home to, by using the only number the old patient could remember. Of course, they wouldn't be able to contact Mavis on that number anyway. Unknown to them, they'd been ringing Bob's own house at Mayfair Avenue and, of course, nobody was at home.

But by the tea-time on the Sunday, Bob was seeming much perkier and more positive, despite him having had a serious private chat with Dr Jamac - about what was in fact a cancer diagnosis. *It's just a routine cough,* he'd kept convincing himself, despite that talk. Nevertheless, he had promised to come back to the hospital on Tuesday morning to see a specialist. For now, though, there was no urgent reason to keep him occupying a much in demand hospital bed. Dr Jamac discharged him, on the basis that the ambulance crew should deliver him home to a caring and able wife.

'And don't forget that Wednesday morning appointment, Mr Horsefield. Nine o'clock sharp in Oncology,' the junior doctor had badgered as Bob finally left the ward, assisted by porter and wheelchair.

'I'll be there. Can't wait,' said Bob smiling drily. But in truth, he was far more engrossed with the thought of being on his way back home to Mavis.

Meanwhile, over at Buttermilk Avenue, Mavis herself was obliviously finishing off watching *Gardening on Sunday* on the BBC. Bob Horsefield, as always, was the furthest thing from her mind as she made a note to get on with planting out her bedding flowers - those colourful bursts of geraniums and chrysanthemums that brought her such joy. Even though her Ken once seemed to have such a better knack than her of making them flourish, that was all a memory now. Because her second husband had passed away some three years ago. She'd now been left as a widow with sole custodianship over the health and welfare of the borders and pots in her modest, but well-stocked, garden. Quite a responsibility - well that's how Mavis saw it. She did miss Ken.

As she switched off her TV and shuffled through to the kitchen to make a pot of tea, through a front window she noticed an ambulance pulling into her avenue. She was momentarily curious, but then carried on with her business, not thinking much more about it.

'Right, here we are then,' said Ollie, the lanky young paramedic sat in the back of the Drabbleton General ambulance with Bob. 'Buttermilk Avenue, home sweet home, yes?'

'Aye, that's it,' said Bob, sitting up on a bench seat with a blanket wrapped around his shoulder. 'Home sweet home.'

Back doors then swung open, Ollie was soon lending a hand to Bob as he descended the two steel steps at the rear of the vehicle and down onto the road. Then, arm in arm, the two men edged their way up the tarmac garden path towards Mavis's front door.

'Have you got your key handy?' asked Ollie, speaking to Bob in a slow, singing voice as though his latest passenger was a simpleton.

'No, sorry,' said Bob, looking puzzled.

'Have you checked all your pockets?' Ollie pressed, patting his own pockets, just so his charge would know where to look.

Bob nodded, *yes, he had.*

'Alright then, you've checked all your pockets. Well done you.' Ollie condescended, smiling. 'Let's ring the doorbell then and give your Mavis a lovely surprise.'

'She'll have been worried about me,' said Bob, frowning as he inwardly chastised himself for causing concern.

After a short wait the ample figure of septuagenarian Mavis appeared at the door, along with her curious little poodle.

'Yes?' she enquired, a little mystified by the presence of her callers.

'Mavis, is it?' asked Ollie, maintaining his patronising tone of voice. 'Look who I've brought home for you.'

The poodle stepped out to sniff Bob's lower trouser legs and yapped twice with unbridled enthusiasm. Must have picked up a whiff of Rocky.

'See, at least your little dog is pleased to see you,' Ollie smiled.

'Who is this?' asked Mavis, looking at her obviously unrecognisable ex, distrust etched across a stern face.

'Mavis, it's me, Bob,' replied the apparent prodigal husband. 'You must have been worried sick that I didn't come home. But it's alright now. I'm OK.'

'Bob?' Mavis started to carefully examine the face at the door. With piercing eyes, she went to work, slowly peeling back the years, the wrinkles and the hair loss. Finally, the ravages of time were defeated, and a look of sudden realisation crossed her own face. '*Bob Horsefield?*'

'Yes, of course, Bob Horsefield. Your husband, you big daft thing!' He laughed indulgently and winked at Ollie as if to make him see that she was just joshing them both.

'See here, Mr Ambulance Man,' Mavis went on, but curtly, maybe taking this joshing thing too far for Bob's liking. 'This indeed *used* to be my husband. But we were divorced some forty odd years ago. I haven't seen Bob Horsefield since.'

'Awkward,' said Ollie, most confused. 'Now, have you been telling Dr Jamac porky pies then Bob?' The discharged patient had obviously lost the plot.

'What's the matter Mavis?' asked Bob, ignoring the young medic. 'I don't reckon you're thinking straight.'

'Me not thinking straight?' Mavis's pained expression spelt only exasperation. 'I think you must have gone quite mad!'

'He has had a dangerous fall,' explained Ollie in mitigation. 'Off a railway bridge and into a passing train, so I'm told. It's a miracle he's still alive.'

Again, Bob merely looked lost. Ollie tried his best to help by speaking his next words extra slowly and mouthing them with exaggerated expression, as if talking to a geriatric deaf person.

'I - said - it's - a - miracle - you - are - still - alive.'

'Oh dear,' said Mavis, now starting to show a modicum of concern. Bob merely looked heartbroken that he was being disowned on his own doorstep.

'Come on you, back to the van,' said Ollie, more business-like now. 'I'll phone Dr Jamac and see what she says.'

He tried to pull Bob away, back down the drive, but the old man wasn't for budging.

'I'm sorry Mavis, I won't jump off a railway bridge ever again. I promise.' He started to snivel.

'Erm, young man,' the old lady intervened, stepping off her doorstep and catching Ollie's arm as he'd turned away. 'Are you saying Bob here tried to commit suicide?'

The medic shuffled his feet, uncomfortable at the bluntness of that question.

'We're trained not to use the *'S' word* in front of them,' he mildly admonished. Mavis's winced, recognising her insensitivity. 'But yeah, looks like he tried to top himself alright,' Ollie confirmed breezily, seeming happy to have cleared that one up. Then he put his nose virtually up against Bob's face. 'You did, didn't you? *I - said - you - tried - to - top - yourself!*'

The medic then turned aside, so that Bob wouldn't hear and muttered to himself. 'Bloody nutter.' But Mavis heard alright, and she tutted in disapproval.

'So, aren't you going to find out where he really lives?' she probed.

'Not my job,' said Ollie, dispassionately. 'He needs his old head looking at by a doc.'

'Mayfair Avenue, that used to be where he lived,' offered the former Mrs Horsefield, helpfully. 'When we were married, that is.'

The gangly paramedic raised his eyebrows, as if grateful for that possible breakthrough information.

'Ring - a- bell - Bob? May- fair Av- en- ue?' Ollie then stared into dimming eyes, checking to see if any lights were on at all. Didn't look like it, as Bob silently rotated his head from side to side.

Mavis looked anxious. 'Where's he going to end up if he doesn't even know where he lives?'

'No hospital beds tonight, except for emergencies. That much I do know.' Ollie checked his watch. 'This time on a Sunday, I expect he'll end up in a homeless hostel or something until them in charge find out more about him.'

'I see.'

'I don't want to go to a hostel. I want to stay here with Mavis.' Bob folded his arms and stamped a foot, regressing to toddlerdom.

'But she's not your wife, is she?' Ollie tilted his head, eying Mavis as if to acknowledge they had both realised by now that they were dealing with an utter fruit cake. Although Mavis herself was no longer sharing the ambulance crew member's faded tolerance.

'Right then,' she announced in a no-nonsense manner, straightening her frame in the doorway. 'I've been in public service myself for thirty years. Firefighter.' Ollie immediately nodded, impressed. 'I've seen many a worse crisis than this. And I certainly don't want to see a potentially suicidal old man, someone who has obviously lost his memory, being shunted off to a hostel. Confused and lonely as he obviously is.'

Bob's eyes started to sparkle in hope. Mavis had more to say.

'Not when I have a small but perfectly adequate spare bedroom. I'll do you a deal. I will take him in just for tonight and in the meantime you people should contact the police and find out who his real family are.'

'That's a very kind offer, Mavis,' Ollie replied, taken aback. 'But I'll have to check with Dr Jamac.'

'Well, you do that, young man. But also tell your doctor that one night is my limit. Then he'll have to go.' She linked arms with her ex-husband. 'Come along Bob, please do come in for now.'

Bob Horsefield then entered the hallowed portal of 21 Buttermilk Avenue, an address he'd been annually stalking for four decades but had never actually set foot in. His face had illuminated, and he was close to tears. In his mind, right at that moment, he was finally home.

21
- NECKS ON THE LINE -

Across the road from the Brimstone's Knightsbridge lavish mansion stood another equally decadent neoclassical property - one belonging to billionaire oligarch and Russian mafia boss, Vladimir Volkov. Or *Mr* Volkov, as he liked to be addressed, even by those closest to him. He was a stocky man of middling height, some sixty years of age, as strong as an ox it was said. Using his own squat hands, he had personally throttled by the throat both the occasional failures he had encountered in his own organisation as well as a selection of assorted enemies - those that had foolishly decided to get in his way over the years.

These staged stranglings, to be witnessed by all available staff, were often carried out right here in the grand entrance hall to his London mansion. His victims were to kneel, blindfolded and bound, on the terrazzo floor at the foot of his Hollywood style sweeping staircase. As a henchman removed the blindfold, they would then see Volkov ceremoniously descending the stairs, penetrating their eyes with his own. The man, who in Madrid once strangled a bull, would then take pleasure over the next three or four minutes throttling his latest human victim, a comparatively easy task but one to be relished for sure. Every gasp, every dying gurgle and rasp was lapped up by the righteous executioner in the name of his own take on justice. And at least these sinners had the pleasure of dying with dignity under the opulence of tiered crystal glass chandeliers, not shot like dogs in some scrubby alleyway. A noble way to die, Mr Volkov reasoned. *Civilised.*

But today, no executions were scheduled and only Dimitri and Lewis waited at the foot of that very same staircase as Mr Volkov descended in an apparent good mood, the elegantly poised Roxanne on his arm. The pair had just completed their first business meeting and from the smiles on both of their faces, Dimitri could see it had gone well.

'Dimitri, you did not tell me that Roxanne here was so beautiful and charming,' said Mr Volkov, reaching the foot of the stairs. 'But not only this, she is very shrewd too. A woman of such sound judgement.'

Roxanne bowed in deference. 'It is a pleasure for someone as inexperienced as I to learn from such a wise business head, Mr Volkov,' she smoothed.

'I suspect you are a very fast learner,' the oligarch chuckled. But he then suddenly appeared a little less pleased as he viewed his illegitimate son's attempt at looking the part in regulation black suit. 'Do up your tie, Lewis. *Standards*, boy!'

Lewis quickly adjusted the offending neckwear. He wasn't taking well to this, his first tie ever. Mr Volkov then turned again towards Roxanne, attempting to force a smile once again across a craggy face.

'I take it your meeting has been productive?' his senior operative politely enquired.

'Ah yes, Dimitri. Dearest Mrs Brimstone has just kindly agreed to invest £10 million pounds into our growing online business venture, Disposals Inc.'

'A most generous sum, Roxanne,' Dimitri nodded in approval.

'Not generous,' Roxanne purred. 'I expect to double my money in three years. If Mr Volkov's projections are realised.' She smiled respectfully towards him. 'Which I am sure they will be.'

Volkov then eyed his chief henchman with purpose.

'Dimitri, it is important for you to know that this money will be realised by liquidating the assets of the Northern England division of the Brimstone business empire.'

'Liquidating, you say?'

'Yes, closing everything down. Selling all assets as soon as possible.'

'Of course,' Dimitri finally caught on.

'That sounds like a lot of people will be losing their jobs, Mr Volkov, Sir.' Lewis's nervous voice had piped up, its owner immediately wishing it hadn't.

'And that matters why?' Volkov sneered in disapproval. 'You are boy of tender years, Lewis. Clearly too much of your mother's son. But life will teach you that business is not a place for sentiment.'

The young man looked to the floor, hoping there was a stone there to crawl under.

'I'd just nuke Drabbleton and everybody in it if it were up to me,' Roxanne interjected, adding what she hoped would be light relief. She laughed. 'That would be doing the rest of the UK a favour in my opinion.'

'Ha ha, very good my dear,' Volkov concurred. 'But even my extensive business reach does not stretch to nuclear weapons.' He paused to mull over that novel idea. 'Well not yet anyway!'

They all soaked in the moment of amusement, even a still awkward Lewis. Then Volkov was immediately back to business.

'So, I understand there might be a problem recovering the body of Mr Bryce Brimstone?' He keenly surveyed Dimitri's face for the slightest sign of duplicity in any reply.

'No. No problem, Sir,' his confident foot soldier replied. Dimitri had long since learned never to show hesitation in front of Mr Volkov. Hesitation was weakness. 'We are collecting corpse on Monday evening. Everything has been arranged by our AI inside Disposals Inc.'

'You are sure about this?' Volkov probed, as Roxanne had previously expressed less certainty to him on the same subject. 'Mrs Brimstone will need her husband's body to secure a death certificate, the pathway to releasing our investment monies.'

'Absolutely sure, Mr Volkov,' Dimitri barked, like an obedient Marine on parade addressing his drill sergeant.

'Excellent.' The oligarch acknowledged his lieutenant with the wave of a hand. *At ease!* Then with that his mood seemed to lighten. He pulled out a mobile phone from his jacket pocket.

'Now Lewis, your first mission has gone well,' he smiled to the trainee. 'A successful hit, yes?'

'Yes Sir,' Lewis seemed to gush with pride.

'Yes, very good.' Volkov was scrolling on his handset.

'Thanks,' he added, only to see his father raise an eyebrow... 'I mean thanks, Sir.' The eyebrow dropped; all due respect paid.

'Yes, I have been looking at the archive photographs on the app.' Volkov was flicking through the images of multiple assassinated victims, knowing their number was increasing by the day as Disposals Inc steadily grew in popularity. 'Yes, this one,' he paused, viewing Northern England's inaugural hit. 'Very good, Lewis, a bullet between the eyes. But it seems your youthful enthusiasm got the better of you with that unnecessary axe to the head. And what is this polythene - or whatever it is - wrapped around the target's head?' Volkov looked at his phone from multiple angles, puzzling over the photograph's irregular details.

'Oh, that wasn't me, that was the other people,' Lewis gauchely replied with a big grin. Dimitri sent him silent daggers. *Idiot!*

'Other people? What other people?' Volkov thundered. 'Why wasn't I told about this Dimitri?'

'The assassination was successful, Sir. The client was happy.' The senior hitman looked to Roxanne for confirmation, an uneasy appeal for help.

'I did not know about others' involvement either, Dimitri,' Roxanne snapped. 'What is going on?' She was certainly throwing no lifeline.

'Indeed, Mr Sidorov. Explain.' Volkov looked ready to literally explode.

Dimitri cast a sideways look at Lewis that was again meant to kill.

'It seems that Mr Bryce Brimstone was very unpopular man,' he continued, trying to sound measured and business-like. 'It seems we were not the only professional killers hired that evening to take him out. Lewis indeed carried out his shot well. But then he was overpowered by others who decapitated the victim.'

'Decapitated? That is awful,' Roxanne reeled in shock. 'I was clearly told it was to be a single bullet to the head. OK, I knew about the axe and stuff, but decapitation? No!'

'This is not happy client!' Mr Volkov complained, putting a comforting arm around the unsettled female beside him.

'My sincere apologies, Roxanne. And to you Mr Volkov.' Dimitri bowed his head in contrition. 'Although, it was the other gang of professional killers who took things too far, not our team.'

'So where were you during this blatant hijacking of our business interests?' The fuming oligarch pulled a scornful face at his failure of a charge. Dimitri continued to keep his cool, humbly adding to his explanation.

'I allowed Lewis to take job alone, as it was kindergarten level.'

'Understandable,' Volkov replied, giving the junior hitman the once over in a way that suggested all expectations were low.

'I waited close by, of course, but then came to his assistance when I suspected he was in trouble. My suspicions were correct, so I burst into room. Then followed a crazy gun fight, during which time I risked my life to rescue Lewis and secure corpse of Mr Brimstone.'

'Is this true, Lewis?' Volkov abruptly quizzed.

At this point even Lewis, out of his depth as he was, could work out he had a simple choice. Either go along with Dimitri's embroidering of the tale. Or watch his mentor - and even himself - face dire consequences. He decided on the former for an easier life all round.

'Yes, Sir. Dimitri came in, all guns blazing.' He mimed two shooters in active combat with the fingers of each hand. 'He saved my life.'

'Really?' Volkov replied, not entirely convinced. He addressed Dimitri again. 'So how many did you take out? Ex *Spetsnaz* trained killer that you are?'

Lewis looked startled. *Please, no more lies!*

'They were very skilled operatives, Sir. Probably ex-CIA or MI5. It was my one gun versus three. They escaped.'

'What, *all* of them?' Volkov had never known his most valued hitman to come away with such a poor return. He huffed and grumbled to himself.

'Yes Sir. Sorry...' Dimitri was watching his boss pace the floor - never a good sign.

'You would recognise them again?'

'I would, yes,' said Lewis, hoping to be helpful.

'Yes, of course,' Dimitri assented as firmly as he could. At which point he wanted the earth to swallow him up. He knew Volkov was going to be speaking his mind. It wouldn't be pretty.

'This is an utter embarrassment to our business,' the oligarch snarled. 'We want people across the world to have the confidence to make Disposals Inc first choice for handling their everyday assassination needs. We need to be a quiet and efficient service, no-fuss, no hitches. And in this very early, reputation building period, you have allowed another gang to muscle in on our territory. What is more, they have seen your faces!'

Volkov stopped to take his breath. His doctors had warned him against getting excited like this. Dodgy heart, and all.

'Are you feeling quite well?' asked Roxanne, noticing the flushed face and suddenly strained breathing of her new business partner.

'Yes dear, I am fine. But thank you.' Volkov dabbed a white handkerchief across a perspiring forehead. But then he steadied himself and was ready for more.

'Lewis, pray tell - has Dimitri here even bothered to teach you the most basic principle of our operations?'

'Not sure, Sir.' Lewis was trembling.

'Yes, Lewis,' Dimitri interjected desperately, now miming *Charades* style. 'You know. Two words. First word, *no*. Second word, w...' He pursed his lips in the *double-u* shape.

'Erm, ...w ...w. Erm, ...worries?' Lewis fist pumped. He had cracked it. 'Yeah, *no worries.*'

'Not *no worries*, Lewis. It is *no witnesses*, cretin!' Dimitri face palmed himself.

Volkov tutted. *Such a shambles.*

'Please do not call my son cretin, Dimitri, even though he is acting like one. I am so disappointed in you.'

'I apologise, Mr Volkov.' Again, Sidorov bowed in deference.

'Should I accept pathetic apology? Let me consider.' Volkov eyed Dimitri up and down with disdain, firstly for botching a simple mission, secondly for trying to conceal his incompetence and thirdly now - perhaps the worst misdemeanour of all - for finally showing fear in his eyes. Never show fear!

'Mr Sidorov, please kneel down,' he requested with mock politeness. Dimitri made a silent gesture begging for mercy. 'I said, on your knees,' the oligarch growled - at which point his henchman meekly acquiesced. Volkov then seemed to be gathering his thoughts as he slowly circled the kneeling minion like a vulture encircling its helpless prey. For a few seconds he said nothing, quite aware that silence only increased the tension in the room. He had played out this scene many times. Roxanne and Lewis seemed to hold their breath, smothered by the unease. Then he spoke:

'Mr Sidorov, you have been a trusted Number Two to me for many years. But this is your biggest failure to date. Are you losing it, my friend?'

'No, Mr Volkov,' came the mumbled reply of a man wondering if he had already been condemned.

'No?' Once more the interrogator paused, letting silence work its cruel effect. He then stood astride the trailing legs of his kneeling quarry, taking Dimitri's neck from behind. He seemed to be caressing it tenderly as he smiled. 'See how frail the human neck is, even on one as strong as you. ...So tempting.'

'Please give me one final chance, Mr Volkov,' Dimitri beseeched, believing he was pleading for his life. 'I can rectify everything.'

'Sometimes giving people a final chance is merely a state of denial that the person you have trusted will only fail again,' Volkov tutted. 'It is weakness. Do you think I am weak, Mr Sidorov?'

'No, Sir. Certainly not.'

'You are right.'

He then slowly squeezed Dimitri's neck, applying fractions of increased pressure by each second, eking out the pleasure for himself - and the pain for his victim. After half a minute the first choking sounds began. More pressure was applied by the vice-like grip until Dimitri began to convulse, a dreadful rasping noise escaping from his constricted throat. Roxanne and Lewis both felt nauseous, each wanting to flee the room, neither daring to do so.

Then a casual release. Dimitri fell forward onto his hands, gasping for breath.

'Only because of your loyal service do I ignore my instincts today,' Volkov asserted, cleaning the sweat from his hands with the handkerchief. 'I value loyalty. But all credits in that respect are now spent. Understand?'

At this point, a reply was physically beyond Dimitri, still gulping for air as he was.

'I said, do you understand?' Volkov kicked his henchmen's supporting arms off the floor, so that a face smashed down against terrazzo floor tiles.

'Of course,' Dimitri finally managed to mutter.

'Good. I will give you a moment to compose yourself and then we will continue our conversation,' he scorned, before then turning to Roxanne with the sweetest of smiles. 'I do apologise for that show of slight unpleasantness, my dear. In my organisation, we call that kind of thing *showing people who is boss.* Unpleasant, but necessary.'

'Yes, I understand,' Roxanne smiled in return, though clearly still rattled. Volkov smiled again, then returned the handkerchief to his Saville Row tailored jacket.

'And do you understand why that was necessary, Lewis?' He caught his illegitimate son's eye, hoping he had not inwardly crumbled.

'Yes Sir, Mr Volkov. You were showing people who is boss.'

'Very good, Lewis. You learn.' It seemed that the disciplinarian father was relieved that the young man seemed to be showing at least a little gumption. There was hope for him yet. Then, to the surprise of both his son and Roxanne, he began to help Dimitri back onto his feet.

'OK Mr Sidorov, playtime over, up you get. Come on.' Two outstretched arms were accepted and the previously fallen henchman was hoisted until he was now upright again, towering over his boss, but feeling very small. Volkov hugged him passionately. 'We are Russian businessmen in a weak country. We must show our strength together.'

'Thank you, Sir,' said Dimitri, returning the hug - with admittedly less gusto.

'Good, very good!' Volkov concluded, patting the back of his still best agent, now restored to duty. 'Water for Mr Sidorov,' he ordered of Lewis pointing to a water jug and glass sitting on an Italianate table nearby. The much-needed liquid was quickly delivered - and gratefully received.

'Refresh yourself, Mr Sidorov. For duty begins again. I order you to return to Drabbleton as soon as possible. You must seek out the rival assassins and wipe them out. What sort of organisation are they? Torture them before killing them - so that we know everything.

And that local nobody I hear you tried to frame for Mr Brimstone's murder. Stupid idea. He must be eliminated also. Let us forget that Disposals Inc were ever involved in this bungled assassination. It is so potentially damaging to our reputation. It is therefore damage limitation time.'

By now, Dimitri had composed himself and was trying to look his serious best. Lewis viewed him in awe. *Mental strength man, respect!'*

Then, Roxanne unexpectedly interrupted, her host gallantly giving way. 'Mr Volkov, I would like to accompany these two to ensure your orders are carried out. It is my money - *our* money at stake.'

'Excellent idea, my dear,' Volkov replied, admiring the determined spirit of his latest business partner. 'You can be my eyes and ears.' He smiled at her with unbridled admiration.

'So then, Dimitri. Return to Drabbleton with Lewis and Roxanne - knowing she is my eyes and ears. You know what to do?'

'Yes, Mr Volkov,' came the efficient sounding reply. 'Recover corpse, find other crime gang and eliminate. Find all who know about this particular Disposals Inc operation and eliminate.'

Volkov turned now to the young man, one doing his best to take all this in.

'What does this mean, Lewis?'

'No witnesses, Sir?' Finally, a confident and strong reply.

'Very good, Lewis. No witnesses.' Volkov silently applauded and smiled. But his face soon straightened again as he addressed his top field agent. 'But Dimitri, if you fail in this you will be meeting me here again at the foot of these very stairs. But the outcome would be most likely less favourable for you. Do you understand?'

Sidorov inwardly shuddered. 'Yes, Mr Volkov, I understand.'

Roxanne noticed the steeliness in her lover's eyes. She approved. This was a man who surely would not fail a second time. Volkov silently concurred.

'I am so pleased we understand each other,' the finally pacified oligarch concluded, turning away to walk deeper into the house. 'I wish your operation every success.'

★

The iconic 99 cone, with its waves of soft serve vanilla ice cream, topped off with a Cadbury's chocolate flake and raspberry sauce, had been the emblem of Gavin's childhood summer memories. Those were the heady days when ice cream vans, with their jangling chimes singing out, would drag people out onto the streets as surely as the Pied Piper of Hamelin attracted his vermin. But then along had come supermarkets and giant domestic fridge freezers. Folk didn't need to go chasing pastel coloured diesel vans down the street if they wanted their ice cream fix - they just needed to open a cabinet door in the kitchen and sweet relief would be duly provided.

But one thing domestic ices have never properly replaced - and that is the 99 Cone. Just too hard to manufacture and store. The 99 can only be ever properly made then and there by a *bone fide* ice cream vendor in possession of a fully operational Mr Whippy machine. And so, Gavin reckoned that now was exactly the time to cash in on what we all must surely believe we have lost. On a hot summer's day, how the good citizens of Drabbleton must have been missing a regular and genuine 99 - its rapidly thawing ice cream and runny raspberry sauce dribbling down hands and even wrists. The delicious race to lick and devour it before the whole thing melts - oh, and then the chocolate, *divine*, but crumbling always onto any clean-on clothes, especially white, staining them for fun! Has there ever a been a more satisfying edible indulgence as the ice cream van 99?

Well Gavin didn't think so anyway. That is why he had chosen this particular model of ice cream van - as not many of them have an eight-foot high, plastic moulded 99 Cone fastened to its roof. *What a marketing ploy.* The punters wouldn't be able to resist. OK, they weren't enamoured much by the giant clown's spinning bow tie illumination that he had installed on his joke shop's roof. But put a bow tie up against a 99 and there is really no contest, the nation's favourite cone winning every time. Therefore, looking back, while he still thought his previous bow tie marketing stunt had merit, you've just got to have the right product. *Schoolboy error.*

So yesterday - the Sunday - had been a day of mixed emotions for him. He'd had to say a sad goodbye to reliable servant, Skoda Lizzie, sold at the upper end of his price estimation. But then he'd said a happy hello to the new mode of transport in his life - one that could also hopefully provide a livelihood - the ice cream van he'd already christened Raspberry, despite its bright yellow paint job. Well, its registration plate featured the letters RSB set together. So Raspberry, after his favourite flavour of ice cream sauce, seemed to be the logical, creative choice. Gavin always thought motor vehicles needed a name and to be treated like treasured pets. Only then would they agree to occasionally start.

This morning, he'd been at the cash and carry stocking up - quite an expense, but he could cover it thanks to the cash received for Lizzie. But now it was already the Monday lunchtime and Gavin had decided to take his new prized possession off to the Town Hall. It was Alice's first day at work there as Tourist Development Manager and he'd hoped to pop in and see her at the now open *Drabbleton Cotton Town* exhibition. All being well they might even be able to take in a spot of lunch at Ted's greasy spoon cafe, if she could take a break. After that he could show off his fantastic new van and treat Alice to its very first 99 Cone served under new management.

So it was, that by mid-day, he was swinging his bright yellow magic machine into Town Hall Square. No sooner had he parked up in a vacant bay and started saying his usual hello to the statue there of James Brimstone, there'd been a tap on the glass window of his van's serving hatch. It was his first ever customer - and he wasn't even officially open yet. Promising. He quickly sidled into the back of the vehicle and slid back the hatch.

'Hello, can I help you?' he enquired of a petite grey lady in her eighties.

'Could I please have a vegan choc ice,' she smiled, ignoring Gavin's hand-scrawled menu on the side of the van. It was still very much a *work in progress* menu. '99 Cone, single flake, £1.50. 99 Cone, double flake, £2.00.' That was pretty much it for now.

'Sorry, I've never heard of a vegan choc ice.'

'Oh, surely you have. Made with plant-based milk.' A passively condescending reply.

'No, sorry. I can do you a 99,' Gavin chirped, always trying to help a customer with a valid alternative.

'Is that made from plant-based milk?' Same tone.

'I don't think so. No.' Gavin shrugged. 'Sorry.'

With a pitying look but no further word, the first potential customer was gone. Gavin watched her slowly walk away, dragging a wheeled shopping bag behind her. The old girl then quickly turned to give this rubbish ice cream van a quick wave - which turned out to be a disgruntled V-sign, actually. But never mind, there's always one, thought Gavin. Just wait until he got set up in Victoria Park this afternoon. Then the 99s would reel 'em in.

So, cash register still empty for now, he crossed the square to the Town Hall and entered through its huge double entrance doors. Along the corridor and he was soon inside the main exhibition space and mingling amongst the odd fellow visitor as well as the industrial looms and spinning machines of Drabbleton's commercial heyday. Just around the corner from a preserved Spinning Jenny, Gavin immediately noticed Alice. His heart skipped a beat. She was sat inside a small glass-partitioned office, obviously having some kind of meeting with Leo - her boss who he'd met the other day. The atmosphere between them seemed relaxed enough as they appeared to be sharing a joke. On that basis, Gavin thought that it wouldn't be too rude to interrupt, and he shuffled across the room to knock on the door. Leo immediately smiled and waved him in.

'Hello there,' the curator said cheerily. 'Not wearing the old skirt today?' He seemed disappointed with the Roman soldier's baggy track suit bottoms.

'No, bit nippy this morning for the mini,' Gavin politely indulged.

'Shame.' An impish smile was flashed.

'Hi Gavin, what's up?' Alice asked, smiling with noticeably less enthusiasm.

'Sorry to interrupt if you're busy,' he replied. But I was wondering, if you had a break coming up, we could maybe do lunch at Ted's across the road?'

'That would be wonderful,' said Leo, bright as a button. 'We'd love that, wouldn't we Alice?'

Gavin fidgeted, avoiding all eye contact. 'Erm... I just meant Alice.'

Social hand-grenade.

'Oh, silly me,' Leo blushed, flapping at his face with a cooling hand. 'How very awkward.'

'Sorry, sorry, big foot in mouth. That's me.' Gavin never knew that blushing was contagious.

'Yes, Gavin. If you like,' said Alice flatly, happy to move things along. 'I'm on lunch in fifteen minutes, so I'll meet you in Ted's.'

'Oh great,' came the relieved reply. With that Big Foot slunk away through the exhibits and towards the door. Only the waxwork figure of James Brimstone, now having been officially unveiled and standing proudly on a display plinth, momentarily caught his attention. But even this impressive creation didn't distract him for long. *That was embarrassing in there. And what is wrong with Alice?*

Gavin at least had a fifteen-minute interval, over at Ted's, to maybe work it all out for himself. He went and ordered just a strong mug of the hot stuff for now, the kind of tea served around here in which you can virtually stand up a teaspoon. Tea for stout souls, not for wimps.

What about Alice, though? Maybe she was sore with him for turning down the invitation to come round, late last Friday. Or maybe things simply weren't going to work out. He picked at a fraying hole in the gingham plastic tablecloth wondering what might be. His appetite for Lancashire's best all-day breakfast, famously served here at Ted's, was diminishing by the minute. And fifteen minutes can be an awful long time when all you have to do is to fret.

Eighteen minutes is even longer, and Gavin had watched every single one of those plod slowly by on Ted's huge, replica fried egg wall clock. At one point he'd tried to distract himself by checking the menu. Did they sell vegan choc ices? Nope, no joy there either. Until… Joy indeed - well maybe - as Alice arrived at the door, at least this time managing something of a sunnier smile. She joined him at the cosy table for two by the window as the young waitress promptly attended.

'I'll just have a latte, thanks,' said Alice. A nod and the server was off. 'I'm really not that hungry today,' she then said to Gavin. 'But you go ahead and order.'

'I might,' he replied. 'I'll just finish me tea first.'

Alice settled herself at the table. Gavin tried not to stare as he admired the attractive woman she undoubtedly was with her deep brown eyes, neat Cleopatra style bob and svelte figure. She looked great today, he thought, in her *first day in new job* navy business suit, with its knee length skirt and sharp creases. He imagined that he would very much like to wake up in a morning, at least now and then, with this lovely lady by his side. But would that ever happen? He wasn't sure.

'So, how's the job going?' asked Gavin, a harmless enough ice breaker.

'Well, a whole four hours in and I'm enjoying it. Plus, we've been rushed off our feet this morning with the grand total of eleven visitors,' she replied with an accompanying sarcastic smile. 'Typical Drabbleton.'

'Eleven is better than nothing, I suppose.' Gavin tried to sound optimistic. 'Early days.'

'Yes, but I think maybe half of them only came in to use the toilets,' Alice sighed. 'All other council loos in town were shut last year due to budget cuts. And I'm counting you too as one of the eleven.'

'Right.' Gavin had a think, but he couldn't come up with the positive spin.

'Yeah, but we've got our first school trip in tomorrow. - Drabbleton Central Primary. Hopefully a class of seven and eight-year-olds will be captivated by old spinning and weaving machines.'

Again, Gavin couldn't see it.

Alice removed eye contact and meaninglessly toyed with the menu for a few moments. Then she quickly drummed her fingers on the table and got to the point. 'But I know you didn't invite me to this fine dining establishment just to ask me about my job.'

'I suppose not, no. Seeing as you're asking...' Gavin's words seemed to ebb away. He wished he'd have spent a bit more time in rehearsal.

'And?' Alice waited, frustrated by the pause.

'Oh, if you want me to get straight into it, I'm just kind of missing you, that's all.' It seemed easier for him to look at his ice cream van through the cafe window than into Alice's eyes. 'I was thinking we'd started something together and, y'know, kinda hoped it might continue.'

Gavin turned from the window in time to see Alice taking a deep breath. She had a look of wearied resignation about her that he wasn't liking very much.

'I've been missing you too,' she said with a sigh. 'But you turned me away from your house...'

'It was a tip at the time. I was embarrassed.'

'Then, in a pretty low state, I asked you to come round to spend the night. But you...' This time it was her words that tailed off. The waitress had brought the latte, quite unaware she'd interrupted an intimate moment. Gavin caught a whiff of grilling bacon and sausage - usually irresistible to him, but which today elicited only disinterest. But these little distractions at least provided enough time for the *case for the defence* to be hastily concocted.

'OK, so I am sorry about the other night. But I didn't want you to do something you might regret. I could hear on the phone that you were sounding vulnerable.'

'You were right, I was.' A bitter riposte.

Gavin started playing with the pepper pot. It didn't help - he knew he just had to get to the point.

'It's been an upsetting time, I know. But I was wondering if we could try to pick up the pieces. I'd really like to."

Alice took the pepper pot out of Gavin's fumbling fingers and firmly rehoused it in the condiments tray. She was demanding eye contact.

'I've had a few days to think, Gavin. I'm still in shock about Bryce.'

'Yeah, course.'

'It doesn't help that all the town seem to think his death is funny,' she winced. 'Do you know there was even a rumour the other night that the *Star of India* takeaway near you had chopped up my brother and made him into a curry? Everybody thought that was hilarious, apparently!'

'No, I didn't hear about that,' Gavin replied as convincingly as he could. 'But yeah, what a sick joke. People can be cruel alright.' He noticed that she seemed relieved by his apparent ignorance of that unpleasant gossip.

'So, us? I don't really know, Gavin. Give me some space and we'll see. Even if that app thing your Freddie showed us was just some elaborate hoax - or even yet another sick joke - I still can't get over we were all wanting Bryce dead. Laughing about it, even me, his sister. Until I saw that photo on your phone. Then everything suddenly became all too real.'

He cupped her hands across the table. 'We weren't to know this was going to happen. I think there's some seriously bad people involved now. Why exactly, I don't know.'

'We do know he had enemies. Somebody like Bryce collects them for fun.'

'I know Alice,' Gavin sighed. 'But now I'm just wishing we could turn back the clock.'

'But this is the thing, and it's killing me now...' She looked to the ceiling as if to catch a tear that was welling in her eyes. 'I'm not sure that I would *want* to turn back the clock. I'm his sister, yes, and there's something in that which means I'm kind of bonded to him. Yet I came to hate him over the years, Gavin. I came to really hate him.'

The tear escaped. It ran down a cheek, but she let it meander away.

'Anyone who knew him could understand that,' Gavin spoke gently. 'Try not to feel guilty about it.' He just wanted to hold her and make everything better.

'Easy to say.' She sounded bitter again. 'He'd controlled my life so much, squashed me down... So that day when I walked out on his job, you know, that was so very liberating.'

'I can see that.' He nodded, admiring the fight in her.

'Yes, I was finally free,' she laughed over the further oncoming tears as Gavin offered a paper napkin to stem the potential flood. 'Thanks,' she said, grateful for the assistance. 'But you came with me too, despite me knowing how much you needed that job. You stuck with me. We were united.'

'We still can be. I want to be.' Gavin helped her dab her eyes with the napkin.

'But no, Gavin,' she replied, steeling herself. 'I may have ruined everything.'

'That sounds unlikely, but why?' *What could be so terrible, come on?*

Alice's tears were now stemmed. She took in a steadying breath and then adopted a matter-of-fact tone.

'See, last Friday when I called you, as I say I was at a low point. I really wanted you to come round. After everything that I'd been through…we'd been through, I thought you'd jump at the chance to be by my side. To hold me… hopefully more.'

'I know, I wish I had come round. Sorry.' He squeezed her hand again.

'But I'd been getting on so well with Leo. We already knew each other from university, actually. Then since, whenever our paths crossed.'

'You never told me that.' Gavin felt a twinge of sudden jealousy.

'Yes, well I didn't want you to think I'd got my job under false pretences,' she replied with a hint of defiance.

'Course not.'

'But anyway. I phoned him, very upset about everything. Very upset about you.' She hesitated for a moment. 'Then he offered to come round. I didn't have to ask,' she added, clearly telling a certain someone what they should have done.

'And then?' But Gavin was hoping there really wasn't an *and then*.

'Oh, I slept with him, that's all.'

'What?' The last dregs of a mug of tea were slapped down hard on the table.

'I slept with him.' Alice freed her hand and stared hard into Gavin's eyes, betraying as they did the myriad of confusing emotions whizzing round his head.

'I heard, but you said *that's all*.'

'It didn't mean that much,' she ventured a casual dismissal.

'I thought he was gay,' Gavin tremored, as he finally felt the certainty of his world shaking beneath him.

'I never said he was gay. That was your assumption.'

'I'm certain he's gay.' Some things were surely obvious, taking a backward Drabbleton perspective.

'I think his sexuality might be what you would call *flexible*, if you get me,' Alice smiled, mildly amused at the conventional soul opposite - determined as he was to keep everything in neat little boxes.

'I don't want to know,' he huffed, out of his depth.

'But I can't say you and I were properly together,' Alice reasoned, now kindlier. 'Plus, you'd turned me down. But I'm ready to apologise if you want me to.'

'I don't know.' More brooding. 'Maybe you should.'

'OK, I'm sorry,' she replied, but only as the defiance bounced back into her voice. 'Even though my brother had just died, I was in a state, and I don't think I'd had sex in almost two and a half years - since my divorce.'

'That's a long time.' Gavin didn't know any of that last bit.

'Anyway, me and Leo - It's not going to happen again. It was a one-off. Something we both needed for our own particular reasons.' Again, her stare was lethal. 'Are you saying you wouldn't have done the same thing?'

'I know that none of us are perfect.' An awkward muttering. 'Certainly not me.'

'But would you or wouldn't you have done the same thing?' An insistent question.

Gavin hesitated. This was the chance for him to come clean about Krystyna. Alice had been honest with him. It was only fair, so he reckoned, that he should now do the same thing. Then again, he didn't like the idea that the woman he loved would think that he'd randomly sleep with just anyone. It had been a whole twenty-eight months since he'd had sex before Krystyna came along, *had that been mentioned?* But neither had his own brother died - well he didn't have a brother, but not the point. It just meant he couldn't claim emotional distress as a defence. Furthermore, even though their love affair had barely begun, if she'd been unfaithful and then it was out there that he'd been unfaithful too, where did that leave them? On the rocks, that's where. But he certainly didn't want that. Maybe avoidance was the best policy - although he now felt only cowardly at that prospect.

'I can't answer that right now,' was all that she could get out of him.

'Anyhow, there it is,' Alice shrugged, having hoped for more. 'I slept with Leo. It's in the open now.'

'It certainly is.' Gavin's eyes were off out the window again. Across the road, in Town Hall Square, a parking attendant seemed to be busy scribbling on his pad. His jaw slacked

'There you go. Somebody else is having a bad day too,' Alice noted casually, deciding to look out of the window herself if she couldn't claim full attention. 'That ice cream van is getting a parking ticket. Serves 'em right. That's a disabled bay.'

'Oh shit. Brilliant.'

'What's up?'

'That's Raspberry, my ice cream van,' Gavin blathered. 'I brought it here to show you. New business idea.'

'Mmm, you seem more upset about the parking ticket than about us being in a mess.' Now it was Alice's turn to brood.

'Course I'm not.' Wooden chair legs scraped gratingly against vinyl floor tiles as Gavin got to his feet. 'Look sorry, I'll just pop over and see if I can stop him writing the ticket.'

'Too late for that, I fear.'

'I'll be back in a minute,' Gavin yapped, so that both the waitress and Alice would hear. 'It's my new ice cream van...' He darted for the door.

Alice remained seated as she eyed him dashing across the road for a pointless conversation with officialdom.

'I hope you and your van will both be happy together. I really do,' she mumbled to herself with a large dose of sarcasm. 'Waitress.... Can I get the bill please, love?'

Gavin did return as quickly as he could. But points in mitigation had needed to be argued out there. The disabled bay signs were definitely faded. He was only dropping off ice cream to Ted's anyway, he'd feigned, so surely commercial deliveries were allowed. Then it was only his first offence. Clearly a verbal warning would have been a more appropriate punishment than a sixty quid fine?

So then, back inside the cafe with the inevitably issued sixty quid ticket stuffed in pocket, he literally kicked himself when he noticed the empty table where he was hoping Alice would still be sitting.

'You've missed her,' explained the waitress. 'She's gone.'

That's right thought Gavin. *She has gone.* He only hoped it wouldn't be forever as he felt a pang of loss that virtually shook him to the core.

★

Bob's own start to this particular Monday morning had been pleasant enough. At around eight o'clock there'd been a knock on the guest bedroom door, which a dressing gowned Mavis then opened carrying a hot cup of tea. It had been over forty years since she last provided morning brew service to her ex-husband, not that Bob seemed to realise.

'Morning dear, he'd beamed as he'd sat up in bed, gratefully accepting the cuppa. 'Tea in bed, as per usual.'

'Two sugars still?' Mavis had wondered, as that's what she'd gambled on.

'Yes, course two sugars, you daft thing,' he'd grinned in bemusement. 'Why wouldn't it be?'

'People do change you know. I'm on sweeteners these days.'

'That's a new one on me. And there's me still giving you three sugars. You should have said.'

'I see you're still in dreamland this morning,' Mavis had frowned, having hoped that a good night's sleep would have brought her surprise visitor to his cognitive senses.

'It's lovely to be here as usual with my wife if that's what you mean.'

Bob's face had been a picture of contentment as he'd then sipped on the lovely, sweet beverage. Mavis had simply shrugged her shoulders before going off to get showered and dressed.

By nine o'clock she was now out in the front garden doing a spot of weeding in the bedding plant borders. Also now fully dressed, Bob appeared on the drive near to where she was working away with garden gloves and trowel. Poppy, the little white poodle, seemed to be following the new lodger around - definitely picking up the smell of Rocky. Bob, however, just thought the family pet had a thing for him. Obvious really.

'I can't find the cereals,' he grumbled. 'Where've you moved them to now?'

Mavis looked up from her kneeling pad with befuddled creases across her brow.

'They're in the cupboard where they've always been,' she declared, not entirely with patience. 'Next to the fridge.'

'I wish you wouldn't keep moving things.'

'I've not moved anything Bob. This isn't your house, remember? You don't live here.'

'You're so funny, Mavis,' he giggled, genuinely amused. '*I don't live here*, indeed! You're a case, do you know that? Next thing you'll be telling me you're not in the fire brigade anymore.' She wasn't of course, having retired from that line of work a quarter of a century ago.

Mavis decided not to reply, continuing to pull up an invading dandelion and hoping her guest would stop bothering her. With luck the authorities would be turning up soon and Bob would be taken off to be reunited with his real family - wherever it was he really did live these days.

★

By the lunchtime, as a fretful Gavin had been driving his ice cream van off to Victoria Park for an afternoon's ice cream vending, a black Mercedes SUV was driving up the M1 Motorway heading north. At the steering wheel, Dimitri Sidorov looked to be in a mood. He had just taken a new instruction from Dizzy, the AI persona from the Disposals Inc app.

'Looks like Mr Volkov is testing us, Lewis,' he stonily spoke to the back seat passenger. 'Two additional hits to complete before we even reach Drabbleton.'

'We'd better not mess up then,' said Lewis, stating the obvious. Dimitri nodded as he viewed his earnest looking apprentice in the rear-view mirror.

'Disposals Inc is suddenly getting very busy,' Roxanne smiled from her front passenger seat. 'Good for my investment.'

'Yes, four more operatives have been flown in from Russia,' informed Dimitri. 'This makes six of us - three teams. Target will be fifty or sixty hits per month, just in the UK alone. That's how much? ...At thirty grand a pop?'

'Sixty hits would be one million, eight hundred thousand,' Roxanne replied, quick as a flash, wads of currency crystallising in her mind. 'Easy to see how this would be a mega-millions business once rolled out across the world.'

'Yes, well that's not really my concern,' said Dimitri deadpan, mustering focus. 'My concern, as Lewis just said, is that we don't mess up.'

'Of course,' replied Roxanne, now with equal solemnity. 'But I have every confidence in you,' she then purred, squeezing Dimitri's left knee, although receiving no response.

The car was approaching the Junction 15 turn off for Northampton.

'This is us,' said Lewis, studying his directions guide inside Disposals Inc. 'Head towards Northampton town centre. Harlow's jewellers are right there on the main high street.'

'Thank you, Lewis,' said Dimitri. 'Let us hope that the assassination of one Gerald Harlow goes more smoothly than that of Mr Bryce Brimstone.'

'I'm sure it will,' Roxanne added in pandering tones. 'You are a trained professional after all. The very best.'

Dimitri's mouth curled into a half smile. Yes, he knew he was the best. A couple of recent little blips couldn't take away that reality, so he was thinking. He just had to click back into the old Dimitri, the machine-like killer that never failed.

★

Around the same time, back at 21 Buttermilk Avenue, a spiky haired teenage lad was walking up the gentle slope that was Mavis's drive. He wore skinny jeans with white sneakers and a retro punk t-shirt picturing The Clash - the latest band he'd discovered in an old uncle's vinyl collection. Under his arm he carried a battered leather, art portfolio case.

'Oh, Charlie, how lovely,' Mavis radiated as she eventually opened the door to greet her grandson.

'Hi Gran, I've bought that painting for you to see.' The young man held up his case and smiled cheerily. 'Hi Poppy,' he chirped, quickly kneeling to give the welcoming poodle a bit of love.

'Goodness, the painting's done already? Well then, you'd better come in.'

Mavis led her latest visitor along the small hallway leading into the living/dining room where Bob was currently sat on a chair reading the *Daily Mail*.

'Bob, this is Charlie, my grandson,' Mavis explained. 'He's an art student.'

'Doing a foundation year,' Charlie waved. 'Hi there.'

'And this is Bob,' Mavis continued, but then paused as she wondered exactly how she should complete her introduction. 'Erm, he's an old friend,' was the best she could do.

'An old friend indeed - *and* only her husband,' Bob grinned, rising to shake the caller's hand. 'You're not a real grandson, of course, are you?' he chuckled. 'You two big kidders!' He was happy to call out the fanciful conspiracy.

Mavis caught Charlie's eye and rolled an index finger around her temple. Luckily the grandson was quick on the uptake - *yep, the old guy was a fruitcake. Never mind, ignore him.*

The portfolio case was then deposited on the mahogany dining table and carefully unzipped by its young owner. A bundle of twenty or more paintings and drawings were stacked up inside and Bob could instantly see from glimpses of various overlapping pieces that the kid had a talent. Charlie then took a mid-sized water-colour painting, one that was sitting on the top of the pile and placed it onto the polished tabletop for his grandmother to see.

'Hopefully, it's true to the photograph you gave me,' said the evidently gifted young artist.

'Oh, Charlie! I don't know what to say.'

Mavis's eyes welled up as fifty years of the consequence of living a life were peeled back from her features. There she was now, in the magical time-machine painting, back in her twenties, the wrinkles and the excess pounds all miraculously erased. She'd been accurately painted with a strong jawline and robust cheekbones, her lustrous brown hair styled in a tight Seventies perm. A handsome woman, confident looking and strong.

'That's my Mavis,' Bob gasped in unfettered wonderment. 'Just like the day we were married. How did you do that?' he asked as he too held back a tear.

'Gran lent me an old photo. It was easy really.'

'Nonsense with your *easy*. I can see you've put a lot of work into this. But I love it, so thank you!' Mavis pulled her grandson towards her so that she could gift him a hug and kiss. 'Thank you. Thank you so much!'

Charlie blushed, but beneath an embarrassed smile he was enjoying the fuss and familial adulation.

'I need it for my end of year submission, but I'll get it framed for you after that.'

'Good lad. That would be grand,' Mavis gushed, dishing out a further kiss.

Just then, Poppy sprung over to the window seat fitted into the front bay window and jumped up on it so she could see outside. She was yapping excitedly. Mavis inevitably wondered what had caused such a sudden stirring of sprightliness in a pet not often, these days, animated by much. Peering through the mock Georgian UPVC window, both Poppy and Mavis could now see that another dog had decided to invade their neatly manicured lawn. The human resident of 21 Buttermilk Avenue immediately knocked on the window to shoo it away, although if the canine resident could have spoken, she would have let it be known that she wasn't at all happy with that.

'Look at that old dog, cheeky blighter,' Mavis griped. 'Go on, off with you!' She knocked on the window again, this time with more force. But the grey mongrel seemed to be barking at Poppy - and she was yapping happily back in return - yet remained quite undeterred by Mavis's scare tactics. Charlie and Bob then turned up by the window, showing marginal interest, understandable for the young man maybe - but not for the dog's owner. As it was indeed Rocky out there on the lawn, calling out doggy style for his lost owner - and possibly that nice little poodle too!

'He seems to like your Poppy,' said Bob to Mavis, seemingly failing to recognise his closest companion. 'Dogs will be dogs, eh?'

'Well, he can hop it!' came the snappy reply, as Mavis went off to the kitchen to arm herself with a sweeping brush-cum-dog-deterrent.

'I'll see him off, don't worry,' Bob casually assured as he too shuffled out of the room heading towards the front door, a brush carrying reinforcement soon behind him and a slightly bemused student bringing up the rear. Poppy stayed on duty at the window, continuing the two-way engagement with the intruder.

Bob only needed to set one foot out onto the driveway when the tatty looking old mongrel was scampering enthusiastically towards him. *What a shame, he's got a limp*, he thought, as he then somehow couldn't help stroking the tail wagging dog jumping up against his legs.

'Hello, boy. You're a friendly lad alright,' he laughed, ruffling Rocky's ears playfully. 'But you can't stay here, sorry. This is not your garden.'

By this point Poppy had decided being inside by the window was no fun at all when there was real action going on outside in the garden. She sprinted for the exit just as Mavis was readying her weapon.

'No need for the brush, Mavis,' said Bob, waving the cavalry member to stand down. 'I'll just give the lad a bit of a pat and send him on his way.'

'Well, he certainly seems to like you,' said Mavis, observing man and dog in perfect harmony and backing off with the heavy weapons. 'But don't make him too fond of you as I don't want another lodger for the day.'

At that moment, Poppy came flying out through the front door and into the garden and both dogs greeted each other with frenzied tails and tongues. Unfortunately for Bob, however, the effect of Poppy running between and catching his legs to get fast access to Rocky sent him wobbling. Gravity soon took over as he then completely lost his balance, toppling backwards, arms flailing and trying in vain to grab Mavis's nearest arm as he fell. Charlie then quickly stepped forward trying to catch him, but his grandmother inadvertently blocked the intended path as she instinctively flinched away from the falling old man. Bob hit the ground, back of head first. He lay there on the concrete driveway, completely out cold.

'Oh, my goodness,' said Mavis, kneeling beside the prostrate Bob. 'Silly girl, Poppy,' she then admonished in a squeaky voice, which in reality was to lead to no telling off at all. 'You shouldn't have made the silly man fall over. No, you shouldn't,' she patiently explained, before then stroking her little dog who'd immediately come over to sniff the guy having a nice lie down.

'I'll get some water,' said a quite flustered Charlie, dashing off towards the kitchen.

'Good idea,' Mavis replied as she checked Bob's pulse. But yes, at least he was still alive.

Rocky limped over now, squealing doggy tears and sniffing his owner for signs of consciousness. Could this be curtains for the long-standing Bob & Rocky partnership? No more late-night walkies to the railway bridge on Baker Street? No more trips to the *Star of India* takeaway for a mid-week sneaky sausage? No more Mr Bob Horsefield, even - Rocky's great alpha hero? This really couldn't be happening!

OK, there was only one thing for it. The *lick of life* needed to be administered, a medical procedure handed down from generation to generation in the genetic memory code of dogs. Mavis immediately gave way. She wasn't going to get in the way of such a potentially lifesaving measure.

So, Bob lay there, quite motionless, as Rocky frantically licked his face and slavered all over his skin, exhaling hot canine breath into his gaping mouth and nostrils too.

Nothing happened to begin with. All seemed lost. But then maybe something deep in Bob's subconscious began to stir as the odour of Rocky's bad breath infiltrated his nose and was then translated into some instinct or other in the dark crevices of his mind. Then he maybe registered the slobbering mess of warm saliva flooding over his face, this too maybe triggering a *call of the wild* type response. His 'pack' were drawing him back from beyond. Something more then stirred from that deepest of retreats and Bob was slowly, yet finally, being pulled back to the Land of the Living.

There was a violent cough and unsightly splutter as he jerked forward into consciousness, before then quickly catapulting back to his prone position. It wasn't exactly pretty - but the *lick of life* had worked.

'Rocky, is that you,' Bob mumbled, as he then managed to open an eye. 'Give over with all your licking will you,' he giggled, quickly recovering, and pushing away his old pet's dribbling snout.

'Thank goodness, you're alright,' Mavis sighed. Charlie passed her the freshly retrieved glass of water.

'Mavis?' said Bob, gozzy-eyed. 'What are you doing here?'

His ex-wife of forty years back looked at him with equal degrees of bafflement. She lifted his head and got him to sip on the water.

'You don't think we're still married then?'

'Ow, me head,' Bob replied, tenderly touching the back of his skull and what was surely going to be an almighty bruise. 'Still married? Course not,' he grouched as he started to view his surroundings. This wasn't home. Where was it? All the garden gnomes? Not Buttermilk Avenue, surely? 'What am I doing here?'

'The answer to that is quite a tale. But if we can get you on your feet - come on Charlie, give us a hand - I'll do my best to help you fill in the blanks.' The young student crouched down and started to support Bob's own efforts to stand up. 'I do think you've got a bit of explaining to do yourself, as well,' Mavis added, as all parties - three people and two dogs - returned to the sanctuary of the neat little bungalow.

Actually, Mavis found herself positioned in the procession behind the two happy canines who were leading the way back inside. It was then that she noticed Rocky's unfortunate affliction.

A limping dog, she wondered. *Now why is that familiar?*

22
- THE HUNDRED STEPS -

Disposals Inc Operations Log - Today View

Job Name: *Harlow, Gerald*

Location: *Harlow's Jewellers, High Street, Northampton*

Agents assigned: *Dimitri Sidorov, Lewis Wilson*

Method: *Standard. Single gunshot to head*

Assassination completed? *Yes*

Time of completion: *1.13 pm*

#

Job Name: *Sharpe, Kim*

Location: *Head Teacher's Office, St James's High School, Derby Way, Stoke-on-Trent*

Agents assigned: *Dimitri Sidorov, Lewis Wilson*

Method: *De-luxe. Torture with lit cigarette. Then single gunshot to head*

Assassination completed? *Yes*

Time of completion: *3.45 pm*

\#

Job Name: *Hargreaves, Gavin*

Location: *21 Mayfair Avenue, Drabbleton*

Agents assigned: *Dimitri Sidorov, Lewis Wilson*

Method: *Standard. Single gunshot to head*

Assassination completed? *Still outstanding*

Time of completion: *TBC*

\#

★

Bob hadn't been expecting to be standing here today with Rocky at the Drabbleton Circular bus stop down at the bottom of Buttermilk Avenue. Now late afternoon, he'd just enjoyed a reasonably pleasant afternoon up at Mavis's sharing old memories with his ex-wife. Oh, and grandson Charlie seemed a nice enough kid too, so evidently making the effort to look out for his gran.

All had been going well as Bob had been tucking into his second fairy cake, all smiles around the room - plus with two contented dogs sharing a rug together in front of the glowing *coal effect* electric fire. But then Mavis's tone had suddenly changed, and not for the better.

'I remember now!' she'd declared, eyes widened, as a light bulb moment sparked out of nowhere inside her head. 'Your dog Rocky with that limp... I knew I'd seen him before.'

'Drabbleton's a small town, I suppose,' Bob had replied, immediately nervous.

'You were the man standing outside of my house the other week, staring in all creepy, like. That's when I saw your dog Rocky limping off.'

Charlie had immediately looked concerned and had left the sofa to stand behind his gran's rocking chair.

'Is this true, Bob? Have you been spying on my gran?' he'd demanded.

Bob had gnashed his teeth and squirmed in his chair. But the look on his face had told his interrogators he was guilty as charged. Explaining to Mavis that she'd been the love of his life hadn't helped either. And neither had informing her that he'd made an annual pilgrimage to Buttermilk Avenue for the past forty years - just to kind of touch base with her in a kind of spiritual way and to make him feel that all was well in the world.

'Stalker!' she'd cried accusatively from her rocking chair throne. 'You've been stalking me for an entire lifetime!'

'That is a bit weird, Bob,' said Charlie, struggling to grasp that level of obsession.

So having seen that Bob's cognitive faculties had been restored, even though this meant he was back to being a weirdo creep, Mavis had decided he should be sent on his way without further ceremony. She'd literally frogmarched him out of the front door and he'd then mournfully trailed away down the drive before both he and then Rocky had turned back to take in one last glimpse of their dearest loves.

A sad end, they'd both thought, to a potentially blissful tale. Such a cruel world!

But before he'd left the garden completely, Rocky had made sure he'd retrieved the lovely bone accessory - hidden behind the apple tree - that he'd been carrying round and feeding on since Friday night. Bob could see that all the flesh from Brimstone's arm and hand had been stripped, all no doubt gratefully devoured by the hungry animal left without dog food - but a pooch, nevertheless, with a noble mission to track down his missing owner.

'Looks like you've enjoyed yourself with that,' Bob had smiled in bemusement as he'd seen the skeletal arm being contentedly carried between what was left of Rocky's old teeth. 'At least the lousy bastard came in useful then. You must have been starving, poor lad. I'm sorry about that. Lost me marbles for a bit. But I'm fine now.'

Rocky had seemed to nod in complete understanding.

So here the love-stricken pair were now standing, moping together, and waiting for the usual bus - just over eleven or so months earlier than they'd expected to be, that's all. Then, sauntering down the avenue towards them came Charlie, art case swinging by his side. Rocky's ears perked up as he'd hoped to see him maybe accompanied by Poppy, but sadly not to be.

'Hello, mate,' said Charlie, slightly warily. He hadn't expected to see Bob at the same bus stop that he needed to be at.

'Hello again,' Bob replied, trying not to imagine what the young man might be thinking of him. 'Any idea what time the bus is due?'

'Any time now. But you never know with the Drabbleton Circular.'

They both smiled nervously. Then Charlie couldn't help but notice Rocky and especially the generous portion of human bone trailing from the tatty creature's mouth.

'Hey, is that a real human arm? Or what's left of it?' The young artist seemed quite captivated.

'Nah, course not,' Bob laughed, waving away the daft suggestion.

'What is it then if it's not real? It feels real,' Charlie added, crouching down to inspect the bones, Rocky not particularly minding.

'What is it then?' Bob repeated slowly, buying much needed time to come up with what needed to be a convincing lie. *Aha!* 'Well, if you must know... It's something I picked up in a second-hand shop one Halloween. The shopkeeper told me it was from the hospital, part of one of those fake skeletons, y'know - those that they use with medical students and the like.'

'Cool, great,' said Charlie, happy enough with that convincing narrative. 'But I wonder what happened to the rest of him?'

'It's hopefully in Poland,' Bob mumbled, mainly for his own benefit as he finally recalled the disastrous attempt to send Brimstone's body parts overseas along with the nightly coal exports.

'Eh?' puzzled Charlie.

'Ah nothing.'

'Actually mate, is there any chance I could borrow this skeleton thing? I'm doing my end of year art installation at the moment. It would fit right in.'

Bob considered the pros and cons of the request. Well on the plus side, this might well be a most convenient way of disposing of incriminating evidence. Nobody would be searching for Brimstone's remains amidst a college art project, after all. And no doubt Mavis would be pleased with him if she were to one day hear that he'd been supportive of her darling grandson. On the cons side, well Rocky would have to give up his latest toy. But nothing that an extra mid-week sneaky sausage from the chippy couldn't take care of.

'I'm not sure about that,' said Bob all the same, shaking his head as further possible benefits came to mind. 'They're expensive, these human bone replicas.'

'Yeah, I bet,' Charlie replied as his face fell in dejection. 'But it would be amazing if I could use it.' ...Nope, he could see that the old man was standing firm. 'Oh well, never mind.'

'Mmm, I might be able to help,' Bob added with a wry smile. 'If you could help me in return.'

'How do you mean?'

'I'd love to get a copy of that painting you did of your grandmother.'

'Oh, I don't know about that Bob. I'm not sure she'd like that at all.'

'Well, she wouldn't have to know. I'm not asking for the original. Just a colour photocopy or something.'

He winked at Charlie, who he could see was already weakening.

'I suppose if it was our secret,' he inwardly wrestled. 'But you have to promise no more stalking. That's the main thing.' He sounded firm about that too.

'Yeah course. Goes without saying,' said Bob, crossing his heart and putting on his best *butter-wouldn't-melt-in-my-mouth* expression. 'So, deal then?'

'Alright yes. Deal.' Charlie smiled, if a little guiltily.

'Deal.' Bob held out the handshake offer which was duly accepted.

But only two minutes later and Bob was unexpectedly waving off both Charlie and the skeletal remains of Brimstone's right arm as they left together on the Drabbleton Circular. Just as he had been about to board the bus himself, coughing his way through the vehicle's usual polluting emissions, he'd realised he hadn't got his bus pass with him. And since neither he nor archetypal penniless student Charlie had any spare change between them, Bob had to give up on the bus home idea and resign himself to a good hour or so's walk instead.

Yep, the walk it was to be then, and as the black and acrid exhaust fumes billowed beyond the arse of the departing bus, Charlie waved back to Bob and Rocky from behind the passenger rear window, himself looking proper pleased with his art materials sourcing success.

'Come on Rocky lad,' said Bob to his slightly downhearted pet who'd had to give up both a love interest and a half-decent chewy treat in one afternoon. 'We could probably do with the exercise. I certainly do.' To be honest, Bob wasn't really minding the prospect of the long walk home. He was just happy that soon he'd be receiving in the post the copy of that lovely painting of the young Mavis that Charlie had promised to send on. Then he'd be able to look at the love of his life, just as she was when he married her, for every single day that he remained alive on this planet.

At that moment, however, the tinny chimes of some amplified music box rang out behind them. The melody being played was instantly recognisable, despite its warped and wobbly sounding rendition. It was, of course, *Greensleeves*- that traditional English pastoral song universally favoured as the ice cream van signature tune of choice since time immemorial. The music box then stopped abruptly, midpoint between the subsequent 'Green' and 'sleeves', providing a less than pleasing listening experience.

Bob was irritated enough by the grating music and its jerky conclusion to turn around to possibly scowl at the driver of the vehicle that had pulled in a few yards behind them.

'What a stupid thing is that?' he scoffed to himself, noticing the giant ice cream cone moulding sat on top of the admittedly sorry looking van, a weathered yellow rust bucket whose best days were undoubtedly long behind it. Obviously, Gavin hadn't seen the same vehicle in such a disparaging light. But Bob's assessment was nearer the truth.

But then the old man saw a familiar figure at the van's steering wheel, mouthing his name as if in slow motion.

'B-o-bbb!' shouted Gavin, only behind the windscreen which ensured his *gone- missing* neighbour couldn't hear him. He waved enthusiastically and pointed to the serving hatch behind him. '*Meet me there!*'

'Oh gawd, he's gone back into retail,' Bob muttered, scratching his head. 'Disaster!' But still he strolled a few yards back down the road, mostly out of morbid curiosity, so he could engage with the white-aproned Gavin who was by now waiting at his hatch.

'Bob, what you doing round here?' the ice cream vendor blurted, sounding a little frantic. 'I've been worried about you.'

'Alright there, Gavin. Long story.' Bob casually shrugged. 'Had a bit of a nap in a railway wagon, woke up in hospital...'

'Oh no, are you alright?'

'Yeah fine,' Bob went on, sounding like this kind of thing happened to him all the time. 'My ex-wife has been looking after me, but I'm off home now.'

'Mavis?' This didn't sound likely to Gavin. He'd heard all about the long-lost ex-wife and the sadness that remained in his old neighbour's heart. 'I thought she was well out of your life?'

'No, we've kept in touch. Once a year like.' Bob nodded, inviting belief in the writing of a new truth.

'That's nice,' said Gavin, quite alright about accepting a happier ending to Bob's lifetime love story. *So, her wanting nothing to do with you all these years was just a lie? Some people!*

'But how did you get on with getting shot of you know who,' Bob enquired, suddenly more enthused.

'Long story, mate. But all good once Dinesh finally came up with a plan, but I'll tell you later...'

Bob nodded, accepting that a public highway was probably not the best place to be talking about their corpse disposal operation. *But Gavin in an ice cream van?* That was a most surprising career change for a Roman Centurion.

'What's this heap of junk all about anyway?' he then asked, with typical Drabbleton bluntness.

'I'm back in business,' Gavin bristled with pride. 'Well trying to be. I got moved on from Victoria Park - no permit. So, I thought I'd try the streets instead. At least there's a bit of money round here.' Gavin smiled as if he still believed he was onto a commercial winner.

Right on cue, a potential customer appeared on the scene - a porky looking teenager on a skateboard, but no doubt a discerning 99 fan.

'Hey mate, giz us a Solero will you?'

'I'm sorry, I don't do them?'

'OK, I'll have a Magnum.'

'Sorry.' Big smile, followed by a confident delivery: 'I can do you a 99 though.'

'Nah mate, it'll melt on me hoody, know what I'm saying?'

Gavin couldn't remember being that fussed about ice cream staining his clothes when he was a kid. But with no more than a frustrated little huff, the nicely laundered skater boy was off on his wheels. At least he didn't throw in the customary departing V-sign. Progress.

'Early days,' Gavin explained for Bob's benefit. 'I might have to tweak the menu.'

'Yeah maybe,' Bob kind of agreed, thinking his wannabe entrepreneurial friend would have a great business if only he could turn up at Blackpool beach on a sunny July weekend. Then turn the clock back to 1965 and change his price to one old shilling. Everyone would want a 99 then! But right now, Gavin's van was failing to entice any further customers from the comfort of their snug District of Riverstone homes. Which meant that today he'd made less than a tenner in sales - after starting out on a minus with the unfortunate sixty quid parking fine. But he had read once that even retail giant Amazon had made an operating loss for years - so one bad day for the ice cream van had to be expected.

But Rocky did like it on the double front passenger seat of the *99mobile* as Gavin drove all wanderers back home to Mayfair Avenue. The fledgling ice cream man had a lot to update Bob about, new business venture apart. In private now, the success of Dinesh's special curry could be revealed, even its apparent appreciation by certain members of the local constabulary. His good luck with Krystyna but bad luck with Alice, on second thoughts, he decided to keep to himself. But tonight was the night when he'd been told to expect somebody or other from Disposals Inc turning up at his house, ostensibly to collect Brimstone's previously delivered body parts. He did tell Bob about that, even though he'd being trying to put it out of his mind over the weekend and all through today. As the evening in question approached, however, *denial* was a less useful strategy.

'Sounds like you've been a bit of an ostrich about it,' said Bob, superciliously, as Gavin finally finished the tale of the threatened impending visit. 'Head in the sand. That's no good, is it?'

'What am I going to do? I obviously haven't got the body anymore - thanks to our clever schemes. They might not like that.'

Bob could see the worry lines indenting deeper into his driver's forehead. 'Well, if they are killers, I don't suppose they would be all that reasonable about it. I hope you've not bought too much Mr Whippy.'

'Why's that?' Gavin looked blank.

'Shame to see it all go to waste after they've bumped you off.' Bob cruelly laughed in self-amusement.

'Very funny,' the ice cream man sniffed. 'Any serious suggestions?'

They were already nearing home. So, Bob, finally feeling sorry for his neighbour, reluctantly put his teasing aside and thought that he'd better come up with something. A plan maybe even better than throwing Brimstone's body off a railway bridge and hoping it would end up in Poland.

'Leave your van parked up the road,' he muttered in hushed tones. 'You don't want them to know anyone's at home. Then you can lay low at mine until they've been and gone. We can even hide behind my sofa in case they look in my window.'

'Brilliant,' Gavin replied, not even sarcastically. 'Hiding behind the sofa at yours. Why didn't I think of that?'

★

On a practical level, Bob needed a few supplies - bread, milk, eggs, as he'd not been home since Friday. Gavin had therefore lent him a few quid so that he could pop into the Co-op and do the necessary. Meanwhile, the ice cream van had been parked up just across the road, its owner and Rocky the dog staying in the vehicle while the modest shopping trip was accomplished.

Gavin was doing nothing in particular, sat there in the driving seat, gazing up at the grey Drabbleton sky and letting his mind go peacefully blank. Always a good idea that, he'd theorised - when there was too much to think about, try thinking of nothing. Great therapy, but something that probably came too easy to him than was often useful.

So, the subsequent tap on his serving hatch glass made him jump, jolting him back to unwelcome reality. Turning around in his seat he was being waved to by yet another potential customer. *Whoo hoo*, two in twenty minutes, that was something.

Sliding back the hatch he was greeted by a young and spindly, tall guy, smiling in his smart black suit - cloth too posh for these parts. His braided locks swung freely as he looked first at the 99 oriented menu and then up at Gavin.

'Hey man, I'll have the two quid 99 please,' said Lewis Wilson. '*Two quid,* that is seriously cheap!'

'Glad to oblige,' said Gavin, eagerly onto his Mr Whippy machine. 'You don't sound like you're from round here,' he added, listening to the accent that was about five or six tube stops removed from Cockney.

'You're talking about a fiver for a 99 where I come from, bruv. I need to live up North!'

'You're welcome,' said Gavin, amused. 'Not many people move to Drabbleton, y'know. Most folk move away!' He laughed sardonically at the uncomfortable truth. 'Two pounds please.'

The transaction was completed, and Lewis stared admiringly at his new ownership of the giant 99 with double flake - *what a beauty*. He held it aloft, like a trophy, so that his two friends could see, sitting as they were in a parked Mercedes SUV over the way. They didn't seem particularly impressed. *Takes all sorts,* Gavin thought. *Southerners of the usual miserable cut, no doubt, unlike this guy here - he's alright.*

'Hey bruv,' said Lewis, turning back to face the best-value-ever ice cream vendor, 'Mayfair Avenue - our sat nav can't find the way in 'cos of the road works.'

'Oh yeah, looks like they decided to dig up the road this morning. Kids have probably nicked the diversion signs.' Gavin's tone was almost apologetic on behalf of the bored adolescents of his town. 'You'll have to go in the back way - down Park Avenue, then Buckingham Palace Road, then first left and you're in.'

'Sounds very posh, mate.'

'The land of millionaires, you'll see for yourself,' he quietly chortled.

'You're having me on,' Lewis winked, catching on. *I get it.* But yeah, you're right if you're saying this place is a bit of a shit-hole.'

Bit harsh, thought Gavin. Locals could think that. But not complete strangers against whom the honour of the town must be stoutly defended.

'It's not that bad,' he sighed in half-hearted defiance. Yet it was the most robust knock-back he could presently muster.

'Anyway cheers!' said Lewis departing, having no interest in further discussing the merits or otherwise of this once grand cotton town. As he crossed the road, a diminutive figure was coming over from the opposite pavement, Co-op carrier bag in hand. The two passed each other like anonymous strangers, Bob not clocking Lewis long enough to realise that this was the guy who he'd accidentally shot in the arm up at Brimstone Mill. Whilst Lewis hadn't even noticed Bob at all, the luscious 99 captivating pretty much his entire attention.

Both men then returned to their respective vehicles, Lewis to the black Mercedes and Bob hopping back into the yellow *99mobile*.

'We need to go via Park Avenue to get into Mayfair,' Lewis informed his surly driver. 'The 99-guy told me.' He took a slavering lick of the ice cream.

'OK,' said Dimitri. 'Well now that your childish sulk about wanting an ice cream has been placated, maybe we can proceed with business.'

'Lewis,' said Roxanne, catching the younger one's eye in her window-blind vanity mirror, 'I don't wish to do Dimitri's job for him, but don't you think it's a little foolish to ask directions for the place where you're going to put a bullet in someone's head?'

'Yes, bloody stupid!' Dimitri chipped in. 'Idiot! I was just about to say so!'

Roxanne raised an eyebrow. She was hardly convinced.

'Sorry guys,' Lewis temporarily moped. 'But two quid, this 99 cost,' he instantly cheered up. '*Seriously*, only two quid!'

Meanwhile, over the road, Bob was back safely ensconced in the van's front passenger seat, alongside the now snoozing Rocky.

'Did you see? I got a sale,' Gavin announced, sounding chuffed. There was mileage in this old van yet. 'The guy over there in the back of that car.'

'What a paying punter? Yay!' said Bob, genuinely pleased for his friend. He then squinted to try to put in focus the blurry car and its passenger across the road - but without his specs, too far out of range for his short-sighted eyes.

'Yep, he's up from the South. London, I'd say. 99s are a fiver down there, so he reckons.' Gavin tutted in disgust.

'Bloody rip off.' That made it double disgust.

'Too right. He was asking directions for our street.'

Bob pulled a confused face. '*Our street?* Why would people from London want to visit Mayfair Avenue?' He squinted again at the car across the way - some kind of quality marque, so it seemed.

'No idea, didn't ask. But now you mention it...' Gavin goggled the sophisticated looking driver and then his even more sophisticated looking lady passenger. She looked familiar - but he couldn't place her for now. *People like that don't come to Drabbleton.* Over in the back seat of the Mercedes, Lewis had spotted them gawking over towards their vehicle. He held up his by now half-eaten ice cream and gave Gavin a big *thumbs up* and accompanying grin.

'You don't think they're the guys coming to collect Brimstone's body, do you?' Bob mused, thinking a bit quicker than his neighbour.

'Don't know, never thought about it. But that stupid app thing told me I was booked in for an evening slot.'

'It must be about half five by now. That's practically evening.'

'Let's go.' Gavin quickly flipped the ignition over and pulled his van away from the kerb. The sudden movement woke Rocky up from his dozing and the old dog immediately sat upright on the passenger seat. As the *99mobile* then curved over by the Mercedes in front of them - now virtually windscreen to windscreen with it - Bob visibly shuddered. For the first time he'd been able to get a proper view of both Gavin's customer and the vehicle in which he was travelling.

'Bloody hell, it's the kid I shot - and it's their car too!' he jabbered in sudden panic mode. He'd then quickly remembered seeing that very Mercedes speeding away from Brimstone Mill as he'd been hiding in the Executive Bathroom - along with Krystyna and Dinesh - on the night of Bryce's demise. 'Step on it!' he urged.

'What you blabbering on about now, Bob?' Gavin asked, screwing up his face in befuddlement. 'You *shot* somebody?'

'By accident!' he flapped. 'Well sort of. But just drive will you. These guys are killers alright!'

Rewinding ten seconds or so, Lewis's eye was caught by the sudden emergence of a dog behind the windscreen of the approaching van. Not many dogs looked as shabby as Rocky.

'Wait, it's that plug-ugly dog!' he blabbed for the benefit of Dimitri who was just preparing to put the Mercedes into gear. He quickly scanned right and *yes* - it was that annoying little guy who'd grazed his arm with a bullet! 'Look it's that midget who shot me at the mill!'

'Are you sure?' asked Dimitri, mentally preparing for action stations. 'I didn't see them, remember.'

'Positive. It's them alright. The midget and his plug-ugly mutt, anyway.' He stuffed the last of the cone into his mouth and chomped it with venom. 'The ice cream guy's new though,' he added, almost indecipherably due to his overly stuffed gob.

'They're coming after us,' Gavin fretted, as through his offside wing mirror he witnessed the Mercedes doing a *Formula One* style hairpin turn and powering off in their pursuit.

'Damn it, he recognised me,' Bob fretted, also observing the oncoming vehicle through the nearside wing mirror.

'This is all down to you!'

'Oh shush,' said Bob, matching Gavin's sudden impatience. 'Have you got a gun in your glove box?' He quickly flipped open said compartment obviously hoping to find a *Beretta* pistol, or even better, a monster *.44 Magnum* handgun. The empty Snickers wrapper he did find was of no use whatsoever.

'Course I don't have a gun, Bob! I'm an ice cream man. You could try squirting their windscreen with chocolate sauce!' Gavin steamed with frustration. It wasn't his fault some nutters were after his diminutive ally.

'Very funny, *not!* You won't be making smart-arse comments when they've put a bullet in your brain.' Bob didn't like taking all the blame at all.

'Why's it anything to do with me? I didn't shoot one of them!'

'Because they're the guys who took Brimstone's body and then obviously delivered it to you, God knows why,' Bob explained, via a patronisingly slow delivery. 'Guess what? They're probably the same guys who are visiting you to get it back.'

'How can you possibly know that?'

'I just know so, that's all,' Bob virtually growled. 'Now drive!'

'I am driving!' But looking in his wing mirrors he could see that the Mercedes had already made up the fifty or so yards start that the chugging *99mobile* had on it when the pursuit had begun. The killers were now right on their tail as they sped through a section Drabbleton town centre's narrow streets, these fortunately too narrow to accommodate overtaking. 'Sorry I forgot to install the turbo charged power pack this morning!' Gavin snapped. *It was still Bob's fault!*

'I'll get rid of some weight from out back,' said Bob, always ready with a plan. He shuffled into the ice cream van's preparation area and grabbed a large cardboard box from a shelf.

'Hey they're my flakes!' Gavin protested. 'Don't you dare throw...'

Too late, Bob had already whizzed the cardboard box out through the serving hatch window, trying his best to make it land in the path of their pursuers.

'Bastards!' Dimitri grunted as he tried to swerve his motor out of the way of the flying box. *Success*, but only at the expense of clipping a street litter bin.

'Careful darling. This is a company vehicle,' Roxanne rebuked, protecting her imminent investment in Disposals Inc and all of its assets.

'Watch it, there's another one,' Lewis yelled, as a second box came soaring through the air towards them.

'I'm not blind, Lewis!' Dimitri spat.

But this time, as the street narrowed further, his evasive manoeuvring was to no avail and the weaponised cardboard box bounced against the windscreen, scattering a hundred ice cream cones on impact.

'Bulls eye!' Bob celebrated back in the van.

In the Mercedes, Roxanne screamed and covered her eyes.

'Bastards!' Dimitri grunted again, nevertheless maintaining a strong and steady course, despite the potentially deadly wafer onslaught.

'Oh no, they're still after us!' Bob cried, frantically tearing at what was left of his silver hair.

'Course they're still after us, stupid! How much do you think a few dozen ice cream cones weigh? Not enough to knock out two tons of Mercedes, anyway.' Gavin bashed his head against his steering wheel. *But no,* he wasn't dreaming.

'At least I'm *thinking*. I haven't heard any ideas from you,' Bob sulked. 'Are you sure you don't have a gun?' He slid back into his passenger seat, stroking an increasingly anxious Rocky on his way, and trying to come up with Plan B. Quickly re-opening the glove box, once again the empty Snickers wrapper offered itself up for service - but was once again turned down. The glove box was slammed shut in disappointment.

'I don't have a gun, Bob. Live with it!'

'Never mind,' said the perpetual strategist as an even better plan came into his head. 'Go that way, quick - down Pall Mall. Then down The Hundred Steps. They won't dare follow us down The Hundred Steps.'

'I'm not going down The Hundred Steps either. It'd kill us! My van would be bashed to bits!' Gavin shook his head, dreading that thought, cold sweat now visible on his brow. Although he did then take the sharp left into Pall Mall, he knew he could later turn right at the end of the road, into Downing Street, therefore avoiding the precipitous slope that was The Hundred Steps pedestrian thoroughfare.

'We need to go down them Steps,' Bob insisted. 'It'll only be like Star Trek; you know, when Captain Kirk orders the crew to steer the Starship Enterprise through a perilous meteorite shower or something. Then Scotty pipes up. *The ship can'nae take it, Captain.* But old Captain Kirk says, *Warp Factor Twenty-Five, Scotty,* or whatever. And by the finale of the episode, they're all safe and sound and the Starship Enterprise doesn't even need a paint job.'

'Bollocks, Bob. Utter Bollocks! We're not going down The Hundred Steps,' Gavin held firm as the turning off into Downing Street approached. 'And besides, it's Warp Factor Eight in Star Trek. Factor Twenty-Five is a sun cream.'

Less than two metres behind them, indifferent to the danger of high speed - or at least *moderate* speed - tailgating, Dimitri had spotted a road sign that the driver of the 99mobile had evidently missed.

'We've got them now,' he grinned, a malevolent glint in his eye. 'The right turn ahead is closed. It's a dead end.' Lewis nodded and readied his gun. Dimitri slowed the car. The ice cream van was going nowhere.

Gavin had already begun to swing the van around into Downing Street when he belatedly saw the line of traffic cones sealing off the road. Behind these, a large roadworks hole in the tarmac meant that any advancement forwards was simply impossible.

'Bugger!' he screamed in blind panic as he instinctively yanked hard left down on his steering wheel, the cones and hole upon him. Bob and Rocky closed their eyes ready to say goodbye to the world. But somehow the van swerved erratically to the side, its brakes screeching and with only the two left hand side wheels touching the ground. Dimitri gawped, expecting the enemy's vehicle to overturn or at least crash into the adjacent pawnbroker's shop. Yet Gavin had tugged again on the steering wheel while cranking on the handbrake. As all its occupants screamed in horror, the 99mobile performed a complete 360-degree spin, dicing with certain disaster and scattering a passing band of pedestrian pigeons. But then it came unceremoniously to a sudden stop, its nose coming to rest inches away from the terrifying rollercoaster style drop that was The Hundred Steps.

'They're history' said Dimitri, believing the point of no return - or no further progression - been reached. 'Let's go.'

He was just about to leave the Mercedes with Lewis, both packing their loaded pistols, when the ice cream van inched forward.

'I'm not going down The Hundred Steps. I'm not going down The Hundred Steps,' Gavin bleated, as he delicately applied the gas, dreading the inevitable.

'It's that or a bullet in the head. They've got guns!' cried Bob, spotting the brandished weapons through the rear window. 'You choose.'

'Sh-i-i-i-t-t-t! We're going down The Hundred Steps!' Gavin was soon wailing as the van was half-heartedly launched, yet went immediately diving and tumbling into its bone-shattering, pogoing descent into what seemed like the Valley of Doom.

'Are they completely irresponsible? There is sign there that says *pedestrians only.*' Dimitri seemed quite happy to surprisingly turn into a law-abiding motorist. Especially as he saw before them the *edge of the world* plunge here at the very top of Drabbleton's valley sunken town centre - a seemingly endless Victorian stone staircase less than eight feet wide but terrifyingly steep. 'We cannot follow,' he wisely concluded.

'Are you mad? Get after them Dimitri,' Roxanne demanded.

'I do not like heights,' Dimitri then confessed sheepishly, showing a kind of weakness to his front seat passenger that she hadn't seen in him before. Nor was she going to welcome now.

'Neither would you like Mr Volkov's angry hands around your neck. Remember that?' She narrowed her eyes and stared at him hard.

'OK, I remember,' he mumbled reluctantly. He edged his car towards launch pad.

'It's called The Hundred Steps,' said Lewis casually enough, reading the street sign. 'Wonder why.'

'Because there's probably a hundred steps, fool!' Dimitri snarled. He took in the deepest of breaths and then went for it.

'Sh-i-i-i-t-t-t! We're going down The Hundred Steps!' Dimitri then screamed while Roxanne just sat back in her seat and closed her eyes, trying to relax through the ride. Hardly possible. Meantime, Lewis was ear-to-ear smiling.

'This is cool!' he whooped. He'd always liked rollercoaster rides.

Boing, boing, boing, boing went the old ice cream van, bouncing down the steps, rattling so badly that it seemed most likely it would imminently explode, shattering into a hundred or more rusted pieces.

B'doing, b'doing, b'doing, b'doing went the plush Mercedes, its passengers benefiting from top-of-the-range suspension that meant their downhill kangaroo hop was only painful, but not excruciating.

The ice cream team had pulled away, due to Dimitri's temporary prevarication, but again the Mercedes had now gained ground - due mainly to the van's numerous buffeting collisions with both brick walls that framed the stairway's descent. Gavin had tried to navigate, but his steering wheel hadn't much wanted to cooperate at that juncture. *Whoops*, there went a wing mirror. *Whoops*, there went the menu board from the side of the van. The passage of the 99mobile resembled that of a calamitous bobsleigh team, on a daredevil run where all the athletes in the cockpit are blindfolded.

'We're going to die!' yelled Gavin.

'Try steering and we might have a better chance,' Bob grumbled.

The van bashed against a wall once again.

'This *is* steering!' the miffed driver retorted. 'Muppet!'

'Then try *not* steering!'

Gavin looked at his passenger for clues. *What?* Bob mimed taking his hands of the steering wheel. *Was he insane?* But then again, could that idea really make anything worse?

'OK then.' Hands free mode was quickly engaged with Gavin instead raising his hands over his head in classic rollercoaster rider pose.

'Good!' Bob congratulated in approval as the van - unhampered by human interference- sailed a steady path down through the last quarter of the stairway, no more buffeting, no more scrapes. The Gods of Drabbleton were on their side.

'Whoooooo!' hollered Lewis in the back of the Merc, also having adopted the rollercoaster ride pose. 'Got to do this again later!'

'Shut up Lewis!' shouted his unexpectedly petrified boss, himself now so grateful that the final steps were about to be traversed. His hands were literally trembling as he gripped his steering wheel with a steel-like grip.

The last of The Hundred Steps exited out into Town Hall Square - and should any vehicle foolishly attempt their descent there would be every chance it would end up careering into either Ted's Cafe on the right or the statue of James Brimstone on the left. Gavin had pictured that outcome in the final few seconds of the perilous drop. Retaking the wheel, he somehow knew to swerve hard right when he then skidded again but missed Ted's shop window by an inch.

'Good driving for a change,' said Bob.

'Thanks.' *Amazing what sheer terror can do for you,* Gavin privately concluded.

Dimitri had no picture of the Town Hall square in his mind, however, and when he came crazily careering out from the Steps passageway his car went heading straight towards the statue. He rammed down on his brakes, which in turn screeched as if in horror. No more than half an inch was the space between his front bumper and the base of the statue's plinth when the Mercedes came to a most fortuitous halt. It then took several seconds before anyone in the car dared to breath or move. Until Roxanne shuddered when she saw the stern face of James Brimstone looking down on her from his platform with seeming contempt and disappointment. The family resemblance to Bryce freaked her out in an instance.

'Come on, reverse, go!' she commanded of her still trembling driver who clearly was no lover of thrill-seeking theme park rides. Another deep breath from Dimitri though and the Mercedes was quickly on its way again - trying to make up valuable lost ground on the 99mobile that had tootled off up Drury Lane.

But all was not well in the still fleeing van as some violent vibration then shook through the whole vehicle so that it might have been in the middle of an earthquake.

'What's that terrible knocking?' wondered a much-alarmed Bob, holding tightly onto an equally frightened Rocky.

'Raspberry's done for I think,' Gavin moaned as if in grief.

'What's Raspberry?' asked Bob, puzzled.

'You're sat in her obviously! It's the pet name for my van.'

'Your yellow van! Called Raspberry?'

'Shut up, Bob.'

The 99mobile managed to limp and hop another thirty yards or so along Drury Lane before the unendurable shrieking sound of its metal axle grating against tarmac coincided with the back end capsizing dramatically to the right. As the now lopsided van ground to an involuntary halt, Gavin and Bob watched, silently stunned, as a chrome hub-capped rear wheel merrily spun on its way past the cab and off down the road.

The Mercedes parked up about ten yards behind them. Gavin and Bob both swallowed hard and expected the gunmen to approach at any moment.

'Goodbye, Rocky old friend. It's been a good life together,' said Bob, stroking the head of his mangy pet.

Over to the left was a small Council owned children's play area - just a row of swings, one little slide and an out-of-order roundabout. Bob's life flashed by in his mind. Surely it was only yesterday when he'd been a child on a swing being pushed by his late mother - just like these few kids with their parents in the mini park today. *Goodbye cruel world!*

Once again Dimitri and Lewis readied their guns. But this time it was Gavin who'd been the thinker. Suddenly the warped and cacophonous strains of *Greensleeves* filled the air, destroying the peaceful harmony of the play area. Little kids, who seconds ago had been happy enough to enjoy a harmless go on the swing or slide, now turned into demanding little brats. Parents' faces fell as they inwardly griped at the underhand tactic of an ice cream van stopping outside a children's playground.

'Ice cream! Ice cream!' half a dozen demonically possessed sproglets sang in unison

Outwardly, the parents were all smiles of course. None of them wanted to be the one meanie mum or dad who was seen to be denying their little treasure an ice cream treat when all the other kids were being indulged. Ice cream vendors knew how to press all the blackmail buttons alright. But there was really nothing any of them they could do.

So, the occupants of the black Mercedes sat back in frustration as Gavin's lopsided van was quickly surrounded kerbside by a small gathering of suckered in parents and their little piggies.

'Now what?' groaned Lewis. 'We can't shoot 'em in front of kids.'

'We wait a while,' Dimitri replied, inwardly simmering. 'He can't serve ice cream all night.'

'Yes, but the longer we wait around here the more people will notice us.' Roxanne observed with a snap. 'Not good.'

'Valid point.' He tried to smile sweetly to his clever clogs girlfriend. 'OK, we wait for ten minutes, then move on. But he'll have surely served this lot by then.'

In fact, only five minutes later and Gavin was getting well through the queue with no fresh punters seeming to be appearing on the horizon. Dimitri smiled, biding his time. It wouldn't be long now.

But just then somebody had decided to recover Raspberry's back wheel from the grass verge over the road and was helpfully bringing it back to its original owner. Gavin and Bob had been so busy serving customers with what little was left of the flakes and cones that they hadn't noticed a marked police car pull up in front of them. It was actually the hugely framed PC Duckworth carrying the wheel as PC Chabra – half his size - trailed along a little way behind him, not really cut out for physical work. The two constables waited patiently for the last of the parents to be served but then approached the serving hatch.

'You two again,' said Duckworth, remembering the jump-start favour he and his colleague had helped out with the previous Friday. Plus, hadn't they seen the taller guy outside the chippy?

'Small world,' said Gavin with a welcoming smile. He'd never been happier to see Drabbleton coppers.

'Hello,' said Chabra breezily with a token wave.

'Time to go,' said Dimitri in the Mercedes still parked just a few yards away, eyeing Duckworth and Chabra with contempt.

'These guys are *so* lucky!' Lewis complained. He really did want to get imminent revenge on the little guy who'd embarrassed him on his first ever hit.

'Not for long. Tomorrow we will soon track down an ice cream van with such a silly statue on its roof. You can use your friendly way with the locals, Lewis. Somebody will know where this ridiculous ice cream man and his friend are living.'

'Sure, boss,' said Lewis, pleased that his line manager at least thought he was good for something.

'If we torture the midget before killing him, we will learn the whereabouts of the other two professional killers - the Polish lady and Muslim gentleman who incapacitated you, right? No witnesses!'

'Yes boss, good idea boss.' Lewis kicked himself for not thinking of that. He would have just popped the tiny guy by now.

'Tomorrow then,' Roxanne assented.

'Yes tomorrow,' her lover and Volkov's chief hitman confirmed. 'But first we have appointment with one Gavin Hargreaves at 21 Mayfair Avenue.'

He then engaged gear and slowly glided the Mercedes away past the ice cream van and off down Drury Lane. Gavin and PC Duckworth were too busy in each other's company to clock that smooth exit, although Bob did finally notice. Breathing more easily he gave his ally a furtive little nudge in the ribs and nodded towards the disappearing vehicle. Gavin got the message and a sense of relief physically rippled through his entire body. At least nothing else could go wrong today. Could it?

'Is this your vehicle, sir?' PC Duckworth wanted to know.

'Yes, it is!' Gavin was proud to admit. He waited to hear the officer's praise for this fine example of a classic, commercial automobile.

'And is this your wheel?' the PC continued, holding said piece of evidence aloft.

'Again, yes!'

'I expect you know then that it is a criminal offence to be in charge of an ice cream van on a public highway - if one of its wheels has come off. Sir, I may have to arrest you.' PC Duckworth seemed very pleased with his efficient execution of traffic policing.

'Are you sure it's a criminal offence?' Bob pulled a puzzled face.

'Mmm, I think so,' Duckworth replied, maybe already less assured.

'Not sure about that myself,' Bob almost sang in a patronising voice that suggested he knew better. 'Is it in the Highway Code?'

'Not ice cream vans *specifically*,' Duckworth backtracked.

'Right,' said Bob, looking like a virtual giant at the serving hatch, despite his mere sixty-three inches of actual height. 'It might not stand up in court then if you can't be *specific*. The Law is usually very *specific*.'

'That's true, I suppose,' said the fast-deflating officer.

'Yes. So, if you arrest him, it might all be for nothing. Plus think of all that paperwork you'd have to do down the Station. Coppers on the telly are always moaning about paperwork.' Bob shook his head in sympathy for the administratively burdened.

'That's also true.' Duckworth was shuffling around not really knowing what to say. It was time for Gavin to come to the rescue.

'I tell you what, Officer, why don't I treat you both to a lovely 99 each and we'll say no more about it.' He beamed out a sunshine smile.

'I am partial to a 99, it has to be said,' the PC weakened, but was still thinking things through. 'Hang on though. You're not trying to bribe *Officers of the Law,* are you?'

'No, course not,' Gavin crossed his heart. 'I wouldn't dream of it.'

'Oh.' Duckworth sounded disappointed. Was he talking himself out of a free 99?

'Actually, it's his first day in business,' interjected Bob, back on form. 'Guess what? You are his 100th customer of the day.'

'*I wish,*' muttered Gavin to himself. Mind, after that late flurry at the playground he was now on an improved minus thirty quid for the day, taking into account the parking fine. Bob nudged him in the ribs so that he'd stay focussed on the charm offensive.

'The lucky 100th customer always gets a free ice cream for him or her, plus a friend or colleague,' the small PR guy chirped.

'That's different,' Duckworth gushed. 'Blimey! I never usually win anything!'

'It's your lucky day then! Congratulations,' said Gavin, handing over a hastily assembled 99 cone.

'Excuse me Harry,' PC Chabra meekly interjected. 'Weren't we supposed to be looking out for a swanky black Mercedes?'

'Yes, we were. *Murder suspects.*' Duckworth bloated his chest, expecting the ice cream guys would be well impressed with the seriousness of the crimes he and his colleague were playing a part in tackling.

Bob and Gavin both nodded, as if in awe.

'Only a swanky black Mercedes has just driven off down the road.'

'Why didn't you say something, for Heaven's sake?' Duckworth suddenly flipped to being irked, no more showing off. DI Slater would have them for this.

'I didn't want to interrupt your conversation,' said the polite junior.

'Did you get its reg plate?' Duckworth clung on to the hope of any small crumb of comfort.

'Some of it,' Chabra momentarily smiled, although this quickly fell away. 'But then I got distracted when he mentioned a free 99.'

'OK, well we need to radio in whatever you've got,' the elder officer was growing impatient. 'What *have* you got?'

'P...' Chabra proudly announced. 'There was definitely a P in it. Or it could have been B - as they're quite similar from a distance.'

Duckworth stared at his astute and brilliant colleague in admiration. He could go far, this kid and Bob seemed to be agreeing – as the brightest buttons in Drabbleton obviously came in small packages.

'Good work, lad,' he boomed, heartily slapping Chabra's back. 'Let's get on it.'

'Don't forget your ice cream,' Gavin smiled to the rookie PC as he offered up the second 99 cone.

'Cheers, thanks,' replied the agreeable young man.

With that the officers were on their way. Soon all operational police cars in Drabbleton would be on the lookout for a black Mercedes SUV now known to have the letter P - or maybe B - somewhere on its number plate. Surely the net was inexorably closing in on Dimitri and co?

Half an hour later, Gavin and Bob had finished off jacking up the van and replacing its wheel. Miraculously, Raspberry had seemed to be over its traumatic Hundred Steps misadventure. They headed for home, enjoying trouble free motoring, but fearing that the Disposals Inc team may well have beat them to it. The van needed to be hidden for the night. Then they, in turn, needed to lie low.

23
- UNWANTED CALLERS -

The eight feet high ice cream moulding affixed to Raspberry's roof didn't exactly make the old van easy to cloak away discreetly. But underneath the Victorian railway arches, at the bottom of Mayfair Avenue, a series of garages and workshops seemed to offer the perfect solution. Luckily, Gavin knew the owner - one Spanner Tanner, the local mechanic who for had done his best over the years to keep Lizzie on the road - despite the odds. For a tenner, Tanner had been more than happy enough to offer Raspberry a week's parking under Arch 16c - a timber doored, secure lock-up that was just the ticket for hiding attention seeking ice cream vans away from professional assassins.

Having completed the necessary with Tanner, and then having parked Raspberry safely out of sight, Gavin, Bob and Rocky were now on the five-minute walk down Mayfair Avenue back to their homes.

'So come on then,' Gavin started out reviving unfinished business, 'you're saying you seriously shot that kid. I think it's time you explained.'

Bob inwardly groaned. The Bodysnatchers had been doing so well at keeping their joint murder efforts a secret. But that black Mercedes and its occupants inconveniently turning up, just as it did, had seemingly changed everything. Serendipity aside, both men and dog could have died today. So annoying though it was, Bob conceded that maybe his friend was owed the truth.

'OK, so I didn't expect to be seeing him again for a start,' he sighed. 'I thought he'd have well scarpered after what he did.'

'And what was that?' Gavin saw his septuagenarian neighbour take in a deep breath.

'See, it was all kicking off at Brimstone Mill last Monday. The kid was part of a hit team who'd come to shoot you-know-who. And he did. He stuck a bullet right between his eyes, pro killer style. But only after I'd tried suffocating the bastard first, you know, that cling-film idea I told you about.'

'It's hard to believe that worked,' Gavin screwed his face, trying to picture that unlikely scenario.

'Tough, it did!' came the emphatic confirmation. 'But probably cos your mate Krystyna had apparently rat poisoned him - well that's what she's saying. He wasn't putting up much of a fight to be honest.'

'Krystyna? No way.' Gavin balked as he realised he been recently sharing intimate moments with a murderer.

'Yep, it's true. She hated Brimstone, apparently, like the rest of us. Like you too, hoping to bump him off with that silly app.'

'I'll give you that,' came the muted reply. *Maybe Krystyna wasn't so bad, after all.*

'Just like Dinesh as well.'

Gavin's eyes dilated and he stopped walking. The two men faced each other in the street.

'What's he got to do with it?'

'Well, your sweet little Indian takeaway owner who everybody thinks is the nicest guy in Drabbleton - well he only stuck a meat cleaver into Brimstone's skull, didn't he?'

Gavin remained silent for several seconds as he processed this flummoxing fact.

'No way! *Bloody hell.* Dinesh, the killer chippy man!'

'All true.'

'But how come you didn't tell me all of this before now?'

Bob tutted. Did he have to spell *everything* out.

'If you are in on a co-murder and are hoping to get away with it, you can't go round town blabbing all about it, now can you? But then you could have been shot today 'cos of me. So, yeah... sorry for dragging you in, like.' Bob awkwardly kicked a littering Coke can into the road.

'Yeah, but I do think I was already involved. Fair enough though.' Shock over and apology accepted, Gavin purposely recommenced the walk home; Bob quickly skipped along after him. 'But I get it now why you were so willing to help me get rid of that body. Bit of self-interest there. Pub quiz team - *bollocks!*' he scoffed, almost bitterly amused at his own naivety.

'Alright, don't be sulky about it. Because we *did* help you Gavin,' Bob asserted, throwing out an emphatic arm gesture. 'And we will help you again, if necessary.'

'Thank you,' Gavin finally conceded, after yet another processing pause.

'I suppose we are all in this together now. But I don't expect Dinesh and Krystyna will be that thrilled that I've told you everything.' Bob suddenly looked concerned.

'We've been chased today by people trying to actually kill us. I think we can handle a bit of pub quiz team whingeing.' Gavin smiled at his feisty old neighbour - *the cling film murderer.* He really didn't think the little guy had it in him.

'Good one, you're right,' Bob chilled.

Gavin's house was now coming into view. The gate was open, so it didn't take long for the pair to notice that the front door was slightly ajar too. But no car out front. A little nearer and they saw that the door itself had probably been forced - its latch was hanging askew of obviously jemmied screws.

'Damn, looks like they've already been round,' said Gavin, saying hello for the second time in a day to spasms of anxiety gripping his insides.

'Let's wait here for a minute,' Bob said, pulling back on his friend's arm and crouching behind the bonnet of neighbour and market trader Mike's white van, parked in its usual spot across the road. 'Someone might still be in there.'

Gavin nodded and bobbed down out of the line of sight of his house. They then patiently waited and watched.

*

Compared to his opulent Knightsbridge abode, Loom House was a relatively modest seven-bedroom Gentleman's Residence acquired by Bryce Brimstone, two years ago, as his Drabbleton base. Situated on the outskirts of the town, it had been built for a minor industrial merchant during more prosperous historic times - when mock Gothic architecture saw houses built with pointed arches, fancy stone carvings and heavy mouldings. In contrast to the radiant marble floors, neutral walls and daylight enticing windows of the London house, here we had dusky, flocked wallpaper, swathes of dark oak floors and panelling - the dimness inside only made grimmer by opaque stained-glass windows and stern window shutters. This was a joyless and grim abode, suitably bleak for Drabbleton maybe, but a place quite incompatible with the tastes of a modern A-lister wannabe and former super-model such as Roxanne. She inevitably hated everything about it.

Yet here she was today paying her only second ever visit to the house on only her second ever visit to Drabbleton. Following her first brief stopover, on Bryce's invitation last year, she'd promised herself never to return to this life-draining and grimy eyesore of a town and the equally miserable pile that her husband had chosen here to live in.

But Roxanne was nothing if not pragmatic, so she'd put all those detestations aside for now. Bryce's business affairs did have to be settled and his Will released. On the latter, Roger Payne, of Payne & Cheetham's solicitors, was based here in Drabbleton and had so far been robustly guarding details of the Will from Roxanne - as per his brief. She'd therefore concluded that a personal visit might help. Persuading men to come round to her point of view had always been one of her talents.

Plus, of course, herself and her Disposals Inc associates needed discrete lodgings for a few days while they took care of business on Mr Volkov's side of the arrangement.

Mrs Joyce, the middle-aged local and housekeeper, had been expecting Roxanne. But it was a little later than expected when she finally answered the doorbell to welcome the three London guests. Well, she wasn't to know how they'd been delayed, after all, by a hot pursuit of an ice cream van down Drabbleton's perilous Hundred Steps. They did all look tired though, almost bedraggled there on the doorstep, poor things.

'Ah, Mrs Joyce,' said Roxanne, not exactly gushing. 'We meet again.'

'Good evening, Mrs Brimstone,' the thickly built housekeeper replied politely. 'Yes, it has been a while. But welcome back to Loom House.'

'Thank you.' Roxanne pointed to her suitcases, so that Lewis would jump to order.

'Do you need help with the luggage?' asked Mrs J, stepping gamely forwards onto the gravel.

'No, we are strong men,' smiled Dimitri, himself carrying three of the hefty items. 'We are fine with a few bags.' He entered the cavernous but dismal entrance hall. He liked the place. More like home in Russia.

'Hi,' said Lewis as he then bundled himself through the doorway, clumsily scraping the flock wallpaper with Roxanne's huge and weighty suitcase.

'Careful Lewis, that is *Dior* luggage!' Roxanne scolded. 'That cost more than you earn in months.'

'Sorry, Mrs. Brimstone,' Lewis mumbled. 'Cool place!' he quickly recovered, however, grinning at the housekeeper.

'I am so sorry about the news of your husband, Mrs Brimstone,' Mrs Joyce continued, after secretly nodding at Lewis in amusement and closing the huge mahogany door behind them all. 'It was such a shock. It must be very upsetting for you.'

'Yes Mrs Joyce, thank you.' Roxanne could easily play the part of the grieving widow. Such an easy actress. 'A big shock indeed. But we all must cope.'

'We'll do our best,' said the housekeeper, admiring the younger woman's stoicism.

'Good.'

'I have ordered in the salmon for you, as requested.'

'Thank you. We will eat at eight sharp.' A matter-of-fact command.

'As you wish.'

Mrs Joyce seemed to have the prim and proper air of waiting staff from years gone by about her. This, only because she had quickly learned from Bryce that the toffs from London seemed to enjoy imagining they were Lords and Ladies from a Jane Austin novel. If they were going to mix with the Drabbleton peasantry, then the least they could expect was deference and a smattering of good old-fashioned subservience. Mrs Joyce was only too happy to play this part as she was a skilled actress herself. Besides an adequate salary for cooking and cleaning for the late master, she'd enjoyed suitable private accommodation in a suite up in the eaves of the house. Here she was comfortably bringing up her teenage child, following a messy divorce some years back. Her only hope now was that her employment might somehow continue.

'Please show these gentlemen to their rooms,' Roxanne required of her. 'I have a call to make.

'The drawing room is ready,' said Jane Austen's housekeeper. 'I have lit the coal fire.'

'At this time of year?' It was late Spring after all, thought Roxanne.

'This house needs a fire all year round, pretty much. No central heating.'

Mrs Joyce inwardly smiled at the shocked faces of the two Southern softies - although this Russian bloke seemed nonplussed.

'OK, thank you for now,' Roxanne concluded as the gathering dispersed and Mrs Joyce started a small tour of the house, for the benefit of Dimitri and Lewis, as she led them off to their spacious but stylistically grim bedrooms.

Roxanne quickly took herself off to the drawing room, another darkly panelled cavern whose focus was a substantial stone fireplace, complete with gargoyle carvings. A coal fire raged within, its flames rising as if to reach the enormous oil painting on the wall directly above. It was a painting that her husband had taken pride in showing her on her previous visit last year - his specially commissioned portrait of himself, no less. From his pride of place on the wall, he looked down at his wife with a supercilious smile, reminding her only too well of his constant scheming and manipulation. But Roxanne knew she had positioned herself in the ascendancy now. As she reached for her phone, she laughed back, scorning her demised husband, hoping these flames in the hearth were merely reflections of those that were perpetually burning him now in Hell.

Alice had been expecting her call.

'Hi, sister-in-law, I've arrived,' Roxanne heralded herself into Alice's previously peaceful evening.

'Roxanne. Good journey?' came the less than enthusiastic enquiry.

'Not exactly.' A heavy sigh. 'Still, here we are.'

'So it seems,' said Alice, flashing back to the last time the pair had met the previous year, over at the bungalow. On that occasion, Roxanne had laughed at its pokiness and ditsy provincial decor. Far from reining her in, Bryce had only joined in on the disdain, expressing his disbelief that someone as successful and powerful as he was now had been brought up in 'this little hovel.'

'Thank goodness you escaped, darling!' Roxanne had sympathised, before disappearing from Alice's life for a whole year - until such time as her email yesterday pre-empted this call.

'Anyway, cutting to the chase, can you meet me here at Loom House at ten in the morning,' Roxanne enquired, realising that small talk was both pointless and quite unnecessary.

'I'm working in the morning. But I can take a lunch break at midday and see you shortly after that.'

'We need to discuss Bryce's commercial affairs, his Will, stuff like that.'

'I know.'

With the briefest of goodbyes, the bare-boned conversation was over. Alice wondered if Roxanne knew what exactly was in the Will. She herself had no idea but considered that it was well within her sister-in-law's means to have found out the full story by now. She wasn't expecting good news. Nor did she particularly care, as Bryce's fortune had never been something she'd ever had her eye on.

★

As the telephone conversation between the less than congenial sisters-in-law was concluding, Gavin and Bob were still taking cover behind Market Mike's van, still not yet entirely sure that it was safe to venture towards the clearly encroached house.

'I've got an old Nazi pistol over at mine,' said Bob. 'Do you think I should get it?'

'*What?*' It took a moment for Gavin to realise that his old neighbour wasn't joking.

'Yeah, it belonged to Brimstone. I nicked it from his cupboard and that's how I came to shoot the kid in the arm. I didn't think it was real. But then I thought *I'm well keeping this,*' Bob chuckled.

'I think you should have stuck to cling film, myself,' Gavin tutted. 'I don't see you and guns mixing well, somehow.'

Bob looked insulted. It was his skilled shot that had put Lewis out of action up at the mill, after all. As such, he considered himself quite the firearms expert. Not one to have to tolerate being lectured to by armed combat virgin, Gavin Hargreaves.

'OK, Negative Nelly,' he grouched, so say we meet these bad guys in a dark alley. One of them's got a gun, I've got a gun. That's evens. Then the second one's got a gun and you've got what? A *disapproving stare.* You tell me where it all goes wrong.'

'Fine then,' said Gavin, hiding his eyes in a hand. 'Go and get your stupid gun if you're going to make a big deal about it!'

Bob grinned. A finely argued victory. 'I will, then!' he rejoiced as he then furtively hopped over the road as if across dangerous enemy territory, swinging his Co-op carrier bag as he went. He'd wisely left Rocky safe with his younger neighbour. Too dangerous, this operation, for family pets. On reaching his own doorway, amazingly unchallenged by sniper fire, he turned to send Gavin a confident thumbs up - *so far so good!* Then he disappeared inside his house, only to reappear less than a minute later brandishing a Nazi Luger in his right hand.

'For crying out loud, try and be a bit discreet about it,' uttered Gavin to himself as Bob crouched and crept between the two houses, gun held aloft. Luckily no passers-by were around to witness Bob's ensuing armed assault on 21 Mayfair Avenue. But waving Gavin and Rocky to quickly join him, he took in one last deep intake of air before shouting '*Go! Go! Go!*' and wildly charging - commando style - through the already ajar front door and towards whatever peril lay in wait.

'Bloody hell, hang on!' cried Gavin, hardly expecting this sudden burst of energy and dynamic lead from the front from Bob. He belatedly dashed across the road as fast as he could, realising that if intruders were inside, then Bob would be meeting them at any second. He braced himself for the inevitable manic exchange of gunfire.

As Gavin threw himself into his hallway, fully ready to employ his *disapproving stare* any moment now, Bob was already casually sauntering back towards him, pistol at ease.

'There's nobody here, pal. But your place is trashed!'

Rocky then appeared, a puzzled reinforcement but one mainly hoping to find a place for a nice lie down. The lounge was a good bet, but as he and Gavin both ventured inside, they could see that Bob wasn't exaggerating. *What a mess!*

Chaos reigned, the sofa had been turned over, all the drawers in the sideboard pulled out - their contents scattered - and the coffee table upended. Similar mayhem in the dining room and kitchen. Gavin was miffed. He had only cleaned and tidied up on the previous Saturday. He shouldn't have even bothered. Meanwhile, Commando Bob was already 'sweeping' upstairs - same mess, but all clear of enemy hostiles.

'Look at this,' said Bob, as he then descended the stairs holding up a picture frame recovered from his neighbour's bedroom. It was a photograph of Gavin and Freddie, together in a bumper car when the Easter Fair had come to town last year. The glass inside the frame had been purposely smashed.

'That's just petty,' Gavin complained, taking the picture into his hands for a sorry inspection. 'Why've they broken that thing?'

'Well now you'll know they've seen what you look like, I guess,' ventured Bob, stroking his chin wisely. 'They'll know Gavin Hargreaves and the ice cream man are one and the same too - if they recognised you from earlier, that is.'

'Damn it! I bet they did.'

Out in the car crash of a kitchen, every cupboard and drawer turned inside out, Gavin then noticed that a certain solitary piece of crockery seemed to have survived the recent onslaught. The Disposals Inc murder souvenir mug sat there on the sink's draining board, last man standing. A rolled-up note stood proud of its rim and was soon being snatched at by an anxious householder eager to read its contents, be they for better or worse.

'What does it say?' asked an edgy Bob, coming up behind the reader.

'Give me a minute,' Gavin replied, unfurling the roll, then squinting his eyes trying to decipher the barely legible scrawl now before him. He then did his best to read aloud:

'Gavin Hargreaves. You have failed to return corpse as ordered. This is very serious. You MUST now contact us immediately on the Disposals Inc app. You MUST return the body.

PS. Very nice ice cream van. Very nice son.'

'Shit, I'm dead,' Gavin crumbled. 'And what do they mean, *very nice son?*'

'Don't go there,' said Bob, patting his friend's back. 'Mind games probably.'

'They're working, games or not.'

Gavin frantically pulled his mobile from a pocket and opened the darned app. But what could he say if he made contact? Not the truth anyway - *by the way, folks, Brimstone has been curried. Sorry 'bout that!'*

He closed the app.

'Shit! I don't know what to do!'

'Do you want me to help you put your stuff straight?' Bob tried to smile and just be practical. *Things could be worse - they could be dead already!*

'Nah,' Gavin sighed, failing to see the purpose. Instead, he pointed out towards the front door and a more urgent priority. 'Let's just try and get that lock screwed back on. I can't stay here - they might come back.'

Bob tucked his pistol into a trouser pocket, feeling it might be needed again any time soon.

'Bring some bedding and you can sleep in my spare room tonight,' he suggested, as breezily as he could manage it. 'They don't know where I live, so they won't be trying to find you there.'

'Thanks,' said Gavin, preoccupied with this sudden threat to Freddie. 'I'll take you up on that one, cheers.'

A toolbox was imminently on hand and the latch lock remedied. Soon the lights were extinguished on number 21 for the night as the front door was finally secured. Now it was time for both men to keep the lowest of profiles round at Bob's.

24
- CAPTIVE AUDIENCE -

At around 12.15 on the Tuesday morning, Alice's shiny little hatchback motor vehicle tootled up the quarter mile inclined drive that arced up to Loom House. The late Spring sunshine glistened on the river that ran through the grounds and busy songbirds darted through the clusters of mature trees, tending their nests. The mock Gothic residence that sat at the top of the hill, with its pollution-stained black stone, seemed to Alice to be the only less than pretty thing in these entire acres of otherwise unspoilt Lancashire woodland.

She stopped her car just by the steps leading up to the house, by the black Mercedes already parked there. Mrs Joyce was at the door to greet her.

'Oh, Ms Brimstone, how are you?' said the housekeeper as Alice ascended the small flight of sandstone stairs. 'Good to see you.'

'I'm fine Sheryl, thanks, how are you?' The two women seemed to be on good terms, mainly on account of Alice being the only Brimstone that Mrs Joyce could really tolerate - so unlike her brother as she was. The two had met each time Alice had turned up for dinner with Bryce, which wasn't that often. But after two years, the cumulative visits had nevertheless slowly stacked up and had led to some easy familiarity by now between the pair of them.

'I'm good, thank you - in the circumstances.' She ushered Alice in through the mighty timber door. 'It's all been a bit of a shock, all a bit new. But I am so, so sorry about your brother.'

'Thanks, yes,' said Alice, touched by the small gift of genuine concern. 'It's not an easy time.'

'If there's anything I can do...' Mrs Joyce tilted her head, as if in sympathy.

'Thanks. I'm fine just now,' came the typically Alice stoical reply.

Mrs Joyce smiled and was even considering giving Alice a little hug. But no, that would be crossing a boundary too far. The supportive smile would have to do for now.

'Mrs Brimstone is waiting for you in the drawing room. I'll bring through tea in a moment.'

'Thanks Sheryl,' said Alice, removing her beige raincoat and leaving it on the carved oak hanger in the corner. 'How's your Charlie doing by the way?'

'Great thanks. Last term of his art foundation year coming up. Then he's off to uni.'

'How exciting. Good for him.' Alice seemed sincerely pleased, genuinely interested. Yes, concluded Mrs Joyce, *so* unlike her brother - who had barely spoken to Charlie in the two years he'd been living with his mother in the staff quarters of the house

'Oh, to be young,' mused Mrs J, clearly proud of her son.

'Quite.' Indeed, since reaching forty years of age, Alice had often looked back on her younger existence both with nostalgia and longing. She really did envy someone like Charlie, just setting out on the new adventure of adult life, no blemishes in the copy book, no regrets yet about what might have been.

Mrs Joyce then disappeared down the corridor towards the kitchen as Alice, in turn, crossed the opulent crimson Indian rug in the hallway and entered the drawing room. Roxanne was standing over by the huge bay window but immediately hurried over to her sister-in-law, arms wide open. Alice was hardly expecting such a gushing welcome - quite out of character for Roxanne. *What was she after?*

As this awkward sisterly reception was then playing itself out, just over by the river, young Charlie had set up his easel and was painting a landscape watercolour. He'd liked this idyllic spot, perched as it was high above the distant town's grime. Here, he thought he could capture the beauty of relatively unspoiled Mother Nature in this woodland, then hint at the barbarous intrusion of mankind beyond - the scars on the once unsullied countryside as ugly industrialism made its mark. Which meant he'd paint the shit-hole called Drabbleton in the background, basically.

'Hey mate, that painting is sick,' said Lewis as he approached the young artist from behind, catching him unawares and making him totter slightly on his stumpy wooden stool. 'Oh, soz, didn't mean to make you jump, man.'

'No, whatever, it's OK,' said Charlie, steadying himself. 'Not used to seeing people out here in the grounds.'

'Yeah, soz man.' Lewis smiled clumsily.

'Are you one of the guys up from London with Mrs Brimstone?' Charlie eyed the smartly attired young man standing before him - and there he was in his denim and t-shirt scruffs, feeling suddenly under-dressed.

'Yeah, that'll be me. Couple of days, then you'll be back to your peace and quiet.' The intruder thought he'd better offer up a handshake. 'I'm Lewis, by the way.'

'Charlie, hi...' The briefest of weak handshakes was duly exchanged. 'My Mum's the housekeeper here.'

'Nice one,' said Lewis, scrutinising the work-in-progress watercolour. 'Very cool painting. Love them colours.'

'I'm having to get my finger out at the minute,' Charlie replied, starting to relax. 'Trying to get all my end of year submissions in at College.'

'You're doing good, looks like. I was pretty rubbish at school, myself,' Lewis laughed. 'Bombed my GCSE's. But the only thing I was good at was art. I'd have loved it if I could have been a painter. You know, a proper artist like you.'

'I'm hardly that,' Charlie laughed, slightly embarrassed. 'But you're only young.'

'I'm nineteen already.' Lewis seemed to think he was already ancient.

'Same as me!' The painter clearly thought that this new acquaintance might have a few years left in him yet. 'Do you do art stuff in your spare time? You don't need qualifications to be allowed to do your own thing.'

'I'd like to,' Lewis exhaled a wistful sigh. 'But this new job I'm doing - all very serious business and stuff - ain't going to leave me much time for hobbies.'

Charlie looked over at the sharp-suited visitor. He may have been wearing togs that cost maybe all a term's student loan, but he didn't seem very happy at all.

'If you still have a passion for painting you should go for it. There's adult evening classes that even my Mum had a go at. She loved it. There's probs something similar near you, well maybe.'

'Yeah, evening class?' Lewis's brain put that on his *maybe* list.

'Sure. Maybe Google it.' Charlie nodded in friendly encouragement.

'Nice one man, might well do that. Cheers for the chat,' Lewis waved and was then on his way. He was meant to be cleaning down and oiling the *Makarov* semi-automatic pistols in the systematic way that Dimitri had taught him. Time to get back to work. 'Enjoyed that,' he turned to wave again. 'Laters.'

Charlie returned the wave and returned to his own work. He felt so lucky he had a few years ahead of him to create art and then have fun at uni. That guy there had grown up too soon!

Meantime, as Lewis marched purposefully back up to Loom House, the conversation over tea and biscuits in the drawing room was now in full flow.

'I know you keep saying I must know what is in the Will, Roxanne. But I really don't know at all.' Alice was on the defence, but assertively standing her ground. 'Bryce was only fifty-two remember - but determined to live forever. He'd never think to discuss such a thing across the dinner table. Mr Indestructible, as he thought he was.'

'Yes, ironic really,' Roxanne smiled wryly. 'But I was sure you'd know something.'

She sighed and tried a softer approach.

'He claimed to love us both - well in your case that was certainly true, actually. You were his little sister and very big favourite.'

'Oh, I don't know about that,' Alice almost blushed. Roxanne saw her weaken.

'But why has he kept his Will, of all things, secret to both of the women who dearly loved him and were dearly loved in return?'

Nope, Alice could see she was going too far now. *Less of the melodrama please!*

'He'll have had his reasons. I've never really thought about it,' she casually dismissed.

'But it is so frustrating that his multi-million-pound estate is as good as frozen for now. I can't even get my hands on any cash - and I am his wife, for God's sake.' Roxanne replaced her bone china teacup a little too forcefully on its saucer, causing a minor liquid overflow. *Never mind!* she grimaced. 'Tony Payne, his solicitor, says he's professionally bound by the terms of the Will to only release the details of its contents in the event of Bryce's death.'

'Well then,' Alice shrugged. 'The police are pretty sure he is dead.'

'*Pretty sure* is not certain. We need to produce a body and a coroner's report.'

'I understand your problem,' said Alice, sounding irritated again. 'But I can't help you there. I don't have my brother's body hidden in my wardrobe.'

Roxanne threw up her hands in a dramatic apology for possibly overstepping the mark. 'No, of course not Alice. I wasn't suggesting...'

She shook her head like a braying horse. 'Forgive me for getting a little carried away.'

'No problem. Difficult days, eh?'

'Yes indeed,' she continued in more hushed tones. 'I did love him, you know. In my own way. And he loved me in his.'

Alice thought about that. *Love?* That wasn't a word she'd necessarily choose to associate with Bryce and Roxanne's relationship. For her brother, surely it was about the bragging rights of having pulled a renowned beauty a generation of years his junior. For Roxanne, the term *gold-digger* always came to mind - but maybe she was over-simplifying things? Probably not, she quickly concluded.

'That's all between the two of you. None of my business,' she replied, not really wishing to dwell any further on the question. 'But yes, I'm sure you both connected, as you suggest, in your own way.'

Although it seemed as though Roxanne was keen to continue to sell in this idea of an imperfectly perfect marriage. A loving wife would hardly have her husband bumped off, after all. Third party perceptions were important - especially so when it came down to the family.

'He was quite the character, wasn't he? Playful in so many ways,' she continued with the propaganda.

'A character, yes. But playful?'

'Well yes,' Roxanne laughed a little, as if recalling past evidence. 'His playfulness was usually at someone else's expense alright. But I enjoyed his pranks.' She raised her eyes, seeking out a pertinent example. 'Let me see... We were having a Charity Ball at the Knightsbridge house one evening. Full of boring celebs and dignitaries. This lecherous old MP - Hubert Devizes - had turned up with a high-class escort. Must have paid her a fortune, as she was gorgeous and he was the ugliest fruit to fall from the ugly tree, if you get me. So, he only sneaks her off to the bedroom after dessert. But Bryce was onto him and got a load of us to sneak upstairs to this viewing point he'd set up on top of the two-way mirrored ceiling. When the dirty old toad was having his todger orally serviced, Bryce turned on the lights in our upper room. Poor Devizes nearly had heart attack as he then saw twenty odd fellow guests lit up behind the mirror staring down at him. God, we all fell about killing ourselves as he struggled to get his wrinkly old thingy away while the horrified escort girl slapped his face thinking it was him who'd set the whole thing up. Happy days...'

'I'm not sure about that. I don't think London life would suit me.' Alice merely looked dismayed.

'Nonsense. You'd love it,' Roxanne snickered. 'Mind, I did hear he tried to have his fun here in Drabbleton too.'

Yet another angle aimed at building rapport with Alice.

'Wasn't there some poor bloke he made dress up as a Roman Centurion, for instance? In a bloody Call Centre, I ask you. What a loser he must have been,' she snorted.

'No, he was a nice bloke actually. Just needed the money.' Roxanne wasn't to know she had hit on a nerve.

'Come on, how low can you go for a few pounds a week?'

A millionaire wife, former supermodel from Knightsbridge, was hardly qualified to make judgements on the lives and compromised decisions of ordinary folk here in Drabbleton - that's how Alice saw it.

'Let's just say that Bryce and I didn't see eye to eye on that particular prank. Gavin was a nice, honest guy, as I said. Not some horny old corrupt MP from Westminster.'

'Gosh. Have I touched on a sensitive subject?' Roxanne seemed to enjoy anyone wriggling on the end of her line. But that *name* again?' Gavin, you say?'

'Yes, Gavin Hargreaves, I'm sure Bryce may well have bragged to you about how he humiliated him, alright.

'You're right, he did.' She remembered that precise phone call, in fact.

'Well please don't mention it again. Gavin and I walked out on our jobs at the Mill together, telling Bryce where to go, actually. From there we became a bit of an on-off thing.'

Now this was *useful*, Roxanne immediately thought.

'Yes, lots of girls have a thing about men in uniform, don't they say?' she gently mocked. 'But are you on or are you currently off with this Gavin fellow? If you don't mind me asking. I'm just a nosey bitch if you really want to know,' she cackled.

'We're *on-off,* as I say. We do have strong feelings for each other, but circumstances keep getting in the way.' Alice spoke quickly - clearly an uncomfortable situation for her to clarify.

'Ouch!' said Roxanne, indulging herself perhaps too much. 'Circumstances, eh? Well good luck with him if that's what will make you happy.'

'Thank you,' said Alice, grateful to see this little interrogation coming to an end. 'With a bit of better luck, I do think we could be happy together, I really do.'

'How very sweet.' A patronising conclusion, but Alice was by now past caring.

Roxanne then wrapped up the meeting fairly sharpish. She'd initially thought that this lunch time rendezvous had been a complete waste of time. Alice knew nothing of the Will that was of material use, so it seemed. Plus, her efforts to convince the sister-in-law of a secretly happy marriage she shared with Bryce hadn't come to much either. But this last revelation concerning one Gavin Hargreaves. Now that could change everything. Roxanne was then, after careful reconsideration, very glad indeed that she had invited her dearest sister-in-law here today for such a pleasant chat.

As Mrs Joyce saw Alice out and the two women traded farewell pleasantries on the driveway, Roxanne was swiftly on the phone to Dimitri - a quicker solution than tracking him down in the sprawling house. The information she had to impart concerning Alice and Gavin Hargreaves was succinctly delivered. Due to the lunchtime visitor's departure being delayed by friendly tittle-tattle with Mrs Joyce, by the time her hatchback was nearing the front gates Dimitri was already jumping into the Mercedes, Lewis at his side.

Alice, it seemed, would not be going far.

*

Cruising obliviously along the tree-lined country lane that would eventually lead her back to the grimness of Drabbleton town, Alice had just been replaying in her head the conversation about her and Gavin that she'd just exchanged with Roxanne. She'd surprised herself how quickly she'd been prepared to come to his defence once he was belittled by yet another Brimstone. She missed him, badly even - she realised that. But it was about time they both got whatever they had back on track. She called him on her hands free, determined to take the initiative.

'Hi, Alice,' Gavin answered almost immediately, sitting there bored on a sofa in next door's little front room. Bob raised an eyebrow. His neighbour didn't seem to be too good with the ladies. *This should be fun.* 'Great to hear from you.'

'Hi, thanks,' Alice cheerily began. 'Calling because I've just been talking about you with someone.'

'Who? Leo?' Gavin couldn't let it go.

'No, not with Leo,' Alice tutted. 'With my sister-in-law, Roxanne, up at Loom House - you know, Bryce's place. She's up from London trying to sort out some of his affairs.'

'Oh yeah, *Roxanne*,' Gavin replied, digging up a memory from deepest somewhere. 'His trophy wife. She visited the Call Centre just the once. Quite something,' he teased.

'If you like those cliched super-model looks, great legs, fantastic tits - yeah, well I suppose she is,' said Alice, taking the bait.

'I didn't actually notice, sorry.' One-nil.

'Very funny. Yeah, I bet.' But Alice had decided she wasn't to be derailed. 'Anyhow, I mentioned you to her - and to cut a long story short, it made me realise that we need to sort out this thing of ours, Gavin. Whatever it is. I'd really like us to be together.'

Gavin pulled the phone away from his ear and shook it, playing up to the keenly listening Bob. Did he just hear correctly?

'Well, course,' he finally affirmed, trying not to overdo the enthusiasm for the benefit of the audience.

'And I'm sorry about what happened with Leo.'

'Don't mention it again,' the shamelessly sanctimonious one whispered.

'You're being very good about it,' said Alice, growing a little tearful. It had been such a relief to her that Gavin hadn't just hung up.

'These things happen,' he said, sounding very worldly wise. But there was no way after this that Gavin would be confessing to his dalliance with Krystyna. *No way!* 'Sounds like that Roxanne's been talking some sense into you,' he ventured.

'I wouldn't say that exactly. But let's do dinner at mine tonight. I'll cook. Won't be as good as your Indian cuisine, mind.' She smiled, as if remembering an almost perfect evening - well some of it was perfect anyway.

'Hang on, Alice. Hang on,' Gavin suddenly interjected. He had just been trying to picture Roxanne from the one and only time he'd seen her - last year sometime when Bryce was giving her a tour of the Call Centre and much to her seeming dismay at the time. *That's why* he'd vaguely recognised the woman in the Mercedes yesterday.

This was a big problem.

'When you went up to that Loom House place there wasn't a certain black car on the drive was there? A big, posh Mercedes SUV?' Gavin was increasing his pace of delivery.

'Well yes,' Alice replied curiously. 'It was Roxanne's probably, or one of her team's I suppose.'

'Are you still there now?' came the urgent question.

'No, I'm driving back to work. Why?

'Just don't go back there again,' Gavin pleaded, his voice grave and emphatic. 'These are not good people.'

'Oh, do stop it,' Alice half laughed, her first instincts hoping some kind of punch line would be coming.

'I'll tell you later,' continued the deadly serious voice. 'Just stay away from Roxanne and anyone with her.'

'All very cryptic,' said Alice, but only a little less dismissively now.

Before she could think any more about it, in her rear-view mirror she noticed that she was being repeatedly flashed by another vehicle trying to catch her attention. In its passenger seat a suited young man was holding up and pointing to her own beige mac.

'Actually, that very car's behind me now. Two guys. They want me to stop. Looks like they've got my raincoat. Silly me, I've gone and left it behind.'

'Be careful, Alice.' Recalling the Hundred Steps pursuit, only yesterday, Gavin feared the worst.

'Don't be silly. I've just been there. What are they going to do now, *kidnap me?*' She giggled in the bliss of ignorance. 'I'll call you later.'

'Alice, stay on the line...' Too late. She'd hung up.

As the light blue hatchback pulled over onto the grass verge, under a canopy of great oak trees along this stretch of scenic country lane, the Mercedes then pulled up right behind. Lewis jumped out of the rear car's passenger door, carrying the forgotten item - and was soon waving at Alice through her own nearside window. She in turn smiled back at the pleasant looking young chap holding her coat and released her automatic door lock. Lewis nodded a thank you back at her and hopped into the adjacent seat.

'Mrs Brimstone sent us after you 'cos you'd forgotten your coat,' Lewis explained cheerily.

'Thanks. It's such a nice day I'd forgotten all about it. Chuck it in the back for me if you don't mind.' Alice looked very pleased that there were still some thoughtful people in the world.

Lewis obliged and bundled the raincoat over onto the backseat. As he leant over, though, his jacket fell open revealing first his crisp white shirt but then totally exposing his shoulder holster and gun. He then saw the sudden alarm on Alice's face, although she quickly looked away, freezing, and pretending she'd seen nothing. Gripping her steering wheel tightly, her whole body then tensed further, and she rigidly held a forward only view, nervously revving on her accelerator pedal - a quite involuntary reflex.

'Man, I hate doing this,' sighed Lewis, removing his gun from its holster and pushing it hard against the driver's ribs.

'Oh God,' Alice trembled, crumbling too in an instant. 'Are you going to shoot me?'

'I wouldn't be pointing it at you if I wouldn't use it,' Lewis scowled now, totally abandoning the nice young man persona. Alice snatched on a sharp intake of air, looking utterly petrified. Her abductor could see right then that she'd be no trouble. So, he moderately relaxed the gun's pressure against her rib cage. 'But look missus, the gun's just insurance really. If you behave yourself, you won't be harmed. If you mess with us, different story. Yeah?'

'Yes, of course. What do you want me to do? Drive?'

'Course, drive. Back to the house, nice and easy. I think you'll be staying with us for a while.'

Alice nodded, shaking still, but she did manage a neat three point turn on the quiet lane and was then back on the way to Loom House. As they passed the still onward facing Mercedes, Dimitri half-smiled at Lewis. *Nicely done.* He then flipped his own car around to steadily follow the hatchback.

Down by the riverside, Charlie was still painting as the two vehicles journeyed back up the gravel drive some fifty of so yards from his vantage point. He glanced up but thought nothing much of it. There were always comings and goings whenever guests were staying at the house. Nothing to do with him. But Lewis did see that he'd noticed their return. It bothered him.

At the top of the drive, the apprentice henchman then instructed Alice to veer away from the front of the house and off towards a building just to the right - a disused coach house that he'd discovered on his exploration of the grounds this morning. Mrs Joyce was well out of the way, Roxanne keeping her occupied, as agreed, with an unexpected interest in the vegetable garden. Knowing this, Lewis momentarily left the car - gun still in hand - and hauled open the two partially rotted wooden doors and then beckoned Alice to drive forwards. As Dimitri finally turned up, having left the Mercedes in its usual spot out front, Alice was getting out of the hatchback, hands in the air.

'No need for hands up,' said Dimitri, entering the building. 'We don't expect you are armed!'

'Nice one boss,' Lewis smiled. 'Didn't think of that.' Dimitri sighed.

Alice lowered her arms, not really knowing where to put them. She fidgeted nervously.

'Please, Lewis,' the senior kidnapper barked. 'Go get a nice chair so that the lady will be comfortable.'

The old coach house had obviously been a bit of a dumping ground for the main house for many a year. A disorganised pile of discarded items took up half of its floor-space. Lewis went rooting amongst old fridges, beds, wardrobes, home gym equipment, boxes of crockery, a lawn mower, a mirror, so on and so on, until he retrieved just the thing - a retro walnut, French bistro chair. He dusted it down with a bit of ditched ancient curtain and offered it up to Alice. She sat without thanking him for his efforts.

'I apologise for this,' said Dimitri, taking a small bunch of cable ties from his pocket and binding Alice's compliant wrists and ankles to the chair. 'It is mainly for the photograph. So too this…'

He then produced a leather ball gag and strapped it firmly across the freshly kidnapped woman's mouth, clearly not a pleasant sensation for her as she then moaned and wriggled in discomfort.

'Is there really any need for this?' Roxanne then demanded as she came striding into the cobweb infested outbuilding. 'Poor darling looks like she's in a porn movie!' She stared hard at Dimitri less than impressed. Alice sent a similar weaponised look, but in her sister-in-law's direction.

'If you had arrived one minute earlier you would have heard me say this is mainly for the photograph,' Dimitri snapped back. 'Please do not interfere. I am professional.'

'Sorry, I'm sure,' Roxanne smirked. 'Sensitive as ever?'

Dimitri ignored her.

'Good afternoon again, Alice,' she then beamed. 'I'm very sorry for all of this dramatic palaver, but you've only got yourself to blame really. You see, your *on-off* boyfriend, as you call him, seems to have stolen Bryce's murdered corpse. We had hoped the police would have found him with it and then charged him with murder - leaving us off the hook. And then we, in turn, would have conveniently retrieved the body from the police themselves. And then I'd have inherited my millions. Simple!'

She then turned suddenly angry.

'But the police in this wasteland of a town are too stupid to follow a simple tip-off. Just as your boyfriend seems to be reluctant to return Bryce's dear remains, for some reason quite beyond my comprehension. So, there you are. A problem. But also the full story!'

Alice continued to glare at Roxanne with contempt, not quite sure what elements of *the full story* to believe - but certainly furious that her sister-in-law might just have confessed to Bryce's murder. Then, how dare she have these brutes tie and gag her in this totally degrading and most uncomfortable way?

'Well, luckily for us, we've got you to help us to persuade him to do as he's told.'

Alice's expression suggested contempt might now be quickly turning into pure hatred.

'Found it,' said Lewis, fresh from the hatchback again where a quick rummage inside Alice's handbag uncovered her mobile. He tossed it over into the welcoming hands of his boss.

'No need to smile,' said Dimitri a few seconds later as he opened the phone's camera app and snapped away in Alice's direction. 'This is not birthday photo.'

Happy enough with his quick composition he then quickly found Gavin's details in *Contacts* and attached the image to a blank text. *Send.* So easy. Now... just wait.

In fact, the waiting game was even shorter than expected, as less than sixty seconds after he'd sent the pic the expected incoming call came pinging back.

'Who is this?' Gavin agitated. 'Who's this with Alice's phone?'

'Ah, Gavin Hargreaves. We speak together at last,' Dimitri replied, the essence of calm and in complete contrast to the mood of the caller. He flipped the mobile onto loudspeaker for the benefit of the room. 'You know who we are. Disposals Inc. You also know what we want. But now, as you have seen from our fun little picture, we have something to trade.'

'You had better not harm her. That's all I am saying.'

'Or else what? You will maybe come at me armed with an ice cream cone? But how good is ice cream cone against Russian made, *Makarov* semi-automatic pistol. I would win, I imagine.'

'I need time to sort out what you want,' said Gavin, somewhat breathlessly, but immediately disconcerting Alice that he may well indeed have Bryce's body. *Why hadn't he said something if it wasn't his fault?*

'You have already had time, Dimitri growled. 'We gave you fair notice of the collection, which you then failed to complete.'

'I need more time. But I can get you what you want.' The ensuing silence only made Gavin squirm a little more. 'Please,' he eventually murmured.

'Finally. English manners,' Dimitri grinned. 'OK you have one day. Twenty-four hours. We will meet tomorrow at one o'clock. Bring what we need. We will text location one hour before.'

'Right, got that,' said the caller, clearly relieved.

'But no tricks, or Alice dies. No police, or Alice dies. Only corpse of Mr Brimstone, please. Or...'

'Yeah, I get it,' Gavin interrupted. 'Alice dies...'

'Fast learner. Good!' Dimitri laughed. 'Until tomorrow then' He killed the call and placed the handset in his jacket. 'Finally,' he then fist-pumped. 'Progress!'

'Good work, yes good work, I will give you that,' Roxanne said as she pecked her lover on the cheek. 'Now can we at least remove that porn mask from Alice's face? It's making me quite sick to look at It.'

'Lewis,' Dimitri barked, clicking a finger to indicate that the request should be carried out. The young man got to work unfastening the mask. 'As I said, this was for photograph - and I am professional at this. It is often easier to restrain people with merely emotional and psychological shackles. As I am sure Ms Brimstone here will undoubtedly agree. After all, she wouldn't want Mrs Joyce or her son to come to any harm.'

The fear in Alice's eyes assured Dimitri of her compliance. Roxanne evidently approved of this proposed less primitive approach and kissed Dimitri once again.

Three miles away, over at Bob's, Gavin hadn't needed to have his own phone on loudspeaker. His diminutive neighbour had snuggled up against him, literally cheek to cheek.

'Now what?' said Gavin, as his thinking process tried to kick into overdrive. 'I'm stumped.'

'What did you say OK to them for?' Bob chastised. 'You can't give them back Brimstone's body in twenty-four hours. You can't ever give it back!'

'Don't you reckon I've been thinking about that problem myself over and over? Especially since they mentioned Freddie in that note.'

Bob puffed up his cheeks and then blew out the air. 'Yeah, 'spose,' he conceded. 'But now they're holding Brimstone's sister, they'll hopefully see no benefit in getting kids involved.'

'There is that,' said Gavin, happy to clutch at any straw. 'But them having Alice isn't exactly good news. Mind, do you know something? I do think they're holding her at Loom House - that's Brimstone's old pad.'

'I know, I heard. Good one. Why not tell the police?'

'Too dangerous,' Gavin fretted. 'Would you put the life of a loved one in the hands of Drabbleton's numpty police force?'

'No chance!' said Bob, pinching himself for his stupid suggestion. 'Then again, what chance have we got with only one bullet left in an old Nazi pistol?'

Only one bullet. Gavin pondered that sadly inadequate arsenal - in fact the entire sorry situation.

'We need to apply brains, not brute force,' he concluded. An instantaneous flash of inspiration wasn't exactly igniting inside his head. But the first glimmer of a potential idea was at least trying to get started.

'I think I'm coming up with a plan,' he finally half-smiled. 'It needs building on though.'

'Great,' Bob cheered. 'I'm your man for that. I do like a plan.'

'I'm going to need practical help too,' Gavin added, grabbing a pen and paper to start sketching out his idea. 'You, Dinesh and Krystyna - with luck.'

Well, I'm in. Dinesh and Krystyna will be too. I'd put money on it. Yeah!'

'Cheers, pal. So, this is my idea...'

Gavin took the pen and began to draw a map of Drabbleton. Bob eagerly watched on. *This could be fun!*

But back at Loom House, Lewis had no plan whatsoever about what to do about Charlie. He knew the young art student had seen Alice's hatchback returning just earlier. But had he spotted himself in the car with her? Of that he really couldn't be sure. Best to simply report the matter in. Dimitri would know what to do.

'Well observed, Lewis,' his boss commended later when he passed on the info. 'But what did Mr Volkov say was our golden rule?'

Oh no. The apprentice hit man hadn't thought this through, so he was immediately realising.

'No witnesses? You mean *that* golden rule?'

'Precisely,' Dimitri nodded, pleased that his apprentice was finally catching on. 'I will leave it with you then. Choose your moment, then *bang!*' Dimitri mimed shooting some poor victim's brains out. 'The more of these disposals you do, the easier it will become.'

'Harsh man,' Lewis grimaced. 'Very harsh.' But he understood very well now what had to be done in the name of expedience and the firm's motto. *Bad luck, Charlie. Seemed like such a nice kid too.*

25
- JAMES & GERTRUDE -

Bob had wasted no time in contacting Krystyna and Dinesh on that same Tuesday afternoon, but the latter wasn't exactly thrilled to hear his call to arms.

'But I have done my bit,' Dinesh had complained. 'Brimstone got axe in head and then I made him into very nice curry. Job done.'

'Yes Dinesh, I get it. But because of you Gavin has no body to give back to the London mob. They might do him for that now. Alice an' all.'

'Maybe they're just bluffing.'

'No Dinesh. We both saw that kid shoot Brimstone in his chair. He wasn't to know we'd already finished the old sod. They're pro killers, him and his mate. They've already trashed Gavin's place looking for him. Not only that, but we had a very close shave earlier. Could have easily been shot if a couple of coppers hadn't have turned up on the off chance.'

Dinesh had listened, reluctantly processed, and then had finally realised there was no point in being in denial.

'Yes alright. I know they are bad. I maybe should not have curried Brimstone after all.' He'd started to sound guilty.

'I wouldn't say that. It was a great curry,' Bob had chuckled, hoping to make the chippy man feel better.

'OK Bob. I will be right over,' Dinesh had sighed. It was a matter of duty now, he'd concluded.

Krystyna, on the other hand, had been easier to convince.

'I am in,' she'd said as she'd listened to Bob on the phone. 'I cannot trust you not to go falling into railway wagons, for a start. But Gavin is nice guy. I guess he deserves to live.'

'I'm sure he'll be pleased to hear that,' Bob had replied, slightly annoyed that Krystyna had blamed him for falling into that train. Along with Gavin and Dinesh, she'd been part of the inattentive team who'd lowered him below the arch of the bridge just as the thundering locomotive had approached. They were the ones to blame, surely! But he'd realised that this was not the time to start bickering. *Keep her sweet. She's in!*

By only about half past two that afternoon, then, Gavin's miniature army had been fully briefed round at Bob's. All three of them had expressed nagging doubts about the unusual plan's viability. But none of them had come up with a better idea. *What the hell, in for a penny...*

As a result, here they were now, Gavin at the wheel of Raspberry, Krystyna and Dinesh sitting side by side on the front passenger double seat and Bob crouching down in the back, just behind the handbrake. But following on from his departure from script on their last outing - legging it, having filched Brimstone's right arm - it had been decided that Rocky would be best off being left at home. Therefore, on this occasion, Bob had sensibly said toodle-oo to him, leaving him snout down, sulking on the rug.

'I have never been in ice cream van before,' said Krystyna as they trundled on their way to their first stop - Drabbleton Town Hall.

'Really?' said Gavin, happy to see any shared enthusiasm for his new World of Wonder. 'What do you think, then?'

'I think it is second most shit vehicle I have ever been in throughout my entire life.'

'Well at least it's not *the* worst,' the proud owner consoled himself.

'No, for sure. That was last car you had. That was the most shit.'

Gavin winked at her, maybe thinking that this ultra-critical banter was just a leftover bit of sexual chemistry from their last evening together. He checked to see if there was a glint in her eye. But all the stars were vacant, Krystyna's face sombre and a little grumpy. Their little moment had evidently been consigned to history.

'But this one is shit too, Gavin. An old rust bucket that will be our death if bad guys come after us.' Her features fell further, pulled down by the gravity of disappointment.

'You'd be surprised what she can do!' chirped in Bob, having had the recent experience of riding rough in this bad baby, and initially for the better too. 'As long as the wheel doesn't come off, like yesterday,' he reflected on second thoughts. 'She's not at her best if that happens, admittedly.'

'I fear the fall off the railway bridge has failed to cure his stupidity,' said Krystyna, covering her eyes. Bob just pulled his tongue out at her, hidden from her line of sight.

'I actually think the van is very super, Gavin,' said the second front seat passenger.

'Thanks Dinesh,' came the driver's reply, him happy to hear that at least someone round here had good taste.

'I wonder if it would make a good mobile chippy? I could get one, maybe.'

'Ice cream and chips! Half-decent business idea, that!' Gavin's mind started racing, new entrepreneurial fantasies starting to hatch. 'Could be thing of the future!'

'Yes, but you'll be thing of the past if you don't focus on job in hand,' Krystyna carped, pulling the dreamer back on track. 'Tell me - this waxwork of James Brimstone, it definitely looks like Bryce? The two were obviously born much more than a century apart.'

'Don't worry, you'll see for yourself,' Gavin confidently assured. 'The family resemblance is frightening really.'

'Does James Brimstone have a twisted nose too?' wondered Bob, always thinking.

'No, but I've got a workaround for that. My ex-wife, Marie. She's a beautician and hairdresser, right? She can do something cosmetic with the nose. Then restyle his wig so it's all modern-day Bryce-like.'

'Sounds good.' Bob was convinced.

'I still can't see Roxanne Brimstone believing a wax dummy is her dead husband,' Krystyna continued to grumble.

'She'll only get a brief look at it in the coffin we're picking up later,' Gavin replied, determined to stay positive. 'It'll be fine. Plus, we only need to distract them long enough to get Alice free.'

Sounds great to me,' said Bob, doubly convinced.

'And then what?' asked Dinesh, looking for the happy ending that he feared may not exist.

'Well Dinesh, *and then what* is the rest of the plan we haven't come up with yet,' Gavin affirmed conclusively - failing to provide the questioner with any conclusion at all.

'But keep thinking everyone,' encouraged Bob. We're good at plans. *Remember?'*

The ice cream van then rumbled into the cobbled square fronting the Town Hall. The commanding statue of James Brimstone stood there to welcome them, Gavin secretly fantasising that Drabbleton's founding father would no doubt have approved of the ingenious plan that they were about to execute this afternoon.

'OK, we're here. Has everyone got what they need?' Gavin scanned his troops and saw that all were ready for action.

Creeping forwards, stealth-like, they soon found themselves inside the *Cotton Town Exhibition*, mingling among artefacts and machinery from the Drabbleton's industrial past. Despite Alice's best efforts at putting up publicity posters and delivering leaflets, only one adult member of the public seemed to be currently visiting this grand collection of historical marvels. But she was making a beeline for the Ladies loos. The other adult, quickly spotted by Gavin and much to his irritation, was a uniformed attendant inconveniently standing right next to the plinth where the waxwork target was positioned. *Damn it!* Krystyna, however, took this as her cue to return to the van to prepare the necessary, as previously agreed.

But then further into the exhibition space, just around a corner and in front of his glass-partitioned office, curator Leo was holding court to twenty or so early Primary age kids. Gavin immediately assumed that this must be the school trip that Alice had mentioned would be arriving today when he'd met her at Ted's only yesterday. But the team had talked about this - including what to do. It was time for Sergeant Bob to spring into action.

Now when he'd closed his joke shop, some two years back, Gavin had kept a little stock back and out of the mitts of the ravaging bailiffs. You never know when a whoopee cushion or fake parking ticket might come in handy, after all. Well, some of the stuff might come in handy today, actually - that's what the demised shop's former owner was hoping.

As Bob furtively approached the teaching area, where twenty-odd seven and eight-year-olds from Drabbleton Central Primary were sat on benches showing various degrees of engagement, Leo was off on his mission to educate the unwashed masses.

'Right, children. Who's clever? Who can tell me where cotton comes from?'

There was an awkward pause. Blank faces grew impatient.

'The shop,' then shouted out a bright button of a little girl.

'No, not the shop, but good try,' Leo empathised.

'It does come from the shop. My mum's bought cotton from the shop. I've seen her,' the class's A-student persisted. Disgruntled mutterings of support filtered across the room

'Yeah, and this school blouse is cotton,' chipped in her best friend, in sisterly defiance. 'And that came from Tesco's. And that's a shop.'

'This is stupid,' sulked the clever one.

'Now, now, Emily Wright, that's enough thank you,' Miss Tomkins, the class's accompanying young teacher firmly intervened. The admonished one promptly folded her arms, on strike.

'Yes, well before it got to the shop,' Leo patiently tried again, 'where did it come from?

'Sheep!' cried out Kalvin Bradshaw, a hefty eight-year-old not to be messed with.

'No not sheep.' Leo corrected, much to the whole class's annoyance. *What does this posh bloke know, anyway?* There was much huffing and shuffling of feet.

'Cows then,' Kalvin persisted, gamely.

'No not cows either,' Leo politely smiled, not particularly noticing the pint-sized pensioner creeping around behind them. Bob was doing his best to appear totally engrossed in the workings of an adjacent Spinning Jenny machine. *Yes, invented around 1720, how fascinating.*

Leo then helpfully decided to provide one last clue for the struggling kids. 'Begins with the letter *P*.'

'Poo!' Kalvin hooted, just for the hell of it. 'Cow poo!' As he expected, the whole class then burst into fits of hysterics, each shouting out 'cow poo' over and over, each repetition seeming to be increasingly hilarious to them all.

'Stop saying it,' begged little May Somers, doubled up with stitch from laughing so much. 'I can't breathe.'

'Cow poo! Cow poo!' most kids chanted. They all fell about.

'Kalvin Bradshaw! Everyone! Stop at once!' ordered Miss Tomkins, blushing. She could get into trouble if this tale of wild disorder got back to the headteacher.

Bob had already spotted the opportune moment to strike. He swept in like a bird of prey, one graceful strike and he was off. Amidst the chaos of the cow poo hysterics, he wasn't even spotted. But he'd dropped his load alright - two *Mr Stinkies* right behind the back row of kids. As he swiftly retreated to safety, the rancid and intense smell of rotten eggs wafted mercilessly amongst the children and their unfortunate instructors. *Nuclear stink bombs!*

'Urghhh! That is real cow poo!' smirked young Kalvin, holding his nose. 'Who's farted? *It's him!*' He pointed accusatively at Leo, who wasn't by any means cut out for Drabbleton rough-housery. He seemed to visibly wither, this frail and genteel academic who had never dreamed of farting in public in his entire life. But the whole class then guffawed again, making vain attempts to waft away the rancid smell or copying the beefy class clown's wise example of holding nostrils tightly shut.

'*Emergency exit!*' cried Miss Tomkins in full-flap mode as the disgusting stink engulfed her and she teetered on the verge of fainting. She was reading the illuminated sign above the fire door at the back of the room. Leo got the message.

'Yes, that's it, Miss Tomkins! Everybody out!'

Twenty odd kids, a teacher and a traumatised curator then dashed towards fire door freedom, the putrid stench of two Grade A *Mr Stinkies* still left on their clothes and in their airways - but hopefully that would soon pass, so they all prayed. Gavin watched on with quiet satisfaction from a distance. He knew he only sold *quality items* from his old joke shop. What better confirmation of that fact could he ask for than this? And to get one over on the slimy bloke who'd slept with Alice behind his back... Nice work all round!

'Don't you think you'd better see what all that fuss is about?' Dinesh enquired of the uniformed museum attendant, the lone jobsworth stubbornly refusing to leave his post. Also in this, the still smell-free area of the exhibition space, the old lady who'd come in to use the loo was already on her way out again - so this one official was the only obstacle in the way of mission accomplishment.

'Nay, these exhibits are worth thousands, some of 'em laddie,' said the greying attendant in his sombre Scottish accent. 'I cannae risk anything being stolen on my watch.'

'Hello, Jim, is it?' Krystyna perkily enquired as she then appeared from nowhere, wearing a white apron from the van and reading the attendant's name badge. 'Aye, that's me. Who told you?'

'The pretty one upstairs? *You know!*' Krystyna boldly gambled. She was holding a delicious looking 99 inside a small tissue in her hand.

'Oh, Jeannie, you mean? In Housing?'

'Yes, *that's her*,' Krystyna confirmed, inwardly sighing with relief. 'She said I'd better not miss you out if I'm giving away these.'

The Scottish attendant eyed the 99 with unbridled desire.

'Aye well, she always looks after me, does Jeannie,' he literally salivated. 'What's the story anyway, hen?'

'A complimentary ice cream cone!' Krystyna answered cheerily. 'The Council are doing trial in some departments. Free ice cream treat - but only to staff members nominated by their colleagues for going above and beyond. And lovely Jeannie nominated you. Here.' She handed over Jim's obviously well-deserved award.

'She's an angel alright is that Jeannie lassie,' the uniformed attendant gushed before tucking straight into the ice cream delight.

'I'll just have quick look around while I'm here,' said Krystyna, as she departed Jim's side. 'I'm very interested in history of Drabbleton.'

'You be my guest,' smiled the proud 99 owner. 'Aye, be my guest.'

So then, Krystyna casually sauntered over to a fine example of a preserved Arkwright's Water Frame, a giant spinning machine that brought textile automation up to a new level when it was invented by Richard Arkwright himself in 1775 - or so the complimentary ice cream girl was reading on the card pinned to its side. Blah, blah, yes, yes, a drive from an external pulley propels eight spindles. *Oh, do get on with it!* She was waiting for Gavin's special sugar to work.

Over by the photograph carousel, Gavin and Dinesh looked at monochrome photos of Brimstone Mill in the late nineteenth century. Well, they kind of looked, but without really noticing anything much. They too were waiting for the special sugar to work.

Then Jim smiled at the apparently engrossed diminutive pensioner walking by him. So nice, he thought, to see such genuine interest in the museum's exhibits at last. But little did he know that Bob too was only killing time and waiting for the special sugar to work.

Inside five minutes, Jim felt the first stomach spasm. He flinched but then stood upright, initially determined to appear unruffled. Then a second spasm hit him. Then another and another. He could suddenly hear his gut gurgling and bubbling like a hot volcano waiting to blow.

'Are you OK there, Jim,' Krystyna sweetly enquired, noticing the 99 had by now been totally devoured.

'I'm nae quite sure!' cried the doubled over attendant, not wishing to elucidate on the place where an explosive pressure was rapidly building. Holding his abdomen and already starting to unbuckle his trouser belt, the only thing left to do was to make an Olympic standard dash for the gents. Besides the two *Mr Stinky's*, they weren't going to be the only pungent smell to be left behind in the exhibition hall today. Jim was about to make an epically odorous contribution himself from inside a cubicle - where the debilitating power of Gavin's *Shit-A-Lot Sugar* finally took effect. Another joke shop classic!

When she'd mixed the sugar into the Mr Whippy ice cream just before, Krystyna had read the label and the product's promise to produce *mild laxative effects with just one sachet.*

'*Mild* laxative effects,' she'd grumbled aloud to herself. 'What use are *mild* laxative effects? Bah!' so Krystyna had gone for it. Not one sachet, but a perhaps more than generous three. It now seemed likely that poor Jim's toilet door *engaged* sign was likely to be stuck on red way past museum closing time. But although whoopee cushions weren't part of the purposeful prank, in some ways, it certainly sounded like they could have been.

But not to dwell on the unfortunate casualties of critical operations, Bob had already quickly nipped out into the corridor to check that the coast was clear. He waved the others to proceed with the conclusive stage of the action.

Gavin hopped onto the plinth on which James Brimstone's waxwork rested and took the weight of the figure's upper body upon him. Dinesh and Krystyna grabbed a leg each, again as previously planned out. They then made a hasty exit, leaving the distant toilet strains of Jim behind them. Outside in the Square, Bob had opened Raspberry's serving hatch and had then jumped into the van itself ready to receive the incoming mannequin. Seconds later, the removals team were at the hatch and James was shoved - probably a little unceremoniously for his liking - headfirst into the vehicle.

'Got him!' said Bob, as the waxwork was bundled in and then wrestled onto its feet - facing outwards through the hatch. Gavin, Dinesh and Krystyna then took a momentary step backwards to admire their work. But this was no time for snoozing on the job, as a petite female pensioner somehow familiar to Gavin approached the van.

'Have you got any vegan choc ices in stock yet?' the old lady enquired of James. For some reason, Bob decided to duck down behind the hatch out of view. The others watched on, bemused.

'No, but I can do you a vegan 99,' said Bob in a muffled and high-pitched ventriloquist's voice. He was shuffling James's body from side to side like it was some giant puppet.

'What, made with plant-based milk?' asked the old woman, almost in disbelief.

'Yes,' said Bob - or was it James? 'Glant glased-nilk,' he confirmed obviously trying hard not to move his lips, which was quite unnecessary, given he was completely out of sight.

'Shameless!' muttered Gavin quietly, jaw totally dropped.

'How wonderful,' glowed the delighted old lady.

Bob then got to work, manoeuvring James's body around in the serving area while covertly working the Mr Whippy machine himself. He then somehow managed to get the *genuine* vegan 99 into the right hand of the waxwork and this was in turn passed out towards Mrs Vegan Choc Ice.

'Thank you,' said James. 'Gye-gye.'

The tiny, grey-haired pensioner departed with a spring in her step. James Brimstone had made her day - with a little assistance from Bob, that is. Gavin almost applauded. He always knew that getting James involved in his life would be a good omen. And the great man was already proving his mettle. *Excellent!*

Next stop, home. A bit of trashed house tidy-up for Gavin. Then onto Stage Two of the plan, later tonight. Once it was dark, they would be off to Barry Greenwood's Funeral Home. The small trifle of a coffin needed to be acquired.

★

While Raspberry was ferrying Gavin and friends to the Town Hall this afternoon, onwards on their waxwork acquisition mission, meanwhile over at Loom House, Lewis was also springing into action. Through the large bay window of the library, he'd just spotted Charlie setting off down the driveway, art case in hand. Though the thought of actually killing the young artist and recent acquaintance filled him with dread, there was no point delaying the inevitable. He needed to get it over with asap - then expunge the deed from his mind, just like Dimitri had tried to teach him during training.

'Charlie!' he presently shouted to his target, who'd already made good progress down the first section of the quarter mile gravel thoroughfare. 'Do you fancy a lift?' He was now standing by the Mercedes, waving a car key above his head.

The suggestion was greeted with a smile and thumbs up and so, in nearly no time, Charlie found himself sat next to the considerate, impromptu taxi driver.

'Cheers for this,' he grinned, as the car moved onwards. 'It's a good fifteen-minute walk to the bus stop and - typical me - I'm cutting it fine!'

'I'll get you there, no worries. You off to college then? Well, looks like it,' said Lewis, nodding towards the art case that Charlie had temporarily deposited on the back seat.

'Yeah, we've got a still life model coming in. Old wrinkly. Gotta pencil-draw him once he's got naked.'

'Sounds gross!' Lewis cringed, trying not to dwell on his own job in hand.

'That's the trouble with this course. Too many old willies to draw. I think our teacher, Mrs Graham, has a fetish for them. She's got 'em plastered over all the studio walls - drawings from previous students. Shrivelled willies everywhere! Pervert!'

They both laughed. 'You're putting me off wanting to take up art myself now!' Lewis said in mock protestation.

'Soz,' came the amused half apology. 'But talking of which, I looked up evening classes in Greater London. Not sure which part you live in, so I searched a wide area. There's loads if you fancied trying your hand. I did a printout and stuck it by your bedroom door.'

'Ah man, that's pretty nice of you,' Lewis replied, clearly touched. 'Not used to people being thoughtful, y'know what I'm saying?'

'No probs.' Charlie shrugged his shoulders, *it was nothing.*

'Nice kid,' mused the distracted driver. 'Very nice.'

The driveway stretched out before them, veering to the left through a densely wooded area. This would make a reasonable location for what needed to be done, thought Lewis. The body could be easily hidden in the undergrowth - and not likely to be discovered before he and his party were well on their way out of Drabbleton, hopefully by tomorrow evening.

Back in the house, no more than ten minutes or so later, Roxanne and Dimitri were chatting together in the drawing room as Mrs Joyce brought through a small silver tray of afternoon refreshments.

'What on earth was that?' Roxanne then jolted in the Queen Anne armchair. A single gunshot had just rung out from the near distance, cutting through the peace of the moment.

Mrs Joyce sighed, unflustered. 'It'll just be the farmer in the next field. He's got a fox problem, nothing for us to worry about.' She deposited the tray and casually left the room.

'Sorry, I must be a bit nervous with all that's going on,' Roxanne said to Dimitri, once they were alone.

'Don't mention it my dear,' Dimitri smiled. 'I think my mentoring of young Lewis might not have been an entire waste of time.' He nodded with smug satisfaction.

In the woodland, a trainee assassin looked up at the pale Drabbleton sunshine as it filtered its rays through the trees. Such a beautiful sight, such a beautiful day. He only hoped that he would not come to regret the big decision he had made just now.

★

Dinesh left Mishka to finish off the evening's chippy business when, around 10 pm - and under the helpful cover of darkness - Raspberry pulled up round the corner from the *Star of India.* Gavin, Krystyna and Bob, plus the recently 'borrowed' waxwork of James Brimstone, were already all on board as the final member of Gavin & The Bodysnatchers clambered into the cab and took his usual seat by the nearside window.

A minor backfire or two from the engine and the crew were then on their way to execute the next stage of Gavin's master plan. This was to involve a visit to Barry Greenwood's Funeral Home on Bond Street, chosen for its specialisation in one particular kind of coffin.

'Barry Greenwood was the first undertaker in Drabbleton to introduce American style caskets,' Gavin explained.

'Yeah, I read somewhere that the US has an obesity problem,' Bob chipped in knowingly from the back. 'So, what are these, then? Coffins for fat bastards?'

'Nah,' Gavin smiled, 'but isn't Drabbleton supposed to be the *Fat Capital of Lancashire?*' he reconsidered. 'According to the *Bugle*, like. So yeah, maybe old Barry was onto something with that.'

'Long may they all stay fat,' beseeched Dinesh, certainly one beneficiary of the townspeople's fondness for large portions.

'*Anyway,*' said Gavin, diversion put aside, 'besides their extra robustness, the main difference between these caskets and your bog-standard coffin is the door gubbins on the upper section of the box. So, when a corpse is laid out to rest, family and friends can pay their respects to late Uncle Alfred, or whoever, and they get to see his head and upper torso propped up through the open door.'

'Right, seen 'em on telly,' said Bob. 'Creeps me out, that does. I prefer a coffin with a nailed down lid any day. That's what I'm having.'

'If you need a volunteer to hammer down the nails, I'm your man,' Gavin couldn't help but cheerily offer - as he continued to steer Raspberry through the narrow streets of Drabbleton Old Town.

'Smart arse,' Bob sulked, - Dinesh tried to suppress a chuckle.

'American casket, I like,' said Krystyna, ignoring the banter. 'It is dignified way to say goodbye. But this helps us why, Gavin?'

The answer had been well worked out.

'It gives us a quick way of showing off old James here - once he's been transformed into what we hope will look like the corpse of Bryce, that is. One of us can whip open the lid, the kidnappers can then have a quick nosey in, then before they get too close with their inspection, we can slam the casket shut again, then scarper off with Alice. By the time they realise they've just taken custody of a waxwork model, hopefully we'll be well on our way out of it.

'Then what?' Krystyna pressed.

'Hide, mainly.' Gavin nodded smugly, impressed by his own infallible strategy.

'Yes, well done. Hiding is very good idea,' said Dinesh, equally impressed. Although Krystyna less so:

'Hiding? Hiding is for wimps. We need to do better!' She squeezed down her eyelids, looking mean and focussed.

'Yeah, Gavin. It's a bit shit, that,' concurred a moaning Bob. 'How about we just kill all the bad guys?' he proposed, matter of fact.

'How about you stop watching *James Bond* movies, Bob?' Gavin clipped back. 'We are not licensed to kill. We are certainly not murderers!'

'Speak for yourself,' Bob muttered.

'Yeah, speak for self, Gavin,' Krystyna laughed, suddenly caught by the funny side.

'Indeed, speak for yourself,' said Dinesh, in reconsidered support of his Brimstone nobbling accomplices and suddenly excited. 'We are three murderers - and one who ordered a murder on an assassination app. A *wannabe murderer.* Some would say we are kick-ass bad! We will fear no-one!'

He clenched a fist and punched the glove compartment.

'You tell him, Dinesh. *Kick-ass bad*, that's us!' Bob concluded triumphantly.

Gavin finally laughed, almost with relief. Here he was, spending all this time with three real life killers. But they were just so *ordinary*, just like himself really. Together, just a bunch of unassuming Drabbleton folk going about their business. Which tonight, just happened to be robbing a coffin from an undertaker. Nothing to make a big fuss about, anyway. But his crew were right - they were certainly courageous, all of them.

'OK, we'll work on a better ending for the plan - you win!' he conceded on reflection as he then swung Raspberry round onto a patch of wasteland just by the rear of Barry Greenwood's place. 'This is it? Have you got your tools, Bob?'

'Yep!' the old man grinned as he pulled from his pocket a ladies hair clip and credit card. 'Dah-dah,' he sang. 'I've watched that YouTube video on lock picking so many times this evening, I could mime along with the script.'

'Very good prep, Bob. I put my trust in you,' said Dinesh earnestly. Gavin resisted the temptation for the easy put-down. It was time for teamwork. He jumped out of his cab and around to the serving hatch where Bob was already bundling through the waxwork of James Brimstone. The crew had mutually decided that they would take It with them into the undertakers to make sure they selected a spare coffin that precisely accommodated such a sizeable mannequin. It really wouldn't do if its feet were sticking out of the end, for example, as in reality that rarely happens at funerals and the like. Authenticity was going to be important.

Krystyna then turned up by Gavin's side and helped with the slightly ungracious unloading of Drabbleton's most treasured forefather. Dinesh, on the other hand, had been designated as look-out guy and eagerly shuffled over to the driver's side of the van.

'Don't you go touching buttons and stuff,' Gavin shouted over to him as he saw him merrily jiggling the steering wheel, pretending to motor on. 'It's a complicated machine is this, not for novices!'

'Raspberry is in very safe hands with me,' Dinesh crossed his heart, relishing his responsibility. 'You have nothing to worry about.'

'Mmm,' Gavin wondered. But yes, Dinesh was mostly reliable he had to concede and yes too, they definitely needed a dependable look-out. Then, with Bob also out of the van - hair clip and credit card at the ready - the three would-be burglars set off carrying the horizontal waxwork towards the front door of Barry Greenwood's Funeral Home.

Luckily, Bond Street was pretty quiet at this time of night and the undertaker's itself was the only surviving business on this parade of otherwise boarded up retail premises. Death was one of Drabbleton's few still flourishing trades. The baby clothes shop next door had long been gone.

With most streetlights out, courtesy of brick throwing kids, Bob's subsequent efforts to pick Barry's five lever mortice door lock with a mere hairpin was carried out in the darkest of shadows - a nonchalantly passing cat the only witness.

'How you doing?' enquired Gavin, as the master lock picker wriggled and twisted the hairpin in a well memorised sequence, listening carefully for giveaway clicks that would indicate progress. The credit card would not be needed tonight, as that was only on standby if there was a back-up latch style lock to tackle. But just the mortice lock to beat, in this case. Simple. Unless…

'Trickier than I thought,' whispered Bob, a tinge of frustration creeping into his voice. 'The YouTube guy would have been in by now.'

'Try harder twist,' said Krystyna, already impatient.

'Damn!' Bob then cried as something snapped and he was left holding a fractional hairpin.

'Damn!' Gavin agreed, cursing their luck.

'Let me try Polish way,' grumbled Krystyna, shoulder-budging the tiny pensioner out of the way. 'Mind!'

'Oi!' Bob complained as he fell aside against the doorframe, but just in time to get out of the way of one almighty kick by Krystyna that smacked hard against the door itself bursting it instantly open.

'See! Polish way is best,' the impromptu human battering ram smirked, swishing her hands together. Clean job!'

'Can't argue with that,' said Gavin, in begrudging admiration. The intruding threesome then wasted no time in manhandling James into the entrance hallway.

'No alarm, that's good,' said Bob, as he crept forwards under torch light. A torch? *Of course,* the canny pensioner was meticulously prepared.

'Yeah, who'd bother to rob an undertaker?' Gavin casually laughed, opening the subsequent connecting door.

DANGA-LANGA-LANGA-LANGA-LANGA!!!

The intruder alarm's siren blared out, if later than expected. The entire building shook as the sudden and extreme decibel level threatened to literally wake the dead.

'Do something!' Krystyna yelled at Gavin, seeing him stunned, momentarily frozen.

'Quick, where's the control panel?' Bob called out, shining his torch round the main parlour room, briefly illuminating a succession of coffins on trolleys, his beam then resting on one body container in particular. This one was open, American casket style. An ashen faced corpse was propped up on her back within, raised so that its upper body protruded through the coffin door as though perkily sat up in bed.

'Creepy!' Krystyna cowed, pushing Bob's lingering torch beam away from the embalmed and lifeless face. 'Stick with finding alarm panel!'

'It's here,' Gavin shouted, opening a small cupboard in the corner of the parlour.

'Nice one, lad,' said Bob, running over to stand before the illuminated keypad. 'Quick, put the code in.'

'How can I put the code in? Are you stupid?' Gavin yelped in exasperation.

'Try one-two-three-four, obviously. Loads of people use that?'

Gavin looked dubiously down at his optimistic co-burglar with not much hope in his own heart. But what was there to lose? He banged in one-two-three-four into the pad. No response.

'Three-two-one,' offered Krystyna. 'That is alarm code at Brimstone Mill.'

'Brilliant,' said Gavin, without sarcasm. The newly proposed sequence was promptly entered. But again, no joy. The alarm screeched on.

'Try one-nine-six-seven!' Bob exclaimed, apparently sensing a breakthrough.

'Why is one-nine-six-seven even relevant?' Gavin flapped. 'It's just bloody random, that.'

'It's not random, actually. Nineteen sixty-seven. That's the year that Mavis and me got married,' Bob asserted with all confidence. Gavin shook his head, unable to reply.

'Oh, just try it,' Krystyna squawked most testily. Once again, she barged the obstructing male out of the way- this time, Gavin - and quickly inserted Bob's suggested digits into the box.

Something happened. It was *silence,* actually. Complete and utter silence as the alarm siren was immediately killed. Success!

'Told you!' said Bob, bathing in an immediate glow of self-satisfaction.

'Jammy little sod,' cried Gavin, kneeling by the cupboard in disbelief.

'Well done, Bob,' said Krystyna, amazed and relieved in equal measure. 'What are the odds of that coming off?'

'I was pretty certain about it,' Bob crowed. 'Especially when I noticed *that!*' He pointed to a post-it note stuck to the inside of the alarm cupboard. His partners this evening both quickly read said note:

Alarm Code - 1967.

Bob guffawed. But neither Gavin nor Krystyna would even speak to him - and both just walked off in disgust.

The main parlour room in which they now found themselves was too small to comfortably house all the eight coffins stored in there, all on trolleys, some probably or most evidently occupied, others currently vacant. Gavin switched on a small table lamp that was resting on a mahogany administrative desk - so that a low but nevertheless useful level of light was initiated. Meanwhile, Krystyna averted her eyes as she wheeled to one side the American casket containing the upright and quite ancient female corpse previously spotlighted by Bob's torch.

'Reminds me of my grandmother,' she squirmed, brushing by the white haired and spasmodically toothed deceased. 'I cannot look.'

'What's going on with that casket there?' asked Gavin, as he followed on in Krystyna's footsteps, pushing to the side the trollied coffins of no interest. He pointed to one of two American caskets right by the obviously occupied one.

'I will see,' said Krystyna, approaching the larger, glossy black coffin and reaching for its upper door release. A second smaller casket needed to be pushed aside.

'I like that one instead,' said Bob, pointing to the more diminutive coffin, eager to join in again and needlessly still shining his torch.

'Yes, but you're not choosing a coffin for five foot three you - disappointing as that may be. You are choosing one for six foot three James here,' Gavin scolded, still miffed by the alarm code caper and pulling the imposing waxwork with him across the room. 'Try using your noggin.'

Bob didn't answer. Now it was his turn to be in a huff.

'Yuck,' said Krystyna as she opened the larger casket's upper section only to come face to face with a prostrate corpse within - a very large octogenarian gentleman, or at least his remains, with opened wild eyes and scars across his bald skull where the pathologist's saw had most likely been to work. The embalming and prettification process on this fellow would be a long job, for sure. No wonder his display door was closed. But right now, the poor guy looked like he'd escaped from the set of *Frankenstein's Monster.*

'He's a sight alright,' said Gavin, catching first glimpse of this seemingly unworldly ghoul.

'It's Harry Braithwaite,' cried Bob suddenly, holding his own head in shock. 'I knew him back in the day. He was the lead singer in a rock and roll band that used to play in the local pubs and clubs way back in the Sixties. *Handsome Harry and the Tornados*, they were called. Girls fell at their feet. Harry's feet especially.'

'Lucky bugger. But I don't think Handsome Harry will be going out on the pull again any time soon,' Gavin sympathised, as all three coffin snatchers gazed on the now monstrously autopsied face of a heart throb of his era. 'But he's a big lad. Same as James. Let's be having him then.'

'We're not taking him out of his own coffin, are we?' moaned Bob. 'Poor Harry. He looks like he's had a rough enough time lately.'

'Do not be sentimental Bob,' Krystyna pronounced, wagging an admonishing finger. 'We agreed we would do this if necessary. Harry won't know anything about it. He is quite dead.' She quickly overcame her squeamishness and knocked on the deceased unfortunate's head with a swift triple rap. As expected, no response. 'See - *dead!*'

'Aw, sorry Harry,' said Bob, as soothingly as he could. 'But needs must mate. Hopefully you're up there somewhere having a good old singalong with Elvis.'

'Come on then, heave,' Gavin coaxed, grabbing the lifeless rock and roller from behind his shoulders and dragging him so that he was sitting upright in the casket. 'He's a proper weight!'

Harry's trolley then went all over the place, knocking its other wheeled neighbours flying, as the three much challenged team members got to work tugging and pushing, lifting and squeezing until they somehow removed the huge rock god corpse from his current place of rest. One Gertrude Biggins, the other upright corpse in the adjacent casket, was then disturbed so abruptly that she slid down into her container and its lid smacked down firmly closing her in.

'Sorry, missus,' said Bob, realising that it was his own clumsy wrestling with Harry that had irreverently knocked poor Gertrude out of view.

'Come on, stick him in here,' said Gavin, groaning with the strain of the effort as the towering corpse was pulled across the floor a little further, towards the broom cupboard in fact. And in there he was unceremoniously propped up with just a brush, a mop and a bucket for company.

By comparison it was a breeze to fit the waxwork of James into Harry's gallantly vacated casket. It was a perfect fit too. Gavin closed the display door and the three all finally smiled at one another, proud of a job relatively well done.

But at that very moment the silence was broken. Outside, the warbling wailing of *Greensleeves* started to play through Raspberry's amplifier.

Ever vigilant, from his look-out post in the ice cream van, Dinesh had been delighted to have had a go with an otherwise out of bounds button on the dashboard - and the agreed warning signal had been triggered.

'Someone's coming!' said Gavin in a sudden panic. 'Good lad, Dinesh!'

But the diligent lookout could only watch on with trepidation as a black undertaker's hearse pulled up outside the funeral parlour. The three coffin burglars weren't to know that its driver was in fact young Jason Greenwood - Barry's eighteen-year-old son - who'd been auto-summoned by the intruder alarm's telephone alert system. So here he was on call-out duty, arriving relatively promptly on the scene and ready to investigate any potential problem.

As he left his vehicle and approached the door, he turned to wonder why on earth an ice cream van would be playing its *come-and-get-me* tune at this odd hour. It wouldn't be getting any customers tonight, that was for sure. Dinesh spotted him looking over and quickly ducked and hushed *Greensleeves*. *Very odd,* thought Jason. *No wonder ice cream guys are an endangered species.*

But the young man was more perturbed to discover the kicked in door of the parlour. He picked up an empty milk bottle on the doorstep, a makeshift potential weapon and nervously proceeded inside. With every step he was thinking he would just leg it if there was trouble. Maybe better to come back with his much bigger and braver Dad who had always been up for a bit of aggro.

Meanwhile, Gavin, Bob and Krystyna had taken refuge behind a floor-to-ceiling, red velvet curtain that ran along one wall of the parlour itself - a simple but opulent backdrop against which the open caskets were displayed when grieving relatives came along for their appointed visits. All other coffins then temporarily shunted out of the way, of course. But here tonight, Jason hadn't spotted the intruders- *yet*.

'Hello,' he croaked, holding the menacing milk bottle aloft. 'I know you're in here somewhere, so come on out.'

Bob looked at Krystyna from behind the curtain just to confirm that they shouldn't comply. *Nope*, he didn't think so. *Just checking.*

'You've made a proper mess here,' Jason then grumbled, eyeing the jumbled coffins and caskets that had been sent into various positions of disarray during the only just completed manhandling of Harry the corpse. The young man hated disorganisation and promptly rearranged the wheeled trollies so that they were once more placed into two neat and regular rows of four. That done, he continued his search, maybe starting to sense the intruders had already left after all.

Best to check out the broom cupboard though. Again, he fully cocked his milk bottle. But in just another second, he was screaming in terror. For as he quickly swung open the door, a mop handle first fell across the width of the door frame, so that when Harry's propped up corpse came jolting forwards it acted as a barrier which the deceased torso flopped across. But not before the scarred skull of the much taller Harry slapped itself nose to nose with the face of the smaller, junior undertaker.

'Aaaaggghhh!' Jason shrieked in mortal fear, as he momentarily froze in a face-to-face hideous encounter with the *Beast of the Broom Cupboard.*

'Whooooo!' spookily wailed Bob from behind the velvet curtains, raising his hands and head up into the material in the manner of a melodramatic pantomime ghost.

'Aaaaggghhh!' screamed Jason again, further terrified by the terrible *Spectre of the Velvet Curtains.*

Seconds later, from his look-out post inside Raspberry, Dinesh watched on in bemusement as the now petrified Jason came racing out of the funeral parlour like a man who'd just seen a ghost, *two even.* He was quickly into the hearse, slammed door behind him and then rocketing away via a brake screeching getaway - until all that was left here on Bond Street was silence and routine calm once again.

Until such time that Gavin, Krystyna and Bob then appeared beyond the door, noisily encouraging each other on, briskly pushing along a large American casket on a trolley.

'Great job, guys!' Dinesh waved towards them in delight. The wide smiles and thumbs up he received in return told him that this next tricky stage of their mission had been successfully accomplished. *What could possibly go wrong at this late stage?*

Well, it wasn't easy getting a bulky casket of this size and weight through Raspberry's serving hatch for one thing. Dinesh was quickly joined by Bob on the inside, while Krystyna and Gavin provided the greater muscle on the outside, until with one mighty heave they almost got the coffin up onto the counter, but not quite. It slipped back, crashing at an angle on the ground.

No matter, they needed to go again. The whole team steeled themselves, totally focussing on what had to be done. This damned casket was going through that bloody serving hatch, and nothing was going to stop them now! *Absolutely nothing!*

Except a couple of familiar Drabbleton policemen, maybe. They might at least delay matters a bit.

'Good evening, Mr Whippy,' sniggered PC Duckworth, noting the coffin's lack of progress towards its apparently hoped for destination. 'You look like you're having a bit of a struggle!' He shook his head in disbelief. *That's no way to put a coffin through an ice cream van's serving hatch. They needed to go in horizontally, not from below at a sharp angle. Amateurs.*

'We'll be fine, thanks officers,' said Gavin. 'Nice to see you again, by the way.'

In their bubble of single-minded focus, none of the coffin snatchers had noticed the marked police car gently gliding in behind them. There'd apparently been a call from a neighbour in relation to Barry Greenwood's activated alarm and PCs Duckworth and Chabra had been radioed to check it out. Annoying really, as they were hoping to have made a sneaky appearance at The Anchor pub, it being quiz night and all.

'Don't suppose there's any complimentary 99s going tonight?' asked PC Chabra gamely.

'Sorry, I don't have a licence to serve ice cream after ten,' Gavin drily advised.

'Really? I didn't know you needed a licence for that,' Chabra moped

'Erm, he's being sarcastic, mate,' Duckworth suddenly bristled. 'Nobody likes a clever dick,' he humourlessly warned Gavin. 'What's in this coffin anyway?'

'It's just a waxwork model of James Brimstone, *ye olde* founder of this here Drabbleton,' Gavin prattled, trying to sound relaxed. 'The exhibition at the Town Hall asked us to sort a coffin out for him, seeing as he's dead like. So, we have done. We've just sorted it with our old mate, Barry Greenwood over there.' Gavin pointed to the obvious premises from where a coffin would be sorted.

'Yeah, but we've just been radioed because there might have been a break in at Barry's. Alarm going off and everything,' Duckworth persisted, smelling a rat.

'I hear no alarm,' said Krystyna, cupping her ears.

'Nope, me neither,' Bob confirmed from the hatch.

'That's true, pal,' said Chabra to his senior partner. 'You know, maybe it's just been a false alarm - in more ways than one.'

'Maybe,' Duckworth replied, mulling it all over, sagely stroking his bristly chin. He seemed to be lightening up, remembering his *hundredth customer* good fortune from only yesterday. 'Yeah well, that ice cream prize I won was certainly the *dog's bollocks,* there is that. But go on then, just show us the waxwork of James Brimstone in that coffin and we'll be happily on our way. We've a quiz night we could still catch the last half hour of.'

Both coppers looked towards their favourite Mr Whippy with expressions that signalled *get on with it!* Krystyna then gave him a similar look. *If they wanted to see the waxwork in a coffin, well just show them the waxwork in the coffin.*

No problem, officers,' said Gavin, as he casually manoeuvred his arm towards the casket's upper door handle. 'Quiz night, you say?' he asked, as though the exposure of the waxwork was nothing more than incidentally going through the motions. 'Sounds good. We were hoping to be at that too. Never mind. Maybe next week.'

'Yes, we'll definitely be there next week,' said Krystyna, purposely invading Duckworth's personal space so that he could smell her perfume and see the curves of her breasts inside her tight Lycra top. Maybe he'd forget about the casket, just in case...

'Now...' he fought the blatant distraction. 'Open the coffin, please.'

'Here you go,' said Gavin without hesitation, swinging open the heavy casket lid.

'Aagghhh!' screamed Duckworth as he immediately stared down at the haggard and decidedly unsightly corpse of one Gertrude Biggins. Gavin, Krystyna and Dinesh looked on too, each horrified and gobsmacked. Only Bob kept his cool, starting to work out something of what might have just happened.

When they'd finally emerged from behind the velvet curtain in the funeral parlour, they'd seen that the young undertaker had re-tidied the coffins into the neat rows that they'd clumsily disturbed. They'd clearly just assumed that James's casket was where they had just left it. But even now, how was Bob to know that Jason's coffin OCD would mean he'd always put female corpses to the right of the parlour and gentleman corpses always to the left? So, he'd only inevitably gone and switched James and Gertrude around. In their haste to leave, the wrong casket had been selected and filched. Unfortunate, but these things happen to even the best of coffin robbers.

'Weirdo perverts!' yelled PC Chabra. 'What the hell were you planning to do with an old woman's dead body?'

'No, it's not like it looks,' Gavin protested. 'You've got it all wrong.'

'Weirdo perverts indeed,' Duckworth decried, pulling out his radio to call for back up. 'In which case, I'm afraid you lot are all under arrest.'

'No wonder you called your pub quiz team *The Bodysnatchers*,' Chabra chastised, not really wishing to dwell on any possible next stages of the depraved crime they had just intercepted. 'What a sick joke.'

'It's just a misunderstanding,' countered Gavin as Duckworth decided he should then be the first to be handcuffed. 'Ouch,' came the whimper as the cuffs snapped firmly closed, nipping skin.

'This is what you call getting caught red-handed. No misunderstanding about that,' Duckworth firmly held ground as Chabra then cuffed the still confused Krystyna. 'Anyway, you're all nicked,' he confirmed, adding the customary caution.

Once back-up arrived, the apprehended culprits were then taken off in two police cars to Drabbleton Police Station - where DI Slater had been very interested to hear about the arrest of Gavin Hargreaves. Maybe he'd underestimated his criminal capability after all.

26
- THE NOSE JOB -

Then by midnight, each member of Gavin & The Bodysnatchers found themselves sitting together in a cold and featureless interview room down at the police station. They'd been offered a local solicitor from the on-call pool, so with them now, feigning interest and taking the odd note, was the portly and greying Trevor Freckleton - whose main objective this evening seemed to be to get to bed as soon as possible.

'Probably best just to admit to breaking and entering and stealing the corpse of Mrs Biggins and her coffin,' he'd advised just before DI Slater and crew had entered the room. 'Given all the facts, I can't see any way out of it, sorry to say.'

'But stealing Mrs Biggins was a mistake,' Gavin protested. 'We went off with wrong the coffin, that's all. If you get the police to check, they'll find the waxwork of James Brimstone in another casket back at Barry Greenwood's.'

'That's not exactly helpful,' tonight's solicitor countered. 'The police already know that the *Cotton Town* exhibition have reported that particular item as stolen as well. I just read their incident book. But you weren't caught in possession of the waxwork, so I wouldn't be adding that to the charge sheet if I were you.'

'OK, we haven't got much of a leg to stand on,' sighed Gavin on reflection. 'What about the rest of you? He scanned his co-accused sitting beside him.

'We're guilty as charged, I fear,' Dinesh replied, looking quite ashamed, head down in his arms resting on the table.

'Yes, guilty,' said Krystyna, disconsolately. 'Let's just get on with it.'

'Bob?' Gavin wondered why the normally vocal pensioner had been so quiet.

'Still thinking about it,' he mumbled, appearing deep in thought.

'Good, guilty it is then,' Freckleton briskly concluded, blatantly ignoring Bob's hesitancy. At this rate the old brief could be snuggled up in bed by 1 am.

The door then swung open and in marched DI Slater, a note-bound DS Haslam and PC Duckworth - the latter who remained standing against the back wall, whilst the interview conducting officers took up their seats at the table opposite tonight's suspects.

'Well then, not a very clever bunch, are we?' Slater commenced scornfully, after Haslam had turned on a tape machine and announced for the recording's benefit the attendees in the room. 'You have read them the charge sheet, Mr Freckleton?'

'I have,' replied the sleepy solicitor.

Just then there was a large bumping sound as the interview room door was briskly pushed open by the force of something that had just battered against it. Another thump of wood on wood was heard as the front end of a moving funeral casket was then clumsily shunted into the room, quickly followed by its trolley pusher, PC Chabra. Seeing his colleague struggle to steer the trolley with the proverbial *mind of its own*, PC Duckworth came to his much-needed assistance. Mrs Gertrude Biggins, propped up as she was in full view, would have been most grateful for the then smoother ride - if only she were alive.

The glossy black casket came to rest in the centre of the room.

'My God, PC Chabra, what is this?' DI Slater exploded, while DS Haslam simply held onto her chair on the verge of fainting.

'Evidence, Sir,' the young policeman proudly announced. 'You told us to make sure we always collect the evidence.'

'Yes sir,' added Duckworth helpfully. 'We would have bagged it up, like you've told us. But none of the bags were big enough.'

'Are you both mad? You can't bring in here a corpse in a coffin as evidence!' Smoke seemed to appear out of the craggy DI's ears.

'But last week when that Sean Higginbottom lad stole a bottle of whisky from Aldi, you said where's the evidence?' Chabra made his best shot of his sulky defence.

'This is completely different, you moron.'

'Why?'

'Why? Why?' Slater was so incensed that he'd momentarily lost his ability to construct a coherent argument. 'Oh, you tell him, DS Haslam,' he flapped.

'Because this is a deceased human being who should be treated with dignity and respect,' said Haslam, shakily. 'Not one to be wheeled round on a trolley through the corridors of Drabbleton Police Station.'

'Very good, Judith,' her DI congratulated. 'That's *exactly* what I was going to say.'

'Sorry sir,' moped Chabra.

'And you should have known better PC Duckworth.' Slater eyed the so-called senior officer with disdain.

'Sorry sir,' came the embarrassed reply.

'Well get her out of here, go on! And take the poor old girl back to Barry Greenwood's first thing in the morning, hopefully before her family finds out about this!'

The casket was then bundled back through the door from where it had just made its dramatic entrance. Slater calmed himself.

'I'm sorry about that,' he muttered to the assembled accused and brief. 'Sometimes our officers can be a little on the over enthusiastic side.'

'A first for me,' said Freckleton, looking impatiently at his watch. 'A corpse in an interview room. But it's late, can we just get on with it.'

Chabra and Duckworth then crept surreptitiously back into the room, edging slowly against the back wall until they were in their positions behind the interview desk - uniformed witnesses and arresting officers as they were. Slater passed them one last disparaging look before proceeding with business.

'So where were we Mr Freckleton, before we were rudely interrupted?

'You asked me if I have read the charges to my clients. I replied in the affirmative,' Freckleton thinly smiled, relieved to be finally progressing. 'In any case, the group have decided to totally co-operate with your good selves and will plead guilty as charged.'

Duckworth smugly nodded to his PC colleague. *A good night's coppering, after all!* Gavin, Krystyna and Dinesh seemed to sink in their chairs.

'We didn't actually say we were guilty,' Bob suddenly objected. 'In fact, we are very much *not guilty.*'

'Really?' said Slater, as surprised as everyone else in the room. Freckleton groaned.

'Yes!' Bob continued, accelerating into full flow. 'In fact, we were merely returning the coffin when we bumped into those two.' He pointed towards a quite baffled Duckworth and Chabra. 'Tell me this, officers. When you arrived on the scene did you not see the coffin actually falling out of the ice cream van?'

'Yes,' Duckworth replied, 'it did fall off the hatch. But that's only because your mates weren't strong enough to shove it in because of the stupid angle they were coming in at. That's why you lot dropped it.'

'Sorry,' said Bob. 'That's just your assumption. If you were in court the judge would expect you to say what you actually *saw* happen, not what you *presumed* to have happened.'

'That's true,' Slater somewhat testily confirmed.

'So did you or did you not see the coffin sliding off the serving hatch counter and falling to the ground?' pressed Bob, only longing for his gown and wig.

'Well yes, you could say that...' Duckworth flummoxed. 'But...'

'Then I rest my case,' Bob signed off, very pleased with himself. Watching all those daytime TV Court dramas had certainly paid off. Freckleton covered his face - *there goes the early dart.*

'Is this true, PC Duckworth? Might it be that you actually saw these defendants *unloading* the coffin, not loading it after all?' Slater was already imagining any hopes for this case hitchhiking off over the horizon.

'Well, if you put it like that...' The senior PC was blushing.

'The coffin did actually fall out of the van, now you come to think about it,' said Chabra gauchely. Slater and Haslam eyed both of their uniformed colleagues with a little more than mild contempt.

'See the thing is, there were we aiming to join in on the final round of the pub quiz down at The Anchor,' Bob confidently continued, 'driving along, minding our own business in Gavin's ice cream van. Then we see this coffin in the road at the bottom end of Bond Street. Isn't that right, Gav?'

'Yeah, it's right enough. It's like what he says,' Gavin garbled, hoping he wouldn't be asked to continue the yarn. But Bob was on it.

'So, then I says, I bet some kids have nicked that from Barry Greenwood's for a laugh. And Krystyna says - didn't you love? - she says, *oh, how awful. We must take it back to Barry Greenwood's straight away.*'

'Yes, straight away, I said,' Krystyna confirmed, warming to the elaborate tale.

'Aye, so we loaded it into the ice cream van and thoughtfully drove it back to the top end of Bond Street, back to Barry's place. And then, just as we were unloading it again, along came those two clots and arrested us.' Bob gave the two officers a withering look.

Duckworth and Chabra cringed.

'Most unfair of them!' chimed in Dinesh, better late than never. 'We were just being responsible citizens and now here we are arrested like common criminals!'

'But you could have said something at the time,' Duckworth griped. 'In fact, didn't you try and fob us off, saying the corpse was a waxwork, or something.'

'You said we had a right to remain silent,' Bob fired back. 'So at the time, that's what we did. Nothing about a waxwork from us. We exercised our legal right to button it until we could consult with our learned lawyer friend here.' Freckleton momentarily perked up. Nobody had called him *learned* before.

'Anything more to add?' Slater pointedly addressed the two now sheepish looking uniformed officers. Only blank faced expressions served as the reply. 'Well, if that story is true,' he grouched, 'I suppose we owe you all an apology. Stop the tape, Judith.'

'Interview concluded 12.09 am.' Haslam let out a huge sigh of disappointment and pressed the machine's stop button.

Chabra looked towards his senior oppo looking for inspiration. Surely there was something to be done that might redeem themselves this evening. But Duckworth offered no help, currently bracing himself, as he was, for Slater's post-interview rollocking. It was then left to the younger PC to clutch at the straws.

'Wait,' he bumbled in the direction of DI Slater, 'aren't you going to ask *that one* about making a curry out of Bryce Brimstone's corpse?' He pointed an accusative finger in the direction of an instantly mortified Dinesh.

'What's this?' said Slater, eyebrow immediately raised. Duckworth darted a *please shut up* look to the junior PC, but all to no avail.

'The rumour round town was that this man had the body of Mr Brimstone in his chippy,' continued PC Snitch. 'And yes, he made it into a special curry and sold it for a quid a shot. Half of Drabbleton queued up to bagsy a portion.'

'That was just a bit of a joke - a publicity stunt,' pushed back Dinesh, nervously laughing, maybe unconvincingly so. 'Because everybody hated that Brimstone fellow. Besides, you two officers bought a portion yourselves if I remember. You obviously didn't take the menu too seriously.'

'Is this true, PC Chabra - and Duckworth? People believed they were going to be having Bryce Brimstone for supper and you didn't even inform me? Then you even had the bare-faced cheek to turn up at the chippy for a serving for yourselves?'

'Well sir, it was only a quid,' muttered Duckworth. 'Like giving it away! But course not, no we didn't take it seriously, and quite rightly. Tasted like chicken, actually.'

'This should have been properly investigated. I should have decided if it was serious or not!' Slater practically exploded. 'Which it obviously wasn't,' he tried to steady himself. 'But that's beside the point! You're making the Drabbleton Police Force look like rank amateurs. It's bad enough that our own Chief Constable has called in some Southerners from the National Crime Agency to take over the case. He reckons we're out of our depth. From Thursday we're off the job.'

Haslam clenched her fist in frustration. No more murder case glamour for her - she'd already heard the news and taken it very badly.

'Sorry sir,' said Duckworth, inspecting his size nines.

'Sorry sir,' added Chabra, wondering what else could be said. Nothing probably, that was his belated conclusion.

'*Southerners?*' Bob interjected. 'Why can *Southerners* do a better job than you lads up here?' There seemed to be no irony in his question.

'I know. It's bloody insulting,' Slater bitterly replied. 'Over thirty years keeping Drabbleton's streets safe and now I have to put up with some fresh-faced kid from Oxford coming in to try to show me how useless I am.'

'We're gutted about it,' said Haslam. 'This was the biggest case round here for years - the double murder of Bryce Brimstone and young Darren Eccles.'

'Posh boy Southerners shouldn't be butting in up here with their fancy ideas,' added Bob, surprisingly feisty about the subject.

'Precisely,' Slater agreed, warming to the spirited pensioner, *Drabbleton through and through*. 'Especially as we were on the verge of a breakthrough. Some Russian guy in a black Mercedes, but sorry I shouldn't be saying...'

'What black Mercedes is this?' asked Gavin, suddenly curious.

'Ah, nothing,' Slater waved away his last comment. 'I think it's time you gentleman - and lady - were on your way.'

Thank God for that, thought Freckleton. *I thought you'd never shut up.*

Gavin was thinking things through at a pace his brain couldn't quite keep up with. But it was something along the lines of getting the Drabbleton Police involved, despite previous reservations, in the rescue of Alice. And if this guy in the Mercedes was also someone

Slater was considering a prime suspect, well it was potentially win-win.

'I'd just like to say, speaking for me personally, I've always thought Drabbleton coppers to be a pretty switched-on bunch,' said Gavin, a little disingenuously, but especially fooling PCs Duckworth and Chabra who slightly puffed out their chests with pride. 'Let's put tonight aside as a little blip. 'Cos I do agree with Bob here that posh boy Southerners shouldn't be meddling in the work of our own town's most excellent boys in blue. Especially, as you say, you're so close to catching your guy.'

'That's very nice of you to say so, Gavin,' smiled Slater as he caught sight of Haslam at his side nodding in keen agreement.

'Maybe,' Gavin went on, 'just maybe we might be able to help each other out. Do you mind if we have a private off-the-record little chat?'

Krystyna and Dinesh wondered what was going on but kept their powder dry. It was time to trust Gavin. Bob, on the other hand, sniffed out the makings of a nifty plan. He did like a good plan.

Inside a minute a grateful Trevor Freckleton was well on his way to bed and the two *excellent after all* PCs were on their way too. No tape machine was at work as Gavin & The Bodysnatchers then got down to the serious business of discussing how Drabbleton Police Force could assist in helping to free the kidnapped Alice. And how they, in turn, could help Tom Slater and assistant nab their prime suspect - itself an especially splendid potential outcome. Because, if the Mercedes mob were convicted of Bryce's homicide, then poisoner Krystyna, cling-film killer Bob and meat cleaver murderer Dinesh would be in the clear for good.

*

'**Y**ou actually had the body of Bryce Brimstone, all along? Slater palmed his forehead, taken aback. *I knew it,* thought Haslam. *Told you we should have sent in the dogs.* 'Well, you're a bloody good actor, that's all I can say.'

'But this is all off the record, as we agreed,' Gavin bravely asserted. 'If you charge me later, I'll deny everything.'

'Yes, of course,' Slater pragmatically agreed.

'But it was this app, see - Disposals Inc.' Gavin passed his mobile over to the DI who immediately scanned the open home page, seemingly instantly engrossed by what he was seeing. 'You can use it, supposedly, to order assassinations of your most hated enemies. Or even somebody you've taken a mild dislike to. They don't ask you for a reason.'

'Sounds a bit like ordering a pizza,' mused Haslam, as she leaned over to view the app for herself.

'I thought it was just an internet spoof, actually, but have to say I enjoyed putting in Bryce Brimstone's name, all the same,' Gavin laughed. 'Felt sort of liberating really, after everything that had gone on between us at work.'

'Yeah, I heard about that from Bryce's sister,' Slater recalled, still preoccupied by the app, and secretly wondering what would happen if he nominated the Chief Constable.

'But then I got a contact from the app asking for thirty grand as the hit fee.'

'Wow,' Slater balked at the price. Historic unfortunates in the Drabbleton area had been bumped off for as little as a couple of hundred quid and a crate of Boddingtons. And he had thought technology was supposed to mean progress.

'I know!' Gavin agreed. *Scandalous.* 'When I couldn't pay though, I then got Brimstone's chopped up body in the post. Two arms, two legs, a torso - but no head, strangely.'

'So where is the head?' wondered Haslam.

'No idea. I've never seen it,' Gavin was able to genuinely swear.

'Nor me,' Dinesh quickly interjected, a little too eagerly. Bob mimed *zip-it* across his mouth, and the message was quickly received and understood.

'So where's the body now?' asked Slater.

Gavin hesitated and felt his heart suddenly palpitate. *Whoops*, he actually hadn't had time to think this bit through.

Don't dob me in, please, Dinesh silently prayed.

'Well, we came home yesterday from selling ice creams, and guess what?' Bob helpfully intervened, convivially addressing Slater and Haslam but looking sideways at Gavin encouraging him to catch on. 'This one's place had been broken into. Trashed.' He stuck out a thumb in the direction of *this one.*

'No!' said Haslam, mildly aghast - but quickly remembering that Gavin's house was already looking pretty trashed last time she saw it. What could have made it so much worse?

'Yes, trashed!' confirmed Bob. 'They didn't even use a hairpin to pick the lock. The door had just been kicked in, brutish as you like.'

'Animals,' tutted Krystyna.

'And the body had been nicked too,' said Gavin finally latching onto Bob's ruse - the latter sending him an approving nod. 'Gone!'

'You reckon these Disposals Inc people stole it back? the DI speculated. A reasonable guess.

'I don't think it was them this time,' Gavin seemed to fret. 'Because of what's happened since. But maybe it was the same sick kids who stole that Gertrude Biggins' body and left it lying all alone in the street. Poor old girl. But there's a pattern there.'

'Bodysnatchers. Sickos,' Haslam denounced.

'Exactly! Sickos!' Gavin agreed. 'See though, this is where it all gets even nastier. The app gang are saying I've got to give them back the body. So they obviously don't have it yet. But now they've kidnapped my girlfriend, who happens to be Alice Brimstone. If I don't do as they say, then they're threatening to kill her.'

'You know that how?' Slater's face betrayed the fact that his interest level had suddenly risen a notch. *Kidnap as well as murder. In Drabbleton? Now we're talking!*

'A phone call yesterday, plus a picture.' Gavin retrieved the handset that Slater had still been holding and flicked through to the image of the bound and gagged hostage that was Alice.

'You've convinced me,' said the DI, gawping with Haslam at the compelling evidence that this single photograph represented.

Then, once Gavin mentioned Loom House and the fact that an angry crew in a black Mercedes had also chased him, Bob and Raspberry down The Hundred Steps, everything seemed to fall into place for Slater.

The DI was then quite keen to show Gavin and team CCTV stills from both Waterloo and St Pancras Stations which had captured Dimitri - the latter image most likely recorded when the Russian had phoned Slater, trying to implicate Hargreaves in Brimstone's murder.

'Is this the guy who pursued you in that Mercedes?' the question was plainly asked.

'Yep, pretty sure that's him,' Gavin affirmed. 'Nasty looking bugger.'

'Yeah, I'd recognise that mean face anywhere,' agreed Bob.

'Interesting,' Haslam took over, showing another CCTV shot of Dimitri, this time obviously near Brimstone Mill and him grappling with some unlucky third party. 'We've had the lab work on this - from a local door cam. We think this is the moment when the suspect murdered Darren Eccles. Reason, unknown.'

'Poor bugger,' said Gavin, not dwelling on the grainy yet still brutal photograph for too long. 'Nice lad, was Darren,' he added, giving the deceased the dubious benefit of the doubt.

'We've had all this run through national facial recognition computers, and we've come up with a name,' said Haslam, proud of her initiative on the case. A step up from Duckworth and Chabra for sure.

'Yes. He's known as Dimitri Sidorov,' Slater announced with something of a swagger. 'Part of a Russian crime syndicate controlled by a very big Mr Big indeed - one Vladimir Volkov. Both have been arrested before, but on each occasion any evidence against them seems to have mysteriously disappeared. Or witnesses have miraculously changed their story. Anyway, Sidorov here is the right-hand man of Volkov. It would be a massive win for Drabbleton if we could bring him in.'

'And not let some Johnny-come-lately Southerners steal your glory. Especially after you've done all this work,' crowed Bob, Drabbleton Police's newest fanatical supporter.

'That's exactly it,' Slater agreed, almost wanting to hug little Bob. But now you've mentioned Loom House, how come they're holding Alice at her own brother's house? What's the connection? I think I can guess.'

'Alice went to see Roxanne up at the house,' Gavin went on. 'The Mercedes was in the driveway - she told me on the phone. Then the kidnap happened and right after that the ransom call.'

'So Roxanne must be in on it. That's where my mind's going,' said Slater, joining the dots.

'She was definitely in the Mercedes that chased us through town,' Gavin confirmed. 'I remember her from a visit she made to the Call Centre last year.'

'Sir, Mrs Brimstone must need the body of her husband for the death certificate,' offered Haslam, enthusiastically. 'You know, so she can claim life insurance and the like. Plus, free up the Will.'

'Good thinking, Judith.' Slater smiled at his definitely improving apprentice. 'First, they try to frame Gavin here with Mr Brimstone's murder, a crime they actually committed themselves. Then when that fails, they go to extreme lengths to recover the body.'

'You've got it, sir. All makes sense,' said Haslam, finally reckoning that the teamwork with her boss was on the upward trajectory too.

'But how did you propose to make them think you could still give back the body. If that's what they're demanding?' Slater mulled, addressing Gavin, but turning to his Sergeant before he could even answer. 'I think it's time we went in with the armed unit.'

Haslam beamed. *Proper action!*

'No, wait!' Gavin promptly interjected. 'We do have an idea, but you'd just have to trust us. If you go in with armed police, there's a good chance that Alice would be killed. If we go in and give them back what they think is Bryce, maybe they'd let us walk out with her. And *then* you could go in - with no danger to her, or us, or any member of the public.

'I think we should just go in, sir,' asserted Haslam, not wishing to pass up the chance of an armed skirmish. Next week she'd be back on the likes of petty shoplifters and park-run flashers. This was an excitement level that she might have to live on for years.

'No, hang on Judith. This could be my last big case,' said Slater, slamming on the brakes. 'And it's your first biggie too. We don't want a dead hostage on our hands and being remembered forever as the stupid local coppers who messed up on their big chance. Not if there's a way of getting Alice Brimstone out safely - as Gavin here says.'

Haslam knew her boss was making sense, but somehow wished he'd be a bit more gung-ho for once. Never mind though, armed coppers were still going to be involved. She'd never seen the guns raised in anger here in Drabbleton. *Bracing stuff!*

'Tell me more about your plan,' Slater continued, eying Gavin purposefully. 'But if you are going in, you do know you'd have to wear a wire, yeah? We'd need to know you weren't in danger. But if you could get Dimitri or Roxanne to confess anything on tape, all the better.'

'No problem,' said Gavin assuredly. 'Are we all in?' he asked of his crew.

'We're in!' said The Bodysnatchers almost in unison. It was just a matter now of the team convincing Slater and Haslam that they knew what they were doing with just a borrowed coffin, a fake wax corpse and a convincing bit of chat.

★

Slater had tried not to dwell too much on some of the details. Gavin and his friends had needed a casket - and they'd just been arrested tonight in possession of a casket. A coincidence, no doubt. They'd also needed a waxwork that looked a bit like Bryce Brimstone. And today there'd been a report that the waxwork facsimile of James Brimstone had been stolen from the Town Hall. Another amazing coincidence. But the wise old DI definitely concluded that if busting this last mega case of his career meant overlooking the odd relatively petty misdemeanour, then that he was willing to do.

It had been well past 1.30 am by the time Gavin, Krystyna, Dinesh and Bob had got off to bed. Before that, a duty police officer had kindly driven them back to where Raspberry was still parked, across from Barry Greenwood's. The last action of the night - after the taxi driver PC had innocently left the scene - had been for Gavin and Krystyna alone to sneak back into the funeral parlour to retrieve James. Luckily, the undertaker's door had been still unlocked, on-call Jason Greenwood having been too freaked out by tonight's paranormal experience to have even considered returning.

That smoothly done, on this occasion, and with James and the correct casket subsequently and finally ensconced inside Raspberry's serving area, a successful night's operation had been duly declared. They all needed a good night's sleep now. But they'd agreed to meet at Gavin's again, in the morning around half ten. There was a whole lot more planning and preparation to be done before tomorrow afternoon's expected moment of deliverance.

Nobody, in fact, slept that well at all.

*

Marie had received Gavin's early hours text with less than a cheerful welcome.

'Yer bleedin' tool!' she'd griped as she awoke and saw the time on her phone. 'You've woken me up for this!' Alberto beside her, snoring in bed, had groaned like a horse in a state of semi-disturbed slumber.

'Please call at mine tomorrow at ten. Bring your beautician's kit and hairdressing gubbins.'

'If this is just for Alice, I'll kill him, so I will,' she'd quietly muttered, before throwing her phone to the side and getting back to hard-to-retrieve sleep.

But now this very Wednesday morning, despite her nocturnal grumpiness, Marie was promptly on the doorstep of her former marital home, 21 Mayfair Avenue, at the requested time. She rang the bell and waited. Then waited some more. She rang again, less patiently.

Gavin's silhouette eventually appeared behind the smoked glass upper panel of the front door and the scruffily robed man himself then stood before his ex-wife, screwing his eyes in the shock of daylight.

'Aw, Marie, it's you. What's up?' said Gavin, smacking his face to aid the waking process. Even his caller's perkily pink tracksuit seemed to be too dazzling a sight for his eyes to take.

'You texted me in the middle of the night. Or were you too drunk to remember? You said to bring this lot!' She held aloft a glittery and sequinned gold case, obviously the bling-box container for the tools of her trade.

'Ah course, sorry love,' Gavin came to his senses. 'Long night...'

'Tell me about it!' Marie grumped, remembering seeing her alarm clock at three in the morning, still not back to sleep after Gavin's interruption.

'I'll put the kettle on. Come in.'

Over a much-needed soothing brew in the kitchen, Marie then patiently listened, mostly drop-jawed, as she was made to realise that she had a lot to catch up on. Brimstone's body parts arriving in the post, the failed attempt to get rid of them via the coal wagon, Bob going on an unintended rain journey, the *Ride of Death* down The Hundred Steps and then, worst of all, the kidnap of Alice. But, despite all, there had been one completely successful element amongst all these shenanigans - the disposal of Brimstone's corpse via the digestive systems of the game folk of Drabbleton, courtesy of Dinesh's *Special Curry.*

'So how can you be giving them back the body if it's been eaten already?' asked Marie, caught up in the story and clearly perplexed. 'Oh, and by the way, I had some of that curry myself. Delicious.'

'I'll tell Dinesh,' Gavin smiled. 'We won't be giving them back the body though. But we'll make them *think* that they've got it.'

'How?'

'Step this way. There's the latest bit of the story that I just left out,' he winked. 'But I've got a little job for you.'

Gavin then led the way back through the hallway before he opened the until now closed door of the front lounge.

'Oh. My. God!' Marie put her hands on her head, gawking aghast. There in the centre of the room was a polished black casket sitting on an undertaker's trolley. The upper door of the casket had been left ajar so that the incumbent could be viewed in all his pomp. Propped up at an angle, the head and topmost part of James

Brimstone's waxwork torso was reclined there formally on display. 'How've you got this fellah? And the coffin, jeez?'

'Long story,' said Gavin, 'but he's not real, course.'

'I can see he's not real. Looks a bit plastic.' Marie stepped forward to tentatively touch the waxwork's face.

'This was the guy who built Brimstone Mill back in the Nineteenth Century,' Gavin explained. 'You know, James Brimstone.'

'Never heard of him,' Marie blanked.

'Well, you would have if you'd have been brought up round here. Looks like Bryce Brimstone, yeah?'

'I'll give you that much,' Marie confirmed on an instantaneous inspection. She then put her nose in front of the waxwork's face, studying its strong jawline, mostly handsome features and jet black, wavy hair coiffured in a style of its Victorian day. '*Very* Bryce Brimstone, I'd say.'

'That's because he's this guy's great, great, great grandson. But Bryce had that crooked nose thing going on - some fight or other as a kid, it's said. Plus, this hair is all wrong.'

A look of sudden realisation then crossed Marie's face.

'Is this why you wanted me to bring my kit?'

'Yes, hun. That's exactly it,' Gavin affirmed, happy to see she'd been quick on the uptake and was already opening her bling-box. 'I've got a photo of Bryce from the *Drabbleton Bugle* somewhere. Can you maybe reshape the nose and bring his hair up to date? Make his skin less shiny, maybe?'

Marie mulled over the prospective task in hand. She'd never done a cosmetic and hair double job on a waxwork before, of course. But something inside her fiery spirit relished the challenge. First thing, the easy bit - a haircut.

'I'll have a try, for sure,' she said, reaching for her scissors. 'Oh, and those lamb chop sideburns will have to go for a start - if I could borrow your leccy shaver.'

Gavin was only too happy to oblige. 'Nice one, cheers for this,' he gratefully spouted as he left the room to find that newspaper photo and retrieve the shaver.

Marie instantly flipped into her chatty hairdresser mode, beaming smile, almost singing voice.

'So, Mr Brimstone - been anywhere nice on your holidays?

★

By the time Marie had shaved off said lamb chop sideburns and smoothed over the remaining bristles with cream foundation, Bob had turned up and was now in the adjoining dining room rooting through a couple of cardboard boxes.

'I don't know why you want to go through this lot again,' Gavin bemoaned. 'We're not going to outmuscle the Russian Mafia, if that's what they are, with an electric shock handshake buzzer and a whoopee cushion.'

'You never know,' Bob replied, as he gamely rummaged through the leftover joke shop stock that Gavin had once hidden from the bailiffs. 'That stink bomb at the museum worked a treat. And what about that *Shit-A-Lot* sugar? Classic! Have we got any left, by the way?'

'Nope, I think Krystyna used up the last of it on that poor security fellah.' Gavin winced at the thought.

'Shame. Very effective stuff that. Could have worked again,' Bob moped. But he then lapsed into one of his recently worsening coughing fits. Gavin instantly realised that he hadn't been very thoughtful at all.

'It's Wednesday, course,' he belatedly recalled. 'Weren't you supposed to have seen that cancer specialist at nine?' He'd been informed all about that appointment during the less eventful element of their ice cream van ride together, just on Monday.

'Yeah, yeah,' Bob replied, almost with disinterest. 'I knew it was a routine cough, told 'em so all along. Anyway, the cancer doc just gave me the all-clear. Surprise, surprise. Bloody hospitals,' he grumbled.

'That's great news mate,' Gavin smiled with relief. Although he did closely scrutinise Bob's face for any sign of awkwardness. Nope, nothing doing there.

'Right then,' Gavin continued, convinced by Bob's explanation, and so getting back to business. 'I think the idea is we just hand over the supposed body, but then get out of there. No need for anything clever.'

'But what if they start getting nasty or stop us scarpering?' Bob seemed determined to find something useful in this damned box.

'Hopefully, that won't happen,' Gavin seemed to wishfully think. 'But even if it did, well then that's when the police would take over.'

'Always good to have a Plan B,' Bob persisted. 'What about this?' He was holding a small silver pistol, or at least a joke shop replica of one.

'That's not what you're hoping it is. It's just a cigarette lighter, here...' He took the gun from his diminutive friend's hand and pulled the trigger. A little gas flame then ignited and glowed away out of the end of the gun's barrel.

'Oh, we'll take it anyway,' Bob sighed, having hoped for more gusto. 'It might look real from a distance.'

'Yeah, OK,' Gavin replied, not fussed either way.

'I'm hoping you won't be relying on a fag lighter to save your lives, Jeez,' piped up Marie from the adjacent knocked-through room as she carefully trimmed James's bushy eyebrows with her clippers.

'Me too,' Gavin assented, glancing over at Marie's work in progress. 'He's coming on, isn't he? I think you've got the hair right now.'

'Not bad so far,' said Marie, heavily engrossing herself once again in the transformation.

The waxwork's Victorian coiffure has been remodelled in the contemporary wavy styling of Bryce's picture in the *Drabbleton Bugle* - the image that had appeared under this week's latest front-page headline: *Brimstone Murder. Police Look for Mercedes with P or B In Number Plate.*

'But look at all these balloons,' said Bob suddenly gleeful as he got stuck into the latex delights hidden inside a second cardboard box. You've got hundreds of 'em.'

'They're left over from my children's entertainer days. I used to do balloon animals, y'know,' Gavin shrugged.

'Love them! Brilliant!' Bob enthused. 'Do you still have any helium?'

'Yeah, I've got a big canister in the shed. Why?' Gavin scratched his head.

'Don't know. But there might be some way we could use it in emergencies. I'll have a think.' His eyes twinkled as his imagination went into overdrive. 'Nah,' he concluded after a quick brainstorm, 'maybe not with the helium, but we could always blow them up.'

'How could we blow them up?' Gavin laughed, but actually taken aback.

'I used to be a steeple-jack, remember. How else do you think we demolished factory chimneys? But when all that finished, I took home a souvenir stick of dynamite - yeah, I did! You hang onto that, Bob, I said to myself. That might come in handy one day.'

'No, no, no, Bob,' Gavin pushed back in horror, hardly trusting his accident-prone mate with dynamite on the job. 'If there's any serious stuff to be done, let's leave that to the armed coppers.'

'You might regret it,' griped Bob with a sigh. But he could see that his co-schemer was quite serious in the push-back.

The doorbell rang. Another Bodysnatcher reinforcement, no doubt. Gavin was quickly on his feet, leaving Bob to fantasise about twisty balloon dogs and dinosaurs.

'Wow, hi!' said Krystyna addressing Marie as she entered the lounge, her eyes immediately drawn to the casketed waxwork. 'That hair job is brilliant.'

'Thanks,' Marie smiled, looking more than a little pleased with herself.

'Marie, Krystyna - Krystyna, Marie,' Gavin provided the swift introduction. The two women nodded, *pleased to meet you s*tyle, but with Marie instantly giving the new attractive visitor the once over. '*No way did Gavin sleep with her, the liar!*'

'I'm having a little trouble with his feckin' nose though,' Marie complained, back to business, as she massaged James's perfectly protruding facial snout. 'It needs misshaping, like in the piccy. But this wax is set pretty damned hard.'

Krystyna and Gavin studied the folded newspaper that Marie had propped up in the casket right by James's head. Looking at the front-page photograph, Bryce's nose was hideously disfigured alright. Marie had her work cut out, for sure.

'You're probably doing the right thing rubbing it,' Gavin encouraged. 'I was hoping it would be like plasticine if you worked it a bit.'

'Yeah, that's what I was hoping too,' Marie grimaced, as she upped the ante on the friction.

'Why don't you try melting it a bit,' said Bob, stepping forward through the open double-doored alcove and into the lounge. He was holding the pistol cigarette lighter.

'No, definitely don't do that,' warned Marie. 'Definitely not! This is a delicate job.' She then seemed to have a sudden brainwave. 'I know, I'll get my hairdryer from the car.' She literally sprang out of the room while the others were left temporarily peering into the coffin, admiring the skilled metamorphosis to date.

'Oh, just try warming it up with the flame,' said Bob, elbowing his way into prime face-to-face position. 'A hairdryer will take all day.' He pulled the trigger and a small fire candle instantly flickered to life.

'Are you sure, Bob? Marie doesn't like people messing with her work,' Gavin warned, knowing his ex-wife's single-mindedness in these matters all too well.

'She'll thank me for it in a minute,' Bob persisted, holding the ignited lighter towards the all too straight nose. 'It'll be lovely and soft when she gets back. Like veritable putty in her hands!'

'Be very careful, Bob,' Krystyna gasped as the flame briefly brushed against the waxwork's replica skin.

'I know what I'm doing, *thank you*,' Bob replied, a little crabbily.

WHOOSH!

Right at that very moment the waxwork head exploded into flames, not just the nose but the entire coconut. Marie then screamed as she re-entered the room, welcomed by the sight of dancing fire and acrid smoke.

'Aagghh!' yelled Bob, as he instinctively smacked down on the fiery head, trying to undo his terrible wrong, but only singeing his skin. He screamed again.

'Put it out! Put it out!' wailed Gavin, quickly grabbing a cushion from the sofa and using it to punch down on the burning face over and over. 'Noooooo!' he then shrieked as the cushion did no more than catch fire itself, flames quickly snapping at Gavin's hand. He instantly chucked the fiery cushion away from him, anywhere would do. Anywhere except up against the unhelpfully flammable curtains would have done, actually. But now the foot of the drapes themselves started to burn. Bob leapt into further action, quickly repositioning himself in the heart of the new danger - where he managed to dampen down both the burning cushion and curtain flame with a tatty woven throw that was conveniently waiting there, flopped over the sofa.

Meanwhile, Krystyna had been the quickest thinker of them all. She came running from the kitchen carrying a large pan filled with cold water.

'Look out!' she cried, as she used it to drench the waxwork's fireball of a head. The flames hissed like an angry dragon as they were doused, a final puff of steam and smoke rising towards the ceiling. Krystyna's intervention was indeed successful, and the fire was instantly killed.

'Well done,' said Gavin. 'I thought we were done for just then.' But then his face, only just now filled with relief, quickly turned to one filled with anger. 'I did say *not too close with the lighter Bob!*'

The smoke began to clear and as they wafted the worst of what remained away, the firefighting foursome then eyed the blackened and smouldering head, all facial features melted completely away. It seemed nothing more than the uppermost part of a burnt-out carcass, a disfigured and unrecognisable ashen skull.

'I was as careful as I could be!' Bob backtalked, turning green.

'Did I not say *definitely* don't use the lighter? What are you, feckin' deaf, man? Marie went into combat mode - all her work ruined because of this eejit. 'I put alcohol on the skin to clean it up, didn't I? Inflammable alcohol!'

'You could have said,' Bob moaned. 'How was I to know?'

'Well, when I said *definitely don't use the lighter*, that should have feckin' been enough for yous!'

'Don't come at me with your feckin' this and feckin that,' Bob started to fight back. They'd never really liked each other, he and Marie. 'Foul mouthed, little madam!'

'Do you want to come outside for a fight then? We're just about as tall as each other, are we not?' Marie was inwardly exploding as she raised her fists and danced on her toes.

Gavin quickly enfolded her with his arms. 'Steady on, tiger! It'd be better if we all calmed down.'

'He started it!' yapped Marie, wriggling free from Gavin's hold.

'I did not start it! Bob retorted. 'Well, OK …I started the fire, I'll give you that much,' he reconsidered.

'None of this is helping! Please people, stay calm,' Krystyna intervened. 'We need to think. Our plan is ruined. We must abort mission.'

Everybody paused, their eyes pulled once again towards the charred and scorched out void on the waxwork where a face used to be. There was momentary silence as the shock of the fire incident gave way to gloom and disappointment as the reality of Krystyna's words hit home. The plan was done.

The doorbell then heralded another caller - no doubt Dinesh, mused Gavin as he nudged himself through the dolour to go see. Marie and Bob stood there glaring at each other, so Krystyna took it upon herself to stand between them, just in case. The noise from the direction of the front door suggested there was more than one new visitor.

'Oh my! Oh my!' cried Dinesh as he then entered the lounge, followed by his sympathetic looking wife, Mishka. 'What has become of our handsome prince?'

'This does not look like James Brimstone,' Mishka wailed, looking at the burnt-out disaster. 'Nobody would believe it could be so.'

'We had a bit of an accident,' said Bob, eyes downward. Marie scowled.

'Mishka knows everything now,' Dinesh confessed to all. 'I am sorry, but as we will be putting our lives in danger today, I thought she had a right to know.' He looked close to tears.

'It's alright mate,' Gavin soothed, putting his arm round his emotional chippy man mate. 'It doesn't matter now, anyway. We're sunk.'

'Well, my husband,' Mishka squeezed her eyelids, looking mysterious, 'you say you have told me *everything*. But not exactly *everything*, have you? And I do think it is time now for you to confess something to your friends. It might prove to be very helpful in the circumstances.'

'What are you talking about, Mrs?' Dinesh seemed genuinely confused.

'Mr Head,' Mishka mischievously smiled.

'Mr Head?' Dinesh looked blank.

'Yes,' Mishka insisted. 'Mr Head.' Dinesh suddenly looked sheepish. 'As if I didn't know about your daily pilgrimage to the freezer. *Who is laughing now, Mister?* That is how you would be forever crowing to the head of Mr Bryce Brimstone.'

'Oops,' said Dinesh avoiding eye contact with Gavin and the rest of The Bodysnatchers.

'She knows about Mr Head?' asked Bob, incredulous. Dinesh silently nodded. 'So you've still got Mr Head?'

'You promised us you were going to get rid of that head. You promised it was going into the curry,' rebuked Krystyna. 'Liar!'

'A bit low that, Dinesh,' added Gavin, less harshly. 'We trusted you.'

'A thousand apologies to all,' Dinesh whimpered, holding out his hands in prayer. 'I struggled with my conscience every day, knowing that I should really do the right thing and get rid of Mr Head. But every day and every time I asked, *Who is laughing now?* of that monster, I did not want it to be the last time I would ever say it.'

'He did put you through a lot,' said Gavin, relenting and putting his arm back around Dinesh's shoulder. 'I can understand that I guess.' Bob looked on nodding, seemingly sympathetic - Krystyna, less so. Marie, on the other hand, still hadn't entirely got the hang of this Mr Head thing.

'But maybe it has been Allah's will, all along, that I have still the head,' added Dinesh, seeing beyond the mist of guilt and through to a potentially sunnier outcome. 'He has been leading us to our destiny!'

'Yes, finally,' said Mishka. 'You are seeing what was obvious to me from the first second.'

'No need for bragging, dear wife,' Dinesh mildly countered. But he was grinning broadly all the same.

Within the hour, Dinesh and Mishka had driven back to the *Star of India* to collect the necessary. Marie had then completed her work on the real head of the deceased Bryce Brimstone. From the thawing of the entire noggin with her hairdryer, to the clever work with cream foundation and other make-up to provide that freshly embalmed look, all ensured that her presentation was just as good as that afforded to any expertly displayed corpse in any better end funeral parlour. Bob and his lighter were kept well away throughout. But most importantly, when Marie went on to working on the join at the neck that knitted together Bryce's head and the waxwork's torso, her cosmetics expertise shone through. A seamless conjoining.

'That's brilliant,' Gavin congratulated his exhausted ex-wife.

'He looks like the real thing,' said Bob, most impressed.

'That's because he is real thing! Dope!' Krystyna stung.

All that was left now was to wait for the call from Disposals Inc, inform Slater of the time and place of the rendezvous - then for Gavin himself to catch up, en-route, with whichever officer was going to fit him with his 'body wire'. The plan, for sure, was back on track.

27
- UP IN SMOKE -

Tom Slater had by now taken the expected call from Gavin and had gathered Drabbleton Police's small but elite team of Special Operations Officers - all six of them firearms trained and hungry for real action. It had been so long since they'd had their guns out in anger, Slater had called them in earlier this morning for a bit of target practice on the firing range. While he hadn't been entirely impressed with the deadly accuracy of the sharpshooting at his disposal - only two beer cans and one milk bottle finally being hit during an entire hour session and over two hundred rounds expended - he knew the team would have needed a bit of a warm-up. But right at the death, one young PC, the small and slender Amira Iqbal, had arrived late due to unavoidable traffic duties. There had been only time for her to practice with one round of six shots. But this girl had the knack.

'Bloody hell, PC Iqbal, where did you learn to shoot like that?' Slater had gawped as five out of six beer cans had gone flying.

'It is just focus, Sir, that is all,' she'd replied. 'I was engaged for two years to Abdul, the love of my life. Then he cheated on me the week before our planned wedding. So, when I take aim, I imagine I am aiming for his dick.'

'Great initiative, well done Officer!' Slater had congratulated, consoled that he might have just discovered what could be today's ace up the sleeve.

Back at the Ops Room, it was now time to brief the team on the final details of what was to come. Besides the firearms team, now all present, the covert surveillance vehicle needed to be manned. Slater wasn't entirely thrilled when PCs Duckworth and Chabra walked into the room, the only two available and on-duty officers to have had training for that rarely used Listening Van.

'You two had better be on your game today,' he warned them. 'Lives are at risk.'

'You can rely on us, Sir,' Duckworth assured him confidently. Chabra just smiled weakly. No point over-promising, he reckoned.

'OK, Judith, get on with it,' Slater then instructed Haslam as she stood next to an overhead projector ready to pass on the gen.

'Yes Sir,' she was happy to finally begin, illuminating the large white screen at the front of the room with her slide. 'This is a zoomed-in satellite image of Loom House, the Drabbleton residence of Mr Bryce Brimstone. The kidnappers have told our man, Gavin Hargreaves, that they are holding Alice Brimstone in this building, here.' With her pointer tool, she indicated to the coach house building some forty or so yards away from the main house. 'As you can see, the only vehicular access to the Loom House estate is here.' She then pointed to the front main gates and the quarter mile winding drive up to the house. 'Coming in with cars from this direction is a non-starter as there's no cover and we'd stick out like a sore thumb. But the surveillance vehicle can park here, in this lay-by, twenty yards from the main gates.'

'Do you understand, Duckworth, Chabra?' Slater bellowed. 'No matter what happens you will remain silently and diligently in position. Then you will alert the firearms team when one of two things happen. Either when Gavin Hargreaves tells you, via his wire, that he has Alice Brimstone safely clear of the coach house. Or if you hear that he and his team are in trouble. Got it?'

'Got it, Sir,' Duckworth acknowledged. Chabra smiled, pleased that his senior oppo sounded a bit more confident than he himself was feeling.

'But as you can see, the coach house itself is surrounded by open fields.' Haslam was busy with her pointer again. 'The firearms team will need to approach on foot, coming in from this woodland area some hundred yards away, then through this field of grazing cows.'

'There's a good chance we'll be spotted, Sergeant, if they're using a lookout. Which is a given,' said Officer Tony Rishton, a wider than average policeman who'd realised he'd be hard to miss in such circumstances.

'Don't worry, we've got the latest camouflage gear for you. You should blend into the background perfectly,' Slater convincingly reassured. 'Just get as near as you can to that coach house. Worst case scenario, you'll be going in there shooting. Best case, the kidnap gang will surrender and there'll be no blood spilt.'

'If the firearms team follow me, I'll issue you with your camouflage kit,' added Haslam, readying herself to depart the room.

The highest profile and most dangerous operation that Drabbleton Police had ever undertaken was about to be launched. Slater knew there were a lot of sweaty palms right there in that Ops Room. He was a bit hot under the collar himself if truth be known.

*

At 12.30 pm, as instructed by Dimitri, Gavin & The Bodysnatchers - the originals, no Marie, Mishka or Rocky - approached the wrought iron double gates to Loom House in Raspberry. In the back of the van, the highly polished, black casket - carrying the remainder of James Brimstone's waxwork and the latterly affixed replacement human head of Bryce Brimstone - rattled on its trolley as the bumps and lumps in the road were traversed. As they passed the unmarked, covert surveillance vehicle that they knew would be parked nearby, they received a friendly parp on the horn and wave from PC Chabra sat in the driver's seat.

'What are you doing?' yelled Duckworth from the back of the listening van. 'We're supposed to be undercover!'

'Hi guys,' replied Gavin, from inside his own van and talking into the wire concealed under his sweatshirt. 'Just testing you can hear me.'

'Hi Gavin, all good here,' Chabra shouted towards the two-way radio mic out back. 'See, they're not the bad guys. They're on *our side*,' Chabra reminded his senior colleague via a whisper. 'I was only saying hello.'

'Do you want Slater to kill us? We were told to remain silent, remember!' Duckworth complained to his over-enthusiastic, yet naturally affable colleague.

'Sorry, forgot,' Chabra mumbled to his mate. 'Hope it all goes well, Ice cream man and friends. Over and out,' he added more loudly, for the benefit of the mic.

'Very nice boy, that PC Chabra,' said Dinesh. 'Regular customer of mine. *Chicken Vindaloo, Naan Bread and Mango Chutney.*'

'Well, he wasn't very nice last night, when he tried to get you done for currying Brimstone,' Gavin reminded. Dinesh mused over that awkward conundrum.

'I can hear you know,' Chabra then interjected via Gavin's two-way wire. 'It's different now, anyway. Today you are on our side. I'm with you all the way.'

'Oh good, we are saved,' said Krystyna drily. Gavin just grinned as he then pulled Raspberry onto the grass verge just before the gates. It was time for a brief pause for a final check.

'OK guys, have we got everything?' he enquired, in down-to-business mode. 'Helium gas?'

'Check,' replied Bob, patting the cylindrical canister he'd been holding steadily between his knees in the back.

'Balloons?'

'Check,' Bob confirmed once more, eyeing the cardboard box he'd brought with him from Gavin's lounge.

'Shaving cream?'

'Check,' - Bob, once again.

'I have got cigarette lighter pistol,' Krystyna drawled. 'Why? I do not know.'

'It makes us look dangerous if we need, like I told you,' Bob chided. 'Might come in useful.'

Krystyna remained unimpressed. 'Plus, wire cutters,' she added, sounding happier with that particular accessory. 'Good in case I get tied up!'

'And I've also got something special up my sleeve, if needed,' continued a suddenly mischievous looking small pensioner.

'That something special had better not be that stick of dynamite you told me about,' Gavin warned, remembering this morning's conversation on the subject. Bob looked deflated.

'Course I've not bought a stick of dynamite. You did tell me not to and I am a *team player*,' the former steeplejack and demolition expert sulked, trying to claim the moral high ground.

'Sorry pal,' said Gavin. 'I'm just a bit nervous that's all.'

'Understandable.' The apology was accepted, and the crew were united again, back on track.

As they were parked there taking stock, their van suddenly buffeted with the backdraft of three speeding vehicles passing by, each turning into the gates of Loom House.

'Hey up, what's that lot about?' said Gavin, as he and his passengers viewed the small convoy with immediate trepidation. Each car was a black Mercedes SUV, identical to the one that had chased Raspberry through Drabbleton's streets just the other day.

And in each one, four black suited and very mean looking gentlemen were being carried towards a possible rendezvous that it would probably be advisable for most people to avoid.

'Reinforcements!' said Bob. 'They must have called for back-up.'

'It is a small army,' Krystyna noted, face falling. 'Not good.'

While Gavin and team then debated what to do about this sudden escalation in the danger stakes, the passenger in the leading Mercedes was looking at his phone, tracking something via GPS.

'It is that building there,' the gruff voice of one Andrei Balakin directed his muscular driver, as the coach house came into view beyond the top of the drive. The car approached, the two other vehicles right behind.

'We've got company boss,' Lewis swiftly spouted as the triple Mercedes mini convoy turned onto the mud and gravel courtyard. The craggy featured and bald Balakin and his eleven burly foot soldiers quickly left the cars and swarmed into the neglected building where Dimitri, Roxanne and Lewis were guarding their bound and gagged prisoners. It was apparent that Mrs Joyce had also been kept out of trouble by having to share the same fate as Alice, secured by her side now on an adjacent chair.

'Andrei, you should have said you were coming,' Dimitri smiled bitterly. 'Mrs Joyce here could have made tea.'

'Good day, Dimitri, we are here on Mr Volkov's say so,' Balakin spoke, no emotion in his tone.

'And you found us precisely here, how?'

'Your phone is being tracked. Mr Volkov always knows where you are.'

Dimitri pulled his mobile from his pocket and viewed it, chuckling caustically. 'Of course,' he muttered, as Balakin's men took up armed positions by the windows and doors of the mezzanine floored coach house.

'We are about to recover the body of my husband,' Roxanne spoke out. 'Dimitri has everything under control.'

'No, I am afraid Dimitri does not have everything under control, Mrs Brimstone,' Balakin replied, courteously, yet with firmness. 'When he told Mr Volkov on the phone last night of the hostage exchange idea all confidence was lost. We are not dealing entirely with rival gang members here - hardened criminals. He has involved an amateur - a frightened member of the public who will no doubt have gone running to the police.'

'It is exactly because Gavin Hargreaves is frightened that he would not dare involve the law,' Dimitri growled, indignant about this questioning of his professional judgement.

'Mr Volkov asked me to tell you that I shall be taking over this mission now. Your days as his Number Two are coming to an end.' Balakin was relishing breaking the news and seeing the beads of sweat break out on Sidorov's forehead. 'His contacts have discovered that you will be facing an armed police response today.'

'We can handle a backwater police force, such as the morons of Drabbleton - who I have already gauged the quality of, do not worry,' Dimitri scoffed, remembering that this local rabble weren't even bright enough to go and collect the body of a murder victim when it had been put right under their noses.

'But Mr Volkov does not believe you'll be facing Drabbleton Police,' Balakin dismissed. 'He has heard that *The Invisibles* have been called in.'

Dimitri's face immediately whitened. OK, maybe just he and Lewis would indeed have been no match for an entire unit of *The Invisibles* - the UK's most elite but secret firearms unit.

'What are *The Invisibles*, for God's sake?' asked Roxanne, not enjoying this rude intrusion into her day at all.

'Police killing squad,' Dimitri explained, bowing his head, ashamed that he did not see this one coming. 'They exist to eliminate organised criminals.'

'Called *The Invisibles*,' Balakin was happy to continue, 'because they arrive unseen, like ghosts in the night. They take no prisoners, then spirit themselves away, disappearing into thin air. We fear them. Even Mr Volkov too.'

'I understand now why he has sent all his best men,' said Dimitri, as he noticed Lewis trembling in the corner. 'But I still have this operation under control.'

'Not anymore, Dimitri. I am in charge,' Balakin asserted, clicking his fingers to two of his men, indicating to them to take up position on the mezzanine balcony.

Meanwhile Alice and Mrs Joyce looked on, terrified. If they were hearing right - in addition to now seeing a dozen black suited gangsters preparing their weapons - they might soon find themselves in the middle of a gunfight. Mrs Joyce began to mutter her prayers.

From a raised vantage point, some two hundred yards away, and lying behind a felled log, Slater and Haslam had both seen the arrival of Volkov's reinforcements through binoculars.

'There's too many of them, Sir,' Haslam had fretted. 'Don't you think it's time to call this off?'

'No,' Slater insisted, sounding determined. 'We still have the element of surprise on our side. But if we do pull out now, I would fear the worst for Alice Brimstone, Gavin and all.'

'I agree with that,' replied the DS. 'We've no choice really.'

At that point, a bright yellow Ford Transit ice cream van pulled up in front of Loom House, its occupants obviously having voted on proceeding with the today's mission after all. It parked next to Dimitri's Mercedes and both Gavin and Krystyna alighted. From the serving hatch, Slater watched on as Dinesh and Bob manhandled the casket up onto the counter. Moments later - seeing as a wooden box containing a waxwork and human head is much lighter than one carrying the hefty remains of Mrs Gertrude Biggins - the casket was on the already unloaded trolley and ready to be steered wherever. Although, if truth be known, the thing did seem heavier than it had done in rehearsals. Must just be the tension of the moment, Gavin concluded. He realised that tension was gripping the entirety of his body.

Lewis then appeared into view, walking towards the main house. 'This way, please,' he directed, pointing towards the distant coach house. As previously agreed, Krystyna then joined Gavin pushing the trolley - while Bob and Dinesh remained behind, having other matters to attend to. A helium canister would be needed.

'OK, Black Bull to Brown Cows,' said Slater, taking all of this in and talking into his two-way radio. 'Proceed with extreme caution.'

From their concealed woodland position, the cunningly camouflaged members of the firearms unit then moved slowly forwards.

'These costumes are bloody stupid,' grumbled PC Rishton. 'We'll be like sitting ducks.'

'I think we'll be fine, at least while we're mingling with the other cattle,' young PC Iqbal replied, having no time at this point for waverers. 'DI Slater knows what he's doing.' She covered her face with a paper mache cow's head. PC Rishton huffed and adjusted his udders before lifting Iqbal into position at the front of what sceptical observers might be calling a pantomime cow. But that would be to denigrate the painting skills of DS Haslam herself, whose considered brush strokes had transformed these otherwise potentially comic outfits into authentic looking members of the local livestock community. Well from a distance, at least, they looked mildly convincing. Although Haslam had been most grateful to Drabbleton's Grand Theatre for their assistance with retained costumes from their Christmas production of *Jack & The Beanstalk*.

As previously briefed, now before the six officers of the firearms unit lay an open field filled with docile dairy cows, happily grazing away in the mild afternoon sun. From a lookout window, up on the mezzanine floor of the coach house, one eagle eyed member of Volkov's troops spotted three cows casually wandering beyond the woodland, heading towards the rest of the herd from which they had obviously become unattached. The cows looked strangely odd to him for some reason, but whatever, as he squinted, he could see that they were obviously just cattle - well, of course they were. English cows must look a bit different to Russian cows, that's all.

He was no farm animal enthusiast, but what else would be contentedly grazing there in this rural haven? He scanned the horizon instead, searching out any first move from the formidable and notoriously wily *Invisibles* themselves. After that, he was completely oblivious to the sight of the same three cows sauntering in a meandering but steadily onward pattern towards the coach house itself.

'Brilliant work, Judith,' said Slater, more than surprised by the life-like credibility of the three fake heifers.

'Thanks, sir,' his DS replied with pride. In any case, the Russian lookout was blessed with more brawn than brains.

Meanwhile, the large double doors of the coach house were swung open as Gavin and Krystyna approached, followed by Lewis - who'd by now recognised the previously sword brandishing female from that fateful night at Brimstone Mill. He'd be glad to see her come to a nasty end, that was for sure. But for now, he just bided his time as the casket was wheeled forwards, until the new visitors were immediately startled - not only by the sight of the tied and gagged Alice and Mrs Joyce, but by the realisation that they were now surrounded by a dozen or so armed henchmen.

'Alice, are you OK?' Gavin instinctively called over. She nodded without fuss, trying not to add to his alarm. Everybody needed to stay calm right now.

'So, we finally meet, Mr Gavin Hargreaves,' said Dimitri. 'I trust you and your friend have brought us what we need.'

'We have,' Gavin answered as clearly as he could muster.

'Very nice casket,' said Roxanne. 'A quality item that Bryce would have approved of, no doubt.'

'Thanks, we wanted him to have the best,' Gavin tried to sound genuine. Krystyna smiled with sarcastic sweetness by his side.

'Good,' Roxanne continued. 'Now may I see my darling, please?'

'Yes, of course.' Gavin nodded politely and efficiently went about unfastening the side catch to the upper section of the casket and pulling open the viewing door. Using the inner sliding back mattress, he was then able to prop the Bryce/James mishmash up quickly and effortlessly into a typical and dignified funeral parlour viewing position.

'Oh, sweetheart! wailed Roxanne, melodramatically. 'It *is* Bryce, indeed. What terrible thing has happened to him?' She inspected the head and touched its freshly styled hair and embalmed skin, courtesy of Marie. Then she rubbed a hand over his Victorian gentleman's starched white shirt, his chest feeling muscular and firm - just as she'd always remembered. Yes, it was her dearly departed husband alright. The crocodile tears commenced as she then cupped Bryce's head in her arms.

Lewis looked on from behind Gavin, slightly pleased by the accuracy of his shooting. The bullet hole he'd put into Bryce's forehead on that eventful evening at Brimstone Mill had been perfectly placed - *bullseye*, right between the eyes!

'Good job, Mr Hargreaves,' commended Dimitri, wondering how - at this point - Bryce's head had suddenly turned up. But quite happy that it had, so no need for questions.

'We were so in love,' sobbed Roxanne, maybe practicing for the life insurance company - although only Gavin in the audience was taken in. He hadn't known their marriage was an entire sham, after all. 'I do miss him very much.' Meanwhile, Krystyna was ready to dish out an Emmy Award. Now she *did* know that the Brimstone marriage was one of inconvenient convenience. Bryce had told her often enough, before or after their sex games.

'If we could be leaving now with Alice, that would be good,' Gavin asserted, his team's part of the bargain fulfilled. He stepped forward to the side of his on-off girlfriend and touched her shoulder. The sight of seeing her tied up like this was making his stomach turn.

'I am in charge of this operation now,' Balakin suddenly intervened, pushing Dimitri aside. 'I don't know what pathetic arrangement you had with this one.' He eyed Volkov's fallen Number Two with contempt. 'But I am afraid I work on the basis of *no witnesses!*

Gavin and Krystyna froze.

Just north of the main gates, in the covert surveillance vehicle, Chabra in particular had been studiously listening not so much to this latest development, but more to Roxanne's tragic drama where the grieving, widowed wife comes face to face with the remains of her murdered husband. He'd found it all very moving. Too much even - like a weepy Christmas episode of *EastEnders*.

'I'll never meet a man of his like ever again. Never, ever!' Roxanne continued to sob, ignoring Balakin's intervention and only leaving Chabra in urgent need of his handkerchief. He pulled said item from his pocket and blew on a very snotty nose, then dabbing the already then soggy cloth on his falling tears.

'Steady on mate,' said Duckworth, leaning over the control panel to put a comforting arm around his distraught junior oppo's shoulder. 'It's a tough job is coppering, at times.'

At this point, neither of the TV Soap loving PCs had noticed that the trailing handkerchief had pulled up against the two-way radio switch, suddenly turning a listening device into a broadcast mechanism.

'Oh, it's all too sad,' snivelled the young officer, uncontrollably. 'Poor, poor woman!'

PC Chabra's words and simultaneous blubbering were instantly transmitted out of the small speaker hidden inside Gavin's clothing, the latter trying in vain to mute and smother the unhelpful interruption. But everyone in the coach house had heard Chabra's emotional outpouring.

'He is wearing a wire. Get it!' Balakin furiously boomed out to his nearest henchman, himself a giant brute of a guy - who in turn roughly pulled up Gavin's sweatshirt and ripped the surveillance device from its wearer's body.

'We're in trouble!' Slater edgily exclaimed, speaking into his own radio. 'Brown Cows get ready to go!' he ordered. Three armed heifers, cleverly concealing six armed police officers - like some latter-day Trojan Horses - ambled forward with increased focus.

Inside the coach house, Balakin's anger erupted, as did his gun, which he fired above his head in a display of uncontrolled aggression and frustration. 'Line up all the civilians against the wall and shoot them!' he ordered. Half a dozen men hurriedly moved to corral Gavin and Krystyna into their place of imminent summary execution.

'Brown Cows, go, go, go!' yelled Slater on a surge of adrenaline. From his observation point he could see that two of the bovine cavalry were already in position at the side door to the building. Meanwhile, the other cow - aka PC Iqbal and PC Rishton - had taken up their own position behind a nearby stone cattle trough. In the split second after he had given the order, he imagined his entire armed unit moving onwards as if in a slow-motion movie and all heading for certain death. They were outnumbered by more than two to one, after all. But too late to retract the order now.

Across and beyond the other side of the coach house, Bob and Dinesh jumped in their boots as they heard Balakin's first shot fired in anger.

'Oh my!' Dinesh panicked. 'Where are the police?'

'This might help,' said Bob doggedly. He pulled a small, plastic control box from his trouser pocket and without delay pushed down on the red button in the centre of the console itself.

Explosion!

Both men fell to their knees, shocked by the noise of the blast.

Inside the coach house, pandemonium had set in. Bob had triggered an explosion alright - inside the casket itself, blowing the waxwork of James and the wooden box into a thousand pieces. Roxanne had been thrown across the floor, inadvertently taking with her the head of Bryce that she'd been cradling and now sat against a junked mattress, dazed and incoherent. Thick clouds of white powder were swirling around the room, which were in fact the six bags of self-raising flour that Bob had popped out to pick up from the Co-op earlier. If Gavin had wondered, just before, why the casket had seemed heavier - well here was the explanation. But he was currently momentarily prone, like Krystyna, literally floored by the blast - as was everybody else in the building.

'Bob, no!' Dinesh wailed in anguish. 'You have killed them!'

'Unlikely,' replied Bob, maybe more in hope than certainty. 'But yeah, that was a bit louder than I was expecting!'

The two nearest brown cows then stormed the side entrance, guns blazing and darting for cover as soon as they entered the flour dust and debris filled room. Two Russians went down in the first two seconds.

'Look out, the cows - they have guns!' cried a third henchman, floundering.

'They are not cows, you morons!' Balakin bemoaned. 'They are *The Invisibles.* Again, they have swept in out of nowhere. Kill them all!'

Despite the assertive order, fear instantly filled the eyes of his small army.

Meanwhile, now partially out of costume, from the sniper point behind the feeding trough, PC Rishton opened fire at the obviously disoriented lookout at the upper window. Six rapid shots, all missed. More beer can practice probably required! But his target was in fact stung into life by this hopeless spraying and returned fire himself, immediately hitting Rishton in the shoulder.

'Aagghh!' he howled in pain, instinctively dropping his rifle and palming his wound. PC Iqbal ignored her partner's squirming discomfort, calmly adjusted her rifle sights and fired. One shot. The Russian fell from the window, quite dead.

'One of ours down - PC Rishton,' she informed Slater, via her radio - although he'd already seen as much through his binoculars. 'I'm going in,' she continued.

'Be careful, Amira,' said her bloodied colleague. 'These guys mean business.'

'So do I!' she replied gutsily as she ditched the rest of the brown cow outfit and dashed for the side door to reinforce Brown Cow 1 and Brown Cow 2.

Inside the coach house, with the air still flour-dust befogged, Balakin had now fallen into unconsciousness due to his proximity to the nastier bottom end of the casket where Bob had placed the dynamite. Two other Russians had died instantly when brass coffin handles had flown on a lethal trajectory to their heads at some thousand miles an hour. Right now, it was left to the dazed survivors, Dimitri, Lewis, and six still-standing Volkov henchman, to take care of what they thought was the UK police's almost mythical unit of elite hot shots. As such, as the bullets hailed across the room - a cacophony of gunfire without interruption - Dimitri could only wonder why more of his own had not been already eliminated.

The foot soldier immediately to his right stopped to reload. PC Iqbal was now in position behind a long forgotten about moped. Her flour-faced target fell within the second. The jarring racket of more gunfire from the weapons of those with a less polished aim continued.

Gavin suddenly recovered enough wits about him to realise that neither he nor the other so-called civilians were the current focus of attention for Volkov's preoccupied men - concentrating, as they so obviously were, on their own survival. He locked eyes with Krystyna. She was obviously thinking the same.

'I have my wire cutters,' she whispered, displaying these gamely for Gavin's benefit.

'Go for it,' he replied, optimism once more returning to his own flour-encircled eyes.

They both crawled over to where Alice was lying, her chair having been toppled by the explosion.

'I'm alright,' she answered Gavin's enquiring expression as he released the gag. Meanwhile, Krystyna got swiftly to work, snipping the cable ties that were securing the hostage to the chair.

The henchman nearest to them suddenly noticed the civilian distraction. He momentarily hesitated as, although quickly exterminating them seemed to be the simplest option, he looked towards Balakin seeking the OK - but his boss was groaning on the floor, only just now regaining consciousness. The fleeting delay was to prove costly. He carelessly wandered into Iqbol's rifle sights. A second later he was dead.

'Who is this?' asked Krystyna of Alice, eyeing the middle-aged lady prone beside her.

'It's Mrs Joyce, Bryce's housekeeper,' came the hurried reply. 'Roxanne didn't want her snooping around while this was going on.'

'I will cut cable ties, yes?' Krystyna asked.

'Yes, of course,' said Alice, remaining crouched on the ground, but now completely free. The wire cutters snapped into further action.

At that moment, Balakin had finally stirred himself sufficiently well to be able to rise to his feet. Immediately spotting the escape plan, his anger ensured that any concern for his own immediate safety was promptly discounted. If these civilians escaped, then his first big Commander-in-Chief mission for Mr Volkov would have failed. His whole mobster future was at stake - and not least his professional pride. So, he took his gun, cocked it, and strode over towards the cowing civilians - seemingly invincible against the streams of bullets whizzing past his head.

Just as Krystyna cut Mrs Joyce free, Balakin was holding his *Makarov* semi-automatic pistol against the housekeeper's head. She screamed.

'No witnesses will leave here today!' Balakin bristled, ready to shoot.

'Not! So! Fast!' hollered a cocksure voice coming somewhere from the vicinity of the front entrance. But impenetrable flour dust was still swirling in the air. The newly promoted chief mafioso squinted to view the cause of this inconvenient distraction. But as he did, a single gunshot rang out. As the flour fog thinned in the vicinity of the firing weapon's source, the last thing that Balakin saw was the white faced, ghostly silhouette figure of a diminutive old Teddy Boy holding a Nazi Luger revolver. The shot to the heart, with the very last bullet from Bob's stolen gun, was lethal alright. Balakin bit the dust, mortally wounded yet whispering with his final breath:

'You *Invisibles*. Ghosts in the night. I will see you in Hell!'

He was gone.

'Bob, awesome!' Gavin shouted over to his sharp shooting neighbour, who was by now casually blowing the smoke away from the end of his weapon, old cowboy style.

'What are you waiting for,' Bob then yelled to all on his side. 'Let's get out of here!'

While the alleged *Invisibles* provided ample gunshot cover, Iqbal expertly taking out yet another henchman - her fourth of the day - Gavin, Alice, Krystyna and Mrs Joyce made a daring dart for freedom, fleeing through the now clearing flour dust towards the retreating Bob and even better, towards the waiting Raspberry. Dinesh too, it seemed, had come up with his own bit of quick thinking - bringing the getaway vehicle into the coach house courtyard.

'They're getting away, boss!' Lewis yelled over to Dimitri, as he saw the escapees finally leave beyond the double doors and off into ice cream van refuge. But neither of them could easily do anything about it, as sustained gunfire was pinning them into their corner, their only defence shield - a rickety, discarded piano.

'Come on, roll this thing,' ordered Dimitri, suddenly seeing an option. 'We can use it as moving cover.'

Lewis was quickly onto it and the two men, recoiled behind the old upright and edged its wheels in the direction of the exit. Discordant notes rang out as the piano strings took the full brunt of the incoming fire.

'Come with us,' Dimitri called to Roxanne, who was still sat against the mattress, but now mostly recovered from the shock of the blast. She quickly saw the opportunity and scurried over to the mobile piano as it headed for the door, happy to shield behind its protective buffer.

'Do you have to bring that thing? It's freaky!' balked Dimitri, looking at Brimstone's severed head being nursed in a wife's nursing arms.

'Of course, I need to bring it,' Roxanne snapped back. 'Isn't this what today's disastrous palaver has been all about?'

'I suppose...' Dimitri conceded as he then looked beyond the coach house. Raspberry was being speedily driven away by some Indian looking guy. Every single civilian had escaped - no doubt confirming his own death sentence by strangling at the hands of Mr Volkov. The only consolation he could see was that Balakin was already dead. But then that got him already wondering if he could blame his intruding rival for the bungled mission. Yes, there could be life left in the old dog yet. That said, it still meant that Hargreaves and his interfering friends would all have to perish. *No witnesses* was Volkov's minimum requirement, of course.

At that point, the piano was clear of the double doors and out into the courtyard, now safely beyond the sights of the *Invisibles*' rifles.

'Come, we must catch them,' Dimitri called out, beckoning Roxanne and Lewis to run with him towards his waiting Mercedes.

Behind them, the remaining three members of Volkov's miniature army continued to hold the inevitably falling fort. He only hoped that their futile last stand would continue for long enough for he himself to escape, along with his junior partner - who had shown great bravery today in the face of an armed enemy. Plus Roxanne, of course, and their potentially golden egg laying goose - the severed head of Bryce Brimstone.

As those three approached the front of the main house, Dimitri noticed that the ice cream van had already journeyed downhill to almost reach the front gates to the estate - a quarter of a mile away. There seemed to be some passenger exchange going as a tiny red car had turned up and its driver had left the vehicle to meet someone from the van. Whatever, it meant that the escapees could still be caught as Dimitri remembered that the ice cream van might be tricky, but it was certainly no racing machine. But then he turned to notice the state of his own car.

'What is this?' he snarled, as he espied the Mercedes, its entire interior filled with balloons and its windscreen covered in shaving foam.

'Ha! It's like a newly-weds motor,' laughed Lewis. 'We did this to our mate Jamal when he was off on his honeymoon.'

'This is not funny!' Dimitri fumed. 'Get these balloons out now.'

As Roxanne stood by bemused yet frustrated, nursing Bryce's head, both Dimitri and Lewis hurriedly tried to rid the car of its hundred or so spheres of multi-coloured, inflated latex. It wasn't that easy, as Bob and Dinesh had been very productive with the helium canister but had then cunningly stringed together abundant clusters of balloons. These had in turn been tied, tightly knotted, to multiple available anchor points - steering wheel, handbrake, headrests and door handles.

'Hurry up! It's taking too long!' Dimitri blustered as he managed to rid the car of just three balloons on first attempt. Lewis had done better - maybe another six. Just another seventy or so to go. Meanwhile, the armed battle in the coach house was apparently ongoing, gun shots continuing to ring out, echoing throughout the grounds of the estate.

'Oh, do get in! We'll have to go like this, or they will get away!' Roxanne intervened in a temper as she continued to shake flour dust out of her hair and off her dress. She then bundled herself into the passenger seat, knocking bunches of balloons out of her way, yet looking decidedly uncomfortable in there. Only her nose and eyes seemed to be clear of any rubberised obstacle.

Taking her example, Dimitri and Lewis quickly took up their seats, equally hampered by Dinesh and Bob's purposely aggravating work. Barely able to see above his obstructed steering wheel, the very miffed driver decided to get the wiper blades to work on the double. But the shaving cream just smeared into white, sticky goo over the windscreen barely improving visibility at all.

'Classic stuff!' Lewis giggled, appreciating the opponents' master stroke 'They've only mixed glue in there to make it harder to shift.'

'Shut up, you idiot,' barked Dimitri as he made the decision to drive on having only cleared a narrow-arced strip of visibility, maybe only a couple of inches wide. But until the wiper blades completed a more thorough job, he would only dare proceed at less than ten miles an hour. Hardly ideal for a pursuit vehicle.

'I can't drive like this,' he shrieked, unable to change gear easily due to the balloon obstacles. 'Pop the damn things, Lewis! Use your knife.'

'Keep your hair on,' His underling complained, but nevertheless - and much to Roxanne's annoyance - began systematically bursting the offending items.

Now as this balloon and shaving cream complication was being tackled, in the couple of minutes prior to the Mercedes crawling back into action, Raspberry had pulled up fifty yards or so ahead of the main gates. The little red car that had been advancing in the opposite direction into the drive carried a couple immediately familiar to Bob.

'Stop! It's Mavis!' Bob had hollered as the ice cream van slowed down to give way to the small saloon on the narrow driveway.

'It's Charlie and Mum,' Mrs Joyce had called out. 'We can't let them go up to the house!'

Gavin had been instantly blaring on his horn, obviously startling the oncoming driver, but ensuring her vehicle came to a prompt halt.

'Thank you for saving my life,' Mrs Joyce had then said to Bob, who she'd been sat with in the serving area. 'I'll always consider you to be my hero.' She'd promptly planted a kiss on the hot-shot pensioner's cheek, leaving him immediately blushing - and then had risen quickly to her feet, being ushered out of the van by Gavin.

'Mum, stop. You can't go to the house,' Sheryl Joyce had stood shouting in front of her mother's car, frantically waving. Almost instantly, Mavis had left her driver's seat and had one foot out of the car, supporting herself as she stood leaning against its upper door frame.

'What on earth's happened to your face, your clothes?' Bob's ex-wife had fretted on seeing her daughter's flour dusted condition, then the similarly whitewashed state of Gavin and everyone else in the ice cream van.

'Are you alright, Mum? What's happened,' the young man had piped up, by now stepping himself out of the passenger seat.

'I'm fine, Charlie - fine. But we need to go *that-away*,' his mother had demandingly pointed to the exit route, back out beyond the main gates.

By now, the Mercedes had been making its tentative way forwards down the drive. Bob had spotted its departure, relishing its tortoise like progression thanks to his own deviously employed hinderance of shaving cream, glue and helium filled balloons.

'I'll go with them,' he now announced to Gavin as he jauntily hopped out of the van in favour of the red saloon. 'Someone needs to keep them safe.'

'I guess you're the man,' said Gavin, smiling with unusual respect at his unlikely tiny warrior of a neighbour. 'You know what, Bob? All these years and I thought you were just a useless old windbag. But today, you were blinkin' brilliant!'

'Don't mention it,' Bob smiled awkwardly, but then when Gavin dished out a huge bear hug, he felt more awkward still. 'Gerroff, you stupid bugger!' he cringed, swiftly wriggling out of the embrace.

'Even though you did nearly kill us all with that explosion. You did say you hadn't brought the stick of dynamite,' Gavin only mildly admonished.

'I didn't bring the stick. I brought only *a quarter of a stick.* If I'd have used a whole stick, well yeah, that would have killed you.' He grinned smugly just as he heard his name being called.

'Bob Horsefield! What are you doing here?' asked Mavis, squinting her eyes in disbelief as her ex-husband came into view, whitened face and all.

'This man saved my life,' glowed Sheryl. Mavis looked shocked. Charlie too.

'But we need to get away from here now,' Bob spoke quickly and with urgency. 'These guys behind us mean business!' he sternly voiced, pointing to the Mercedes making its slow but steady way down the hill. He shooed Sheryl, Charlie and Mavis back to the little red car. 'See you at the Police Station, if we make it,' he finally called back to Gavin, before queuing behind Charlie to get into the car.

That had been the plan, as suggested by Slater in fact, that if there was anyone in pursuit of their vehicle then they should try to head for Drabbleton Police Station. They'd be safe there. Well, maybe.

Back in the Mercedes, Dimitri was doing his best to see through his smeared windscreen and, as well as he could manage, he looked keenly ahead at the figures about to disappear into the little red saloon.

'Lewis, I hope that's not that Charlie kid I am seeing down there,' he simmered, focussing harder as the apprentice mafioso in the back was still busying himself with balloon popping duties. Dimitri then took in a deep gulp of air as he confirmed to himself that it was indeed young Charlie. 'You have lied to me, Lewis,' he roared - or rather squeaked. For it was not actually a deep gulp of air that Sidorov had just taken in, but rather a deep gulp of helium. The Mercedes cabin was filled with the stuff, in fact, as the frantic balloon busting activity had released voice altering levels of gas.

'Don't yell at me about it!' Lewis angrily hit back, himself now in squeak mode. 'I didn't sign up for this so I could kill kids.'

'Your father will be furious when I tell him!' Dimitri yelped, higher pitched than ever.

'Tell him, see if I care!' Lewis virtually squealed. 'I will quit!'

'Why are you both talking funny, you cretins?' said Roxanne, talking funnily herself, fury then rising across her face when she realised she'd done so and must have sounded pretty damn stupid.

'It is the helium from the balloons,' Dimitri hollered, in ear-splittingly high tones. 'Open your windows!' Oxygen then gushed into the cabin as the automatic window motors did their trick and the impromptu squeaky voice show was almost instantly over.

Yesterday evening, when Lewis was ostensibly taking Charlie off to the bus stop, he'd learned that the young student artist was, in fact, planning on staying overnight at his grandmother's house and not returning until the following afternoon. Well, Lewis was hoping that he and the crew would be well on their way back to London by then. Charlie had been decent to him, digging him out those evening class details - and in fact seemed like a nice kid all round. Pointless killing him if he didn't need to, or just to satisfy Dimitri's warped sense of satisfaction. So he had, in truth, dropped off Charlie by the bus stop - but then immediately afterwards had driven back by the woodland where he had fired his gun in the air, faking the hit.

Now that Dimitri knew about his deception he expected to be in big trouble. But right now, there was nothing he could do about that. The helium had made him feel quite woozy and he took in successive deep breaths of fresh air.

'We will talk about this when we are back in London,' said Dimitri, voice restored to its baritone grump.

'Whatever,' moped Lewis, looking out of his side window, most balloons by now cleared or popped. But he then saw that Dimitri was leaping from the suddenly halted car and was manically scraping away the gunked up shaving foam with a credit card. Through the then quickly clearing windscreen, the distant little red car and ice cream van could be seen exiting the main gates at the bottom of the hill.

'Hurry, they are getting away,' Roxanne carped, pointing to the obvious for the benefit of Dimitri.

'I am not blind!' he remonstrated, thumping the bonnet. 'But I will never catch them if I cannot see through this mess of a windscreen!'

'Rub harder then,' Lewis added mischievously, happy to further wind up the boss. It worked, as the resultant fury in Dimitri's eyes seemed capable of making him internally combust. Then, within another five seconds, windscreen cleared to a half reasonable standard, the inwardly raging driver was back in his seat and the Mercedes screeched off, rocketing forwards, normal service resumed.

'Good, we're finally getting somewhere then,' Roxanne niggled. Dimitri just ignored her. They were already on the last stretch of driveway towards the exit of the grounds, the Mercedes accelerating with each passing second. But right then, the covert surveillance vehicle suddenly appeared like a rabbit out of a hat, its occupants having seen the ice cream van successfully leave the arena of operations. PC Duckworth and PC Chabra were valiantly taking it upon themselves to block the main gates - preventing any unsavoury Mafia types from pursuing innocent members of the Drabbleton public.

'Are you sure we're supposed to be doing this?' asked a very nervous Chabra, as his senior colleague took charge of the heroic driving. Well actually, both officers knew that they definitely *shouldn't* be doing this. Slater had specifically told them to leave any intervention down to the armed officer unit. But Duckworth, it seemed, was preferring to see that specific order more in the realms of *guidance* than mandatory instruction.

'It's not our fault that the armed guys didn't finish the job. We can't be letting kidnappers and murderers onto our streets. Not on our watch!' Duckworth spoke with determination as he brought the van to a pronounced halt straddling the gap between the open wrought iron gates, nose on to the Mercedes.

'He doesn't look happy about it though,' Chabra gulped, observing the fuming Russian driver in the advancing car. 'But look at that! There's a blinkin' P in that registration plate!' he added in amazement.

'See, you were right all along,' said Duckworth, once again congratulating the younger officer on his incredible powers of observation. 'These are the bad guys alright!'

'Shoot them! Now!' Dimitri barked at Lewis from inside the Mercedes as he slowly advanced towards the unhelpful obstruction.

'What, seriously? Here, with a main road just behind them?' Lewis challenged, remembering his training instruction that use of firearms should be only discretely employed wherever possible.

'Yes, shoot them! It is the local police we saw the other day,' Dimitri bristled as he recognised the two officers he'd last seen by that bothersome ice cream van. 'I have had enough of their annoying interference once and for all!'

'OK, have it your way,' Lewis sighed in resignation as he then leaned out of the window and fired three swift shots through the windscreen of the police vehicle. As glass shattered Duckworth and Chabra had managed to instinctively bob down below the line of fire.

'Bloody hell,' Duckworth gasped for breath. 'They're mean bastards, these lot!'

'We should have listened to DI Slater. I want my Mum,' Chabra whimpered as he tried to improbably contort his body so that it might just nestle in the refuge of the passenger footwell. It wasn't going to happen. 'What now?'

By the terrified and bewildered look on Duckworth's face, it was clear that no productive answer would be forthcoming. But then the van started to shake and vibrate. Something new was afoot.

Dimitri had, in fact, edged the front bumper of his SUV into direct contact point with the front bumper of the police van. He was now accelerating forwards against the parked-up obstacle, using the full explosive horsepower of his engine to drive back his enemy inch by inch.

Duckworth and Chabra tentatively popped their heads above the makeshift parapet, just enough to be able see Sidorov's reddened face seemingly match the fury of spinning and screeching Mercedes tyres and the heat of the resultant burning rubber. But their van was being pushed inexorably backwards and there was nothing they could do about it.

'Put the handbrake on,' squealed Chabra.

'It is on! And it's in gear! *Hang on!*' Duckworth reeled, as the police vehicle was then pushed directly backwards, beyond the gates and into the line of an oncoming articulated lorry - which blared out its deafening siren horn, but then swerved to the right, avoiding impact by no more than a hair's breadth. The black SUV then quickly reversed, before then speeding forwards and clear of its vanquished opponent - off in the direction of Drabbleton, back in pursuit of the escaping witnesses.

Duckworth and Chabra practically fainted. But if they had had managed to stir their failing wits, then thirty seconds later they'd have noticed a police squad car speeding by, swiftly followed by an unmarked vehicle carrying two familiar detectives. The gun battle in the coach house was now over, the last of Volkov's resistance efficiently taken out - mainly down to the hotshot skills of Officer Iqbal. The five uninjured members of the armed response team had now been instructed to track down the fleeing Mercedes. They'd taken to this, buoyed by the already bagged successes of the day, with great enthusiasm. Slater and Haslam, in the car behind, were definitely having trouble keeping up with their speed freak colleagues. Although they weren't to know that Dimitri was now driving the target vehicle even faster.

'That took you long enough,' complained Roxanne, meanwhile, in the Mercedes, blowing out a sigh. 'We'll never catch them now.'

'We *will* catch them,' spat Dimitri, accelerating the car to twice that of the local fifty mile per hour speed limit. 'It is time to *drive*!'

Meanwhile, in the slightly more relaxed environment of the only forty miles per hour advancing ice cream van, as Dinesh competently handled the driving, his passengers were engrossed in important conversation of their own.

'That was amazing back there, Gavin,' said Alice turning round from the front passenger seat to face Raspberry's owner, himself sitting behind her in the serving area. 'You too, Krystyna,' she added, smiling at the co-rescuer sitting in between her and Dinesh. 'You could have been killed going in there like that.'

'Just another day in the life of a Drabbleton ice cream man,' Gavin twinkled smugly. 'But I knew I had to do something. Luckily, I have got some very brave friends who helped me make it happen.'

Krystyna and Dinesh silently acknowledged each other in approval.

'Well, I couldn't be more fortunate,' Alice continued, seemingly close to tears. 'Gavin, I didn't know that you cared so much. I really didn't deserve that - you risking your life, especially after - well you know...' She tailed off, but despite her coaxing nods of encouragement, could see her brave hero wasn't filling in the blank. 'You know, my little slip last Friday night with Leo,' she finally helped out, muttering awkwardly, and wishing that this could have been a more private conversation altogether.

'Don't mention it, you made a mistake, but I'm over it,' said Gavin, sounding admittedly too self-righteous and immediately sparking Krystyna's curiosity.

'It's none of my business, Alice, but no man that I know of is perfect either,' came the supportive, sisterly response.

'Maybe,' Alice mused. 'But I actually think that Gavin *is* perfect. He'd never do what I did and sleep with someone else behind my back.'

'Is that so?' Krystyna replied, eying Gavin with both amusement and disdain.

Dinesh blushed as his eyes widened. He didn't get this level of detail during his therapy sessions down at the chippy.

'Would you darling?' Alice sought affirmation. 'I said you'd never do such a treacherous thing, now would you?'

Gavin floundered, unable to read Krystyna's expression. Was she wanting him to own up? *What now?* Or was she happy for him to simply brush the whole thing underneath the carpet. He reached for the brush.

'Course not,' he finally blurted, seeking Krystyna's encouragement. 'I'm definitely not in favour of playing away. But can't we talk about something else?' he bumbled clumsily.

'So, you feel pretty shit about one night's indiscretion, huh Alice?' asked Krystyna flatly.

'Yes, dreadful actually.'

'And you say this was when - last Friday night?'

'Yes. Why does the particular evening matter?' Alice looked especially quizzical.

'Why don't we just change the subject,' Gavin intervened with pointless wishful thinking. 'Alice has maybe had enough excitement for one day. Maybe we all have.'

'Friday was very interesting night for Gavin too,' Krystyna pressed on mischievously, though clearly on a mission. 'Tell her, Mr Hargreaves.'

Alice sought out assistance from said Mr Hargreaves, but only a befuddled face greeted her.

'Well now, if you had asked Gavin last Friday how long it had been since he had last had sex, what do you think would be answer?' Krystyna persisted.

'That's easy,' Alice laughed. 'It was an open secret.'

'Twenty-eight months,' Dinesh chuckled.

'See, even the chippy man knows,' Alice beamed.

'But how long is it *now* since he last had sex?'

'The same of course, plus a few days,' came the innocent reply. *Where was this going?* 'Still twenty-eight months, I expect.' But Alice was starting to feel less than comfortable.

'No, not twenty-eight months,' said Krystyna with a purpose. 'Tell her Gavin. It is only fair.'

'Really?' The ice cream man froze, cold as a veritable 99 itself. Krystyna was offering no respite. 'Erm, five days, I guess,' he eventually managed to splutter.

'Five days? What are you saying?' Alice responded, but only in the way of someone whose foundations on this earth had instantly crumbled beneath their feet. 'Take it back, Gavin. That's not true!'

'I can't take it back, love. It happened.'

'Congratulations, Gavin. Finally!' Dinesh guffawed, missing the sensitivity of the moment. 'Only five days. That is only one day more than me!'

'We're not really interested in your happy marriage at the moment, Dinesh. This is serious!' Gavin hushed his currently unhelpful friend.

'Who?' Alice pressed, clearly hurt. 'Who did you sleep with?' She seemed to be fumbling blindly for past clues. 'Not Marie? I knew you two were a little too cosy?'

'Course it wasn't Marie.' Gavin's eyes rolled.

'It was me, Alice, sorry,' Krystyna owned up, speaking gently. 'But I had to say something. I couldn't have him being all *Mr Perfect* when you were so obviously feeling just guilty and worthless. Men shouldn't be able to get away with such shit!'

'You? You slept with him?' Alice was suddenly trembling. 'Though I'm glad somebody in this van thinks honesty is of mild importance. But amazing, Gavin. You were batting above your average there!' she laughed bitterly, glimpsing at Krystyna's obviously abundant womanly assets.

'He was pretty poor batsman, if truth be told,' the boyfriend borrower twisted the knife.

'Oi, do you mind! There's such a thing as privacy, you know,' complained Gavin. *No wonder he hadn't had sex for twenty-eight months if he's crap in bed,* thought Dinesh.

'Same goes for Leo,' Alice continued, despondently. 'All that guilt trip stuff later and for what? A few hot and sticky grunts and thrusts - then *bam!* It was all over before I was even warming up.'

'Exactly! I don't think men are very good at sex at all,' Krystyna frowned, staring blankly beyond the windscreen at the Drabbleton gloom.

'Pathetic, most of them,' Alice huffed.

'I'm completely off men I think.'

'Me too.'

As Alice concurred, turning her back on Gavin, Krystyna put her arm around her new, potential soulmate - who in turn snuggled her head across the taller woman's Lycra clad chest.

'Maybe we should have dinner together sometime,' Krystyna casually suggested.

'That would be nice.' Another sigh, sounding more like *relief*.

The two women then brushed lips, kissing gently for less than perhaps two seconds. But an age for Gavin as he helplessly watched on, gobsmacked - while Dinesh had to concentrate extra hard to maintain anything like a moderately straight course.

That fleeting yet special moment over, both Krystyna and Alice then burst out into hysterical laughter. They were losing control! But as they cackled on, Gavin was clueless as to whether or not the pair had, in fact, just started a love affair before his very eyes. It certainly looked that way. On the other hand, was it all a cruel joke to punish him, the latest flaky but only occasionally useful male in their lives? He really couldn't tell. Dinesh, meanwhile, was well out of his depth. He couldn't wait to get home to Mishka - and his maybe boring but comfortingly predictable domestic lot.

As Alice remained nestled in Krystyna's long arms, smiling contentedly, Gavin wondered if even she really knew what was going on. Krystyna would definitely know though. But again, most definitely, she wouldn't be saying.

'Sorry to interrupt, ladies and gentlemen, but I think we have company,' Dinesh suddenly piped up, spotting in the wing mirror the Mercedes speeding into view behind them - and now only some thirty yards away. By now the ice cream van had reached the built-up area of Drabbleton, the little red saloon still tootling on its way just ahead. Yet the police station, and hopefully more assistance, was still more than a mile away.

'The bad guys are catching Gavin's ice cream van,' Bob spouted out as he too then spotted the advancing SUV out of the rear window of Mavis's car. Although, as her motor now trundled along the cobbled streets, just besides Brimstone Mill, the diminutive pensioner was blessed - or so he reckoned - with the inspiration of another great idea.

'Pull over, I need to get out! We can confuse them if we split up.' he shouted, adrenaline pumping yet again. But Mavis didn't look so happy.

'You can't be getting out, Sweetie Bag,' she counselled. 'You could get killed out there.'

But the gung-ho volunteer could only grin. Mavis had just called him *Sweetie Bag*. He hadn't been *Sweetie Bag* since the Seventies. Blimey!

'No, I know what I'm doing, *Snuggle Bear*,' Bob finally insisted, reciprocating on the historic pet names. 'I'm on home turf here.'

With some reluctance, Mavis brought her car to a halt, and in just a jiffy, Sheryl had left her front passenger seat so that Bob could negotiate himself out of the tiny vehicle from the back seat. An assisting tug, courtesy of Mavis's daughter, and he was up and at it.

'You be careful out there,' Mavis finally called out, waving to the ex-husband who had today unexpectedly risen in her estimation to new heights. Her new hero – now and forever.

'I'm on it, Snuggle Bear. Don't you worry,' Bob waved a breezy cheerio and started to jog - well more of a brisk walk really - in the direction of Brimstone Mill across the street.

'Where's he off to?' wondered Gavin, bemused in the back of Raspberry. Just ahead, Mavis's car was then back on the move, veering off into a side street, but one definitely not on the route to the police station.

'They must be splitting off from us,' suggested Krystyna. 'Diversionary tactics. Good thinking Bob,' she muttered in admiration. 'Keep straight ahead, Dinesh. They can't follow all of us.'

The consequence of an apparent quick discussion in the Mercedes was then made clear as, after a momentary stoppage, Lewis stepped out of the vehicle and ran ahead in the direction of Bob's retreat. Dimitri had then obviously decided to ignore the red saloon decoy and went off in pursuit of the ice cream van. So, for now, at least, it seemed that Mavis and family were out of harm's way. Not so Bob, as Lewis was already drawing his pistol as he dashed on, entering the courtyard of the factory.

The sprightly septuagenarian, of course, knew Brimstone Mill well. Back in his days as a steeplejack, he used to regularly service the old chimney. Finally, in the Nineties, a development company who'd purchased the building decided that the towering structure needed to come down. But English Heritage had intervened, this being one of the last remaining historic mill chimneys in this part of Lancashire. On the very day of its planned demolition, a preservation order was duly served and the old smokestack was reprieved. Bob hadn't minded. He still got paid and didn't have to put up with the horrendous noise of the explosion, plus all those filthy clouds of brick dust. Double win!

Just as he'd gambled today, as he turned to see if he had company, he saw the young co-murderer Lewis in sole pursuit. Part one of the plan was already complete - to draw away one of the two remaining gangsters from Mavis, Gavin and gang. Plus, kids today don't get sent up chimney stacks and the like. They're just softies, so Bob reckoned. He been anticipating that it would be the teenager Lewis sent to deal with him. Hopefully, the dizzying height up there on the tower would be all too much.

But Lewis had other ideas as he stood by the gates of the courtyard to see that Bob had already scaled the steel ladder affixed to the boiler house building. He could see that the old pensioner was scurrying over the roof and heading for a similar, but much longer ladder that was attached to the colossal chimney that rose into the Drabbleton clouds like Jack's beanstalk.

'I'm not going up there, man,' Lewis mumbled, with his own more pragmatic solution to hand. 'No thanks.' He raised his pistol and just as Bob set foot on the first rung of the chimney ladder, he took aim and fired. His target had been bang in sights, the shot was aimed perfectly. He saw Bob stumble on the ladder - but then, annoyingly, only quickly recover. Lewis heard the harmless click of a trigger attempting to fire a gun that had run out of bullets. He hadn't checked, but he'd loaded his last cartridge in the mayhem of the coach house shoot out. The three bullets he'd expended to take out the police van's windscreen, back there at the gates to Loom House, were in fact the last of his supply.

'Sod it!' Lewis cursed and fumed, ramming the now useless pistol back in his pocket. So now it had come down to the knife, which he rummaged for instead. But he gulped hard as he dwelt on the task ahead. Bob had guessed right and Lewis, it was true, was no fan of heights.

'That chimney is high, man,' he grimaced. Still, he didn't fancy facing his father, or indeed Dimitri, having to confess he'd let a feeble pensioner witness escape as he'd dipped out of climbing up a ladder. He took in a deep breath, tried to let his mind go blank and then made a dart for ladder number one - attached to the boiler house.

Bob was already halfway up the second steel ladder, the one fastened to the chimney itself, quite oblivious to the brief moment when his head had been firmly fixed in the sights of a *Makarov* semi-automatic pistol. He needed a rest, realising he wasn't quite so good at climbing these things as he had been a quarter of a century ago. The view up here of Drabbleton town was already quite panoramic. As he caught some much-needed air, he looked out across the unremarkable landscape where he had spent his entire little life. He could see his grey, old house at Mayfair Avenue, the block of sheltered retirement flats where he'd hoped to live out his final years

- then over in the greener part of town, Buttermilk Avenue, where Mavis had gone off to live all those years ago with lucky Ken the plumber.

The whole of Drabbleton looked so damn small from this vantage point. But it made Bob, somehow, feel small this day too. It was as if he could see the map of his entire life etched out in the streets and avenues below him. A sudden realisation seemed to hit him.

'I should have moved on,' he muttered to himself. 'Not stayed sitting here in this shit-hole waiting for Mavis to return for all of my life. Lovely as she is.' He sighed a very long and wistful sigh - but then spotted the little red saloon parked up in a cobbled street below. No sign of the Mercedes, it seemed. That was something, so he supposed. Mavis was safe, at least for now. That was his gift.

'I'm coming for you, you old bastard,' yelled Lewis, now at the foot of the chimney ladder, and ruining Bob's quiet moment of reflection.

'Come on then, if you can handle it!' the former steeplejack shouted back in quickly summonsed defiance. 'Well done, you're on about rung ten there. Only another *two hundred and ninety* to go. See you at the top!' Bob grinned wickedly, having enjoyed seeding the idea of a potentially terrifying three-hundred-foot climb in his adversary's head. He then turned with assurance to continue his steady ascent.

'I'll be there, no worries!' Lewis retorted, trying to blank out that unsettling detail. But this still didn't stop him nervously counting...'Eleven, twelve, thirteen...'

'If you don't bottle it. Wuss!' came the last word from the far more confident climber who was already too high in the atmosphere for Lewis to even contemplate.

But the young pursuer did manage to continue to rhythmically scale upwards, quickly getting the hang of a new survival technique. By keeping his nose as near to the chimney's brickwork as possible, his brain had no concept of height. He suspected this might all go to pot if he dared to look down - fainting might even be inevitable, so he wisely kept his eyes glued on bricks and mortar. But even that smart strategy failed to prevent him from feeling increasingly aware of his pumping heartbeat - and the clamminess of his palms as he gripped hard onto successive stretches of cold steel ladder.

After several minutes of start-stop climbing, occasional praying, and pauses for air, a much perspiring Lewis finally managed to pop his head above the apex of the Victorian giant of a chimney, some three hundred feet above ground level. As he struggled to get to his feet and steady himself on the smokestack's rim, a twenty-foot-wide black circular void lay before him - the once smoke-filled chamber of the monumental industrial tower itself.

'Don't go falling in there, lad,' said Bob, standing diametrically opposed to the novice climber on the chimney's rim. 'It's a certain drop to Hell.'

Lewis was tightly gripping a handrail at the top of the ladder. If he let go of it, he knew that only the proficiency of his balance and the steel of his nerve would save him from the probable deadly plunge.

'I'll be over there in a minute,' he threatened, maybe less than convincingly as he fixed a stare on the old man opposite. Lewis was holding his knife in his free hand and shook it menacingly to compensate for the obvious lack of conviction.

'You won't be letting go of that rail,' said Bob, himself holding onto a flagpole that was today, as always, proudly flying the *Brimstone* flag. 'I can wait here all day and you won't be coming.'

'You see if I don't,' said Lewis, riled by the goading. But still he didn't let go of the handrail as an untimely, yet quite moderate, gust of Drabbleton wind buffered against his body making him only grip the steel structure tighter. He wished he hadn't done so, but he'd let out a little scream.

'Yeah, bit windy up here lad, be careful,' Bob laughed, showing off by standing on one leg and waving.

But then Lewis somehow decided to take in the view himself, disregarding his own survival instinct to never look down. Bob fully expected to see him go toppling at any moment, overcome by vertigo. But instead, the young man seemed to be having his own quiet moment as he tentatively, yet bravely, gazed out across the Drabbleton vista.

'Look at the view,' he gasped. 'Sick!' He didn't know any of the town's landmarks, of course. But everything looked so small from up here, from the Lego scale buildings to the insect like people. Everything looked so damn insignificant. Just like he'd felt back in London, collecting trollies in a car park for a supermarket. He suddenly realised that he didn't want to feel small ever again. And this whole thing made him remember the chance he'd been given by his dad, Mr Volkov, to make something of himself. He stared hard at Bob. He wasn't going to let a decrepit nobody of a pensioner make him fail. He wasn't going back to being a nobody himself. He let go of the handrail.

'Very brave,' Bob goaded still on the opposite side of the circular rim. 'People who fall from heights like this don't get picked up, by the way. They get mopped up!'

'You ain't scaring me,' Lewis barked back, surprising his adversary further by edging forwards around the perimeter of the stone ledge. But with every step he took forwards, his target took a corresponding step on the other side of the circle. Apprehending him would be even more difficult than he thought.

'You might be wondering how an old fart like me can hop around the top of a chimney like this?' said Bob, happily. 'I used to do it for a living, that's why. Climbing terrible heights is like riding a bike for me.'

'I'm not interested, mate. You're going down!' Lewis threatened, waving his knife again and growing more confident himself with every step. He was definitely now moving a little quicker around the dangerous perimeter than even Bob.

'This here chimney was primed to be blown up by me. Years ago,' the former steeplejack continued, upping the pace of his retreat from the advancing knifeman. 'See you can still see the explosives are here today.' He pointed to what Lewis thought might well indeed be strips of dynamite, but most probably instead would have been any old piping that used to get put in old chimneys like this in the olden days.

'You're having a laugh, mate. Do one!' Lewis laughed and sent his target the single finger.

'They never paid me to move it, and since I wasn't going to do it out of the goodness of my heart, well here it still is today. Now why am I not surprised?' Bob then kneeled down to reach deep into a crevice under the inner rim of the chimney. He fumbled for a second or two. 'Got it!'

When he rose to his feet, he was carrying what was obviously a push-down ignition device. 'I wondered if this would be still here,' he mumbled, a tad self-absorbed. 'I hid it up here out of harm's way.'

'Yeah, well that's not scaring me either, cos you're not going to blow us both up, now are you?' Lewis spoke with unaffected bravado.

'Why not?'

'Because then you'd be dead too.'

'So?' Bob looked genuinely puzzled.

'So, you wouldn't want that would you?' For the first time in this latter exchange, Lewis started to look apprehensive.

'Well, I'll give you a tip young man. Never chase a terminally ill man up a chimney stack, especially if he's armed with dynamite.'

'What you talking about?' Lewis started to panic.

'Only got two or three months left to live. That's what the cancer doc said this morning. I'm done. So, I think I'd rather go out today, if it's all the same with you - if that means someone I love will be safe.'

Bob smiled serenely and, kneeling again, placed both of his hands onto the T-handle of the ignition box.

'Don't be such a bonehead!' cried Lewis, making the connection between depressing the box's detonator and its terrible consequence.

'Goodbye Drabbleton. Goodbye Mavis,' Bob calmly uttered as he pushed down on the trigger.

Lewis screamed for the second and last time today - in fact, it was the last scream he would be making, ever.

Brimstone Mill's gargantuan chimney, that had shadowed over the town since 1850, was in a single explosive instance literally blown apart, most of it collapsing downwards in a concertina style crush - ton after ton of Victorian masonry noisily plunging down to earth. Whilst some debris rocketed chaotically into space too, showering across the sky like comets. Over one hundred and seventy years of history destroyed at the push of Bob's tiny lever. Drabbleton shook. It was as if its heart had been brutally ripped out.

'Holy shit!' cried Gavin in Raspberry, as the sudden explosion boomed across the entirety of the now smoke filled Drabbleton sky like a thunderstorm sent from some angry Gods. 'I hope that's not Bob's doing.' Dinesh and Krystyna felt suddenly sick, Alice merely sunk in her seat.

They weren't to know, but the upwardly rushing element of the explosion had sent Bob Horsefield flying towards the heavens. But not before his body had been flung against the heavily embroidered BRIMSTONE ensign flying proudly from the top of its pole. The force of impact ripped the flag away to form a shroud around the human form that had involuntarily just collided with it. Now both Bob and tangled wrap were jetting vertically into the clouds, a bullet-like projectile - before gravity inevitably and meanly intervened.

Stunned, but miraculously not yet dead, Bob flayed his arms and legs inside the fabric swaddling, instinctively trying to break free. By now, Mavis, Sheryl and Charlie had left their car, stunned by the giant explosion that had rumbled through the ground where they were parked like an earthquake. Staring into the sky they could see the tiny dot of a human figure dropping to earth as surely and quickly as did the stones just now of the collapsed chimney. But then the speed of descent somehow seemed to slow. Could it be true? Was that tumbling personage, that Mavis suspected might well be Bob, miraculously descending by parachute?

Falling still as he was, from up there high in the air, Bob fought against his own pain and confusion to cling desperately onto two diagonally opposed corners of the flag. A makeshift parachute was indeed what had been created.

'It's Bob!' shouted Charlie, the first to visually confirm the identity of the impromptu airman. 'He's still alive!'

Mavis muscled forwards, flexing her almighty hulk of a frame. 'Mind yourselves, I need to catch him,' she hollered in a manner that nobody was going to argue with. She then manoeuvred herself underneath the entity that was still fast descending, despite the upward resistance of the flag parachute. 'I used to do this in my sleep.'

She was fondly remembering back to her firefighting days. She'd long been famous around these parts as the girl who'd caught falling cats and babies from whichever height they might be dropping. It had been a few years, admittedly so, but she was still up for the challenge.

'Be careful, Mum!' squealed Sheryl as Bob's rapidly descending body was upon them in seemingly no time.

'M-a-v-i-sss!' yelled Bob, as he finally caught sight of the love of his life - only two seconds before he fell into her strong and outstretched arms.

'Gotcha!' shouted the former firefighter who'd still remembered a few old tricks. But strong as she was, even Mavis had never caught a human being who'd virtually dropped out of the clouds before. She tumbled backwards, but still managed to hold on dearly to her ex-husband. A moment later, she had assumed a more dignified position, kneeling, and sat back on her feet, but nursing Bob's prone body across her lap.

'Oh, *Sweetie Bag*,' gushed Mavis, stroking the tiny Bag's furrowed brow.

'Oh, *Snuggle Bear*,' said Bob, with the look of a man who had just found Paradise.

But as she held onto her ex-husband's torso, Mavis felt some sort of wetness dribbling over her right hand. In an instant she'd confirmed that the suspect liquid was nothing less than blood. Then, peeling back the stained cotton shirt covering Bob's chest, she quickly identified the source of the issue. A sharp shard of chimney brick had impaled itself, shrapnel like, below the improviser parachutist's breastbone - most likely having penetrated the heart. Bob's life was draining away, right there in the arms of his lifetime love.

'I tried to save you, Bob,' Mavis convulsed, suddenly weeping inconsolably.

Bob paused, choking on blood, but smiling all the same. He looked up into the sweet eyes of his former wife, only pushing back the years to see the exquisite image of her that Charlie had recently painted. The most beautiful woman in all the world. Just as she had always been to him. 'You did save me, Mavis.' he swore. 'You did save me.'

And with that sacred affirmation, Bob Horsefield's eyes closed forever. As Mavis sobbed, both Sheryl and Charlie huddled around her, stroking her hair and praying. The Drabbleton sky surely darkened further. Inside the still fleeing Raspberry, Gavin Hargreaves felt a jolt in the Universe. He gulped on a sharp intake of breath. He was still trembling from the aftermath of the massive explosion that had heralded the demise of the Brimstone Mill chimney. Somewhere deep in his being, he now somehow sensed that old neighbour Bob might well be gone.

Meanwhile, snuggled on a familiar rug in front of his owner's customary rocking chair, in an otherwise empty house on Mayfair Avenue, a dog called Rocky settled down for his longest ever sleep.

*

'It is nothing more than demolition work,' grouched Dimitri as Roxanne continued to be shaken by the power of the explosion. 'It is time this entire dump of a town was demolished in my opinion.'

'That's true,' Roxanne wholeheartedly agreed. 'But this isn't right.' She pointed ahead to the chunks of masonry in the street that had fallen from the sky because of Bob's over-zealousness on the old dynamite front. 'This could have killed someone.'

'Killing people - how terrible,' Dimitri smirked, only to receive a barbed look from Roxanne in return. *Nobody likes a smart arse.*

Both Raspberry and the Mercedes had come to a sudden halt during the sudden heavenly shower of falling bricks, both drivers concluding that driving head on into the chunks of descending debris was far more dangerous than just staying still and hoping for the best. Raspberry had, in fact, got away with it. The Mercedes had fared less well - and a large dint and partial hole was now disfiguring its bonnet, the consequence of chimney rock crashing into it like a meteorite dropping to earth. Bob would have enjoyed that. Just another few inches towards the windscreen and his last action on this planet would have seen his grand explosion not only taking out the unfortunate Lewis, but the despicable Dimitri and Roxanne too.

The damage only to the Mercedes was at least some consolation though, as when Dimitri tried to get his motor going again something was clattering and banging inside the engine. He could get the thing moving alright, but he'd lost some of the furious speed that would have seen him catching the ice cream van at any second.

'Now what have you done?' Roxanne whinged, blaming Dimitri for the mechanical disappointment.

'Something's catching in the gears or whatever. It's not my fault!' Sidorov smarted, fully depressing the accelerator pedal only to be greeted by an even louder clunking noise and merely moderate speed.

'Well, you're the one who's driving,' Roxanne persisted with self-righteous criticism. 'I wouldn't have parked in such a stupid place with all those rocks coming at us.'

Dimitri's face, not for the first time today, turned bright red. But he bit his tongue and chose to ignore this carping female beside him and concentrate on his professional job - to eliminate every witness in that blasted ice cream that once again was getting away.

'Looks like their car has taken a hit,' said Gavin, noticing the afflicted pursuing motor coming up behind them with less vigour. 'Step on it Dinesh,' he added whilst steadying the helium canister that had come loose from its temporary station, tied to the Mr Whippy machine.

'Yes, come on Raspberry,' encouraged Krystyna, finally coming round to the idea that being nice to vehicles does indeed make them perform better. The ice cream van literally purred.

'Turn here into the Old Town,' said Gavin to Dinesh, somewhat breathlessly. 'The streets are so narrow they won't be able to overtake.' The 99 vendor was, of course, remembering back to the previous pursuit, Raspberry vs Mercedes, that had ended in an almost fatal sojourn down the perilous Hundred Steps. 'But whatever you do, don't go down The Hundred Steps,' Gavin anxiously advised his otherwise utterly focussed driver.

'Do you think I am madman, my friend?' Dinesh laughed. 'There is no way this thing would survive The Hundred Steps.'

'She's done if before. But yeah, let's not expect miracles to strike twice,' the veteran of The Steps concluded, receiving relieved nods of assent from both Krystyna and Alice.

As Gavin had expected, as the van steadily climbed the Old Town streets, the thoroughfare was increasingly narrowing. Raspberry trundled past rows of shabby Drabbleton shops, offering no opportunity for the gaining Mercedes to overtake. What he hadn't expected was what was to happen next as Raspberry's rear window shattered a split second after the sound of gunshot blasted out. As Alice screamed, a bullet lodged itself in the sun visor just above her head.

'You'll bloody well pay for this!' an angry Gavin yelled at Dimitri, leaning out through the frame of the entirely destroyed rear window and shaking his fist. The Russian hitman had his pistol tucked out of his own driver's side window and took another shot, the bullet this time grazing Gavin's right ear. 'Owww!' he shrieked, belatedly realising that it would be best to duck at this point. 'We need a gun!'

'Well, I have only this,' said Krystyna, holding up the silver pistol cigarette lighter - surviving relic from Gavin's old joke shop. 'Most useless.'

'Brilliant,' Gavin failed to agree, but grabbed the pistol with enthusiastic gratitude. He stuck his upper torso out of the shattered back window and shook the pistol wildly in the direction of Mercedes' windscreen. He looked like a man possessed!

'He's got a gun!' yelped Roxanne. 'Swerve!'

Dimitri instantly took evasive action and veered his SUV onto the pavement, mowing through a row of cafe street furniture that was thankfully unoccupied. A disgruntled Pall Mall Cafe owner ran from her premises, only to see the manically driven Mercedes noisily yet steadily speed away in the direction of Downing Street. Then, a passing beat bobby was immediately on his radio.

'Damn, they're still coming,' Gavin sulked as he eyed the still advancing pursuit vehicle gaining on them yet again. Shame he didn't have bullets in that joke shop pistol. Ah well, couldn't be helped. 'Dinesh, there's road works on Downing Street,' he then called to out front, remembering his near collision with these just the other day. 'Turn left at the T-junction into Westminster Street instead.'

'Got that, Captain,' Dinesh acknowledged as he approached the very end of Pall Mall a little too quickly. But the adrenaline had well and truly kicked in, what with the Mercedes getting ever nearer, the shattered rear window and bullets flying this way and that.

'Slow down, mate!' Gavin warned as he realised Raspberry was bearing down too quickly towards the ravine like drop of The Hundred Steps pedestrian thoroughfare. 'Get ready to turn left. Now!'

As Dinesh did precisely as told, right at that moment it became instantaneously clear that Westminster Street was not going to happen. It was currently amply occupied by the full musical ensemble of Drabbleton Colliery Brass Band - who were merrily marching and playing their hearts out in a parade to celebrate the 150-year anniversary of their inauguration. There had never actually been a mine in Drabbleton, incidentally. But other towns had brass bands for their miners, so why should this town be left out? That's what some resourceful mill workers had thought anyway, a century and a half ago. So that if they did ever get a mine, then Drabbleton would have its very own Colliery Brass Band all ready to go.

'People in the street!' yelped Alice, covering her eyes as Dinesh's abruptly erratic driving made her somehow think of sudden death. The whites of the eyes of the fronting members of the brass band were upon them, all looking aghast as the Mad Ice Cream Man drove his crazy machine towards them, ready to send them scattering like skittles. Musician's dived for cover, trumpets and trombones went flying and the tune, 'Amazing Grace', was completely ruined altogether. Dinesh had surrendered, his body seizing up and completely failing to function. Like Alice, he instinctively covered his eyes. But within a split second, Krystyna grabbed the steering wheel and yanked it forcefully to the right. Raspberry's left tyres left the ground as it performed an acute arc of a wheelie. Almost inexplicably - and to the sheer astonishment of the very relieved brass band - all casualties were avoided as the ice cream van swerved beyond the cusp of Westminster Street. However, the centrifugal force that drove it, as it continued its two wheeled feat, was now unstoppable. There was only one small gap to which the van was inevitably heading - the entrance to the precipitous and deadly Hundred Steps themselves.

' Sh-i-i-i-t-t-t! We're going down The Hundred Steps!' Dinesh then screamed while Alice just gasped and prayed.

'Well steer, you idiot,' Krystyna shouted, slapping the supposed driver round the ear, hoping to bring him to his senses. As Dinesh flinched in pain, he was somehow prompted to have a shot at the old steering once again, but less than successfully, as the van now buffeted and clattered against the walls of the steep yet all-so-narrow passageway.

'Bloody hell, look at that,' said Gavin, who for some reason was looking up at the Drabbleton sky - maybe just in a futile attempt to distract himself from watching how he might be likely to die at any second. 'That cloud up there. It's Bob Horsefield!' He pointed to the heavens.

High above the shops and houses, a fluffy Cumulus cloud had taken on the outline shape of a familiar pensioner. Small in stature, slightly crooked spine, thin legs and 1950s straggly, rock and roller long hair. By his side, a smaller cloud was floating along - it just had to be a favoured mongrel.

'It's Rocky too!' Gavin virtually squealed.

'It is Mr Horsefield and Rocky! I can see it!' beamed Dinesh, not entirely concentrating on his steering - the plunging van battering the wall yet again.

'It's a *sign*,' said Gavin with gleeful assurance. 'Let go of the steering wheel, Dinesh. That's what Bob would have wanted. And he's up there, trying to tell us. *Trust the Horse!*'

'Yes, I can feel it,' Dinesh agreed, at one with the spiritual universe and raising his hands from the wheel. 'Indeed! *Trust the Horse!*'

'I am in an out-of-control ice cream van surrounded by morons!' fretted Krystyna. 'Not you of course, Alice,' she quickly corrected herself.

'No offence,' came the whimpering reply.

Meanwhile, Dimitri had yet again pulled up the Mercedes on the edge of The Hundred Steps drop.

'You're not being a scaredy cat again, are you? Just about a few bumpy steps!' Roxanne crowed in admonishment. 'Get after them now!'

'It's alright for you,' Dimitri moaned, staring at the dreaded drop ahead. 'But ever since we went down there the first time, well I've been having terrible nightmares.'

'Damn it, Dimitri!' Roxanne stamped her stilettos in the footwell. 'Just think of the nightmares that Mr Volkov will give you if this lot get away. And then decide.'

'Good point,' the reluctant roller coaster passenger conceded, coming to his senses. Yes, things could indeed be worse if Mr Volkov were involved. So, all very tentatively, he nosed the Mercedes forwards to the tipping point of the drop - the point of no return.

'Sh-i-i-i-t-t-t! We're going down The Hundred Steps!' Dimitri screamed in the manner quite unbefitting of a senior mafioso. But if you don't like heights, you don't like heights.

'Oh, shut up,' said Roxanne. 'I've heard a rumour that you can actually steer these things if you use that leather covered circle thing in the middle,' she sneered.

'Very funny. This is steering!' he snapped back as the car bashed against the wall and kangaroo hopped down the irregular and no doubt evil minded steps.

However, the journey in Raspberry was by contrast smoother now that the Horse itself had been trusted. No more buffeting against walls, even the steps themselves seemed to be paving out a flusher pathway. All the same, the incline remained at the severest of angles as it had always been - and so the consequence of a clearer run was obvious according to the Law of Physics: *increased speed!*

'Dinesh, you're going too fast again,' warned Gavin, anxious once more. 'It's a very tight turn at the bottom of this lot.' He was remembering the danger ahead as The Hundred Steps flattened out in the lead into Town Hall Square. Unless Dinesh could tame Raspberry's speed, then a head on collision with the statue of James Brimstone was inevitable.

But Raspberry came rocketing down the final unresisting steps and into the square, her brakes seemingly failing to make any impression at all.

'Steer Dinesh, steer!' Gavin beseeched for all he was worth. '*Pull sharp right!*'

'It is OK, Gavin,' Dinesh replied, both hands still held well clear of the steering wheel. '*I am trusting the Horse!*'

Unwisely, as it happened. Raspberry failed to turn sharp right, propelled by the mystical power of the universe, but instead bulleted straight ahead - its front end making a crumpling impact with the plinth of the historic statue. James Brimstone, up there on his perch, tottered, badly shaken indeed. But he did not fall. Although inside the now half crushed ice cream van, driver and passengers were groaning and nursing their luckily minor impact injuries.

'Is everyone alright?' Gavin breathlessly enquired, nursing a bruised head to go with his bullet grazed ear. Assenting grunts and mumbles partly assured him that all was reasonably well with his mostly shaken crew.

'I don't think I am insured to drive this van,' piped up Dinesh suddenly. 'Many apologies, my friend.'

Everybody tried to chuckle. They were just so relieved to be alive. The detail of an insurance claim was a long way down the priority list. But the mildest of merriments was short lived. As it happened, Dimitri had made a successful re-entry into the reassuringly horizontal terrain of Town Hall Square, skilfully veering off to the right by Ted's Cafe - niftily avoiding a concertina style pile-up into the back of Raspberry.

The van's driver side door was unpleasantly yanked open.

'Out! All of you!' Dimitri ordered, pistol in hand. 'Out of the van now.'

At the opposite end of the square, Slater's car was crawling carefully along. He'd been tipped off about the ice cream van's possible destination by live reports on his police radio. Apparently, the Colliery Brass Band were nearly all mown down by a nutter in an ice cream van. *Had to be Hargreaves*, thought Slater. And said nutter's van was then escaping off down The Hundred Steps. A likely tale, but worth checking out as he and the armed response unit had lost all track of the much too fast for them Mercedes. But now, here was his back-up team too, efficiently answering his own call just made previously. *'All available cars to Town Hall Square.'*

On his order, unseen by Dimitri, the armed team then took up sniper positions behind parked cars some fifty yards away from the shaken Brimstone statue. Meanwhile, Volkov's sometime star hitman had been leading his death sentenced prisoners into the street. As he stood with his own back against the opposite side of the plinth to where the van had just crumpled, he'd lined up Gavin, Krystyna, Alice and Dinesh to be executed right then and there on the cobbles.

'Any last words, Hargreaves?' Dimitri snarled.

It seemed that Gavin had no last words at all. If he'd been asked earlier, he'd have prepared something. But no, nothing was coming to mind right now.

'How you have wasted my time in this Hell hole of a town,' Sidorov vented. 'But now it will be goodbye.' He raised the pistol ready to fire as Roxanne watched on by his side, taking much pleasure from the moment - and still cradling her husband's severed head.

'You are surrounded by armed police,' Slater shouted through a megaphone, possibly all too late. Dimitri jolted, yet not enough - seemingly - to deter him from his calculated task.

The ensuing blast though was terrifying. But this did not come from the barrel of Dimitri's deadly weapon, nor from the trained rifle of Iqbal or any of her colleagues. From their own vantage point, in front of the statue, it was quite impossible for Dimitri or Roxanne to tell what had happened - well in that significant split second anyway.

But the fluffy cloud in the form of Bob and Rocky definitely had a great view. It now seemed as though the heavenly pair were looking down with joy, giving their blessing to the outcome of this momentous turn of fate.

When DI Slater had made his urgent call for all cars to head for Town Hall Square, this was picked up by PCs Duckworth and Chabra. They'd headed off from Loom House just as soon as they'd recovered from the shock of a near collision with a juggernaut lorry and, in fact, were speculatively touring the Old Town in search of the rogue Mercedes when Slater's order came in.

The quickest way to Town Hall Square from the Old Town was via The Hundred Steps, a strictly pedestrian route, even Duckworth and Chabra knew that. But demonstrating bravery typical of

Drabbleton's finest - or maybe stupidity, as Slater would later wonder - they'd headed their vehicle with gay abandon down the dangerous thoroughfare. And there they'd stoically taken every peril that the *Drop of Doom* could throw at them.

But no way were they going to steer safely out of that plunge. So, screaming their heads off all the way down, when they'd finally come propelling out into the square, there was only one resting point to which they were destined. That would be the back end of Raspberry, its own front end already smashed against the plinth.

So, the almighty bang that everybody in the square had heard, just as Dimitri prepared to pull his trigger- and just as Slater readied his snipers - was the violent collision of police truck metal crushing into ice cream van rust.

'Aaaaggghhh,' Duckworth and Chabra had screamed in unison as they'd shot forward into the deafening smash. Their bonnet was now crumpled against the back of Raspberry, almost as if the two vehicles had become one, not an inch of daylight between them. The two PCs now remained in their seats, momentarily stunned and incoherent.

One second on from impact and its mighty force was just too much for the rusty fixings that were weakly securing Raspberry's iconic feature - the giant 99 cone that sat erect on her roof. The eight-foot-high ice cream was therefore catapulted forwards so that it struck hard against the back of the Brimstone already tottering statue. Sidorov heard the grinding disturbance of bronze and stone behind him and turned just on cue to see multiple tons of historic statue toppling off its plinth on its way to earth. With no time to move, he could only screech in horror as he stood there directly under the weighty drop. He was horrendously crushed in an instant - as Roxanne watched on helplessly, screaming herself in denial as falling mass met human fragility. Sidorov's entire being was indeed squelched like an insect underfoot. *Death by 99* - well indirectly, anyway!

Gavin Hargreaves immediately paid silent homage to James Brimstone, his hero and inspiration. And now his actual saviour too.

Then, in a blind panic, still wailing hysterically and carrying Bryce's head, Roxanne ran for refuge somewhere - anywhere would do. Inside a moment she was shutting herself off inside what was left of battered Raspberry - as Gavin and friends darted for cover by the parked cars sheltering the sniper police.

'Mrs Brimstone, once again I repeat you are surrounded by armed police,' shouted the business-like Slater through his megaphone. 'Please surrender yourself to avoid harm to yourself or others.'

But Roxanne had already switched from panic mode to one of fury. How dare this Drabbleton low life interfere with her plans to become even more mega-rich, courtesy of her husband's carefully planned demise. She wasn't sure exactly what to do - but at least she could *unleash*. Although, in her rush to enter the ice cream van's serving area, she hadn't noticed that she'd kicked over the helium canister, breaking off its valve stop. Gas came gushing out, quickly filling the entirety of the van. She noticed it now though - but was too angry to even bother about the damn thing.

'Now look what mess you've got me into,' she hollered, holding up her husband's noggin by its recently coiffured hair and pressing her nose against his.' As she spoke, the effects of the helium contorted her voice once more, and she grew ever squeakier by the second. 'Don't you look at me like that Bryce Brimstone! You took me as a child bride, a super-model trophy wife. And all that I ever asked for was *all of your money*. You selfish, old bastard! And now look where we are,' she squealed like a baby pig. 'Completely screwed, and all because of you!'

By now, Slater had ordered the armed unit to slowly approach the ice cream van, while one of the team had gone to the aid of Duckworth and Chabra, ushering the two dazed heroes away from the wreckage. Roxanne looked up to see combat police rifles trained on her person.

'Get back, or I'll shoot! she cried in an unnaturally high-pitched yelp, snatching for the silver pistol that Gavin had earlier discarded on the van's floor. She manically waved the weapon in the direction of this crouching officer and that. But only the previous occupants of Raspberry, still taking cover across the street, knew that Roxanne's gun was merely a joke shop cigarette lighter.

'On my order,' shouted Slater.

But the cornered suspect was not going to let the police have the pleasure of gunning her down. Not those worthless insects! Nor was she going to jail - *how humiliating!*

'I am Roxanne Brimstone!' she yelled with a defiant squeak. 'I dazzled you all!'

She then turned the silver pistol towards her head and pulled the trigger. In a micro-second, Roxanne would not have sensed that a bullet had not blown out her brains. But as the humble flame from the joke shop lighter ignited, the van full of helium gas went up too in an inevitable and instantaneous chain reaction. Both Mrs Brimstone's brains and the rest of her body were blown to veritable smithereens - as was what was left of the ice cream van too.

'Raspberry! No!' Gavin bleated as shards of his treasured motor exploded into the sky, scattering far and wide across Town Hall Square, and a small mushroom cloud settled over the shell of his lost *Mr Whippy* dream.

'I will miss her,' said Krystyna, uncharacteristically mournful and staring on in disbelief. 'Best ice cream van ever!'

'Hopefully you are insured for fire,' Dinesh offered helpfully, still kneeling for cover behind a random saloon next to his friend.

'Not really,' moped Gavin, as he watched both flames engulf the remains of his business hopes and then miscellaneous debris fall from the sky. But Dinesh didn't hear his reply. He'd just spotted something falling from the heavens that nobody else had. It was a fast-descending sphere that had now landed in the bus stop litter bin just a few feet away. It was, in fact, Brimstone's flour dusted and now smoke smeared head. He grabbed its hair and pulled it from the bin.

'Who is laughing now, Mister?' he grinned wildly. *'Who is laughing now?'*

Somebody had stuffed an empty brown paper takeaway bag into the refuse container. He pulled that out too and, making sure nobody was looking - which they weren't - quickly deposited Brimstone's recaptured head inside. For Dinesh, happy *status quo* was restored. He was so looking forward to showing off his recovered prize to Mishka and placing it into what would now be its permanent pride of place - third shelf up in main the freezer at the *Star of India* chippy.

Gavin Hargreaves finally left his sheltering position behind the row of cars across the street and slowly walked towards the flaming wreckage of his dreams. He remembered back to that spurring chat in Bob's front room, two years ago now. On the back of Marie's departure and the impending bankruptcy of his joke shop, he'd promised to fight back and make something of himself. Just like James Brimstone had made something of himself, although Gavin never had such lofty aims. He'd just wanted to set up a decent business that would moderately prosper. And he'd wanted, once again, to find love. But none of this had transpired - especially as he'd now concluded that he'd totally messed things up with Alice. Besides which, she seemed more fixated with Krystyna than with himself. Although he hadn't seen that one coming, for sure. Then to top it all, his hopes of ice cream glory were now literally melting before his very eyes and - completely uninsured as it was - would not be making a Phoenix style resurrection any time soon.

Basically, he was buggered.

'Are you alright, Gavin?' asked the soft voice to his left.

'Not really,' he mumbled in return, staring into Raspberry's dying embers. 'I feel like my life is just going round in pointless circles and getting nowhere fast.'

'Sorry about the van. But you're not getting nowhere,' Alice Brimstone countered. 'I thought you were definitely getting somewhere. With me at least.'

'Don't be daft, Alice,' Gavin half laughed, not in the mood for games. 'I just saw you with Krystyna. You two were definitely hitting it off.'

'Oh, for God's sake Gavin, we were just messing with you.' Alice grinned as though she'd just pulled off the biggest wind up ever. 'Krystyna's something alright. But she's not my type, if you get what I mean. And I'm definitely not hers either.'

'So, who is your type?'

'OK, if you really want to know, I'm looking for a guy with great legs who looks good in a Centurion uniform,' came the twinkle eyed reply. 'Someone who buys an Indian takeaway for a date and then pretends he's cooked it himself. I'm looking for an ice cream man who doesn't even have a van. They're the best kind, actually. Oh yeah, and someone who can make stupid fuck ups like sleeping with someone else because crazy circumstances got the better of them. Just like me! But most of all, I'm looking for someone who would risk their life for me. Who in my darkest hour would show up with a stupid waxwork in a coffin and a flour bomb - just to give me hope. That same person would surely love me for eternity.'

'*Eternity?*' said Gavin, so obviously feigning indifference. 'Huh, that's a big commitment!'

'OK, a *lifetime* then,' Alice added with pragmatism. 'I'm willing to negotiate.'

'A lifetime sounds more doable,' Gavin casually concluded, despite inwardly feeling at this moment that his heart might just explode with joy. 'On that basis, I'm in,' he belatedly smiled. Then burst into tears, an ecstatic release. 'I'm definitely in.'

Some might have considered that the kiss they now shared was not staged in the most romantic of settings. What, with police marksmen still stealthily stalking the square and the dust and smoke from the bombed-out chimney and ice cream van filling the air - the scene looked more like something out of a war zone. But for Gavin and Alice this single kiss was just perfect, regardless of the backdrop. Because, as they both now shed the tears, they instinctively knew that this was it. No more false starts and painful stops. This kiss would go on and on, etching itself deep into their hearts - and into the history of Drabbleton town, no less - the moment when things would finally start to positively change forever.

Bob Horsefield's fluffy cloud was dispersing into amorphous mist. Its spirit had seen what it needed to. Time now to happily rest in peace.

- ONE YEAR LATER -

Drabbleton was never going to rival the likes of New York or Mexico City for its high propensity of murder or organised crime. So, after this short burst of isolated notoriety - even appearing in the lead story on the BBC News for one day only - it dozily slid away from the limelight once again. Happy to be itself - the Lancashire town that long ago should have visited a Swiss clinic to be put down. Well, maybe a little unfair. Wasn't something new afoot at Brimstone Mill?

In the meantime, there'd be one particular funeral - and later, a wedding.

Precisely one week since Bob had left this world, his soul disappearing along with the Brimstone Mill chimney, his final service had been held at St Anthony's chapel. Charlie had kept his promise and had delivered a copy of that portrait of his grandmother that his recent pensioner hero had admired so much. It had been put inside Bob's modest little coffin and buried with him forever.

As she laid her flowers on his churchyard graveyard this morning, on the anniversary of his death, Mavis couldn't help but think of what might have been. A fine, brave man who had always loved her had passed. Just like her husband, plumber Bill, had already passed. She felt very sad, but also happy and grateful that she'd been loved by - and had loved in return - two such wonderful men. With Bob having saved Sheryl's life, her admiration for him was now immeasurable and her gratitude eternal. They could have shared love again in their twilight years, of that, she was sure. But it wasn't to be - although she never did get to hear about Bob's terminal condition. So, for now she would simply say thank you and goodnight with these simple flowers, cut in the prime of their beauty and emblematic of the beautiful man that she would always consider Bob Horsefield to be.

Her grandson, Charlie, would also be forever grateful to the old pensioner - not least for saving his mum's life. But there was also the gift of the skeleton arm that he'd also gratefully received from his grandmother's ex-husband. He'd gone on to use this as the star feature in his end of year project - which had won a special commendation from his art tutors and guaranteed his place at university. Called *'Dream Beyond Reach,'* the piece itself was part sculpture, part painting and collage mash-up. On a nearby shore, a drowning man struggling in the darkest of waves was so near to the safety of land ahead. And on that land, all he ever wanted was there - stunning women, prestigious houses, fast cars, and a bank filled with his gold. But now, all that could be seen of the fast-sinking human was the figurative skeletal arm clutching out beyond the foam - his hopes and aspirations beyond him as he was about to be taken by the cruel sea forever.

Charlie had, of course, followed the story of Bryce Brimstone in the local news and had learned how that much feared businessman had ruthlessly gone about acquiring wealth and reputation - before his untimely death had stopped him in his tracks. Bryce had therefore been the inspiration for the young artist's sombre piece - as everybody who saw it came to realise. But what they or Charlie didn't realise, of course, was that Drabbleton's least favourite entrepreneur had given a helping hand to its completion. Well, a hand and an arm, to be precise.

In a quiet corner of the canvas backdrop to the installation, Charlie had painted something that hardly anybody had noticed. It was a young man, sat behind a tripod easel and diligently painting his impression of the view out to sea. It was meant to be the version of Lewis had he taken a different path - as a budding artist rather than murderous hitman. Depicted here, with his weapon a mere paintbrush rather than semi-automatic pistol, Charlie had immortalised him in the way that he'd much prefer to remember his new, but now lost friend.

Meanwhile, at Drabbleton Police Station, Haslam was relishing her meteoric promotion to Detective Inspector, earned on the back of her solid coppering on the Brimstone and Sidorov case. It had been concluded that Roxanne had hired Dimitri to murder her husband. Dinesh, Krystyna and - posthumously - Bob were not even in the picture. Then Dimitri was also held to have been responsible for the Darren Eccles murder. With both he and Roxanne - plus sidekick Lewis Wilson - no longer with us, the Chief Constable had considered the operation a resounding success. No requirement to clutter up Lancashire's jails with non-local undesirables, very cost efficient!

So, DI Slater was able to retire, not only with a *Long Service Award,* but with a *Special Commendation for Outstanding Policing* to boot. Similarly, PC Duckworth and PC Chabra both received the *Chief Constable's Award for Bravery.* Their amazing quick thinking in disregarding their own safety and using their police vehicle as a battering ram, thus preventing a civilian massacre, was particularly lauded. Likewise, PC Iqbal's cool sharpshooting skills in the field of action saw her promoted to head up the police marksman training school for the whole county.

Officers from other parts of Lancashire were seconded in to learn all they could from the model of excellence that Drabbleton Police Force clearly had become - its reputation now second to none. And its kudos grew only further, when it became clear that co-operation between Slater and Haslam and the National Crime Agency had led to the arrest and successful prosecution of one of London's most powerful organised criminals. Mr Vladimir Volkov had subsequently been found guilty of facilitating murder via an ingenious app he had developed - something called Disposals Inc. This software, which would have brought routine assassinations within the reach of the masses, had now been well and truly decommissioned. The world was thankfully safe from its deadly threat. But facing the shame of business ruin and a full life term inside a high security jail, Mr Volkov chose the pragmatic option of a cyanide pill. He died in HM Prison Belmarsh, cursing the incompetence of Dimitri Sidorov with his final breath.

Whilst in less dramatic circumstances, over at Drabbleton Town FC, the new owner of the club had cancelled the transfer of Alberto Assini to Arsolia of Latvia. But shortly afterwards, the handsome Italian was surprisingly offered a goalkeeping assistant coaching job with AC Milan. He'd realised that if he accepted the role, not only would this be a first step to maybe better things in the lucrative world of football management - but his lovely girlfriend, Marie, would finally get to realise her dream of living the high life in arguably the fashion capital of Europe.

But, you know, Drabbleton kind of grows on some people - like a wart on the nose, for example, that some might come to oddly cherish because not many other folk have one. Alberto, originally from Milan himself, and Marie from Dublin, had settled down together here and were kind of wearing the town like a comfortable pair of old slippers. Unlikely, yet now prospering migrants. Thanks to some Alice provided seed capital, Marie had set up her own hairdressing business and hers was the only shop in town that would successfully pull off any hairdo as featured in *Hello!* magazine. And Alberto actually enjoyed the grittiness and grime of English lower league football, with its muddy pitches, half-blind referees and ardent supporters soaked to the skin under leaking stands. Who needed to be bottom dog in sunny Milan when you could be two top dogs in glorious, rain drenched Drabbleton?

Well, that's how Marie and Alberto had finally come to see it and they continued to live a happy life together under the grey Lancashire skies. Plus, Freddie was doing well at school too and was popular, with lots of friends. A move abroad would have taken all that away as well as meaning large chunks of separation for the boy from his much-loved dad. So, Freddie continued to enjoy his hometown upbringing, totally oblivious to the behind-the-scenes discussions his mum and her boyfriend had been having as they weighed up the pros and cons of Drabbleton versus Milan. But, come on, *where was the contest?*

Meanwhile, over at the *Star of India* chippy all had been going swimmingly well. The new landlord of the shopping parade had decided that tenants' rents would be remaining the same for the following five-year term. A profitable existence therefore awaited both Mishka and Dinesh, with the latter gaining on-the-side consultancy work in the flavouring department of a new food business that had set up in town - more on that to come.

Then, on the third shelf up of the chippy's freezer, Bryce Brimstone's severed and frozen head continued to be greeted every single morning by Dinesh's gleeful question: 'Who is laughing now, Mister? Who is laughing now?'

Indeed, the new owner of both the shopping precinct and the local football club - and Brimstone Mill itself - seemed to be cut from a different cloth from the previous owner. More likely cut from the cloth of her own great, great, great grandfather - Mr James Brimstone. And now, here she was - Alice Brimstone, sole heiress to the entirety of her brother's assets and fortune. Even if Roxanne had managed to get away with her murderous plan, in any case Bryce had bequeathed the majority of his estate to the sister he loved, despite their differences. He knew Roxanne was pure gold digger by nature and had therefore only left her the bare minimum that the London High Court was likely to let him get away with. But that did not matter now. Once again, after all these years of pain and decline, a kind-hearted and philanthropic member of the James Brimstone ancestral line oversaw a large element of the town's destiny.

And so it was that one Gavin Hargreaves was also to play his own significant role in Drabbleton's future prosperity and regeneration. Alice had wasted no time in closing down the dodgy business concern that was Miracle Sleep Consultants. But none of the staff had lost their jobs. They were all redeployed in suitable roles in the entirely new business that Alice and Gavin had hatched together. An ice cream manufacturing and retailing business known as *Ali's Ices* had been established in Brimstone Mill. Its USP was the delicious flavours concocted by its Chief Flavour Consultant, Mr Dinesh Patel. Not only that, but its fleet of wacky ice cream vans were also just the thing to win likes and shares on social media - and many of the more outlandishly adorned vehicles had already gone viral.

It seemed that everyone wanted to be photographed, for example, by the psychedelic van featuring a rooftop giant 99 being eaten by a moulded, naked mermaid. Other top-of-van designs were similarly adored. The choc-ice eating funny frog was always a winner, as was the ice lolly sucking monkey with the disgustingly long tongue. Every single van in the fleet was completely different, all garishly and personally designed by Director of Transport, Mr Gavin Hargreaves.

International investors had already come knocking. There was talk in the town of Brimstone Mill becoming headquarters to a worldwide business. And the money folk told CEO Alice that they were not only impressed by the flavoursome taste of the product and the winning quirkiness of the retail transport - but the efficiency of the manufacturing plant was a pleasure for number crunchers to behold. This latter business advantage was the sole doing of Director of Operations, one Krystyna Kowalski, who was already receiving invitations to speak at business productivity conferences. This girl was going somewhere.

Whilst in Town Hall Square, the restored and refurbished statue of James Brimstone once more stood on its lofty plinth – the spiritual guardian of the town, as Drabbleton now moved forwards once again after so many years of decline. The townsfolk were often heard chatting that the spirit of James would have been so very proud of his great, great, great granddaughter for redeeming the Brimstone family name and bringing back the good times. But Gavin Hargreaves, whenever he passed by that statue, only had to look into the twinkling eye of James to be certain for himself that was true.

Then so it was that Alice had proposed to Gavin on a date night some six months back now. She'd bought in a slap-up banquet for the occasion from Dinesh's. But you know what? She'd oddly chosen not to pretend that she'd cooked it herself. Despite this weirdness, Gavin had sobbed with relief when Alice had popped the question, adding unnecessary salt to the otherwise perfectly flavoured Vindaloo - but this only an unstoppable discharge of pent-up emotion now that he'd finally found love again.

Word had it that they were actually having sex, too. Lots of it. Not only that, but by all accounts - well Dinesh's account mainly - all was going rather well in that department. *If at first you don't succeed* and all that...

So, the two love birds had mutually concluded that they should get married today, on the first anniversary of Bob Horsefield's death. They wanted to take a sad event and turn it around into a happy one. After all, with his dramatic intervention at the coach house last year, Bob had saved both Alice's and Gavin's life. Only because of him could their love for one another flourish today. To him they wanted to pay tribute.

There wasn't, in fact, room in the church for everyone who'd wanted to attend Drabbleton's most joyous wedding of recent years. But as the bride and groom had attended to the formalities of signing the wedding registry, it seemed that the entire town had gathered outside of St Anthony's chapel, well-wishers filling every corner of today's amazingly sunny churchyard.

Then, as radiant bride and brushed-up groom emerged from the church, confetti, congratulatory cheers, laughter and tears melded in the air. In this grim and battered town, in the end it had only taken a few good souls with hope in their hearts to change everything.

So, as Gavin kissed his beautiful bride, it seemed this lovely wedding would surely be the optimistic symbol of better things to come.

'I love you. You are my very own *Redemption*,' said Gavin to the radiant creature by his side, lump in throat.

'I love you too. You are my very own *Sexy Legs!*' said Alice, laughing wickedly, feeling freer and happier than she had ever been. 'We need to dance!'

So indeed, the dancing went on into the early hours. An outpouring of joy, not only for Alice and Gavin, but for the whole of the town. This jubilant day had been decades in the making. But Drabbleton, the dump that other dumps had long looked down on, was finally back!

All thanks to the great, great, great granddaughter of James Brimstone, the wonderful Alice, ably assisted by the now legendary crew – the amazing *Gavin & The Bodysnatchers*.

ABOUT THE AUTHOR

Michael A. Duffy is a writer from the North West of England. He first came to fame when, at the age of ten, he managed to split the atom using only a chemistry set his parents had bought him from Woolworths.

At the age of sixteen he became the first person to swim the English Channel whilst reciting the *Complete Works of Shakespeare* from memory. His extraordinary skills as a human inevitably brought him to the attention of extra-terrestrial onlookers - and he was abducted by aliens, aged only twenty-one.

He returned to earth, aged sixty, but not before having been the chief architect in negotiating peace between the warring planets of Zengo and Xylog, ending a conflict that had previously raged for thrialeteen nano years.

These days he is to be found lying on a sofa writing novels and songs, his useful days behind him. Bin day is Wednesday, a highlight of his week.

ALSO BY MICHAEL A. DUFFY

Sixth Beatle
– When Music Changed the World

Johnny Litherland was expecting the bullet. So many brilliant musicians die young, after all. Just like his hero, John Lennon, also gunned down all those years ago. But as he lays dying, now aged 40, Johnny recounts his life as a genius musician – creating music with miraculous consequences, no less.

Set in the music and football mad city of Liverpool in the early Seventies, and paralleled with Johnny's fateful last day, in May 2005, 'Sixth Beatle' is about a boy who grew up wanting to put everything right with music. Defying the tragedies that beset himself and his family, he leads an incredible life. All leading to one incredible moment in time - the day when music changed the world.

★ ★ ★ ★ ★

Five Star Rated on Amazon, Kindle & Goodreads

SONGS BY THE AUTHOR

Michael A. Duffy has, in recent years, written a collection of entertaining songs. Some of these are humorous and quirky. Others are bloody miserable and best avoided.

At the time of publication, these can be found on SoundCloud:

soundcloud.com/michael-a-duffy

AND FINALLY...

If you enjoyed reading 'Gavin & The Bodysnatchers, then this here author would very much appreciate a review or rating on your favourite online bookstore.

If you didn't enjoy reading 'Gavin & The Bodysnatchers, my name is Sally Rooney, and this book is really called 'Normal People'.

Thank you!

Printed in Great Britain
by Amazon